I0713590

CRUX

JAMES BYRON HUGGINS

WILDBLUE PRESS

WildBluePress.com

CRUX published by:

WILDBLUE PRESS
P.O. Box 102440
Denver, Colorado 80250

Publisher Disclaimer: Any opinions, statements of fact or fiction, descriptions, dialogue, and citations found in this book were provided by the author, and are solely those of the author. The publisher makes no claim as to their veracity or accuracy, and assumes no liability for the content.

Copyright 2019 by James Byron Huggins

All rights reserved. No part of this book may be reproduced in any form or by any means without the prior written consent of the Publisher, excepting brief quotes used in reviews.

WILDBLUE PRESS is registered at the U.S. Patent and Trademark Offices.

ISBN 978-1-948239-84-4 Trade Paperback
ISBN 978-1-948239-85-1 eBook

Interior Formatting/Book Cover Design by Elijah Toten
www.totencreative.com

CRUX

For Deborah and Herb

Though lovers be lost love shall not;
And death shall have no dominion.

Dylan Thomas
"And Death Shall Have no Dominion"
May 1, 2014

To see a World in a Grain of Sand
And a Heaven in a Wild Flower,
Hold Infinity in the palm of your hand
And Eternity in an hour.

William Blake
1803
"Auguries of Innocence"

A bolt of lightning shattered the Observation Room, but even in the deafening thunder Blanchard heard horrified screams and glimpsed a scientist scramble under equipment that was obliterated by a blinding blue streak.

Blanchard did not think of the machine. He did not think of his job. He did not think of his life.

All he knew was horror.

Someone—it would only be later that Blanchard realized it had been him—ripped open the Observation Room door and then Blanchard half-sensed blurred images flying past his head, the world rolling away beneath his feet. Screams faded, but his horror remained vividly on fire as he staggered, gasping, through another chamber of the facility.

And another, and another …

Magenta lights revolved in every corridor and corner as Blanchard stumbled, screaming, across the main lobby of the facility and onto the black grass beneath white moonlight surrounding the Circle of Shiva—the Hindu goddess of destruction and death poised in the *Tandava*, the Dance of Destruction, that stood upon the bronze body of a demon, in front of the facility. Then, sweating and breathless, Blanchard awkwardly pitched forward and scrambled across the yard in the desperate crawl of a man seeking to escape the attack of some great predatory beast. Finally Blanchard realized he was lying motionless on the wet grass and, with difficulty, he was still breathing.

Shadows rushed this way and that in the surrounding half-light, but Blanchard noted them with only the dimmest awareness. The whole of his mind was still fleeing down corridors past motionless bodies and white sheets of paper floating lazily through the air. Then Blanchard groaned as he pushed himself up on a single elbow.

He gazed back at the facility.

Inside the expansive windows the bluish-purple magenta alarms were still circulating with a calm steadiness that almost mocked the unashamed horror expressed by every face and form. Then uncountable sirens were silenced at once and screams ruled the night.

Blanchard's face twisted as he wiped tears from his cheeks. Then he took long, steady breaths. He swallowed and blinked rapidly, finding his vision clearing. At last he gazed about and his higher logic measured the situation by scientists and engineers staggering as if they had been struck with news of their own deaths.

Blanchard gasped, "*Good god*!" Awkwardly with visible unsteadiness he finally straightened to stare upon the neon-lit center. He shook his head as he heard someone shout, "What happened!"

"What?" asked a woman standing nearby.

"*What*!"

"You asked me what happened!"

Blanchard realized that *he* had asked the question although he had not directed it to anyone. Larger groups of white-coated personnel were now pouring out of the doors, all gathering on the ground surrounding Shiva, most holding hands or embracing; the eeriness of the scene reminded Blanchard of the horrible, final moments of victims trapped atop some kind of towering inferno who chose to leap to their doom rather than perish even more horribly in the blaze.

Sensing a presence approaching, Blanchard turned to see a beefy security guard from the division that carried weapons. His pistol was in his hand, but his face was white and pasty as if he was utterly unarmed and there was no means by which he might defend himself against what had been unleashed here tonight.

"Mr. Blanchard?" the guard asked coldly.

Blanchard nodded once.

"You're needed inside, sir."

"Are you crazy?" Blanchard stepped back and pointed at the facility. "I'm not going back in there! Not until the place is secured!"

Clearing his throat, the guard said, "Sir, your area is secure. And this is an order from the Director-General."

Drawing a palm across his sweat-slick face, Blanchard bent his head for a moment. Then he nodded slowly, "All right. Just … give me a minute … to pull myself together. Tell them I'm on my way."

"He meant right now, sir."

Blanchard straightened. "I know what he meant! Just give me a damn minute! Okay? I just saw a bolt of lightning tear through that room like we opened the gates of Hell!"

The guard frowned.

"Maybe you did this time," he said.

***

At least a hundred people crowded the corridor so that Blanchard stopped recognizing the color of security badges or even the yellow-white vests worn to distinguish the Emergency Medical Service from the maintenance engineers and physicists. As far as Blanchard was concerned, they were all trapped in this horror and both rank and station had become equally meaningless.

Suddenly and awkwardly aware of how his usual professional comportment had been totally abolished by his horror, Blanchard took a moment in an attempt to straighten his rumpled appearance. Although he usually wore one of his ten-thousand-dollar woven wool suits to accent the very few physical advantages he possessed with his short, stout shape, he had completely forgotten all semblance of dignity as he hastily swept back his short black hair and wiped soot from his face with a torn and blackened sleeve. Then Blanchard, aware of an imposing presence approaching him, turned.

A tall, severe figure appeared in the doorway of the open, smoke-filled Observation Room.

"William!" he shouted.

It was Director-General Antonio Francois.

William Blanchard stopped before Director-General Francois, gazing up. Although Francois was intellectually superior to everyone at the facility, he also had the physical advantage of an Olympic athlete and often used it for no other reason than base intimidation; he was well over six feet tall with a deep chest and a woodsman's arms. His torso and legs were long and muscular like a champion skier. Still, even his dominating presence did not overshadow the aura of his phenomenal intellect, which had contributed significantly to the present engineering of the Large Hadron Collider in which they stood.

"Yes?" Blanchard answered tiredly. "What is it?"

"*What is it?*" Francois repeated the words as if he'd never heard them. "I want to know what the hell happened in here, William!"

Blanchard shrugged, palms uplifted, shook his head and said, "I'm gonna need time to figure it out." He glanced into the Observation Room. "Did any of the hardcopy survive? I know the computers are fried but …"

"*Everything*, and I mean every single piece of electrical machinery in this entire seventeen-mile facility, is fried." Francois pointed at the smoking Observation Room. "I want to know what happened to your crew!"

Blanchard blinked. "To my crew?" He paused, "I thought they were dead."

Francois solemnly shook his head. "Not all of them, no, but some are dead, certainly." He gestured widely. "The others are scattered like sticks all over the compound. And we can't locate seven of them." He stepped forward. "Seven of them!"

"What do you mean?" asked Blanchard. "They weren't killed?"

"As I told you, William, they were not all killed." Francois's expression was remarkable in that it was the perfect embodiment of belief, disbelief, suspicion, and contempt. "Nor do I presume that they were vaporized. Not when every stitch of clothing they were wearing is on the floor at their workstations. So the critical question remains, 'Where is the rest of your crew?'"

Blankly, Blanchard stared around the room.

Francois leaned forward. "I want a report on my desk in one hour. And it better make sense, William, because I am not going to report that we're missing seven physicists! I'll say seven of them were killed in an explosion! I'll be glad to tell them that! But I'm not going to tell the committee that seven of our physicists vanished into thin air!"

Blanchard found it painful to blink, "But what about Swiss Protective Services? Don't we have to notify—"

"Absolutely not," responded Francois, half turning. "Neither the Swiss Protective Services nor the Ministry of Defense will be told anything about this event until we know what happened here and what we're dealing with."

"But protocol requires—"

Francois sprung upon him like a lion. "To hell with protocol! I want answers for the committee! Then I'll follow protocol!"

Blanchard was staring at crumpled clothing strewn across the Observation Room's tile floor as Francois moved past him muttering, "Get on with it, Mr. Blanchard. You have exactly one hour."

After a moment Blanchard was aware that he was still standing in place. He took a heavy breath and released. Then his face twisted into a grimace as he entered the now silent Observation Room.

***

"How the hell is any of this our problem?"

Walter Whitaker, general counsel to the President of the United States, leaned back in his black leather chair in what was loosely referred to in times of peace as "The Situation Room." But in times of alarm it was called "The War Room."

In fact, unbeknownst to the public, and most of those working in the White House, this particular war room is located seven hundred feet beneath the White House. And it is only one of thirty war rooms scattered across North American. Even the three-billion-dollar Air Force One, a virtual flying Pentagon, is equipped to serve as an eternally moving war room. But this particular war room was also Whitaker's formal office and home away from home as he lived here at the president's beck and call 24/7.

Major General Atol Jackman, smoking a cigar, rested a hand on the table as if content to wait forever for an answer he damn well knew he'd never get. Whitaker gestured vaguely and said, "I'll explain that to you in a minute, Atol. But rest assured. This *is* our problem. Mike, would you please distribute the files?" He shook his head. "I hope you're a big fan of science fiction, Atol. Except this isn't fiction. This is as real as it gets."

Black manila folders marked with a red *Eyes Only* warning were distributed. Then Whitaker motioned and said, "All right, Mike. Play the tape."

The room was darkened and a projection blazed to life.

Ignoring the folder, General Atol Jackman leaned back and chomped down on his cigar as he muttered, "Creature features."

In contrast to Whitaker's tailored, professional appearance, Jackman exuded the burly presence of a Grizzly bear. His head resembled a block of granite with short-cut white hair and a sunburned scarred face. And although most career Army officers cultivated a reputation for remaining in poster-boy shape, Jackman was the living image of a Depression-era street fighter. His chest was as deep and wide as a beer barrel and his long arms were heavy and powerful with hulking, intimidating forearms. His hands were large, deeply tanned, and marked by wounds he never mentioned. Yet, despite his barbaric frame, Jackman's uniform was spot-on and squared away with the commitment of a perfect professional soldier.

Seated so closely together, Whitaker looked like a grade-school goodie-two-shoes poised beside a silverback gorilla.

Suddenly on the wall an image of a room was displayed—one not unlike the mission control center at Fort Canaveral. There were thirty-seven physicists at individual workstations not separated by petitions. All were equipped with microphones and headgear but they could communicate directly to one another just by raising their voice. In front of the group was a ceiling-to-floor display that resembled the control panel of a nuclear reactor. There were dozens of small screens, each dedicated to something important since each was monitored by two or three personnel.

For a moment there was no movement in the room. Then a single physicist screamed out what seemed like a warning and every screen spiked into what was commonly referred to as "the red zone."

The soundless video was electrified in cobalt blue and a bolt of lightning crossed the room exploding computers and flinging bodies into the air. Personnel were blown to pieces as others were thrown into the air. When they landed on what appeared to be a tile surface, they began beating at the flames consuming their clothing as still more physicists charged out of the Observation Room without seeming to realize they were on fire at all.

"That's enough," said Whitaker dismally.

Lights were restored and the screen went blank. For a moment no one spoke, then General Jackman focused on Whitaker with, "Okay, Whitaker, the idgets blew themselves up. I figured it was gonna happen sooner or later. And so I reluctantly repeat, why on God's green earth is a bunch of dumbass eel heads blowing themselves up our problem? We're not even official a part of their supercollider society or whatever it is."

With a grimace Whitaker said, "The problem, general, is that there were thirty-seven physicists sitting in that room when they turned the Large Hadron Collider up to full power. And when they turned it off, there were only thirty. You understand? There were only thirty physicists remaining." He stared. "It's true, some were blown to pieces. Killed deader than a wedge. We counted all of them. And some ran off. We counted them, too. But seven couldn't be found anywhere on that compound. They weren't found that night and they haven't been found to this day."

General Jackman chewed his cigar. "So?" He lifted a hand to the darkened screen. "Some of 'em got blown up. Clear as day. And the rest, well, I woulda' been makin' tracks, too, if I had bolts of lightning splittin' the crack of my ass."

"But that's not what happened, Atol. When I imply that seven physicists were no longer in the flesh, what I'm saying is that *they disappeared into thin air*. But all their clothing, their jewelry—wedding rings, earrings, bracelets, necklaces—even their porcelain fillings were recovered at their workstations."

Jackman stopped chewing.

"You see the problem?" asked Whitaker.

It was not a question.

Jackman shook his head. "It ain't our problem, Whitaker. Somebody's been warning those fools for a hundred years that they were gonna open up a black hole or the gates of hell or whatever you wanna call it and half of 'em were gonna get sucked up like Spam in a can." He chomped down hard. "Well, they got what they were looking for. Adios. Arrivederci. Sayonara. I'll call your folks for ya. It's their problem."

Sitting forward, elbows on the marble slab, Whitaker calmly said, "Well, Atol, the president considers it our problem, too."

"*Why?*"

"Because these physicists obviously opened some kind of portal to another dimension," said Whitaker. "Or something like that. The science is beyond me. In any case, they let something into our world that walked away with stuff that didn't belong to it. Therefore, the president suspects this situation could mushroom into a problem for him in the very near future. And, as you gentlemen very well know, our president dislikes problems as much as he dislikes surprises." He folded his hands. "Gentlemen, we cannot have mad scientists destroying the world as we know it. That is not acceptable."

General Jackman retorted, "So what does the big guy want us to do? We didn't build the damn thing. I personally don't even know who controls the place, but it definitely ain't us." He looked around the table and saw mostly shrugs before he lifted a hand. "You see that? Nobody knows who controls that place! It's like its own political fiefdom with the biggest, most expensive, most dangerous machine in the world under its control and those clowns turn that thing on and off like it's a light switch. Now," Jackman pointed, "if you want my boys to disable it, that's a hat with some dynamite under it."

"I don't think it would be that easy, Atol," stated Admiral Jason Waters, seated like the ultimate executive officer in white at the far end of the slab. "It's the most powerful machine in the world and it's guarded more closely than the Federal Reserve. To get a strike team in there will take an act of God."

Jackman turned toward him. "I know how powerful it is, Jason. But if somebody built it, somebody can break it. And the more moving parts, the easier it is to screw up. You could probably just throw a shoe in the thing and they won't have it up and running till Jesus returns."

"And the unequaled security of the place?" continued the admiral. "You do realize that the security of Fort Knox pales in comparison to the security of that installation? In fact, there is not a facility on earth so closely monitored and guarded."

Jackman hesitated. "Yeah," he admitted, "I know. Security would be a problem. Getting in there ain't gonna be easy. But, on the flip side, destroying that thing won't ultimately resolve this, either. This ain't the only supercollider in the world."

"Atol, you make a very salient point," Whitaker enunciated slowly. "The Hadron Supercollider in Geneva is only one of thirty-nine supercolliders operational or under construction. But since this incident happened in Geneva, the Hadron supercollider will receive the misery of our attention."

Blanchard swiveled his chair right to left. "Gentlemen, these fools have proven, however inadvertently, and I must say tragically, that this machine can tear a hole in our universe and into some kind of alternate universe. And since this video shows us that something can go from here to there, logic demands us to accept the fact that something can also travel from there to here. And it might not be of a friendly nature. In fact, it might be downright murderous. And that's the problem we need to address."

"I saw this mess coming full-tilt boogie ten years ago with its hair on fire," muttered Jackman. "The president's afraid that something alien is gonna come calling and it might wanna open a butcher shop. But what does he expect us to do about it? Bust up every supercollider in the world? We can't dis-invent the thing. The science is already out there. It's like the atomic bomb. Once they knew how to build it, they built it. And if somebody's fool enough to build it, somebody's fool enough to use it."

Jackman scanned faces. "What did you think those guys have been doing up there for the last century? Reading John Newton and singing Kumbaya? Or did you not realize they were gonna build the most insanely dangerous machine in the world and not do something insanely dangerous with it?"

"What I think," Whitaker said, "is that we need someone with scientific acumen to tell us exactly what happened in that room." He gestured, "Mike? Would you bring Dr. Mansfield in here, please?"

The soldier disappeared and within thirty seconds a short, portly, utterly bald man in a white lab coat entered the room. He silently stood unmoving with his hands folded and seemed to be awaiting further invitation.

Whitaker said, "Please, doctor, have a seat."

Dr. Carl Mansfield chose the chair closest to Whitaker, placed his pale hands on the table, and neatly adjusted his wire-rim glasses.

"Dr. Mansfield," Whitaker continued, "Can you explain to these gentlemen your theory of what happened at the Large Hadron Collider a week ago?"

Clearing his throat, Mansfield leaned forward and said in a nasal voice, "Gentlemen, to understand the phenomenon of what happened at the Large Hadron Collider I'll first have to give you a lesson on what the LHC is capable of accomplishing and, more importantly, why it is capable of accomplishing these things."

Jackman relit his cigar.

"May we see the video again, please?" asked Mansfield.

The video was again displayed as Mansfield fished out a laser pointer from his coat pocket. He used it to illuminate a site on a topographical map. "Gentlemen, this is the physical location of the Large Hadron Collider. But of course it's much larger than it appears in this photograph. It is almost one hundred acres and the collider itself is located three hundred to six hundred feet below the surface. The corridor is seventeen miles long and is equipped with 9,300 magnets of various purposes and strength. And we are not talking your average Play Store magnet. These magnets weigh thirty-five tons apiece."

"That's ridiculous," said Jackman. "What do they need that kind of hardware for?"

"Well," continued the doctor, "as you may know, at its inception the official goal of the Large Hadron Collider was to discover the origins of the universe so that we might better understand the substance of elements in our solar system. But that noble public goal, as they so zealously advertised it, was long ago superseded by the hidden agenda of an unknown conglomerate that has expanded the use of the LHC to include experiments of a far more dangerous nature."

Jackman took his cigar from his mouth. "How dangerous we talking?"

"Dangerous enough to destroy the universe," answered Mansfield with no expression. "The collider is under the authority of the European Organization for Nuclear Research, hence the acronym, CERN ..."

"That acronym don't match that name," muttered Jackman.

Mansfield continued, "No, but it was originally named *The Conseil European pour la Recherche Nucleaire,* which was conveniently shortened to CERN. However, that mantle was deemed too foreign, and even insulting, for non-French-speaking partners, hence it was replaced.

Now, to proceed. We only partially understand the nature of the current experiments that are recorded at one-hundred-seventy computer centers located in forty-two countries. But from what I have observed from this video this was the first time they conducted this particular experiment at this power level. Consequently, no one anticipated the outcome. In fact, I would suggest that even the officials who sanctioned this experiment did not expect such a shocking result and are themselves horrified and confused."

Whitaker asked, "Expound on that, doctor. If you will."

Mansfield glanced past Whitaker's blank stare, "We have concluded, based upon this video as well as additional, illegally appropriated materials from satellites, that CERN successfully opened a portal to a parallel dimension."

Expressions were exchanged.

"What kind of parallel dimension?" asked Jackman.

"A horrifyingly dangerous one," the scientist answered. "As we have analyzed it, they opened a door to an alternate dimension made of antimatter." Mansfield paused as if to let lesser minds comprehend. "You see, gentlemen, there is more dark energy in alternate universes than the energy inherent to our own universe. There is also more antimatter in parallel dimensions than the matter common to our universe. Now, under normal circumstances, matter and antimatter would react energetically and dramatically if they came into contact. I have placed scientific articles on these somewhat technical matters in your packets. So, frankly, what they did in this video should have destroyed this world, which begs the question. Why didn't it? Well, the short answer is that we don't know. But we are confident that they opened a door to a dimension composed primarily of antimatter and dark energy, which should have, at least, killed everyone in that room. And yet they survived."

Whitaker spoke up, "Doctor, before we make a decision about how to handle this situation, we need an explanation for why they weren't all vaporized that even a layman can understand. Because I swear before Almighty God that telling the President of the United States that we don't have a clue just isn't going to cut it. It's his job to ask the questions. It's our job to give him the answers."

Dr. Mansfield nodded deferentially. "I understand, Mr. Whitaker. Then let me say that for every positively charged electron in our dimension there is a negatively charged electron in a parallel dimension. We call these negatively charged electrons 'positrons.' But the point is that this universe that we can see with the naked eye is paralleled by an invisible universe that is just as real, just as substantial, and just as alive as the visible dimension we inhabit."

"Then why can't we see it?" asked Jackman. "If this thing is as real as our world, why can't we see any of it?"

"Our most favored hypothesis is that we cannot see it because it is comprised of antimatter, dark energy, and neutrinos of a composition that are outside any light spectrum we are able to perceive," said Mansfield.

"A neutrino?" asked Admiral Waters. "Is that like an atom?"

Mansfield shook his head. "Not quite."

Seated at the far end of the table in his bright admiral's uniform, Waters was the picture of a white-haired elderly statesman. His Service Dress White was perfect to every crease and he wore it like the epitome of an officer and gentleman.

"Expatiate," said the admiral.

Mansfield nodded, "Now, neutrinos are what constitute the most finite anatomy of an atom. In fact, you could fit several billion neutrinos inside a single electron, which is the smallest part of an atom. And which, incidentally, is the smallest particle that we can observe with our most advanced technology."

"Billions?" Jackman asked. "You're telling me that these neutrino things are so small that you can fit billions of them into one electron?"

"Yes," confirmed Mansfield.

"Doctor," Whitaker said tiredly, "please get to the point. Why wasn't everyone in that room killed like a dog when they opened that portal?"

Inhaling deeply, Mansfield continued, "Gentlemen, please bear in mind that what I'm about to tell you is just an educated guess, which is what physics is all about. In fact, you should be informed of an old saying among physicists that states, 'The laws of physics are always right. Until they're not.'"

"Which means?" asked Jackman.

"Which means that there are a great many more laws of physics that we don't understand than those which we do understand," Mansfield elaborated. "For instance, we don't know for certain that neutrinos exist at all. We've never seen one so they're simply a centuries-old, firmly held theory. We don't know for certain that dark matter exists. It is also only a traditional theory. And we certainly can't prove that there is a single parallel dimension although the math seems incontrovertible. The truth is that we can algebraically demonstrate the existence of dark energy and dark matter and at least eleven alternate dimensions, but proving they exist is another matter." He paused. "Entirely."

"This is getting to the point?" grumbled Jackman.

Whitaker groaned, "Please, Atol."

Jackman grunted, "Go ahead, doc. But it seems to me that we're burning daylight on this witch hunt."

"A witch hunt perfectly captures the consequences of this affair," said Mansfield. "We have concluded that the LHC tapped into a very hostile dimension of entities that are just as real as we are. Only, these ghost-entities are composed of antimatter instead of matter. And their dimension is comprised of negatively based dark energy instead of the positively based energy that enables our universe." He gently tapped the table. "Gentleman, what I believe happened in that LHC Observation Room is this. These physicists smashed particles together with sufficient force to open a portal between dimensions, and both dimensions are inhabited by living creatures. One dimension is inhabited by incomprehensibly hostile creatures comprised of antimatter. The second dimension is inhabited by us. And opening this portal is, without question, a very, very dangerous thing."

Releasing a trail of blue smoke, Jackman asks, "As they say, doc, I ain't scared a no ghost. But, explain to me, exactly, why this is so graveyard dead dangerous."

Mansfield stood and walked to the screen, "Can you play the digital again?"

The incident began to replay.

"In slow motion please," Mansfield added. "Steady … Stop!"

The screen froze with the image of a gigantic bolt of blue lightning erupting from a large metallic cylinder and through the LHC Observation Room Plexiglas shield.

"This is the precise moment when they opened the portal," continued Mansfield. "This explosion, or lightning, is typical when you smash a positively charged atom into a negatively charged atom. The particles disintegrate and release their nuclear energy into the surrounding environment. So in my opinion it is clearly a miracle equal to Moses parting the Red Sea that anyone survived this event. And that, gentlemen, means that these physicists at CERN may have come very close to destroying the world. But we've already discussed that. Now I would like to point out to you what was so dangerous about this event."

"There's something *more* dangerous than destroying the world?" asked Jackman, eyes wide open.

"Yes, general, because they succeeded in opening a portal to what we are calling—for the sake of brevity—a demonic dimension. It is also safe to say that the entities inhabiting this dimension are incalculably hostile, more intelligent, and far more physically powerful than we are."

Jackman was scowling. "You do realize you're using the word, 'demon?'"

Without hesitation Whitaker stated, "Dr. Mansfield, would you please show these pilgrims the photograph?"

Dr. Mansfield removed a single eight-by-ten black-and-white photograph from his manila folder and slid it across the table. With teeth locked on his cigar, Jackman picked up the photograph and stared.

"What the hell is this?" he asked.

"It's a demon," said Dr. Mansfield without reservation.

"A demon!" Jackman searched every face. "How do you know that?"

Dr. Mansfield shook his head. "What you see in that picture is what lies on the far side of that portal, General Jackman. It is what reached through and snatched up seven scientists in one-thousandth of a second and hauled them back into its world. And if that's not a demon, it missed a good chance."

Jackman laid the photograph on the table. "Well," he frowned, "I think it's safe to say we're not the only murderous species in the universe."

The image was of a slouching black shape that vaguely resembled a human being but was monstrously more muscular; the face disproportionately elongated with large black eye sockets that held no light. Its six-fingered left hand was prominently visible revealing curved black claws. Its mouth was locked in a tight line as if it were concentrating. At its feet was a blurry image of what appeared to be a naked woman with a single hand upraised as if begging for mercy. But the creature showed no sign of mercy. Rather, it displayed the unconcealed indifference of a beast that had beheld millions pleading for mercy and it had dispassionately destroyed them all.

"It does appear to be quite malevolent," commented Admiral Waters. "Are you sure this is an accurate photograph of what resides on the other side of that portal?"

"Absolutely," nodded Mansfield. "This is a photograph of what's on the other side of the portal, admiral. Or, at least, the portal that CERN opened on that day. There is no way of knowing if there is one parallel dimension, or four, or a hundred. All we know for certain is that this dimension does exist and can clearly be considered a threat of, forgive me, Biblical proportions. I don't think I need to suggest to you what might happen if an army of these creatures emerge from that portal. To put it mildly, I would estimate that the outcome would be, quite simply, the annihilation of the human race. And, perhaps, our universe, as well. Or these creatures might keep some of us alive as soldiers, servants, slaves, concubines, or even construction workers like the ancient Egyptians used the ancient Jews."

For a while no one moved or spoke.

"Well, boys, there you have it in," said Whitaker. "There is something on the far side of that portal, gentlemen, and it ain't human and it ain't friendly. Call it what you will but I'm gonna call it a damn demon because that's what it damn well looks like to me."

"Why did this thing kidnap seven people?" asked Jackman.

"We don't know the answer to that question," Mansfield stated bluntly. "But we believe that this dark power reached through that gateway and snatched up these people for some kind of truly monstrous purpose otherwise it would not have had to kidnap them." He shook his head. "If you ask me, these physicists are not dead."

Jackman rumbled, "So what are they?"

"Again, general, we do not—"

"Yeah, yeah, you don't know." Jackman's scowl deepened well-worn creases in his scarred face. "Doctor, just what the hell do you know?"

Mansfield did not appear to take offense as he lifted his hands. "General, we now have empirical knowledge that this Dark Universe, as some are calling it, is just as real as our own universe. It is simply invisible to the naked eye. We believe it is populated by these monstrous, very intelligent beings composed of antimatter instead of matter. And we believe it is a dimension of tremendous energy capable of tearing our galaxy apart. So we have reached the conclusion that we are facing a vast enemy that is incalculably more intelligent and more powerful than we are, and they have harnessed the power of dark energy—a weapon that can easily destroy this universe if not the entire galaxy."

Ten seconds passed before Jackman turned to Whitaker, "Whitaker, I'm not clear what we're doing here. If something from another dimension reached through that door and snatched seven people into oblivion, then those poor folks are dead. What do you expect us to do about it?"

"The problem," Whitaker answered, "is this. What might happen if these fools at the LHC can keep that portal open for more than a tenth of a second?" He stared solidly at Jackman. "I mean, you saw what happened in a bolt of lightning. What will happen if these eggheads figure out how to keep that door open for five minutes and an entire battalion of those demonic sons a bitches march into our world?"

Jackman erupted, "Come on, Whitaker!" He raised an arm to the screen. "They just opened it for a split second and it blew the place all the way to hell's half-acre! What makes you think they can open it for five whole minutes?"

"Because as of this moment they are reinforcing the superstructure of that collider to withstand over two-hundred Tera-Electron-Volts, or six times as much electricity, Atol." Whitaker shook his head. "Jesus, man, you saw what happened when they turned the collider up to handle the power of just *one* nuclear plant. Right now they're insulating that thing so that it can handle the full power of *six* nuclear plants. And what do you think they're going to do when they're finished with this upgrade? Sit back and open a few bottles of champagne? Or does it occur to you that they're going to turn that thing up to full power, reopen that gateway, and see what happens? Atol, those fools are going to keep that portal open long enough to let a damn demonic army loose in our backyard. And that, gentlemen, is *the* surprise the president doesn't want to be woke up with at two in the morning. So this *is* a military situation, Atol. And a damn serious one."

Admiral Waters' eyes narrowed. "What makes you so certain that this is a living creature and not an illusion?"

"*We're* living creatures," said Whitaker. "It's arrogant to presume that an alternate dimension wouldn't also have living creatures. And something did snatch those people out of that room. Only, that bastard isn't human, by god." He fiercely slapped the photograph. "That's a demon."

"Are we talking about Hell here?" grumbled Jackman. "Now, don't get me wrong. I believe in Hell and I believe in God. Anybody who's been neck deep in combat believes in Hell and, as they say, there's no atheists in foxholes. But is that what we're getting at? That these fools have opened a gateway to Hell and *we*, meaning the rest of the sane universe, have to find a way to stop them from opening it again?"

Whitaker motioned at nothing, "For brevity, we'll call it Hell. I don't know what else to call it. But whatever it is, the president has decided that it is *un*friendly and he wants us to do something to insure this doesn't happen again."

"So why don't we just destroy it?" suggested Jackman again and with more emphasis. "We can definitely put it out of commission. But, like I said, this supercollider ain't the only game in town. A dozen countries are building copies of this thing. And if these fools in Geneva can open a highway to Hell, so can everybody else. The only solution that I see is that we make this world the one place Hell don't wanna' visit. We teach 'em a lesson." He stared. "Let's open this portal again and send through the biggest nuclear warhead we've got. I'm talking one-hundred megatons of our own kind of

Hell. It might not kill all of them, but it'll sure brighten up their day. In fact, why don't we send through every nuke we've got? That'd sure hang up a 'No Trespassing' sign."

"There's a hole in your logic," said Admiral Waters. "These creatures might not even be affected by radiation, Atol, so we have no reason to believe they'd be deterred at all. And we cannot go around blowing up every supercollider in the world. If nothing else, it would precipitate World War III. And, frankly, I'm not sure which would be worse—to let an army of those things through that portal or a global-thermal nuclear war. Either way, it's a party I think we'd all rather skip."

Jackman scowled for a long time before he rumbled, "I hate to admit it, but Jason has a point. Fighting these creatures with nukes on their own ground *or* our ground could be a disastrous tactical move. For all we know they eat radiation for breakfast, so using a nuke is a last-stand move—a *Samson Option*. If we're all gonna die, let's make sure we take all of them with us. On the downside, if something as small as a platoon of those creatures gets through that portal, we'll have to mobilize a battalion of Rangers and fight them with conventional weapons. Sadly, I don't think we have a conventional weapon that would even wound one of them. That bastard looks pretty tough to me. I mean, I doubt that it would survive a Javelin. But anything less than an antitank gun will probably just piss it off."

Whitaker agreed, "I think we're all on the same page, Atol. Fighting these creatures with nuclear weapons is not the best option. Hell, for all we know, they have nuclear weapons, too. And for the love of God we don't want to get involved in an interdimensional nuclear war. So if they get through that gateway and into our world in sufficient numbers, we'll have to fight them hand-to-hand."

Admiral Waters reached out and slowly rotated the photograph without lifting it from the table. "Doctor," he began, "this … creature … is encapsulated by the ATLAS cylinder. Is that correct?"

"Yes."

"And what are the exact dimensions of the ATLAS?"

"The ATLAS detector weighs seven-thousand-eight-hundred tons. It is seventy feet in height and one-hundred-forty-seven feet in length—approximately half the length of a football field, so it is quite large. It has a magnetic strength of about forty thousand times more powerful than the Earth's own electromagnetic field and measures eight hundred million particle collisions per second." Mansfield paused, as if uncertain. "But I digress. Why did you wish to know the size of the ATLAS detector?"

Admiral Waters frowned over the photograph as he asked, "In proportion to the size of the ATLAS detector, what is the size of this creature?"

"Ah," Mansfield nodded, "yes, we have those calculations." He strolled down the table. "From its precise distance to internal cameras and its exact position to measured components inside the ATLAS we estimate the creature to be approximately eight feet tall. We can only speculate as to its weight. But if its weight is proportional to its height and width, then it weighs at least a thousand pounds." A pause. "Or more."

Jackman muttered, "That's the size of a grizzly."

"And these," Admiral Waters pointed, "are claws?"

"Yes, admiral. We measure the claws to be six inches in length."

"And this creature is made of flesh and bone?"

"We have concluded that it's made of what qualifies as flesh and bone in its dimension, admiral. But, in our dimension, it would qualify as some kind of hybrid matter and antimatter so, frankly, I'm not sure that we could even touch it with a weapon and survive the resulting explosion." Mansfield glanced at the image. "Unless …"

Whitaker raised his chin. "Now is not the time to be conservative, doctor. Please speak your mind."

"Well," Mansfield grimaced, "the whole truth is that we don't know that much about neutrinos, which are stupidly called 'the God Particle' by fools who know even less. In truth, the men who originally discovered a neutrino named it something quite the opposite because it was so difficult to isolate. But for the sake of decorum and to facilitate civilized discourse it was tastefully renamed 'the God Particle.' And it's just another theory that neutrinos have any electrical charge at all—positive or negative." He cleared his throat once more. "What I'm saying, gentlemen, is that this creature might be electrically neutral. And if that's the case then it would have no trouble emerging from the portal into our world fully intact. It would be able to interact with any positively charged matter. In other words, it would be just another insanely murderous, demonic creature running loose among us."

"*Another* insanely murderous creature?" queried Whitaker.

"Besides one of us," answered the doctor.

"Theory is all we've got?" asked Jackman. "You don't know *anything* for certain about this thing?"

"We know it is not an illusion, general, but we do not know the electronic nature of the neutrinos that comprise it. As I've said, we've never measured the electrical registration of a neutrino. Some still insist they don't even exist. But I, for one, believe that they do and they're so small you could fit billions of them into a single electron, as I stated earlier. However," he raised a hand, "if this creature were to pass through that dimensional portal, then there is no reason to doubt that it would retain much of its original dimensions by absorbing the neutrinos of this dimension."

Admiral Waters asked, "Do these creatures have the power to assume any shape they wish in our universe or would it retain its relative form?"

Mansfield lifted both hands. "That is a very difficult question, admiral, and we have no answer. But we suspect that neutrinos gather on the basis of the mass of atoms, and Einstein's theory of relativity mandates that atoms comprise all elements specific to their universe. But to more accurately answer your question, I would say that in our universe it would be proportionate in size to a grizzly bear or a gigantic gorilla. And that does not even take into consideration its molecular density, which would determine its main strength. It is my personal belief that because of its molecular density this creature would possess the physical strength of a hundred men."

"What about its intelligence?" asked Jackman. "Can they—wait a minute. Let me put it this way. Do they work as a cohesive unit? Do they think strategically? Do they plan tactically? Or do they just drop like baboons from trees and start railing on you?"

"Baboons don't live in trees, Atol," muttered the admiral.

Turning his head with a sullen gaze, Jackman released a cloud of smoke. "I actually don't give a hoot in hell where baboons live, Jason. I want to know if this thing thinks like a soldier or an animal."

Mansfield sighed as he shook his head. "Gentlemen, any hopes you might entertain that these are just dumb animals are useless. We know for a fact that these creatures possess a very high degree of intelligence. In fact, they're probably more intelligent than we are. And just as we know that they inhabit their dimension, they also know that we inhabit our dimension. And I would suggest that they know our strengths as well as our weaknesses, which is more than we know about them."

Jackman snatched the cigar from his mouth, "Just how in the hell do these bastards know all that about us when we barely know they're out there?"

Mansfield spoke up with supreme certainty, "During that brief interaction between dimensions, one of our detectors received what can only be described as a mathematical code sent to us from their dimension.”

Everyone stared until Jackman exclaimed, *“A code for what?”*

“A code for the means to make the Large Hadron Supercollider more powerful,” Mansfield answered. “Whatever inhabits that dimension is attempting to help us build a stronger supercollider so that we can keep the portal open for a longer time.”

“I’ll be damned,” muttered Jackson, grinding his cigar. “These fools are messing with powers they don’t understand and they’re leaving the door wide open. They *are* gonna get us all killed.”

“Not if we come up with a plan to shut this door forever,” Whitaker counseled. “Be advised, the Large Hadron Collider is the most powerful collider in the world. Nothing else comes close. And, using the total output of energy from a nuclear plant, they can only keep that portal open for a tenth of a second. But if these maniacs can somehow fix that with six nuclear reactors and a gazillion Tera-Electron-Volts, or whatever they’re called, then we might be looking at Armageddon a little early. So what we are tasked with doing, gentlemen, is making sure that nothing from this hell even wants to come through that gateway, which would cover things nicely.”

A somber aura silenced the room.

“Well,” said Jackman finally, “I got no love for the place so I got no objections to any kind of doable plan. But what kind of plan we talking?”

Whitaker folded his fingers in a pyramid as he stated, “The task, Atol, is to make our dimension off limits to them. We prepare our infantry, and if these things begin invading our space, we stomp their guts out.”

Jackman blanched. “Jesus, Whitaker, stomping the guts out of a ten-foot-tall alien ain’t a damn plan! That’s what you do when your plan goes to shit! We need to hit 'em from a *distance*." He paused. "Some serious distance!"

"Then we go to our most reluctant option and send through a one-hundred-megaton warhead and hope for the best," said Whitaker. "I seriously don't give a damn how you get the job done, gentlemen, and neither does the president. He just wants us to shut this door." His eyes widened. "Forever."

"Yes," said Mansfield, "the president does not care how the mission is accomplished. He simply wants it accomplished."

"What about another collider opening this gateway?" Jackman asked. "We don't even control this Hadron Supercollider. And this thing is in Switzerland, for God's sake. If we can't control some gizmo in Switzerland, we need to get a new job. Is this the real reason why they built this thing? So they could contact demons or whatever these things are?"

Whitaker shrugged, "Well, Atol, a lot of us do suspect that that was the real reason for why they built it in the first place. It's a conspiracy that goes back a hundred years to an occult movement that occurred in the late 1800s and is probably still around. Personally I think of it like the Tower of Babel. Man wanted to reach the other side and so they began building that tower. Then God confused their language and they all went their own way and the tower was never finished. But one thing has always nagged me about that old story, not that I'm unduly prone to metaphysical musings."

Jackman grunted, "So what bothers you?" He stared a long moment. "Metaphysically, that is."

Whitaker continued, "What bothers me, Atol, is that if there wasn't genuinely another dimension that was hostile to the human race, and none of those ancient guys stood a chance at reaching it, anyway, then why did God go to the trouble of stopping them?" He stared without blinking. "I'm not a religious man by nature. But a photograph like this can make you come to Jesus real quick.

"In the old days, those fools at Babel were obviously onto something just like these scientists at CERN. I mean, CERN might not be there yet, but my guess is that they're getting damn close to opening a portal to this dimension and keeping it open. And if they succeed, disappearing in a nuclear holocaust will be the least of our worries. At worst, these creatures have some insidious plan to use this planet for a purpose. Then we'll have entire truckloads of dark energy and demons and God-only-knows what kind Hell-born creatures or homicidal, fallen angels loose in our peace-loving world to enslave mankind. And I don't need to tell you gentlemen that that battle may very well be the bloodiest battle this world has ever seen. And we won't be counting empty saddles as we fall back because there won't be any falling back. There won't be any rules. There won't be any retreating or surrender or ceasefires or internment camps because nobody will be taking prisoners. It will be kill or be killed from the get-go and I bet you that it'll be so murderous that it'll be fought and finished in a single day." He shook his head. "Jesus, man, we're supposed to be the emergency team that prevents something as screwed up as this from becoming an emergency in the first place. Why do you think I have to live down here? I probably handle ten godforsaken catastrophes a day but I have *never* faced a situation like this."

For a time no one spoke and then Whitaker added, "I'll tell you what the president suggested to me. And, as we all know, the president is a brilliant man. He's built a thousand Towers of Babel. That's all he did before he was elected president, so he knows his business. And he told me that the surest way to shut down a deal is to lay down conditions that you know the other side will never agree to and, then, don't compromise on a single penny. That's how you end a negotiation. That's how you kill a deal."

"I agree," said Jackman. "But this ain't no building and it sure as hell ain't no negotiation. That thing came and went as it damn well pleased and took seven of those guys with it. And if they're not dead, I bet they wish they were." He turned a frown to the blank computer screen. "How do you stop something that can appear and disappear at will? And take stuff that don't belong to it while it's here?"

Admiral Waters contributed, "The first rule of war is to know your enemy. But, clearly, we don't know this enemy. So before we go launching nuclear warheads I suggest we plant some people inside CERN to collect information on what, exactly, we're dealing with. Then we obliterate the collider. But if that's not possible, and as a definite last resort, we send every nuclear warhead we've got through that portal and hope that wins the day." He paused. "The delicate stage of the operation will be to strategically place people in that Observation Room where we really need them. I don't believe it would serve much purpose to replace one of seven thousand electricians. We have to have someone in the brains of this operation."

Mansfield stated, "Under your president's direction I have already placed two of your best CIA computer people in the Observation Room, admiral. They have been in orientation for one week."

Whitaker's brow hardened. "When were you going to tell us about this?"

"I also spoke with the president directly after this particular incident," Mansfield replied smoothly. "He told me to immediately put someone inside CERN to replace the lost physicists. I obeyed his orders. Just as I am obeying his orders in this moment. I was told to inform you, Mr. Whitaker, of this asset directly before this meeting." He glanced, apparently unaffected by the hostility. "I am still Chief of Human Resources at CERN because no one is aware that my allegiance has been compromised. Director-General Francois does not know I am no longer dedicated to opening a dimensional portal when we have no idea what dangers might emerge. If he did, I would certainly not be alive."

"Tell me something," stated Jackman. "Why did an apparently intelligent man like you join a fool project like this in the first place?"

"Because CERN was, up to that point, just another electromagnetic machine surrounded by a hundred thousand theories," said the doctor. "And, to be honest, I needed the job and the money. The signing bonus made the down payment on my house. But now the proven existence of an infinitely hostile army from another dimension is no longer an empty theory. It is a very clear and present danger." Mansfield shrugged, "I know that what they have touched upon at CERN is a trillion times more dangerous than the Manhattan Project, which began MAD—Mutually Assured Destruction. Rather, what they are doing at CERN might very well be the end of this galaxy, so self-preservation is my motive. And for your information, General Jackman, I am not the first physicist to harbor grave concerns over the destruction this device can deliver to our world. Our past director-general committed suicide after he realized that the supercollider had the power to expose this world to forces that might very well destroy mankind."

"How do you know that's why he killed himself?" asked Whitaker.

"Because that's what he wrote in his suicide note."

Whitaker gaped. "And this didn't make the papers? *With pictures?*"

Mansfield brushed his shoulder as if dismissing a fly. "The mainstream press of every nation in the world is in the pocket of those who control CERN, Mr. Whitaker. The so-called progressive reporters only report what they're progressively instructed to report. They are propagandists, not journalists."

Jackman turned his gaze to Whitaker. "We have full authority and command to do whatever we decide? Including the use of a warhead?"

Whitaker shrugged, "I'll have to clear the last-resort warhead option with the president, general. But I don't anticipate any objection. The mission is ultimately more important than any repercussions."

"Why are you so sure about that?"

"Because he wants this thing dead as King Tut."

"Then I want the new three-stage fission warhead."

Whitaker stared. "That's the most powerful warhead ever created, Atol. But even with this new fuel, the freaking thing weighs five-hundred pounds. It's not something you can tote in your gym bag."

"We can handle it."

Whitaker sighed. "All right, then. I'll see if I can get one for you."

"Good enough," Jackman nodded. "So I ask one more time. *If* any of these things made it through that portal and are running loose in this world, how do we destroy creatures that can come and go in our universe at will?"

Dr. Mansfield collapsed forward, leaning on both arms. He shook his head before raising his head. "General," he said patiently, "This creature cannot come and go at will. The only way, or the only way we are aware of, for it to invade our world is through that portal. They cannot come and go as they please. And they possess the knowledge to make the supercollider more powerful, but they do not have the means or ... or the permission to build their own collider."

Jackman stared. "Permission?"

"From God," stated Dr. Mansfield.

Jackman didn't blink.

Mansfield continued, "Gentlemen, whatever creatures inhabit that dimension are apparently prohibited by something from building their own collider. That's why they need us to do it for them. That's why they sent us the equations for how to redesign our collider to meet their needs. So, to repeat myself, they are obviously more intelligent than us. Perhaps infinitely so. And if photographs are to be taken at face value, they are also physically superior to us. Comparing a human being to one of them would be like comparing a jellyfish to a gorilla. Although they are both dangerous, I'd say the gorilla has a distinct advantage. However, despite their obvious desire to punch a hole into our universe, something prevents them from building a similar collider to accomplish the task. So, after one of these creatures passes through our ATLAS, it's just as imprisoned in this dimension as we are. It cannot return to its own world unless we open the portal again. I suppose you could say that it is trapped. But my most plaintive instinct tells me that *we* are the ones who would be trapped. Because it will be here. In our world. Among us. And its intentions are clearly murderous."

Whitaker's face twisted. "I think it's safe to say this creature bears ill will, doctor. And why the freaking abomination even wants to come here in the first place is one more hellacious mystery to me. But that only brings us back to the main problem. How do we keep these fools at Geneva from opening that portal again?"

"One idea has been used to great success," said Admiral Waters. "Computer sabotage by critically placed spies inside that facility might be our best option. For instance, it doesn't take more than a single computer chip to disable a multimillion-dollar Tomahawk missile—a part that costs less than ten dollars in Taiwan, mind you. But if that cheap little slave-made chip goes down, then the whole nuclear warhead goes down in the ocean dead as a doornail. So why don't we just plant some bad chips in this thing so that it blows up again and it takes them years to get it up and running?"

"That plan was seriously considered," said Whitaker. "The problem is that these people triple-test everything before they fire up that machine, so it's not easy to disable." He frowned. "They have seven thousand electricians babysitting this thing day and night. That's more electricians than you've got on any flattop. And since it blew up the first time and demolished two miles of tunnel and threw over a hundred thirty-five-ton magnets forty or fifty feet apiece, they are acutely aware of the high cost of error. They check everything. Then they check it again. So I don't think throwing a sabot onto the assembly belt and stuffing up the machine is going to work."

"How about we just kill a few of these scientists?" suggested Jackman.

Whitaker released a breath. "It might be worth a try, Atol, but mad scientists are a dime a dozen. CERN can just go back to MIT, grab some more, offer them minimum wage and the fools will be more than happy to work at this godforsaken place."

No one forwarded another suggestion until Whitaker added, "The only thing we can do is disable that machine with military resources. Now, since Dr. Mansfield has already gotten two of our people in the Observation Room—thanks for telling me, doc—maybe they can temporarily disable the security so that some of our elite operators can get in there and blow the thing up. It might not be a permanent solution but it'll buy us five or six years to come up with something better."

Whitaker stared at the table before shaking his head, "I just hope these CIA spooks are more James Bond than Patton and someone has already told them that they have no official sanction to be there." He paused. "I remind you gentlemen that this mission does not exist, nor will it ever exist. There will be no orders cut, no faxes, no emails, no signatures, and no written sanctions you can hide in your safe as a get-out-of-jail-free card. If anything happens, we don't know anything about what you were doing, nor will there be any military funerals or medals or pensions conferred.

You can forget Arlington. You can forget a nameless star on the wall at Langley. As far as we're concerned, you died in a whorehouse." He exhaled. "We all know how the game works."

Nods.

"Good," Whitaker stated. "General Jackman, I advise you to select four of our best men. Or people, rather. And I suggest you choose them from the First Special Forces Operational Detachment."

"Why Delta?"

"Because Delta is more highly trained at working in small groups. Rangers are trained for battalion-size operations. So are Special Forces."

"What about SEALs?" asked the admiral.

"The identities of Delta operators are even more closely guarded than the identities of our SEALs, if that's possible, and I want these people to be unidentifiable."

With a frown Jackman sighed. "I'll get on it. When do you want them on deck?"

"Give me time to advise the president and alert our CIA people," Whitaker answered. "And we'll need some time to come up with a foolproof plan. A plan that doesn't have too many moving parts." He shook his head. "You said it, Atol. The more moving parts, the more can go wrong."

"I'll pick the operators," Jackman nodded. "I'll interview them myself. What are you gonna tell the president?"

"I'm going to tell him we're sending our best people in there to get the job done and I'm going to get nuclear authorization for you."

"But this plan still doesn't take care of the other supercolliders in the world," offered the admiral. "Any of them could do this and then we're back at square one."

Whitaker stood as he began to gather files.

"One Hell at a time, admiral."

***

The door to the small combination coffee shop/bookstore was open even though it was after ten at night. Amanda Deker entered and looked carefully down the aisles. She quietly closed the door and stood in the entryway noting the spectacular array of books for a store that appeared to be so small from the outside but, inside, it resembled the Library of Congress. It also housed a rather cozy coffee shop.

"Yes?" came a polite voice. "Can I help you?"

"Yes," answered Amanda to a shape concealed behind tightly packed bookshelves. "My name is Amanda Deker. I came here to speak with a gentleman named Isaiah."

A man walked from behind shelves. He was six feet tall with medium-length brown hair fighting with his collar. His eyes were green and he seemed to be in his mid-forties although it was hard to determine because he also seemed exceptionally fit. He wiped his hands with a rag as he came forward.

"Well, I'm the only one working in the book section tonight," he smiled. "And I don't know about the 'gentleman,' part, but I'm Isaiah, so I guess we're both in luck. How can I help you, Ms. Deker?"

"Amanda, please."

"Very well, Amanda. Have a seat." He pulled up a rocking chair. "Those might not look comfortable, but they are." He smiled freely. "I also sell them."

"Thank you."

Three rocking chairs lined either side of the entrance and Amanda sat, placing her purse in her lap. "Just out of curiosity," she began, "is Isaiah your first or last name?"

"It's my first name," Isaiah replied. "I don't bother telling people my last name because it's too difficult to pronounce. And I answer pretty well to Isaiah." He took a seat opposite her and laid his forearms on the wooden rests. "So what can

I do for you, Amanda? Our specialty is locating old or even ancient manuscripts, but we're flexible."

"I'm looking for another form of help," she said.

"Okay. What kind of help?"

"I need someone to help me find my missing sister."

Isaiah blinked slowly. "And why does your sister need finding?"

"Because my sister was a leading physicist at the Large Hadron Supercollider in Geneva and I haven't heard from her in a week." Amanda waited before adding, "I also heard a rumor that there was some kind of disaster at the collider and I think my sister was involved." She folded her hands on her purse. "I just want you to find out if she's dead or alive. And, if you can, what happened." She fidgeted. "I can pay you if you're willing to wait … a few months … to cash the check."

Isaiah leaned back in the chair. His eyes narrowed.

Amanda knew he was studying her and was suddenly grateful she had dressed down for this. Not that she was embarrassed by her appearance; she was tall at five-ten and slim because she worked hard to stay that way. Her legs were as muscular and toned as her arms and in the league of a professional athlete. Her brown hair was shoulder-length and she liked to think her somewhat unique cut accented her face and not her body. Also, she consciously wore clothes that were a bit concealing because, frankly, she was so uncomfortable with the acute attention she received otherwise.

Isaiah finally asked, "Why do you think a bookstore owner can help you more than the FBI, Ms. Decker?"

"Again, it's just Amanda."

"Forgive me. Amanda."

"Thank you. And, to answer your question, I know someone that you helped. She told me that you were someone I should come to if I was ever in grave danger. She said you were someone I could trust." Amanda gestured to the books. "I truly have no idea what you do, but I know you helped my friend out of a very bad situation with some very bad people. And I may be paranoid but I think something terrible happened to my sister and the people at CERN are covering it up."

Isaiah's head tilted. "Why do you say that?"

"Because I've tried every legal department of our government and they all say they can't help me. The FBI says they can't get clearance from the Swiss Ministry of Defense to interfere with matters involving the supercollider. No private detective that I've talked to will take the case. They all said that CERN has a very deadly reputation and tragic things happen to people who start asking questions. And please don't get me wrong. I do hold your life in high value. But I'm convinced something has happened to my sister and I have no one else to turn to. And Deborah told me you could … uh … handle yourself."

Isaiah didn't blink.

"Do you know what CERN is?" asked Amanda.

With a dismissive gesture Isaiah said, "It's the site of the world's most powerful particle supercollider and it's built on the ruins of what the Romans called Apolliacum—a temple to one of their more provocative deities. It's houses a seventeen-mile-long tunnel that accelerates protons, electrons, and other particles to 185 miles per second, which is ninety-nine percent of the speed of light. It cools mercury to minus 472 degrees so that there's no electrical resistance in the lines. It has 1,232 bending magnets, 858 focusing magnets, and 7,210 correcting magnets to keep the protons on a dead-on collision course. The designers said it was built to discover the origins of the galaxy, but most people think it has some kind of political or demonic purpose." He paused. "To be honest, I'm not sure what the difference is."

Amanda blinked rapidly. "Is that *all*?"

Isaiah shrugged, "All the data they collect is measured in petabytes per year and analyzed on a computer infrastructure connecting 172 backup centers in forty-two countries. They use ninety-six tons of super-cooled helium to help the mercury cool the thirty-five-ton magnets, which makes the LHC the largest, most magnetic cryogenic facility in the world. It also uses seven neutron detectors attuned to the Higgs boson field, which is simply a field where matter doesn't exist. And they're located in underground caverns dug out by an unknown German-owned engineering firm at critical intersection points for the two beams that comprise the circular collider pipeline. Two of those caverns hold the ATLAS and the Compact Moon Solenoid, which are general-purpose particle detectors strong enough to detect portals to the ten, or more, dimensions that run parallel to our own. But I only know what I've read. And CERN is a physically fluid facility. They're constantly updating the collider, the neutrino detectors, the pipelines, or digging out more caverns. Even America, which only has observer status with their phantom conglomerate, doesn't know what's happening inside the place. Israel probably knows more than we do. They recently joined up with CERN. But I think it's only because Israel is afraid of what they might secretly be doing."

Amanda was gaping, then asked, "You have all that memorized?"

"I have a facility for remembering things."

"Do you have a photographic memory?"

"There's no such thing," laughed Isaiah. "For what it's worth, physicians call it a Highly Superior Autobiographical Memory. So I have pretty good recall of everything I've ever said or read or seen or experienced or been interested in. But my memory is no better than anyone else's if something doesn't interest me. For instance, I can't tell you what color socks I put on this morning. I wasn't interested, so I don't remember."

"That's how it works, huh?"

"With me it is."

Amanda leaned forward, hands clasped, her face showed concerned. "I know what I'm asking is extraordinary. And I'm well aware that you're very reluctant—Deborah told me that much—about sticking your nose into other people's business. But she also told me that you sometimes help people just because no one else *can* help them." She bit both lips. "But I'm asking you to help me because no one else *will* help me. Not the FBI. Not the Swiss police. Not the French police. Not Interpol. Not private detectives. Not anybody. And my sister is autistic. She's a brilliant physicist but she's an autistic savant. Anything terrible could have happened to her and she would have never seen it coming. And the private detectives confirmed the rumor I've heard about the people at CERN."

In a mild tone Isaiah stated, "Yeah, I'm familiar with CERN's reputation for security. But several Halloween-type rumors also orbit the place. They're apparently resurrecting Dracula or opening portals to demonic dimensions or piling up buckets of dark energy so they can liquefy the galaxy, so the possibility that something untoward has happened to your sister is not without merit."

Amanda said, "I'm referring to the rumor that the people at CERN don't like interference and they're experts at making people disappear. And that's another reason why I've come specifically to you. Deborah told me that you're proficient at finding things regardless of … inconveniences. And she said you're very protective."

Isaiah paused a long time. "So you, yourself, want to come with me if I agree to do this for you?"

"I want to come, yes. And I won't cramp your style if that's what you're thinking. It's just that it's my little sister and I have always been close. And now she's missing." Amanda's brow tightened. "I need to know what happened to her."

With a somber gaze Isaiah turned his face aside. He already had a fair idea about what happened to her sister;

a list of the people killed in the history of CERN would probably fill your local library. If anything, the place was renowned more for its murder list than its proton-splitting accomplishments and anyone with a brain knew there was far more happening at the laboratory than the mere observation of atoms. Just the gigantic statue of Shiva, the Hindu Goddess of death and destruction that stood outside the front doors of the building was enough to confirm suspicions about the supercollider's purpose.

With that thought Isaiah measured the odds of looking into this without getting an international hit team sent to deal with him and this woman. His second thought was how Switzerland might handle a lot of dead hitmen if that happened. But he had chosen his path a long time ago and couldn't, or wouldn't, change.

Isaiah said deliberately, "Write down your sister's name, address, date of birth, social security number, and her bank account numbers and credit card numbers if you have them. Write down everything you can think of."

"Will you help me?" she asked.

"First things first, Amanda." Isaiah smoothly rose and walked to the checkout counter where he retrieved a legal pad and pen; he gave them to her. "Write down everything you know including her friends, pets, the last time she changed her locks. And I want to know what her specific job was at the supercollider."

"But I told you. She was a physicist. A scientist."

"I remember. But there are theoretical physicists, mathematical physicists, sub-atomic physicists and cosmological physicists that specialize in astronomical radiation. I want to know what her specialty was at the collider. Can you do that?"

"Yes." Amanda began writing. "And she had several specialties, but I believe her job at CERN was cosmology."

"Do you have your cell phone with you?" asked Isaiah.

"Of course. Do you need it?"

"Yeah."

She fished her phone from her purse.

Isaiah studied it, then snapped it open and removed the battery, broke the SIM card in half, and tossed the pieces in a trashcan. "Sorry," he said, "they can track you by that, so you don't need to be using any cell phone until I say so, okay? Are you staying at a hotel?"

"Uh huh."

"Okay. Don't use your credit cards and don't make any phone calls from your room or the lobby."

"But can't they trace the credit card I used to get the room?"

"It's too late to fix that, and it won't do you any good if I put it in my name. If they're tracking you, they already know you're here. We'll have to live with that one. But don't borrow anybody's cell phone to call anyone you know. Or anybody else, far as that goes. Not until I get back to you."

Amanda paused. "Isn't that a little paranoid?"

"I'm too cautious to get paranoid."

Isaiah rose and strolled back among the shelves. "I'll be right here if you need me." He paused. "And, yes, I'll help you."

Amanda smiled, and imagined that she felt a pleasantly surprising relief. In the moment she realized that asking for his help had been as nerve-wracking as the dread of what she would have done if he had refused. But he hadn't refused.

"Thank you," she said.

***

Leaving staff to lock up the shop, Isaiah saw Amanda back to her room at the Motel 6. After closing the door and setting aside two sacks of groceries that he'd picked up along the way from a conveniently located food mart, Isaiah removed three small, steel wedges from his knee-length leather jacket.

He gave the wedges to Amanda.

"Okay," he began, "I should be finished with your information by morning. Until then, I don't want you to leave this room and don't order anything. When I go, kick two of these wedges into the foot of the door and push one into the casement. It'll make it almost impossible for someone to get in here without causing a commotion. And don't answer the door no matter who it is. Not even if it's the police. They can get a card from the concierge if they're legitimate. If they're not, they probably don't want their faces on camera or in anyone's mind and they don't want a high body count, either, so their options are limited." He placed a hand on the door. "Do not be unduly alarmed. I'm always this careful. And I'll be back first thing in the morning with some breakfast. What do you prefer? Coffee or tea?"

"Tea, please. Are you always this polite?"

"Depends on the company."

"Well, thank you."

"Just make sure you double-lock and then triple-wedge this door. You have to do it all or you won't be as secure as I need you to be." Isaiah pointed toward the parking lot. "And don't be alarmed if you see a very big, very mean-looking Korean dude sitting in a silver Cadillac in the parking lot all night. He's a friend of mine and that makes him a friend of yours. He's just watching your door to make sure you're okay. If anything looks unusual, he'll call the police or handle it himself. And if he handles it himself, I'd advise you not to watch."

Amanda blinked. "Should I be afraid?"

"I'm very protective. Remember?"

She nodded, "I'll take care of the door."

Without another word Isaiah was gone.

Amanda forcefully wedged the door shut at the base, the side, and then studiously double-locked it and backed away, arms over her chest like she had suddenly entered a gray, fast-moving dream. But it didn't feel like a dream.

It felt like a nightmare.

***

After they convened in the war room the next day everyone sat stoically until Whitaker gestured, "Mike, would you please hand out the files?"

In a moment everyone opened another file covered with a red *Eyes Only* qualification inside a red rectangle. No one spoke as the moments passed in silence. Then General Atol Jackman closed his file and gazed at Whitaker. "I thought you morons were gonna come up with a simple plan, Whitaker."

"This is as simple as we could make it, Atol. And, believe me, about a thousand simple plans went down the crapper."

Jackman lifted a sheet of paper, "'Blow it up?' This is what you call a simple plan?" He dismissively tossed the file with a laugh. "Jesus, Whitaker! A monkey could have come up with this!"

"It's the best idiotic idea we've got after going through a very long line of tragically idiotic ideas."

"Listen up, Whitaker. I know you work for the CIA, so you're an idiot from the get-go and you have my sympathies just like I have sympathy for insane people and lepers. But penetrating one of the tightest security systems in the world and starting a chain reaction of liquid nitrogen and liquid helium explosions in an underground tunnel, and surviving, is not a simple plan."

"Well, that's why you make the big bucks, Atol." Whitaker slightly swiveled his chair. "We've come up with a plan. How you implement it is up to you. After all, we're just civilians. You're the professional so you should be able to figure out how to do it. I mean, if you can't fly it, drive it, or shoot it, you blow it up. Isn't that the motto?"

Jackman's tone dropped. "'Surviving' does have a little something to do with it. What's wrong with just dropping a Massive Ordinance Air Blast Bomb on it and denying any responsibility? When I suggested that we destroy the place, that was my first thought. Sending in a team was the admiral's idea. And to be honest I never liked it in the first place."

"Because hitting the facility from the surface won't do the job," Whitaker replied, unfazed. "You have to destroy the collider itself and that thing is located three hundred feet underground. And some parts of it are six hundred feet underground so you have to get your men through the most hellacious security system in the world and inside the corridor that contains the ATLAS itself."

Jackman wearily swept a hand down over his face. He gazed to the side before he stared again at Whitaker. "And this is the only directive? Destroy the thing? We don't need to clear any last-minute details on how we do it? And you do have two hackers in the Observation Room monitoring the security system?"

Whitaker nodded, "Affirmative. And you have an official sanction from the highest authority to use the warhead at your discretion. So, as of this moment, you have full command and authority." He slid an envelope across the table. "These are the access, clearance, and detonation codes."

Jackman pocketed the envelope. "I'm making the requisition through the Department of Energy. And I've picked four Delta operators. Here's their files."

Whitaker simply received and consequently slid the files across the table. "Mike, have the NSA issue four passports per man with matching credit cards and driver's licenses by morning. See that the cards are covered by Pacific Oil Company."

Jackman asked, "When do you want them squared up?"

Whitaker leaned back. "A disguised civilian flight will leave one week from today from McNair. Your team will covertly obtain any equipment you requisition at the American Embassy in Geneva. But, after that, there will be no further contact with American resources. You are to complete the mission and then your men are to make their own way home with their cards and IDs. And there's no budget because the money is unlimited." He emphasized, "Just make sure everyone is crystal clear on the one unbreakable rule."

"We were never there?" asked Jackman.

"Exactly," Whitaker nodded. "You guys were never there in the first place and iron-clad alibis will be provided by people who wrote the script for this rodeo. And if you wind up in heaven—hopefully, I mean, in heaven and not where *we all deserve*—and God sees your alibi, even God will say you weren't there."

"That's no problem," Jackman stated with a bitter edge. "Got the tattoo and the T-shirt."

Whitaker asked with noticeable hesitance, "Atol, and don't take me wrong, but are you going over there, too?" A pause. "No offense, buddy, but aren't you getting a little long in the tooth for this?"

"You don't give someone a mission that you're not willing to do yourself," said Jackman with a frown. "If my operators on this suicide mission don't come back, I don't come back. So bury my heart at Wounded Knee."

Whitaker sighed with a shake of his head. "I know you're a full-blooded Sioux, Atol, and fighting from the front is your natural warrior instinct, but that's how Stonewall Jackson got himself killed, man. And he was a general, too."

Jackman said nothing.

"All right, then." Whitaker shook his head, "Just remember; the same goes for you. If you get killed, there won't be any medals conferred, no combat benefits paid to your family. You and your guys won't even get a five-dollar funeral. And you won't be buried at Wounded Knee. You'll be buried in some cesspool in Switzerland. And, man, that's about as buried as buried gets."

For a good minute Whitaker tapped a piece of paper that lay separate from the files. "And, also, Atol, I think it's fair to tell you that there's something of a wild card involved in all this. And it might prove complicated."

Jackman straightened. "What kind of wild card?" He shook his head. "We don't need no wild cards, Whitaker. This whole damn thing is a wild card. We sure as hell don't need another one."

"It's a civilian affair and it's not easy to shut down without raising a few flags," Whitaker answered. "There was one American working in the Observation Room at CERN when all this crap went down. Her name was Cynthia Deker. She was a physicist. And, of course, she has a very inquisitive and protective sister. Her name is Amanda Deker. It's all in your addendum. Now, Amanda Deker isn't rich so she can't hire a big legal firm to find her sister. But she has approached a mysterious character who's in our DHS files and it might be a grave mistake to underestimate this guy."

"Christ," muttered Jackman, "what does this mystery man do for a living?"

"He owns a combination bookstore, coffee shop," Whitaker said blandly. "But he also has a bar and makes some pretty good ham, turkey, and cheese sandwiches on toast. Or, at least, that's what the guys told me."

Jackman stared a long moment. "A bookstore owner." There was another, and even longer pause. "Are you telling me that some chain-smoking, out-of-shape bookstore owner could be a problem to *me*? When I've got four operators?"

"That's exactly what I'm telling you, Atol." Whitaker opened a manila envelope, removing a photograph and an attached sheet. "To begin with, this man, and the only reliable name we can confirm for him is 'Isaiah,' was approximately six years old during the last days of the Vietnam War. He basically grew up during the most murderous stage of the killing. And he somehow fought his way out of that bloodbath. Then he survived the wholesale holocaust of the Khmer Rouge like some kind of six-year-old Tarzan and made his way through Cambodia before he crossed into Thailand, so we give the guy credit for being real smart and tough as a nickel steak. And, nowadays, he does favors for people no one else will help. People who can't afford a highly trained team of professionals. Only, this guy *is* highly trained and he *is* a professional. It's just that he works for free. And, from what we understand, he's agreed to help Ms. Deker find her sister."

"So how is this a problem?" asked Jackman bluntly. "They have no creds. They have no foreign access to guns or explosives. They probably can't even get through the front door of this Hadron Supercollider." He shook his head. "Having a couple of amateur gumshoes asking the wrong people a bunch of questions ain't no problem. And we probably won't even see 'em, so I ain't gonna worry about 'em."

"Well," Whitaker answered, "I still have an obligation to make you aware of this potential threat because this man's no joke, Atol. DHS says this guy's IQ is off the map and he's *very* capable."

Jackman hesitated. "What do you mean by very capable?"

"We've attribute forty-seven deaths to him and almost all of them were KGB, Spetsnaz, Romanian Secret Police. All of them were shooters with serious trigger time, experience, and skill sets. He's also planted a fair share of corporate hitters and mercenaries. None of them were civilians. All of them were pros. So this guy can kill like lightning but he's never killed a noncombatant. Or not that we know of, anyway."

"So this guy *does* have access to foreign weapons?"

"All we know is that he uses some kind of edged weapon. We don't know what it is. But we know he's very, very good with it." He coughed. "For some reason, he's never used a gun. Or, yet again, not that we know of. Our best guess is that he just doesn't like guns. To tell you the truth we have very little intel on the guy. We know what happened to him when he was young. Then he became a naturalized American citizen and vanished."

"Any record of training? Bosnia? Israel? Russia?"

"No record of it. Not with us or anybody else. And, believe me, we've checked." Whitaker's countenance was vaguely worried. "So nobody knows what he did, or was, between the time he was sixteen and when he opened his bookstore. Social security has no record. Customs only has a smattering. All we know with anything close to concrete is that he was raised in the bloodiest killing of the Vietnam War. We know he survived the last of that insane rampage all by himself and then fought his way through the Khmer Rouge at *six years old*—I say again—and then made his way through that hellacious, mine-laden, booby-trapped inferno called Cambodia and crossed the border into Thailand.

"Now, gentlemen, I give credit where credit is due. Call it noblesse oblige. I think that escaping those homicidal maniacs of the Khmer Rouge after the downright insane bloodbath of the Vietnam War speaks to this man's determination and intelligence and a whole lot more. I think it goes without saying that he's a freaking genius, he's got some real hard bark on him, he's incredibly resourceful and he can probably disappear at will. And I don't know how he might play into this but I wouldn't underestimate him." He paused. "My guess is that he will almost certainly be in Geneva searching for this woman's sister and probably with Ms. Deker. And it goes without saying that we might cross paths with them. But make no mistake. Isaiah and Ms. Deker are noncombatants. There is no green light on them. You can detain them for their own safety or the success of this mission but, and I stress, they are not to be harmed." He waved. "Otherwise just get the job done."

Jackman asked, "Rules of engagement?"

"Our target is the supercollider and the usual rules of engagement apply," Whitaker continued, more relaxed. "We defend ourselves in accordance with the normal force continuum. If they pull a knife, we pull a gun. If they pull a gun, we kill them. But remember, we are not officially there. We do not have diplomatic immunity and so the embassy can't do a thing if any of you get nailed by the Swiss police for killing a civilian. Or anybody else, for that matter. You will rot in a Swiss prison. And, lastly, the president would prefer a zero-body count." He cleared his throat. "If that's possible."

"Listen up, chief," Jackman immediately stated. "Does the president want this demonic son of a bitch destroyed or not?"

"He wants it obliterated, Atol."

"Then I can't promise no zero-body count." Jackman stared. "We can try. That's the best I can do."

"Just try not to leave a trail of dead bodies all the way to our doorstep, all right? The main objective is to disable the thing so that it'll take them ten thousand years to get it up and running. We'll deal with the other supercolliders as they come."

"What about final approval on the bomb?"

"There will be no approval for you or anyone else. As I stressed, there will be no sanction, no orders, no history of room service or even a phone call much less any authorization to use a nuclear weapon. I cannot stress enough that this is not a righteous mission. This is a black ops mission to the horizon. You guys are so off the books, you're not even listed as off the books. But as far as the bomb goes, you have full authority and command. You make the call at your discretion."

"And if *we* take casualties?"

"You are ordered to dispose of our personal casualties at the most covert site available with no ID and no possibility of identification." Whitaker stared. "In other words, if you don't live, you get dumped in the woods."

Jackman leaned back. His left hand was clenched in a fist. He stared at nothing long enough for everyone to shift, watching him.

Finally Whitaker exclaimed, "Good grief! What is it now, Atol?"

"Nothing I haven't dealt with all my life," Jackman muttered. "A typical government operation. Find a way to fit a square peg into a round hole. And the suits don't want a body count, but I can promise you there's gonna be a damn bloody body count, Whitaker, and there's gonna be just as many dead civilians as dead soldiers. So you and the president can expect to count a lot of casualties. Including us."

***

After Isaiah had brought Amanda breakfast with tea in the morning, he told her that she was now free to go to and from the hotel and his shop because she would be heavily guarded by a team the entire way. And since waiting at the hotel had become painfully monotonous, Amanda had decided to pay a visit. But as she walked through the door of the bookshop, Isaiah was nowhere to be seen.

"Isaiah?" she called.

Footsteps were heard on the staircase behind the counter and Isaiah descended. He was dressed as before; blue jeans, a black T-shirt, a thick leather belt, lightweight-hiking boots. He smiled, "Sorry. Everything going okay at the hotel?"

"Yes. Your friend is really quite diligent. He's like a shadow. I haven't even talked to him but I know he's always there. And you mentioned a team guarding me from the hotel to this place but I haven't seen any of them, either. And I was looking."

"Well, they're pretty good at what they do. Come on upstairs. I live up here."

Amanda waved at Isaiah's small staff of clerks and waitresses and climbed the stairs behind the counter. "Save a little on rent, huh?" she asked.

"Yeah," he replied easily, "every little bit helps." He hesitated. "I started this place five years ago with some used books that I'd picked up at auctions and built it up from there. I wasn't making any money, though, until I finally got my permits to serve alcohol and food. Then I turned this place into a combination bookstore, bar, restaurant. And I've stayed in fair shape with the cops, firemen, and city employees by giving them a discount on everything from sandwiches to beer, so things aren't too bad right now. And if you're looking for work, I could always give you something part-time."

"Oh, thank you," Amanda answered, "That's very nice of you but I've already got three good offers. I just haven't decided on which one I want to take yet." She laughed. "In any case, I'd hoped my waitressing days were behind me."

"Fair enough. What's your line?"

"My line?"

"What do you do for a living?"

"Oh." Amanda muttered, "well, I earned my master's degree in friction variations for aerothermal fluid dynamics after I got my bachelor's in aeronautical engineering. My childhood dream was to work for NASA on the Mars program. But I've been a risk appraisal officer for the last eleven years."

Isaiah glanced over a shoulder. "That's quite a career switch, isn't it? From rocket scientist to banker?"

"Not really," Amanda answered dully. "It's just numbers, in the end. Physics is just numbers. Risk appraisal is just numbers. It's all just equations."

"Why'd you switch? Seems like Mars would be more fun."

"Well, it might not seem like a good reason but the money's a whole lot better in risk appraisal."

Isaiah laughed, "That'd be a good enough reason for me."

"Yeah, but I resigned my last job two years ago to help Cynthia get situated in Geneva, which used up a heartbreaking amount of my money, and now I've got to get back to work. But I'm looking for a stronger company. My last employer never truly recovered from the bailout. They didn't go under but they'll never come back, either."

Isaiah glanced down. "Did you see all that coming?"

"Oh, yeah. I wasn't even in risk appraisal then. I was still studying rocket science. But I saw that coming. A blind mule could have seen that coming. Why? Did you lose anything in that mess?"

"Nah," Isaiah shook his head, "I spent seven years in Japan when I was younger, then I just wandered the world for a while so I was barely back in America when the bailout went down. And with what little money I had, I started this store. I only had enough to invest in some books, shelves, rent, and food." He shrugged, "Of course, I have a good little business now but it's still a small business. And the profits prove it. But I've got a roof over my head and I'm not hungry and that's good enough."

"What did you do in Japan for seven years?"

"Studied."

"Studied what?"

"Kendo."

"That's interesting. Why kendo?"

Isaiah's tone was perfectly casual. "Because I believe survival is an art everyone should master in their own way."

Isaiah's second-floor apartment was a spartan one-room efficiency with a kitchen and small bathroom. No bathtub, just a shower. It reminded Amanda of a so-so camper. An old-fashioned Murphy bed was folded against a wall. There was a TV and photographs of what Amanda assumed were friends, but there were no diplomas, degrees, or awards. A quick glance along the single wall of his wide-open kitchen confirmed that Isaiah lived a very sparse life indeed with few, if any, luxuries.

"Do you keep up with the news?" Amanda asked, touching the TV.

Isaiah shook his head, "No, but I like old movies." He began placing items in a black duffle bag. "I don't pay much attention to politics that change like the wind of the sea, unstable in every direction it goes. And I don't like commentaries with a lot of parrots reciting bullet points and can't answer a simple question. Basically, I'm not entertained by bigots and badly veiled prejudice."

"I understand completely," said Amanda somewhat wearily. "So what are some of your favorite old movies?"

Isaiah laughed, "I guess I like westerns like *True Grit. Shane, Wyatt Earp, High Noon.* I sort of identify with the underdog."

"I would think that, owning a bookstore, you'd be reading all the time."

He dropped what looked like a sharpening stone on the bed as he answered, "Yeah, I read a lot for sure. I like honest history and good biographies. And I'll occasionally pick up a newspaper to see if we're at war again. But despite what a lot of people think, running a small business, even one as small as this, takes a lot of time."

"Oh, I imagine it does," Amanda agreed. "Why do you say you like honest history books?"

"Because too many history books are just propaganda. Biographies, too, far as that goes. And I've heard and seen enough propaganda for ten lifetimes. That's another reason why I don't watch the news."

"Do you remember everything you read?"

"No, it's like I said, there's no such thing as a photographic memory. There's a memory continuum of sorts. Some people can memorize a few pages. Some can memorize an entire book with interesting accuracy. But nobody has the native ability to photograph everything they see. At least, nobody that science has ever verified.”

“Not even you, huh?”

Isaiah laughed, “I can photograph a page if I concentrate. But that’s not a legitimate photographic memory. Frankly, I think a photographic memory is just an urban myth. And not many doctors believe in it, either.”

“How many people are there like you?” Amanda sat, leaning forward. “I mean … what did you call it?”

“Psychiatrists call it as a Highly Superior Autobiographic Memory. And I don’t know how many people have it. The psychiatrist that diagnosed me said that there were three other bona fide cases in the world. But that was a while back.”

“If you don’t mind me asking, why did you go to a psychiatrist?”

“Because I was worried about whether I had something wrong with my brain or if I just had an unusually good memory.”

Amanda paused a long moment. “Is it a pain? I mean, does it cause you more trouble than it’s worth?”

“No,” Isaiah shook his head, “I can turn it on or off. If I couldn’t, I’d probably be insane. It would be hell walking around with ten thousand restaurant menus in my head.” He raised a gaze. “Have you finished packing?”

“Not yet.”

“Don’t bring anything you want to keep.”

“Why not?”

“Because we probably won’t be coming back with it. Just bring stuff you were planning to give to Goodwill, anyway.”

“How long will we be gone?”

“Until we know.”

Amanda folded her hands. “You know, you never did tell me what you found out with all that information I gave you.”

"I found out that Cynthia lived alone," said Isaiah. "About like you, I suppose."

"You checked on me?"

"Just guessing," he shrugged. "You don't wear a ring. You don't mind talking about yourself. You don't assume a defensive posture, so I suppose you're single. And I don't see any stray hairs on your clothes so I don't think you have a pet."

"That's about right," Amanda conceded. "I'm single and I don't even have a cat. Anything else?"

"You're smart. Ambitious. From the smoothness of your right sleeve, you write a lot, and you're something of a workaholic. But you do have a long-term plan for your personal life. It's just that you're not close to achieving it."

"Good grief! Why would you guess that?"

"Because you have highly refined social skills, which means you want to make a good impression if you might stumble into somebody's who's lucky enough to interest you. Also, you're more than just a brainiac. You work out hard with a combo of heavy resistance training and cardio. You do interval training like a pro. So you either just like to stay in primo shape for whatever comes down the pike or you've just got gold-plated genetics. And my best guess is that it's a combination. But you don't take anything for granted, which is another reason why you work so hard. You don't cheat yourself. You fully commit yourself to everything you put your hand to do, which is typical of obsessive-compulsive personalities. And that's going to include finding your sister."

Amanda grunted, "You like reading people, don't you?"

"Not so much," Isaiah shook his head. "It's just a habit that I developed for self-preservation. Like always being aware of people and my surroundings. I've been doing it for so long I do it without thinking about it. Now, Cynthia did have a cat but it was rescued by the landlord when her neighbors didn't see her come home for a few days. Out of concern they called the police, then the police called the landlord and the landlord let them in where they found one very hungry cat that the neighbors adopted. But she had no real friends. According to her neighbors, she worked most of the time. And, yes, she was a genius in cosmological physics just like you said and it doesn't get any more complicated, so there aren't a lot of people like her in the world. She must be a genius."

"She is. Do you have any idea why she's missing?"

"Not yet. And neither does anybody else including the Swiss and French police and Interpol. And the FBI won't get involved because of a territorial dispute."

Amanda scowled. "What kind of territorial dispute? The FBI just told me that they didn't do missing person cases. They told me that they do foreign kidnappings, murders, terrorists, bomber plots, all that stuff. But they don't go looking for American citizens who don't happen to show up for work for a couple of days. At least, that was their excuse to me. That's not what they told you?"

"The FBI told me that Switzerland is saying that there's no indication Cynthia went missing on Swiss soil and so they're not granting permission to the FBI for any kind of investigation in Swiss territory. The French government is saying the same thing. So it's a jurisdictional dispute." answered Isaiah "The Hadron Supercollider is located in both France and Switzerland. It doesn't matter where it's incorporated, and in order for the FBI to investigate in a foreign country they have to obtain official permission from that country. And at the moment both France and Switzerland are refusing to grant permission." He paused. "It's logical that whoever's behind CERN purposefully built it on the border in case they ever needed to complicate an investigation, and that's probably what they're doing."

"Does that make it more difficult for us?"

Isaiah tightened the chain at the top of the duffle bag. "That's going to be the least of our problems since I don't give a damn about laws or jurisdictions. The hard part is that these people do have a well-earned reputation for 'disappearing' anyone they feel is a threat. And that includes Supreme Court judges, FBI agents, generals, lawyers, or just people like you and me. So, obviously, someone wants to keep whatever is happening in that place a secret. And they don't mind vanishing people from the planet to do it." He set the duffle bag on the floor. "I want to warn you before we leave."

"Hit me."

"This could get dangerous, Amanda. And I'm not talking about a broken foot or a busted tooth. I'm talking about getting buried in a cave because these people have already killed a four-star army general and a Supreme Court judge. And if they have the will to kill those guys, then they have the will to kill anybody in the world. Plus, they're obviously very capable at making people real dead real fast." He sighed. "A general who even suspects that he's on the hit list of some conglomerate like CERN is not an easy target. Survival is an art he's cultivated all his life and he knows how to protect himself, so snuffing out a general requires operators that can reach anybody, anywhere, anytime."

Amanda didn't blink.

"And if we get put on this list?" she finally asked.

Isaiah shrugged, "I've been called a hard target. But there's a gun behind every corner. And bullets don't have a name. They end up where they end up. Do you understand what I'm saying?" He straightened and stared steadily into her eyes. "Trying to find your sister can get you killed."

"It might get you killed, too," Amanda said. "And you're still going. Why?"

"Because I believe the poor and weak deserve the same protection as the rich and powerful," Isaiah remarked. "Also, I don't fear what might happen to me—or, at least, not like most people—because I've always considered myself as good as dead, anyway. But I wasn't in the mood to die then and I'm not in the mood now."

"Is that a Zen thing?"

"It's just an attitude I learned when I was a kid and it's gotten me through the bloodiest battlefields this world has ever seen." He walked to the closet and removed an aluminum case about four feet long and six inches wide. He sat it on the floor beside the duffle bag. The case had "*Diplomatic Pouch: United Nations Property,*" written in bold, bright orange letters across the top.

"What's that?" asked Amanda as Isaiah dropped a metal clipboard with official-looking, multicolored documents onto the bed.

"Call it a walking stick," he said.

"It doesn't look like a walking stick."

"It's something that's come in handy in the past." Finally Isaiah sat on the edge of the bed, head bowed. "But maybe we won't need it."

With a curious grunt Amanda stood and lifted her purse. "Okay, well, I need to get back and finish packing. What time do we leave?"

"The day after tomorrow. I'll book us on the earliest available flight. But, first, I'll have to find people to cover for me. Then we'll go to Switzerland and find Cynthia and we'll all come back alive."

Amanda muttered as she walked toward the door.

"The 'alive' part sounds good to me."

***

Dressed in civilian clothing General Jackman and his four-member team arrived at Geneva International Airport at sunrise. They dismounted the jet separately and did not make eye contact inside the heavily guarded terminal. They each took separate taxis to various bus stops, changed modes of transportation, repeated the procedure two more times and three hours later they checked into separate rooms at the Hotel Beau Rivage Geneva.

Jackman had chosen the five-star dwelling instead of a fortified CIA safe house because this operation was, after all, off the books even to the CIA. The two agents that had been loaned from the Company had been sent here "on vacation" and, gazing about his genuinely ritzy hotel room, Jackman mumbled, "Holy crap. What a place to go on vacation. No wonder it's costing an arm and leg."

The Hotel Beau Rivage was located only a mile from a CIA safe house if this tour took a tragic left turn. It also provided direct access to the river, which snaked all the way through Geneva. Plus, it was next door to a dozen ports for a last-chance escape by sea. And the customized crowd was a highly affluent array of sultans, princes, ambassadors, and gunrunners each with their own entourage of heavily armed bodyguards. With so many hired guns on the property it would be complicated for a team of hitters to infiltrate and attempt an attack without half the building shooting back.

Five hours later the entire team, including the two female CIA operators, had checked in and at midnight they convened one by one in the general's suite. Jackman poured himself a scotch and glanced up. "Anybody want a drink?" he asked. "We're making our own rules on this one and I'm having a drink. In fact, I might have a couple of them."

Everyone wandered to the bar. In another five minutes they sat casually, all silent, placidly sipping, as Jackman pulled up a chair. He grimly gazed over them. "You do not know the full details of this operation," he began. "The cover story you were given was a fabrication for your families in case you don't come back and it's not the first time that you operators have been deployed in such a way, so we can skip the explanations. Now I'm going to tell you what we're really here to do."

From the war room file Jackman tossed pictures that splashed across the smooth glass coffee table. The photos perfectly captured the gargantuan image of what could only be described as a demonic entity glaring balefully into the video as if it perfectly understood the machine.

Jackman leaned forward to tap the image.

"This bastard, and we suspect he's just *one* of 'em, is using this portal to gain access into our world. They are fighting like hell to get through a dimensional gate created by this Hadron Supercollider and we've been volunteered to make sure this son-of-a-bitch machine is obliterated in a holocaust that will make it unusable until the stars fall from the sky. And that, ladies and gentlemen, is our mission."

Staring at the monstrous image, no one spoke.

Then, finally, Susan said, "Ya know, that sorta' looks like a demon."

"That's exactly what the president said," nodded Jackman. "And that's why we are going to permanently disable the Large Hadron Supercollider. But that's just half of it. And the easy half. Next, we have been asked to keep this to a zero-body count, and if we do have to kill some people, we do it so that it can't be traced back to the good ol' USA. Which means that we have to conceive a plan, execute it by destroying the most powerful machine in the world and, hopefully, do it all without making anybody dead. Then we coordinate our extraction without any official help."

Jackman paused. "But the rules of engagement do apply. If we are shot at, we shoot back. If someone attempts to kill us, we deal with it. This is not a suicide mission. The zero-body count directive was issued to keep down any collateral damage that might be traced back to us. But it's not one of the Ten Commandments. It's a request. Now, why don't you introduce yourselves?"

A muscular man with a bushy brown beard and a Hell's Angel jacket and ponytail midway down his back said, "I'm Major Roy Burris." He motioned to the remaining three men.

"This is Jake. That's Tanto. And this here is Picket. All of us are with the First Special Forces Operational Detachment. Most people just call us Delta."

"I'm Susan," said one woman of hypnotic beauty with long brunette hair and green eyes. "I'm with Central Intelligence and my specialty is cyber-security penetration and counter-computer insurgence. And, no, Susan is not my real name, but on this Kamikaze mission I don't think it matters. Any wrong name on whatever mass grave you drop me into will do." She bent, staring at the photograph. "Just don't let *that* thing get its hands on me. I don't care if you can't kill *it. Kill me.*"

"I'm Janet," said a ponytailed blonde who raised her hand. "I specialize in crippling computer systems, phone systems, security systems. Pretty much any kind of system. But let me tell you something about CERN. There are no outside means of accessing security. It's protected by a multi-tiered defense that is activated by fingerprint, voice, a retinal scan, and a code that they change every day. Now, Susan and I are already cleared for access since we began orientation for the Observation Room, but how we're going to get the rest of you inside without tripping an alarm is beyond me."

"Do any of you know what the Hadron Supercollider is secretly designed to achieve?" asked Jackman.

"Susan and I have suspicions," said Janet. "But this gizmo isn't a Ford. It's the most powerful, most dangerous machine in the world and we're not sure what they might be doing with it. Or even what they're capable of doing with it."

"Well, they're trying to accomplish the worst thing they can accomplish," Jackman continued, placing burly forearms on his thighs as he leaned forward. "One month ago these eggheads opened a gateway to a parallel dimension and something from that place physically reached into our world and snatched seven physicists into thin air." He let that settle; there was no visible reaction. "So, like I said, our job is to get inside this facility, do something that will disable this Hadron Supercollider for a thousand years and, if we get killed, we get killed. I think some of that was explained to you before you signed on and it's true. And since this is a classified mission, our families get no military compensation. You don't get a flag-draped coffin. Like you deserve. We just drop you in a hole, say something poetic, and that's it."

Roy muttered, "About like I always expected to end up."

Susan asked, "Do we have anything like a plan? I mean, Janet and I have space-age security passes and we have active duty inside the Observation Room, but nobody has told us anything like a plan."

"The plan is to get inside this supercollider, do something biblically catastrophic to the thing that will literally put it out of commission for eternity, and then go home as invisibly as we came. And, just so you know, there won't be any paper trail because we were never here and this mission never existed."

Major Burris asked, "Not to seem pedantic, but I'd like to stress Susan's point. Do we have anything resembling a plan?"

"How we accomplish our mission is up to us," stated Jackman, somewhat ponderous. "We have blueprints of this place. We have Janet and Susan inside. We have unqualified access to any weapons we request. But that's all we got."

Roy asked, "What about medical backup if we're disabled and not dead?"

"The CIA has a Geneva-based emergency medical service on twenty-four-hour standby for their people and we're temporarily under their care. That is, if you're still alive. If not, we make sure your body is never found."

"Huh," grunted Susan. "*Sounds* like a CIA operation."

Janet followed, "Well, we can't just destroy a zillion-dollar supercollider without a convenient patsy. There has to be somebody they can point a finger at or they'll blame America just for the hell of it."

"We've got a fall guy," Jackman answered. "We're gonna blame what they call their D-squad of electricians. That way, they can only blame themselves. And it's not a far-fetched idea. Those clowns already blew the thing up once. Disabled it for years. But what we've got to do is a hundred times worse. We've got to put this machine permanently out of commission."

"Disabling the computer system won't be enough to get the job done," stated Roy. "Explosives offer the most certain outcome. And this new brand of Semtex doesn't have any uniquely American chemical elements. Or, in other words, it can't be traced. It doesn't leave a fingerprint. Who has to approve the final plan?"

"We are to design and execute our mission plan without the sanction of any authority whatsoever," Jackman said in a grave tone. "We are outlaws, here, people. And that means that if we take this thing to the trash heap we might as well jump in with it. 'Cause if this goes bad, nobody gets out of jail unless you can escape a Swiss prison. Our families will get a letter saying your son or daughter was killed in a classified training accident and that's the short hairs of it."

He took a heavy breath. "Now, you're all soldiers, so you damn well deserve a last chance to *un*volunteer yourself. So if anybody wants to get their act in the wind, now is the time. But, after tonight, if you decide to take a hike, I'll have to send you to Leavenworth or sanction you. You'll know too much. I won't be able to let you walk. And that's the last order on this." He raised a hand toward the door. "But you're all heroes in my book for even being here. And if you want to get in the wind, that door ain't locked."

"Let's just blow this mother up and go home," said the Delta commando named Tanto who was tall and lean and sported a Fu Manchu mustache. His wild head of dark hair framed a hard, merciless face and his arms were completely covered with tattoos of samurai beheading man and beast alike. "Just another day at the office, sir."

With a scowl Roy asked, "This machine is currently down for some kind of maintenance, isn't it?" He motioned in the general direction of the supercollider. "How about we kidnap a few of the construction guys? We take their IDs, code entries, doctor the pictures. I'm positive that the guards don't know the faces of seven thousand rotating electricians. And an ordinary electrician isn't gonna require a retinal scan. We split up for routine maintenance, coordinate the charges, and blow it. Then we just fade." He gazed around the table. "It's a simple plan. Not much can go wrong except those walls will prevent any radio communications, so we'll have to trust each other and stay on the clock."

Janet commented dryly, "You can't set a bomb with a timer on this machine. If you set anything on that supercollider that has any kind of electrical charge—even a signature as small as a wristwatch—alarms will go off all over the place."

"Can you disable the alarm system?" asked Roy.

Janet paused. "I can disable it for a few minutes. But they'll start searching for the source of the interference and they'll find it no matter how well I conceal it. And when they do find it, it'll lead back to my terminal. So unless I'm out of there by then, I'm dead. They'll just shoot me on the spot."

"A few minutes is all I'll need," stated Roy. "I'll get you out of there before your number comes up."

"But Susan and I are the only Americans in the Observation Room," Janet added. "Won't they eventually blame America just by default?"

"By the time they figure it out, it won't matter," answered Roy. "Eventually they'll discover who did this. There's no stopping that. But we can't worry about what these guys dig up in the future. Someone in the next administration can deal with the fallout."

Jackman stated, "Each of you will have foolproof alibis. Some of you were at the White House with fifty witnesses. Some of you will have papers proving you were on another mission in China. The most important thing—hell, the *only* important thing—is that none of you had anything to do with this. And you'll be able to prove it. Incontrovertibly. With a presidential signature."

Jackman walked across the room, picked up a duffle bag, and walked back to the dining table. He laid out multiple blueprints, a dozen manuals, construction plans. Everything anyone would need to build the Hadron Supercollider.

He motioned, "This is what we've got. We have construction blueprints, plumbing, electrical, breakers, and substations. These pinpoint every nut and bolt. There's also a breakdown of the software with an analysis of the ungodly chemicals they use in that thing." He frowned over the material. "The embassy will supply us with any ordinance we need. Just remember the bottom line. I want maximum destruction and I want an ironclad plan to get out of there before it goes boom. That's it."

"Just one thing," stated Roy.

"What's that, Burris?"

"Are we sanctioned to use the warhead?"

Jackman's frown smoothed down his scarred face.

"That's my call," he said. "But if I do, none of us go home."

***

"You make excellent tea," said Amanda. "I've never tasted anything quite like it. What is it?"

"It's made out of some Chinese herbs and teas that I learned to mix when I was a kid," Isaiah remarked as he reclined into a chair. "Where I grew up, it was nothing special. But all my friends here really like it. They say it triples their energy." He laughed. "One of them wanted to start a website and market it."

"Where was that?"

"Where was what?"

"Where did you grow up?"

"Oh," Isaiah glanced to the side before looking back. "I was born and raised in Vietnam until I was six. Then, after the war, the Khmer Rouge captured me and locked me up in an internment camp. That is, instead of just killing me outright like they killed almost everybody else. I guess they figured I was still young enough for re-education."

"They put you in a prison camp? How did you get out?"

"I escaped."

"What!"

Isaiah laughed as he added, "After I got a little bigger, they put me on a squad digging graves and burning bodies. So, one day, after we began to bury the last one, I slid into the grave and crawled under the body of some politician they'd tortured to death. Then they shoveled in the dirt and I was buried with a decapitated body."

Amanda didn't move.

"It was a unique experience." Isaiah continued. "But, anyway, I immediately started digging my way out because I knew it'd take me a while to claw through all that blood and dirt. And about … oh, I don't know … right after sunset, I guess, I finally broke the surface and crawled into the jungle."

"And that was it?"

"*No*," Isaiah shook his head. "That was just the beginning. After that, I had to sneak back to the cave where I picked up the only thing I owned. The one thing I wouldn't leave behind. Then I grabbed a bag of mangos and rice and started making my way through the jungle, which was the absolute worst bush you can imagine, a killing ground where they still practiced cannibalism. And that was an ordeal. Believe me. There were cannibals and snakes and tigers and unexploded bombs. But eight months later, and half-dead, I reached an American Red Cross station in Thailand and from there I eventually immigrated to the United States. And, in case you're wondering, I am indeed a naturalized American citizen."

"Who were your parents?"

"My mother was French but she died when I was young," Isaiah said with a somewhat sad shrug, the first real hint of loss Amanda had seen in him. "The man who raised me said his name was Coldy Bimore. He was an old man then. He was a veteran of World War II. Then he saw action in Vietnam because he was a super-lifer. He said we might outlast the killing if we stayed low long enough, but the Khmer Rouge found us the day after the last American chopper lifted out of Saigon."

Amanda's eyes had softened. "Did they hunt for you after you escaped?"

"Oh, yeah, they hunted for me. I heard them beating the bush. But I climbed a tree and hid there until they gave up. Then I walked into the jungle and eventually reached Thailand. Fortunately, my so-called father had taught me English and my mother had taught me French and Vietnamese, so language wasn't a problem."

"What'd you do when you got to America?" Amanda asked with a tone of genuine interest. "You had no family."

"I had the name of a relative of my mother. He lived in San Francisco. And I had the one thing my father kept with him his entire life."

"What was that?"

Isaiah signed more deeply. "When my father died, and they ransacked the cave, they failed to find the only thing he valued."

"Which was?"

"It was a sword," stated Isaiah simply. "I thought it was just an ordinary sword, but it turned out to be a Japanese

National Treasure that was supposedly destroyed during World War II."

"Is that what Deb meant when she said you could defend yourself like nobody she's ever seen?" Amanda's eyebrows rose curiously. "You use your sword?"

"I've used it to defend myself a few times. And I did have to use it to defend your friend, Deborah."

Amanda stared at the case.

"Can I see it?" she asked.

"Sure." Isaiah rose and walked to the bed. "I'm not superstitious." He flipped three locks, three switches, and opened the case; the katana was approximately four feet long and the handle, or hilt, was strangely wrapped and very well-worn. The grip was also embedded on one side with what appeared to be a gold dragon.

"I know a little bit about these things," Amanda said, extending a hand. "My father was an avid collector of Japanese weapons. Can I touch it?"

"It's all right with me," Isaiah shrugged. "I don't hold the Japanese philosophy that a samurai's sword is his soul."

Amanda touched the gold dragon, which felt ancient and smooth. "I think I know what this is. In fact, my father talked about it. What's the name of this sword?"

"It's the Honjo Masamune."

"The Honjo Masamune," Amanda laughed. "Yes, I've heard of it. Everyone has. My father was obsessed with this thing. He told me it was made seven hundred years ago by Goro Nyude Masamune." She raised her face. "Yeah, I remember every word he told me because he searched for this sword his whole life. He said it was forged during the Kamakura Period of Japan. It belonged to the house of Tokugawa Lemasa, president of the House of Peers, until an American soldier confiscated it after the war. But there wasn't any record of it being confiscated. Do you think that's because your so-called father knew he was stealing a Japanese National Treasure?"

Isaiah smiled, "Probably. Anyway, the Japanese relative of my mother who raised me thought that my possessing the Honjo Masamune was something like destiny, so he taught me how to use it. He said I was born to be one with the sword since we had each escaped from the grave. And, when I was older, he sent me to Japan to study with an old-world kendo master. The last of his kind. I was in Japan seven years practicing kendo ten hours a day, every day, before I returned to America."

"Like a samurai," joined Amanda.

"More like a Ronin," Isaiah remarked. "And so I've used it my whole life, mostly just in practice but sometimes to defend myself or someone else. And, on a stunt like this, I feel better with it than without it."

"You don't like guns, huh?"

"No," Isaiah stated coldly.

Amanda blew out a breath. "Well, I won't ask. I'm sure you have your reasons. And they probably run deep like everything else about you." Her smile brightened. "So! You gonna call me and let me know what time to be at the airport?"

"No," Isaiah shook his head, "I'll take you back to your hotel and I'll have Sataturi watch you again. Just be ready early tomorrow. And remember what I said about clothes. Don't pack anything you want to keep."

"You don't make flight reservations?"

"No. I'll get the tickets after we get to the airport."

"I forgot how cautious you are. I'm glad I've got you."

With a smile Isaiah shut the case.

"Yeah," he nodded. "You've got me."

***

Muttering a curse, Jackman lowered the binoculars. Beside him, Roy Burris and Janet continued to study the

Large Hadron Supercollider's enormous compound. It was at least a hundred acres and looked like any other town surrounded by snowcapped peaks. There was very little that hinted at what monstrous machine was buried beneath it except for heavily armed guards patrolling the streets.

"There just ain't no way in without being seen by a guard or a civilian or one of them security cameras." Jackson chewed on his cigar. "They got roads, but they're all guarded. All entrances are guarded. They got snipers on the roof of the topside facility which ain't nuthin' but an elevator shaft. The guards inside the building are armed with rifles. Or, for Janet's sake, they've got what civilians call machineguns."

Janet didn't lower her binoculars. "Thank you, general, but I know what a fully automatic weapon is. The guards are in a two-by-two roving patrol carrying a mix of Colts, Zeniths, and Scorpions, all nine-millimeter or two-twenty-threes. They won't stop a rhinoceros, but they're more than enough for stopping a human being. And, the deeper you go, the more security you run into. The only other thing they told us about guns is that there are no armor-piercing rounds allowed inside the compound because they can't risk knocking a hole in the collider. It uses a zillion explosive gases."

Roy muttered, "They may allow tours of this place, but I bet they don't show you the guts of it. Anybody with half a brain would know that no research facility needs a thousand guns to protect it."

With a weary sigh Jackman half-turned on the tiny hill they'd selected from a topographical map. It was far enough to avoid naked surveillance, but if someone were watching through a telescope, they were easily visible. "Anybody got any good ideas?" he asked. Then added, "Hell, I'd be happy for a bad idea."

"Mansfield has got us oriented for the Observation Room," Janet began, "but we haven't been taken down to the collider so we've only got the vaguest idea how we can get the team inside." She hesitated. "I did do some checking, though, and found out that the electricians have to go through a retinal scan, too, so we can scratch the idea of kidnapping a few and using their IDs, hands and *eyeballs*, God help me."

Roy asked, "Can you start a fire or distraction from the Observation Room so that everyone has to leave the building? Something like a fire drill or chemical spill?"

"No," Janet shook her head. "The Observation Room is exclusively devoted to measuring particles in the collider relayed through the proton detectors and the security in the collider corridor itself. It has no connection to the rest of the facility. So, basically, I can do very little from my station to affect the whole compound. I can only do stuff that affects the collider corridor itself."

"What about scrambling the security system to the corridor?"

"Then a bunch of titanium doors shut and they can't be lifted by anything less than a bulldozer. The elevators are shut down. The stairs are locked down. Nobody gets in. Nobody gets out. Everybody grows old and dies in the dark."

"Can you leave your post?" asked Roy.

"I can," Janet said, "but not without them monitoring my every move. To put it mildly, they are obsessed with knowing where everyone is at every second. That's why all personnel wear a badge and every badge has an individual signature that is read by a heavily guarded computer that automatically alerts armed guards if someone wanders into a red zone when they're only qualified to be in a green zone. Obviously, they don't want eyeballs going where eyeballs are not color-coded to go."

Jackman asked, "Why all this secrecy above the ground? I don't see nuthin' above ground worth protecting. All the money is buried."

After a long pause Janet said, "Well, some say these people are a bunch of warlocks or witches. Whatever the difference is. Maybe they have a temple to Shiva or Satan or something and that's what they're protecting."

Roy drawled, "Why did Mansfield get you assigned to the War Room?"

"The Observation Room?"

"I'll call it a War Room until we wrap this up."

"As far as I know, and as far as they know, I'm replacing an expert at detecting reductionistic atomism," said Janet, nonplussed. "Susan is assigned to communications for all of the neutrino detectors, which doesn't sound particularly important, but she's critical to this operation and it's too complicated to break down into layman's terms. No offense."

"Give it a try," stated Jackman.

Janet exhaled, then continued, "Susan monitors the relays sent from the neutrino detectors to backup facilities all over the world, and that system allows her to link up to any satellite. And the satellites are where I plan to hide my command when I put the computer offline. If not, they'll track me down fast. But if Susan can link enough encrypted satellite systems with foreign and domestic detector stations, interlacing all of them, I think I can put the system offline long enough for you guys to sneak inside without them tracing it back to me in seconds."

"You can put the computer offline without triggering the vaults?" asked Roy.

"Yes," Susan nodded curtly, "they're separate programs. And they should be. You can't have fifty security vaults slamming shut every time you have a computer glitch or you'd never get anything done. But, to a degree, they're also interdependent, so if the computer is offline, the security system is also offline without initiating a full shutdown. Now, if security is offline for more than a half-hour, it initiates a shutdown, anyway. That's the second protocol. But I can buy you guys a half-hour before that happens."

"What are we going to do in a half-hour?" asked Roy.

"Get inside."

Roy glanced from the facility to Janet. "*How*?"

"I haven't figured that out yet."

Jackman: "So what is it that you're pretending to be? And, if you don't mind, what the hell is atomic reductionism?"

"We're not 'pretending' to be anything at all, general. Susan is a genuine communications expert and I'm an expert in gamma rays and neutrinos, which are critical to reading the Higgs boson field and the wake fields left by antimatter." Janet continued as if reciting, "The Higgs boson field tracks neutrinos which reveal tiny grams of dark matter, and that's my specialty. I'm also an expert—as experts go—in antimatter, dark energy, and the uses and consequences of interacting with either of them. Basically, general, I'm what they call a real genius and I'm one of the few people in the world who actually understands the very serious dangers of dark energy."

"You know," Roy mumbled, "I've heard that term a lot lately. Dark energy. Dark matter. Antimatter. Can you give me a layman's understanding?"

"Antimatter is just the opposite of matter," Janet raised her binoculars again. "And it's very unstable. If one gram of antimatter comes into contact with anything in our world, which is called matter, it would explode with catastrophic results."

Roy continued staring. "How catastrophic?"

"Oh," Susan answered in a bored tone, "approximately one gram of antimatter would explode with the force of about forty-two kilotons. That's equal to forty-two-thousand tons of dynamite. Let's say it'd make Hiroshima look like a firecracker."

Roy laughed, "Yeah, I know what a kiloton is. But I thought these guys were trying to open a portal to some kind of demonic dimension. Which is it? Bombs or portals? Or is it six of this and a half-dozen of that?"

"For what I've seen so far it appears to be both," Susan replied, "but I can't say why they're trying to build superbombs. If they can perfect the means for dimensional transport, then they could master time travel, as well. And, at that point, they won't need bombs. They'll just go back in time and wipe you out before you're born. Hell, I don't know what they're ultimately planning to do. We're dealing with sociopaths. Maybe they want superweapons because even they're afraid of screwing up the timeline. They might have a secret fear of 'the butterfly effect' and they're terrified they'll wipe out their own existence by changing history. How the hell would I know what a sociopath wants to do with a time machine and an illegal weapons facility?" After a moment she added, "But if I let my rather bizarre imagination roam—not something I like to do—it's possible that antimatter bombs could be used for terraforming."

"What's terraforming?" asked Jackman.

"Terraforming is basically changing the atmosphere and landscape of the Earth. And one way to do it is with weapons of mass destruction. And I mean mass destruction like no one has ever seen. You see, the biggest nuclear bomb ever detonated was fifty megatons. The Russians did it. It was called Tsar Bomba. But that bomb was, relatively speaking, just a firecracker compared to the power these boys are playing with. To put it simply, just two-hundred grams of dark matter would explode with at least sixty-thousand megatons and that's enough force to level a lot of countries. It would make an area the size of Siberia uninhabitable for a million years. But only for human beings, and that's where terraforming enters this."

Roy lowered his binoculars as he asked, "Terraforming? But *not* for human beings? Who are they gonna be terraforming it for?"

"For whatever's on the far side of that portal, Roy."

"They could do that?"

"Yeah, they could. All they would have to do is build some very big antimatter bombs. And after they detonate enough of them, the blasts would terraform the land so these demons would have their own little playhouse off limits to human interference. Or, and this is the most horrible possibility, they could begin mating human beings with creatures comprised of neutral-charged antimatter and create a whole murderous race of hybrid abominations like the ancient monsters of the Bible."

"Monsters aren't in the Bible," Jackman commented.

"Of course they're in the Bible. What do you think Goliath was? Andy Warhol on steroids? No, general, Goliath was a member of a hybrid race. Like Og. And Goliath was a wimp compared to his ancestors. Goliath was only, like, eight feet tall. The Bible says his evil-as-Hell granddaddy, Marduk, was over thirteen feet tall and six feet wide. Now, if that isn't a real-life monster, I don't know what is."

"Where'd you learn so much about the Bible?" asked Roy.

"All serious physicists know the Bible. You guys really don't know crap about physicists, do you? Do you want to know what real physics is, Roy? Because it's the same as the Bible."

"What's that?"

"A whole bunch of unanswered questions. Nobody knows what holds neutrinos together. Nobody knows why this whole planet doesn't just disintegrate into space dust. And no one knows what protons and electrons are composed of. They assume electrons are comprised of neutrinos. But what's a neutrino? What is it comprised of? We're probably a thousand years from answering that one." Janet's laugh was ironic. "Physics is as much theory as provable science, which is generally considered a 'fact.' But for every fact we can relatively prove there's a hundred *suspected* facts that we can't prove and we don't know why, so it's a lot like the Bible. You can have any theory you want about the Bible, but you can't conclusively prove much. And you can't disprove much. Just like physics. The only scientists who claim to understand it all are fakes or uneducated political or religious psychopaths with a prejudice that has nothing to do with genuine science."

Roy was studying her. "How did you get a job in the damn CIA? Why ain't you working at MIT or some place?"

"The money's better."

"That's a joke!" Roy laughed harshly. "I ain't getting' rich doing all this shootin' and lootin,' that's for sure. At least, that's what my ex-wife told me often enough."

"Yeah," Janet smiled, "but they don't pay you what they pay me."

Roy blinked.

Jackman lifted his binoculars. "You get what you pay for, major. Gunfighters are a dime a dozen. But a superspy with the mind of a nuclear scientist comes with a heavy price tag. I bet she even makes more than I do after thirty-five years in the service. But that ain't saying nuthin, either."

Janet placed her hands on her hips, binoculars dangling. "Well, guys, I don't need to see any more. What we should do is go back to the blueprints and come up with a workable plan because the doors are very obviously out of the question unless the major, here, goes full commando. And if you do that, Roy, you guys will be shot dead while you're still in sight of the front desk. Plus that, security vaults will slam shut automatically and it'll take a tank to open them. Or, to put it more comprehensively to you gentlemen, this whole mission will be mocked and scorned by the entire world as a spectacular and humiliating disaster and we'll all spend the rest of our lives in front of a firing squad."

Jackman grunted, "Yeah, there's no way through topside without exposing ourselves. And, just asking, but what the hell is that statue all about? The big one inside that circle in front of the building? Is that Buddhist?"

"It's Hindu," Janet stated. "It's Shiva. And Shiva is a crazy-bitch Hindu goddess, or god, of destruction and death. Mayhem and disaster. Evil and corruption. He, or she, is not someone you want to share a bed with."

Roy asked, "He or she?"

"Shiva is male *and* female. In that statue, the she-bitch is dancing the Tandava that symbolizes the destruction of the old, weary universe in favor of a new matrix that will replace everything that exists. That's why her leg is upraised and her foot is on top of a little P. T. Barnum–style demon. Some people think they installed it here to celebrate, and even advertise, the real purpose of the collider."

"Which is what?" asked Roy.

"The annihilation of this world and the creation of a new world ruled by Shiva and her perverted servants. So, if these people succeed, it's safe to say that all of us are going to die."

Jackman was suddenly motionless. "I've read the science reports, but it was like trying to read a Chinese recipe for Moo-goo-dodo and I didn't understand a word. Just how powerful *is* this collider?"

"That's a frighteningly ignorant question, general," answered Janet. "Powerful enough to propel protons at ninety-nine percent of the speed of light. Powerful enough to handle a hundred Tera-Electron-Volts of electricity when they're finished with this new insulation." She turned to stare at Jackman. "Powerful enough to destroy this galaxy if they collide protons in the right combination. Or, and this is a worst-case scenario, they could smash together particles from alternate dimensions, open a dimensional portal, and keep that portal open so they could remove all the liquid antimatter they want. And anyone who controls that much liquid antimatter absolutely controls the world."

"Elaborate on that statement," said Jackman.

"What I mean, general, is that with nothing more than a half-gallon of antimatter they can create bombs a trillion times more powerful than the Tsar Bomba which, again, happens to have only been fifty megatons and is still the biggest nuclear explosion in the history of the world. And you want to know why the communist regime didn't make it a hundred megatons? Because even those bloodless sons of bitches were afraid of what might happen if they set off a one-hundred-megaton nuclear weapon. I think they were afraid they'd crack the planet in half."

Janet unleashed her normally unexpressed intensity as she pointed at the valley. "With one liter of antimatter those fools down there will be able to create an antimatter bomb that could literally obliterate North America. Nothing would survive. Not even the common cold. We're talking about unleashing the power that fuels the universe. And these fools are stupid enough to tap into the unknown superpower that fuels that! And you don't think that's flirting with the end of the world? The end of the universe? The end of the galaxy?"

Jackman: "What else can they do with it?"

"It can get worse?" muttered Roy.

"It can always get worse, Burris."

Without skipping a beat Janet said, "They'll be able to create black holes that can swallow planets or solar systems or even galaxies. And like I said a few seconds ago, they'll be able to create chimeras, or hybrid creatures. Maybe something that's half matter and half antimatter that will have the physical strength to move mountains. Creatures that might be immune to radiation and age and disease and perfect for some unholy terraforming plan. In short, the people who control this supercollider, once they get it perfected, will be able to create any brave new world they want simply by programming it into the collider. They will be able to create a world ruled by demons, a world ruled by monsters, a world ruled by *them*. And even though I'm thinking they might be afraid of the butterfly effect, I don't think they'll be able to resist the temptation of time travel. And if they do that, they could make it so that the Bible, the Torah, the Talmud and the Koran disappear from history. They might try and make it so that beliefs in Jesus, Allah, Zeus, and Ra never existed. And there is no nation and no weapon that would be able to stop them. If they even *suspect* that you're a threat, they'll just push a button and you'll disappear. Your parents will disappear. The city and hospital where you were born will disappear. Anything that has your name on it and the effects of anything you've done will disappear. In terms of reality it will be as if you were never born and nothing was ever associated with you."

"But you said they might be afraid of this butterfly effect, right?" asked Roy. "So what is this butterfly effect? *Exactly*."

"I personally think the butterfly effect is a *myth*," said Janet pointedly. "But some think it's an inevitable consequence of time travel. Basically, it's a belief that if you go back in history and kill a single butterfly then that will change the entire line of history from that moment forward. It means the world that you knew won't exist from that second onward because you killed a single butterfly that was not previously killed at that split second. But classically educated people don't largely believe in the butterfly effect. It's mostly used as an element of fiction. The truth is, most physicists tend to think time is more like the Mississippi River, and throwing a pebble into the Mississippi River isn't going to change the course of the river. Consequently, changing minor events in the past aren't going to have much of a punch on the future. All the physicists that I know believe the future is comprised of far too many variables for any single event to alter world history unless you change some truly climatic event like the shattering of Pangaea or the formation of the Pacific Ocean or something with equal consequence."

Both Jackman and the major were staring down on her as Roy asked, "All right. Forget time travel. Tell me, have you ever actually seen one of these proton weapons in action? In real life?"

"Yeah," Janet nodded. "Once at Redstone Arsenal in 1987. It wasn't exactly a portable weapon like a rifle. Not like these maniacs are going to produce by the millions. It was a very complex device as big as a house. But they finally got the voltage up to fire off a nanosecond proton particle beam into a ten-foot-thick slab of tempered steel."

"What happened?"

"It was over so fast that all you saw was a blue flash that didn't last a thousandth of a second. Then, after enough checks were done to make sure there wasn't an undue level of radiation, we entered the room to see the results." She grunted, "To put it in terms familiar to you gunfighters, it hit like a bullet. It made an impact hole the size of a fist and it blasted a path clean through that ten-foot wall of steel like it wasn't even there. It even left the remnants of steel in the form of a splash of water—the kind of splash you see when you throw a rock in a pond, ya know? Except this steel was frozen mid-splash with half of it still standing up from the slab. It was fascinating and frightening at the same time."

"How'd they do that at Redstone Arsenal without a particle supercollider like this one?" asked Jackman.

Janet raked back her hair. "They just somehow managed to speed up a single proton, and I do mean *one proton*, to ninety-nine percent of the speed of light. At that speed, anything it hits, it vaporizes. There's nothing on this planet that can resist. No armor. No wall. Nothing. It's the most powerful weapon in the universe and that down there, gentlemen, is the biggest, most dangerous gun store in the galaxy. So if we let them continue, we might as well kill ourselves. Because if they succeed in making these weapons, nothing on earth will be able to stand in their way. All they'll have to do is push a button and they'll vaporize anything you've got—an entire battalion or a landscape of tanks, trains, ships, missiles—whatever you throw at them. Or, as I've mentioned, they *might* go back in time if they're suicidal and manipulate history itself."

"Is that *all* we need to worry about?" asked Jackman.

"No," she shook her head. "They could use 'the Mandela Effect.'"

"Good God. What's that?"

"It's a process by which they use that machine to change the memories of everyone in the world. But if they had perfected the Mandela Effect, we'd all be thinking that there's nothing dangerous about this machine. Our memories would have been reformatted so that we would simply believe whatever they want us to believe."

"Like the butterfly effect?" asked Jackman.

"No. The butterfly effect is the action of *physically* changing history for a desired outcome. The Mandela Effect is simply changing our memories. And if they'd used the Mandela Effect on us, we'd all be at home with no concerns about this place. There would be no reasons, in our manipulated minds, to be here." As they stood in silence staring down at the compound, she added, "Only one thing can stop it."

"What's that?" asked Roy.

"Itself." Janet said simply. "It's like you say, Roy. That thing is fueled by hundreds of tons of liquid nitrogen and liquid helium. And both of them are under dangerously high pressure—we're talking about hundreds of tons per square inch—so if we can somehow sabotage it so that the helium and the nitrogen tanks explode at the same time, we'll put it out of commission. Maybe forever. The cost of repairing it will be billions and I'm not sure any coven of perverted psychopaths, no matter how cozy and crazy these people are, will pay that much after this place suffers another catastrophic failure."

"When did they blow it up the first time?" asked Roy. "How bad was it?"

"They blew it up about ten years ago and it took them a good two years and about a billion bucks to get it up and running again. I'm not sure if enough people will get on board to rebuild it if they blow it up again. And I don't think any supercollider in the world can come close to what this one can do, so destroying this thing might permanently solve our problem. Understand?"

"No," said Jackman. "I don't. What do you mean?"

Janet rolled her eyes. "General, what I mean is that if some country spends ten billion dollars to send a ship to Mars and the entire crew gets eaten alive by a ten-foot-tall Ted Bundy do you think another country is going to mindlessly follow in their tracks with another ten-billion-dollar ship just to see it get eaten up, too?"

"No," Jackman stated curtly. "I don't."

"Well, there you go. Neither do I."

Jackman's head seemed bowed in something more than a displeased stare. He somberly turned away from the compound.

"Let's go," he said. "I've seen enough of this damn death camp for one day."

***

After an uneventful flight, Isaiah departed the Lufthansa jet with Amanda close and they quickly found their luggage and a taxi. They declined the driver's advice—in English, no less—to the best hotels and decided on an overcrowded hostel at the edge of Geneva. The only amenities were a bed, a table with two chairs and a small bath.

Amanda dropped her purse on the bed, pushed down. "Well, it seems comfortable enough. But why this place? It's not exactly five stars."

"Because they have a lot of people coming and going at all hours," Isaiah said as he unchained the duffle bag. "And it's not the kind of place where you'd want to ambush somebody. You'd leave too many witnesses or you'd leave too many bodies. Either way, it'd draw attention from Interpol. And that's the kind of attention nobody wants. Not even the maniacs who run this supercollider."

"That your only reason?"

"I need another one?"

Amanda cocked her head and knelt to open her suitcase. "I guess not." She began hanging her things.

"I wouldn't waste time," said Isaiah. "Just take out what you need to stay warm and leave the rest. There's a good chance we won't be coming back here, anyway, after we do a little reconnaissance."

"Fine with me. I'm getting used to how careful you are, which reminds me. There's something I've been meaning to ask you. That is, if you don't mind."

"Go ahead."

"Why do you seem to know so much about this supercollider?" Amanda paused, staring, one hand holding a wool coat. "I mean, it's like you could build the thing. You probably know as much as the engineers who designed it. I was just wondering why."

"I read about it a long time ago," Isaiah replied, detached. "It caught my interest and so I read a little more."

"What interested you so much?"

"The fact that they were attempting to manipulate the unknown forces that power this universe," Isaiah replied as if recalling it word for word. "And it interested me that there was no formal chain of command for controlling the place, so I guess I found it disturbing that the biggest, most expensive, most dangerous machine in the world was being managed by a nameless conglomerate of faceless goons from unspecified nations and they were turning the end of the world on and off like a toy. And if that wasn't enough to get my attention, they put up a statue of death and destruction at the entrance of the place and said it was a sign of their ambition. But the cherry on top of the cake was a statement made by one of their chief operators."

"What'd he say?"

"He said, 'With this machine we are going to open a portal.'"

"What kind of portal?"

"Hell if I know," Isaiah shrugged. "I don't think he knew himself. But it doesn't matter to me whether it's a portal to another world or another universe or another dimension. The bottom line is that it isn't *this* dimension and I think there's a lot of real dangerous dimensions out there."

"What do you think this means for Cynthia?"

Isaiah stopped unpacking and turned, staring somberly. "I have no solid idea what it means for your sister," he said with obvious compassion. "It might mean nothing or it might mean … something bad."

Amanda was motionless. "But you said she might not be dead."

Gently, Isaiah crossed the room and grasped her arms, directing her to a chair. He sat her down and settled next to her. His voice was calm. "Amanda, I need you to prepare yourself."

"For what?"

"For the fact that these fools might have succeeded," Isaiah stated simply. "Let's just imagine for a moment that they did manage to open a door to another dimension. Well, the thing about doors is that they swing both ways. If they opened a doorway for us to enter another dimension, that same door might have allowed for something to exit that world and enter our world. And if your sister was in that control room, there's a slim chance, and I repeat, a very slim chance that she was either badly injured or killed or something even worse happened when that portal was opened." He shook his head. "This is all just conjecture. I don't know. But you told me your sister worked in the Observation Room, right?"

"Yeah," she nodded. "Right."

"Well, that would be closest room to what they call ATLAS, and that chamber—among other places—is where protons collide. So if there was a disaster it could very easily have affected whoever was in that room. Now, I'm not saying your sister's dead but these fools are playing Russian roulette with powers that created this universe billions of years ago. They don't know what's on the other side of that portal. It could be Heaven. It could be Hell. It could be millions of years into the past. It could be billions of years in the future."

"So why are they doing this?" Amanda asked. "They don't even know what kind of power they're dealing with, right? Or what's on the other side of that portal that they might open? Or *have* opened?"

"Because the people who began this particle collider a century ago were part of an insanely dedicated occult movement of very rich people, and we're talking stupid-rich, who believed that the powers of creatures from the other side were powers they could manipulate. In other words they believed they could use those alien powers for their personal benefit whether it was political or religious or economic. But what they didn't consider is that if they did manage to open a gateway, and whatever emerged was unfriendly, they would be its first meal ticket. And I guarantee you that whatever comes from an alternate dimension is not going to have any love for this one. And it won't be controllable. And it won't be grateful for the opportunity to be here. Instead, it's probably going to destroy anything it chooses to destroy from one end of this planet to the next. And when it's done, this *will* be a brave new world. Only, the people who invited that thing to the party will be served up for Thanksgiving. So if you're asking me why I read up on the thing it's because anything that threatens my personal survival gets my undivided attention. And, in that case, I photograph every word."

Amanda seemed to scan the room before, "But … if that's all true … then wouldn't it mean that hundreds of thousands—no, millions of construction workers and laborers and financiers would have to know about the collider's true purpose? I mean, how could something as terrible as this stay a secret?"

"It's not hard," Isaiah commented. "They kill whoever talks too much."

Isaiah sharply unsnapped the aluminum case and flipped it open. Without ceremony he removed the Honjo Masamune and held it horizontally before his face. Then, with a single hand on the hilt, the other holding the scabbard, he ripped out the blade. And although Isaiah spoke of the sword without any sense of reverence, there was definitely something reverential about how he held it.

Pursing her lips for a moment, Amanda said, "Think we're gonna need that?"

A moment.

"Yeah," Isaiah frowned. "I do."

***

Arms crossed, Director-General Anton Francois appeared distinctly displeased as he stated, "I am required to inform you that very critical people are beginning to ask inconvenient questions, William. What are you doing about obtaining some answers?"

William Blanchard tossed the file he'd been holding onto the table. "Look, Director Francois, I'm just part of the management that runs this place. I don't even understand the math for that machine. But our best mathematicians and physicists have run every equation they can imagine and they don't have any answers, either. All they can tell me is that there seems to be an unknown kind of superpower—as they called it—inside or beyond dark energy and it somehow intervened in the interaction between matter and antimatter on that particular day or we'd all be dead. And maybe the rest of the planet, too."

"Very well," Francois allowed. "I'll give you a little more time. But get me some answers promptly. Now, you were aware that one of our missing physicists, this Deker woman, was an American?"

"Everyone was aware of Cynthia's nationality," replied Blanchard. "But I didn't hire her, director, and had no authority to fire her. Human resources hired her. Nor did I have anything to do with her replacement. That was also a decision of Human Resources. All I did was supervise her work, and her work was flawless. And, then, we had this disaster. And Cynthia Deker vanished with six others."

"Concerns for the others were, for the most part, resolved this morning," said Francois. "But this woman's sister, Amanda Deker, has not been contacted. And now she is in Geneva with a man who is something of an alarming mystery even to our security personnel. And, needless to say, our security people are not easily alarmed."

"I was under the impression that nothing was a mystery to you, Mr. Director," said Blanchard, with a touch of bitterness. "After all, you have the President of the United States in your pocket."

Francois cursed vehemently. "You're talking about the former president. The current president is a sworn enemy of all that is holy because he will never endorse this facility or what we're trying to achieve. But neither is he powerful enough to stop us. Not at this point. Besides, we have enough deep spies inside his government to forestall anything he initiates. So what concerns me is the dismissal of this woman, Amanda Deker, without her raising any flags with the FBI or Interpol." A pause. "She is waiting for you in your office at this moment, William. I want you to talk to her. I want you to explain to her that her sister was very tragically killed in an accident involving the collider. Explain to her that her sister's body was, unfortunately, vaporized along with the bodies of several others when the plutonium rods of our reactor were accidentally exposed."

"We don't use plutonium rods."

"They don't know that! You're dealing with little people, William! Use their ignorance! Not one person in a million has a clue as to how the particle accelerator works! All they have are hysterical theories and groundless accusations. And the world is full of faceless villains and dark conspiracies and make-believe heroes rescuing damsels in distress. They are all meaningless."

"Is that all you want me to tell her?"

"No. I want you to offer her enormous compensation for her sister's tragic death. Call it a life insurance policy. In any case, there is no proof that anything untoward has occurred, so this woman should realize that further investigation is futile. And, if necessary, we will make that painfully obvious."

Blanchard grimaced, "I am quite skilled at lying, director. But if this woman and her soldier of fortune are not satisfied with my explanation, there is very little that I can do to stop them. Further, I do not involve myself in matters of violence."

"As always, William, you will leave such matters to me. That authority is beyond your purview for many, many good reasons." As if talking to himself, Francois added, "Violence is a precious commodity. Like gold, the more you use it, the less precious it becomes until it no longer serves your purpose."

"So you will not kill them?"

"Personally? No. Of course not."

"But they will die."

Francois laughed.

"Everybody dies, William."

***

Hulking, the round-shouldered creature stood before the electric panel.

The substation was black and silent.

At its feet, two guards lay with heads torn from their shoulders, their rifles snapped like twigs. It had, itself, been shot but it was not wounded. It had encountered nothing yet in this world that wounded it. The bullets had bounced off its protective armor to disintegrate into the cement walls. And then the killing was done silently and quickly before it effortlessly ripped open steel mesh to stand before the substation control board. Slowly it reached up to wrap a blood-soaked hand around the main breaker switch.

Its plan was proceeding perfectly. It would continue to control their progress until its master was ready to enter this world with Hell's full army at his command and then they would begin to take back what was theirs, the highest throne in existence. Indeed, they would destroy the Old One's plan. They would take back what they had lost. And when it was over the galaxy would run red with the blood of stars.

It laughed.

Then it threw on the breaker to connect the current.

***

A magenta light installed in the wall abruptly began spinning and a voice echoed clearly over the speakers, "*Alert! Alert! Alert!*"

Francois calmly raised his head. "It appears your presence is required, William."

Blanchard was out the door knocking personnel from his path as he quickly fled down the corridor analyzing a dozen scenarios. Fortunately, the elevator was free. He descended and ran a quarter mile to charge into the Observation Room.

The ATLAS was engulfed in what appeared to be blue liquid lava.

"What the hell!" gasped Blanchard. "I told you to leave the collider down until we finished maintenance!"

"We didn't do anything!" a woman cried.

"What do you mean!"

"I mean that it turned itself on!" the woman shouted. "I mean that we didn't turn on the damn power! *It* turned on the power!"

"Shut it down!" Blanchard cried and didn't wait for anyone to obey his command as he leaped to a huge complex of switches and began to throw every breaker and push every red emergency shutdown button. Then he jumped to another console that was lit with blue sparks and began smashing down levers and suddenly …

The image of lava vanished.

For a long time nobody moved.

Blanchard found himself breathless. Then he somehow, surprisingly, found the strength to ask, "Did … did *anything* register on the neutrino detectors? And I mean on *any* of them? Even in the pipes?"

The female physicist took a moment to rake hair from her brow, then brushed sweat from her eyes and face. "I don't know," she whispered shakily, head bowed, breathing heavily. "Give me a minute."

"Jesus Christ," Blanchard moaned, raising a hand to his forehead. He looked toward the woman again. "Listen, Margaret, I want to be clear on this. Are you telling me the damn thing just turned on the power all by itself?"

"That's exactly what I'm saying, Bill!"

"That's impossible!"

"I was standing right here, Bill!" Margaret slammed a hand on the desk. "We had no breakers on at the substations! No power in the pipes! Nothing! We had a dead ATLAS! Then everything came on at the same time! And before I could even read what was happening that damn blue lava crap surrounded the ATLAS and all hell broke loose! All the alarms went off! I'll be surprised if somebody didn't get shot by security! I *know* those cowboys panicked! They've been in a panic for weeks!"

"Are you sure the electricians didn't accidentally turn on one of the substations? I mean ..." Blanchard gestured to the Observation Room window, "... those monkeys *are* still working on the insulation, right?"

Momentarily closing her eyes, Margaret replied, "I'm positive, Bill. Whoever or whatever turned the power on ..." She shook her head, "is not on the payroll. And no unauthorized activity was recorded on a monitor. Also, we know exactly where everyone was and what they were doing. You know that everyone is accounted for at all times and there was nobody but guards close to any substation."

Blanchard found himself staring at the ATLAS.

Closing his eyes, he shook his head.

"God help us," he whispered.

***

It was late in the afternoon when Isaiah and Amanda were escorted out of the CERN main office building, which was located a good quarter mile from the laboratory and the particle collider.

Although it was all included on the same campus with apartment complexes, shops, grocery stores, everything a small town needed; the entire facility was classified as a laboratory and the perimeter was continually monitored by Switzerland's military.

William Blanchard had broken the tragic news of Cynthia's death to Amanda with appropriate gravity. Then he presented Amanda with a death certificate confirming cause and a letter authorizing her to collect five million dollars from CERN's self-financed life insurance company. Nor did Blanchard fail to mention that the amount of five million dollars was standard for all personnel and it was a matter of proper procedure that Amanda accepts the payment on her sister's behalf.

Isaiah said nothing through the discussion. And as they strolled down the long walkway toward the parking lot, Amanda asked, "Why am I the only one who doesn't believe a word these people are telling us? The other families just took the money. But I don't buy it. I won't. I can't. I mean, do you believe him?"

Isaiah walked in silence, casually scanning the surroundings.

"Isaiah?" Amanda looked over. "Did you believe him?"

"Let's not talk about it," he said.

Amanda glanced to each side. "Somebody listening?"

He shrugged.

"You want to talk in the car?"

"I don't have anything to say right now."

"So you're not talking to me now? At all? What the hell, Isaiah?"

Isaiah glanced at her without expression. "We'll take the car back to town. Then we're ditching it. We'll talk later."

After a moment Amanda softly said, "I don't think I like the sound of that."

Isaiah casually took another step.

Without a word.

***

"There's just no damn way into this collider," said Roy Burris as he leaned back from the blueprints. "Even if we can put the security system offline for a few minutes, we still need a way in that's relatively unguarded."

Angrily he swept the sheets from the table. "This freaking thing is built like Fort Knox inside the Federal Reserve." He grunted. "Nuclear missile silos don't have this kind of security. It must have cost a hundred bazillion bucks just to build the freaking place. And they must have cornered the titanium market. A thousand Virginia-class subs wouldn't have this much titanium."

Janet sighed, "Relax, Roy. I have an idea."

"What's your idea?"

"Okay, hear me out. This place is built on the context of a nuclear reactor, so there's lots of fire exits, right?"

Suspicion narrowed Roy's eyes. "Yeah. Okay. I see where you're going. What's the downside?"

"The downside is that we can't just shut off the alarm to a single fire exit."

Jackman scowled, "What the hell? Do you have an idea or not?"

"Yes," answered Janet, "I have an idea and it will work. But Susan and I will have to shut down *every* single security, fire, and gas alarm in the corridor at the same time in order to get you inside a tunnel. And something that radical is going to initiate a system-wide response that … I can't even guess what will happen. But I'm fairly certain it will rise to banana-balls and we might be imprisoned in that Observation Room until the computers are back online. And then they're going to see that one of the tunnels has been compromised and they'll be coming after you." She scrunched her face. "After they kill Susan and me."

"That's the only way?" asked Roy.

"Yeah," Janet nodded curtly, "that's the only way."

A moment.

Roy finally said, "All right. Then this is how we're going to play it. Both of you go to work tomorrow in the Observation Room. At exactly nine o'clock you reboot the computer and put security offline. Then we'll slip inside an escape tunnel and cowboy it."

Jackman: "Why do we have to cowboy it?"

"Because, sir, the corridor where these nitrogen and helium containers are located has rotating shifts. It's always filled with guards and electricians and mechanics, so the son of a bitch is never empty. I'd say there's at least a hundred people in that tunnel at any time, day or night. So we'll probably have to neutralize a few."

"No," Susan shook her head. "There won't be any personnel in the corridor tomorrow morning."

"Why not?" asked Jackman.

"Because they plan to start up the collider tomorrow morning. By eight-thirty the collider corridor will be empty."

Roy placed a hand over his face for a second, then removed it to say, "Well, if that corridor is empty when the Semtex blows, nobody should get killed except everybody in the Observation Room."

"Like *us*?" asked Susan.

"You two won't be there."

Susan glanced to Janet. "Where will we be?"

"Outside," said Roy. "After you set security offline, we make entry and set the charges. Then we'll come to you, neutralize the guards at the Observation Room, and get you out. When the satchels blow, you'll be with us."

Janet: "Won't some shot-dead guards be evidence that we, meaning *the* United States, did something to this thing and then they'll blame us? And isn't this supposed to be a 'secret mission?'"

"Nobody can trace what country fires a nine-millimeter round into some slow-moving guard. Lead is universal." Roy reached out to tap the blueprint. "Plus that, this tunnel is three hundred feet underground. Some parts are six hundred feet underground. It's insulated from the inside, insulated from the outside. If these liquid helium and liquid nitrogen tanks blow, there's no heat source, no reason for that nitrogen and helium, which is frozen at something like minus four hundred degrees, to even begin thawing out. I wouldn't doubt that they won't be able to open that tunnel for ten years. Maybe more. And, by then, any haphazard bodies they find won't matter." He paused. "Yeah, this should work unless …"

Susan leaned forward. "Unless?"

"Unless we have to change the plan at the last second," finished Roy.

"Yeah. That would absolutely suck, dude. For real."

"Well," Roy allowed, "plans do have a tragic way of going south. And, if it does, I'll have to notify the two of you or you'll die horribly."

Susan asked, "Radios don't work down there, Roy. How are you going to notify us of a change of plans?"

"With one of the corridor telephones," muttered Janet, chin on fist.

Roy nodded, "Exactly. They have hard-wired phone systems in the corridor in case of emergencies. And they're all wired to the Observation Room just like a nuclear plant. So in a worst-case scenario I'll raise you on the phone and Tanto will come for you early because I have to guarantee the charges." He released a deep breath. "I swear to God, they're gonna make me a colonel for this. This is a suicide mission no sane person would accept. We have no delivery, no backup, no extraction. We live or die and it's up to us whether we execute the perfect plan *perfectly*. The only thing missing is that they won't hang us if we get caught. We'll be frozen in a manmade glacier for a thousand years."

"You'll need me to help with the charges," said General Jackman. "And Tanto might need backup, so I'll go with him. We'll get the girls and meet you at the escape tunnel and we'll make tracks. That work for you guys?"

Janet laughed, "Always with a backup plan. That's why you make the big bucks, general."

Roy: "Works for me, sir."

Susan looked at Roy. "Are you guys gonna have enough time to set all seven satchels on the collider?"

"Yeah, but it's really all about placement," Roy answered. "These tanks are interconnected. If you blow them at a juncture, you blow all of them. It's like making a tiny pinprick in one balloon that feeds the air to twenty additional balloons. And it will be impossible to seal seven blown-to-Hell helium and nitrogen tanks before these people get seventeen miles of frozen corridor."

Janet murmured, "Then we'd better be ready to run when you get to us. Pick 'em up and put 'em down. Fleet of foot. Like the wind."

"Sounds good." Roy focused on Jackman. "Sir? With all respect, are you certain that we don't have to clear this plan?"

"Are you crazy, Burris?" grunted Jackman. "No sane person would put his name on this. Hell, even I wouldn't be here if I hadn't gotten volunteered for it."

Silence.

"Well," said Janet, "we do have one thing going for us."

"We do?" asked Tanto blandly. "I'd love to hear it."

"I'm almost certain that these maniacs at the Hadron Supercollider haven't succeeded yet."

"Succeeded in *what*?"

"Succeeded in their ultimate goal, Tanto."

"What the hell is their ultimate goal?" Tanto stared. "Look, I'm just a gunfighter. I just snatch and grab. Shoot and loot. What do you mean?"

Janet sighed, then, "The ultimate goal of these physicists was not just to open this portal and turn these demons into slaves, Tanto." She leaned forward, elbows on knees. "Think about it. This supercollider propels neutrinos and elemental particles to ninety-nine percent of the speed of light, and Einstein proved you cannot surpass the speed of light or gravity will basically vaporize you. In other words, you die. But if these creatures on the other side of this portal know how to enhance the collider so that it can go around the speed of light, then these physicists will be able to travel backward or forward in time. But since nobody hostile to us is here— and I mean here in this room at this moment—to stop what we're planning to do, then they don't know we're here, which means they can't read the future. And if they can't read the future, they can't change the past or we wouldn't be here. We'd be dead somewhere along the highway and that means we don't have to worry about human intervention. But we do have to worry about alien intervention."

Roy leaned back. "Alien intervention?"

"Yes," Janet nodded. "These aliens or interdimensional beings or demons or Nephilim are not helping these people for the good of all mankind. These creatures have their own insidious reasons for telling these fools how to strengthen the supercollider and they are infinitely more intelligent and infinitely more savage than any human being ever was or ever will be. And when these monsters realize what we're doing, and I bet you that some of them are already here, they'll fight to the death. And they only know one level of violence—the absolute annihilation of whatever gets in their way."

Tanto muttered moodily, "I guess we can forget rules of engagement."

Roy lowered his gaze, staring into his empty glass.

"I'd say we're already engaged."

***

It was evening before Isaiah finally found a hovel of a restaurant that he deemed safe and Amanda dropped her new baggage on the floor beside a rather rickety-looking wooden chair. She tiredly took a seat. "Okay," she began, brushing away a widespread handful of wind tousled hair, "tell me again why we had to leave everything at the hostel? And why did we change cars so fast?"

"Because they know you're not satisfied with their explanation about what happened to Cynthia," Isaiah responded a bit obliquely. "And that means they've already bugged our clothes, our car, and our room at the hostel. They've also been re-tasking satellites, which ain't no piece of cake, to keep a visual on us. And within a half-hour they'll have a laser pointed at this room to listen in on what we have to say." He eased back the curtain, peering. "So, in a way, half of this is futile. You can't hide from these people. It all depends on how much interest they take in you. Right now I'd say we're in the middle of the road. But changing cars peaked their interest."

"Why all the caution?" Amanda leaned forward, elbows on her thighs, hands dangling. "We didn't do anything but ask a few harmless questions."

"There's no such thing as harmless with these people," said Isaiah. "They don't like questions, harmless or otherwise. And I've finally decided that your sister isn't missing because of some freak accident. If it was a legitimate accident it would have been explained in more detail. When those helium tanks exploded a few years back, it was all you read about for months. No," he shook his head, "they don't want anyone to know what happened."

Amanda squinted. "So you're back to your theory about Cynthia being snatched up by something?" She paused. "Like, something from the other side? And that's where she is now? Lost in space?"

"I'm not sure. But I believe that there was a very serious accident and something tragic happened to Cynthia and maybe a few more. It was something nobody in that place anticipated and something they don't know how to explain and that's why they're trying to buy our silence." Isaiah leaned back. "Do you still want to stay or take the money and run? Taking the money is the only safe option because after this I can't make any promises."

"Of course I want to stay!" Amanda slapped the table. "I want to know what happened to Cynthia! My sister! Jesus! What a stupid question! Do you think I'm made of snowflakes? I can take a few hits!"

It was the first true anger Isiah had witnessed in her. He eased back the curtain, glancing out, before he said, "I'm only sure of one thing."

"What's that?"

"I'm sure they did something big, and probably outrageously illegal, but it went bad and now they're trying to cover it up because they lost people to something that worries them even more than another scandal. If they could explain what happened, they wouldn't be so scared. But they *are* scared and that means they don't have a clue about what happened to that machine or your sister or anyone else."

"How do you know they're scared?"

"Because paying somebody off is the second to last thing you do if you're scared."

"What's the last?"

"Kill them."

Amanda paused before asking, "So Cynthia is really … gone?"

Isaiah's drew his lips back. Then, with obvious reluctance, he stated, "Amanda, listen to me carefully. I've already told you that this machine is designed to open portals to alternate dimensions. But like I said, that door swings both ways. So it's possible that *nobody* died in what they're calling an accident."

"It's *possible*?" Amanda gaped before shaking her head and raising a hand. "What's not possible, Isaiah? It's 'possible' that my next-door neighbors are aliens! And I think they are! It's possible that you and me don't even exist! It's—"

"Yeah, I got it," Isaiah motioned. "But what I'm saying is that it's more than theoretically possible. I'm saying it's likely that these fools opened a portal to another dimension. Only, it didn't work out like they planned. Instead of getting a good glimpse into the next world, the next world got a good glimpse into them. And I think that when they opened that portal, whatever was on the other side reached into our world and snatched up a few things. Like people."

"But wouldn't that mean Cynthia is dead?"

"Not necessarily," Isaiah replied, rubbing the back of his neck. "But it's not good, either." He glanced along the smoke-singed wall. "If whatever is on the other side of that portal can exist long enough in our world to grab people and retreat to its own universe, then maybe we can exist in their universe, too. And, if that's true, then Cynthia might still be alive."

"But for how long?"

"I don't know. I don't even know if anything I'm saying makes sense. I'm just spitballing, here. But you asked me what I think, and that's it." Isaiah paused. "They built a machine they can't control and now they're playing with forces they don't understand. But what they've actually done is open some kind of gateway and whatever beings exist on the other side of that portal are spectacularly hostile and outrageously dangerous."

"So what do we do?"

Isaiah raised a dead stare. "We've almost taken this as far as we can go without killing somebody to defend ourselves. So we're going to get concrete records of what happened that day and turn them over to Interpol." He shook his head. "Interpol can't do anything with wild speculation. They have to have proof."

"You mean we kidnap Blanchard and force him to give us blueprints to the experiment that made Cynthia disappear? And how are we going to do that?" She placed hands on the table. "Did you not see all those guards?"

"Do you want to find your sister or not?"

"Yeah! But getting killed isn't gonna get the job done! I mean, do you think Blanchard is going to just cooperate with us? I don't!"

"We need to get to Blanchard, but not at his office. We'd have to beat too many guards. And that's not possible."

Amanda lifted an arm. "He *lives* at that office, Isaiah. And we'd have to get below the surface. Without clearance! And that place is guarded by god! I mean, what did we have to pass through? Three guard gates? And there was a dog patrol or something around that fence, wasn't there?" She looked emptily around the room. "It looked like a dog patrol to *me*. There were two guys with German shepherds. I mean, I'm no security expert but—"

"You're right," Isaiah said with a calming gesture. "But there's a way in. We just have to catch the bus."

Amanda hesitated. "What does that mean?"

"It means that we catch a tour bus. They still keep up appearances for the rest of the world to make it look like they're doing something legitimate with that multibillion-dollar time machine. Of course, they don't show people what they're really doing, but it's good public relations. We'll just buy two tickets. Hitch a ride."

Amanda leaned back and laughed. "And then? You think they don't count heads on the bus before it leaves? Oops! We've got two heads missing! Then what are we gonna do? Hide? Where? We don't have IDs. We won't last five seconds in there, Isaiah, before we're detained and arrested and probably shot dead. God only knows how many people are already dead in those hills. It's probably everybody who's ever quit or retired because nobody quits that place. Not after they really know what's going on. They get 'disappeared,' or commit suicide or get run over by a car. At least, that's the vibe I get. Once you go in, you never come out. What do gangs say? Blood in, blood out? Well, that place is even worse. Even your soul doesn't get out. It gets snatched up by demonic entities from some kind of hell."

Isaiah grimaced as he said, "Well, I think this is where you should get off the bus, anyway. I'm going in alone. You're staying here."

Amanda straightened in her chair.

"The hell I am."

"Amanda," Isaiah said, raising a hand, "there is just the wildest, craziest chance that even I can get in there and stay in there without being detected. I can't do this with you tagging along. No offense, but you're not made for this. You might not make it impossible, but you'll make it damn near impossible."

"You're not going in there without me, Isaiah." Amanda stood, hands on hips. "I hired you for this."

"You're not paying me, Amanda."

"Forget that! You're a man of honor! And I didn't come all this way just for you to tell me that my sister got sucked into a demonic black hole and I can go get some Swiss coffee that sucks, anyway! I want some … some …"

"Closure?"

"Justice!"

"For what?" Isaiah waited. "You don't even know what happened! You don't even know if it was Blanchard's fault! Who are you gonna blame? The people who built the place? Fifty thousand of them? The people who work inside it? How many is that? Seven thousand? The people who give the orders to turn that machine on and off? Who's first? Who's last? Give me a name, Amanda, and I'll kill him for you if justice is all you want."

"What do *you* want!" Amanda demanded. "What the hell are we even doing here, Isaiah, if it's not to find the truth about my sister and do something about it? This is not what Deborah told me about you!"

"That's the third time you brought that up," Isaiah said, exasperated. "Just what *did* Deborah tell you about me?"

"She said you killed everyone who was involved in her father's death."

"Did she also tell you that we were being held prisoner by seven heavily armed men who had every intention of killing us?" Isaiah bent forward. "Or did she fail to mention that little detail?"

Amanda impatiently swept back her hair. "She didn't give me all the details, no. She just said you handled it."

"Yeah," Isaiah agreed, a tragic shake of his head. "I handled it, all right. I got shot twice and stabbed three times, but I handled it." He paused. "That's the thing about using violence. Everybody gets hurt. Even if you win, you get hurt. Nobody comes out of a throw down like that unharmed."

Amanda lifted her face and both hands toward the ceiling before lowering them to stare tiredly at Isaiah. "So what's the plan, Isaiah? I am not letting you go in there alone. In the first place, I feel responsible for you, for my sister, for this whole mess. I'm the one that got you into this and I am not going to let you suffer the consequences alone. Call it a Catholic conscience. I just don't want to call it regret. I've got too many, already."

"If you go in there with me, you could get us both killed."

"Live or die, we do it together. It's your choice."

Isaiah sighed. "All right. My plan is to make Blanchard give us whatever records he has. Then we're going to deliver the records, along with a list of the missing personnel, to the Geneva office of Interpol. And then we're out of it. Interpol can take it from there. Or there could be … a doomsday option … if that plan goes south."

"There's a worse plan?"

"If we can get in, but can't get out, we'll probably be trapped inside the Observation Room, so we'll lock the door from the inside. I'm sure that room is damn near impregnable. Then we'll make Blanchard repeat the experiment. But this time I'll go into the ATLAS myself and cross over into this unknown dimension and bring Cynthia back. After that I'll set off every alarm in the place and we'll wait for the Swiss police to get there. And with Cynthia's explanation, and records proving what happened, maybe Interpol will listen to us and escort us out of there alive."

"What if those guys break down the door before you get back?"

"Then they'll kill you and shut down the machine leaving me marooned in whatever dimension took Cynthia. Case closed. Put a fork in it. We're done."

Amanda's shock could not have been more distressing; her hair seemed to rise on end, her eyes were wide with horror. "What are the chances that you can bring her back?"

Isaiah frowned, "I don't know. But if Cynthia is alive, and that's a big *if*, I'll do everything I can to bring her back."

"But you don't have the foggiest what you're walking into."

"Yeah," Isaiah sighed, "I might run into a glitch or two."

"*A glitch or two*?" Amanda's face went white. "If seven people got sucked into a black hole and have never been seen again what makes you think you can go into it and come back with Cynthia?"

Isaiah didn't blink as he stared. "Like I said: It's a doomsday option."

Leaning back, Amanda felt her jaw tighten.

"Good thing you brought the katana, huh?"

***

It hovered at the edge of darkness, watching.

Seven men worked along the pipes that connected the collider to the ATLAS, as they called it, and were diligently wrapping thick black material around new electrical lines. With narrow, black eyes it studied their movements and then one worker dropped insulation, muttered something, and walked toward it.

It had no intention to slow their progress, here, and so it moved further into shadow.

The man continued casually until he reached the part where this subterranean structure emerged into the collider corridor and stepped without hesitation into the darkness. He removed his tool belt and began to …

Abruptly the man lifted his face, staring at the wall.

It was standing less than ten strides from his position, but it did not move. Nor would it move unless there was no longer a reason to conceal itself. And then, faintly, the man's head began to turn, his eyes searching beneath a brow hard as flint. He looked further into the connecting corridor and continued his search before his gaze settled on the gigantic form beside him.

His eyes and mouth opened—

It took a single huge stride, like a leap, and delivered a downward blow upon the maintenance worker's helmeted head—a single hammer-fist that liquefied skull and brains and flesh so that nothing but crimson slush flowed over the torso and soundlessly downward to the cement; the man's body stood for a moment before it fell forward.

With the same gorilla-arm he caught the body and quietly lowered it so that it made no sound. He laid it haphazardly, without reverence, and strode across it to stare down the corridor once more with bright blood descending from its hand, a stark contrast to the black palm, fingers, and talons.

Because the remainder of the work crew had heard nothing and were acutely occupied with their own appointed task, no one yet revealed any suspicions. In time, yes, they would notice one of their crew missing, and begin to search. And they would find the dead man. But it would be gone long before then.

It bared fangs, *for you were created only slightly less than angels …*

It spat.

Slightly less than angels!

Their strength was nothing! They were pitiful, weak, cowardly, ignorant, and arrogant! Even their senses were dulled to where they could not feel Death standing beside them. Instead, these humans placidly continued in their work as if knowing the sun would rise again.

But the day was close upon them when the sun would not rise again, a day when his dark army would see to the end of this world and the beginning of a new firmament far above this wretched wasteland already cloaked with more graves than lives.

And, then, the final conflict would begin.

It inhaled deeply and exhaled with strength.

For this moment, alone, he would leave them to their task. Their work was necessary, and he was not yet so hungry. And that was a new limitation, he'd quickly discovered, to this world. Here, he must eat. But he could not eat of the black manna of the world he'd departed, nor that manna he remembered from long ago.

Here, he must eat flesh.

He was limited in this form, yes, but he was still far more than the inhabitants of this cursed earth. And although he could not continue without food forever, he could last far longer than them. If necessary, he could starve for a thousand years. But he was confident it would not come to that. And, meanwhile, these carrion would provide him with ample food until he fulfilled his purpose by seizing control of that room and beginning what these fools were not intelligent enough to begin.

Slightly less than angels …

The words, written so long ago, caused a frown to bend the edges of its mouth. How it had always hated that term delivered so certainly, joyously, and victoriously. It was an insult that the lesser should rule over the greater, that the weakest should tread down the strongest, or that the sheep should be made the shepherds.

All of it was an abomination. But what was theirs would soon be his.

But not now—not yet.

Its black lips parted.

"*Soon*," it whispered.

Silently it turned and walked into darkness.

***

There was a mild knock on the door and Janet answered.

Roy stood leaning on the frame, a bottle of wine in hand. He smiled wryly, "I thought we might celebrate our last night together."

"Our last night?" Janet smiled. "You don't expect us to come out of it?"

"Well, let's celebrate, anyway." Roy entered as she stepped aside. "Wow," he added, "I'm glad they got us all separate rooms but, your suite is a helluva lot nicer than mine." He tossed his coat. "Anyway, to answer your question, I don't go on any mission hoping I'll survive. I find worrying about living or dying to be distracting and distractions can get you killed. You can find yourself worrying about surviving when you should be concentrating on your job."

"The Army teach you that?"

"Nah, I learned that from an old book on samurais. Those guys were tough. They didn't expect victory. They didn't expect defeat. They expected nothing. A lot of modern operators use the same mentality. Keeps your mind on your mission. Keeps you from thinking about the wife, the kids, or living or dying." He gazed down. "All you got is what's in front of you, so empty your mind. Slow is smooth, smooth is fast. Just do your job and leave. Then you can get back to where you worry about distractions. Get back to the wife."

"But you don't have a wife," said Janet. "Or did you lie about that?"

"I used to have a wife," Roy half-lifted a shoulder. He carefully opened the bottle and just as carefully filled two glasses. "It didn't take. About like everybody else's marriage." A pause. "I'm not totally cynical. Some guys make it work. I just wasn't one of them. But the divorce rate in my unit is ninety-seven percent and I think it's easy for you to understand why. So, I live by another system now."

"What system?"

"As long as I'm doing this cowboy stuff I'm not gonna have a relationship. I'm not even gonna have a whore."

"That sounds lonely," Janet accepted the glass and reclined on the couch. "I'm CIA and even I'm not that cold. At least I bring my emotions to the table."

"I thought spies didn't have emotions."

"I'm not a spy, Roy. I'm—"

"A computer whiz. Yeah. I remember."

"So what do you really think our chances are tomorrow?"

"If you and Susan can crack the door and let us in, I'd say our chances are as good as they ever get in a covert op. If not, we'll have to go loud. And if we do that, we'll have an entire army down on us. I don't think we'll even finish setting the Semtex. Basically, if Plan A doesn't work, we don't stand a chance of getting out of there alive or accomplishing the mission or denying American guilt behind this operation or anything else." He gazed steadily into Janet's eyes. "We'll just have to blow the satchels with us down there. This mission will be a one-way trip and the good ol' USA will take all the blame."

Janet was silent.

"Frankly," he continued, "it all depends on whether you and Susan can put the mainframe offline. Then Tanto and the general better haul ass, grab both of you, and get back to the escape corridor with time to spare. By then the charges will be set and we'd better be making some swift tracks because nothing can stop the detonation."

"Nothing?" asked Janet.

"Nope," Roy shook his head. "Once they're charges are set, the satchels are tamper-proof. It's all but impossible to disarm them." He sighed. "I mean, it's possible if you have a week and a truckload of circuit breakers. But it's not possible if you've only got a few minutes and seven satchels spread over a mile. The only people that can stop them then will be me or Tanto. We'll each have a remote. It's called redundancy."

"Yeah, I'm familiar with that. I think Stonewall Jackson invented it. So how long have you been doing this cowboy stuff?"

"Too long. But I'm not gonna stay too much longer because I don't wanna grow old with nothing but an empty house and a dumbass TV set."

"Were all your years in Delta?"

"No," he shook his head "I was a Ranger for three years, the 72nd. Then I was invited to Delta and qualified. The rest is classified eyes-only stuff locked away somewhere. Even I can't access records on myself."

"Do you like your job?"

He shrugged. "I'm good at it."

"How many missions have you been on?"

"Seventy-four." He laughed grimly. "Wounded nineteen times. Lots of shiny medals that I'll never see. Lots of places that don't exist. I guess it's a lot like being you." He smiled. "How come you joined the CIA?"

Janet smiled. "I actually just sort of fell into it. I was a lineman after I graduated from college trying to save up for grad school."

"A lineman?"

"Yeah. A lineman for the county."

Roy blinked. "You mean, like, a real county lineman? Telephone poles and all that?"

"Yeah," Janet laughed. "I took down poles, installed poles. Ran wiring. Worked substations. Fixed substations and every kind of power outage from sleet, snow, hurricane, or tornado. Whatever was needed. I did it all."

Chuckling, Roy sat back. "So that accounts for why you're in such good shape."

"You think I'm in good shape?" Janet laughed.

"Yeah," Roy nodded. "I do. You're strong." He stared to the side before he shook his head with a smile. "A lineman. Amazing. That's a damn dangerous job."

"You bet it is. A lot of good people get killed doing it. But it pays well and I saved up enough to get my master's. Anyway, I didn't know I was being tested for the Central Intelligence Agency at first. I was at MIT and they just told me it was an aptitude test. I guess I scored pretty high for whatever they were looking for."

"They didn't tell you your score?"

"Nope. Anyway, they put me through every kind of psyche test known to science. And then a lie detector test. And then another lie detector test. And then, after all that mess, they sent me to see a shrink for an in-depth psychiatric evaluation. Then I was put on a six-month probation and had to master a truly astonishing programming system ad nauseam. And, finally, I was assigned to a classified job in a classified complex that doesn't exist."

"Let me guess," said Roy. "Because it's classified?"

"Good guess."

"Did you have a good view?"

"When I took a smoke break."

"So you smash codes all day now?"

Janet laughed. "I can't share that any more than you can tell me how many people you've rescued from who, or when, or how, or how many people got killed in some place we were never at. Isn't that how it works?"

"Something like that," Roy nodded with a sip. "Which just leaves us one thing to talk about."

"About tomorrow, right?"

"Yeah."

"What are you so worried about?"

"First," said Roy, "get this straight. I don't want you getting creative or sacrificial or noble on me. I don't want you thinking you're a hero because nobody's a hero. You just do your job and go home. I don't want you staying behind to make sure the security blackout lasts long enough than absolutely necessary. And right now I want you to be honest and tell me what you wouldn't say in front of the general or the rest of them."

"Why are you talking to me and not Tanto or the general or Susan?"

"Because you're one who's lying to me," Roy answered without expression. "First, I don't like lies. Second, I believe you're in more danger that you're letting on. Third, you could endanger this whole mission. So why don't you tell me the truth?"

Janet almost laughed. "Are you getting sweet on me?"

"Just doing my job."

"I'm touched."

"It doesn't mean we're engaged."

"It's still sweet."

"So why are you lying to me?" he pressed.

"Why do you insist I'm lying?"

"Because I plan to personally look you up when this last tour is over." Roy stared down into his glass. "I've done my time. My tour is almost up and I'm not re-upping. I'm going back to civilian life and my cattle ranch. And I have some extra space if you'd like to see a little bit of Texas. And if I can get you out of this deathtrap alive."

At that, Janet did laugh. "Don't sugarcoat it, Roy. Just tell it like it is."

"That's another thing I'm good at."

"Well, the feeling's mutual." Janet settled back. "I've never gone for heroes. But I kind of like cowboys."

"Good enough," he nodded. "Now talk to me. Tell me what you didn't tell the general at the meeting."

Janet released a long, slow breath as if focusing on the unwanted inevitable. "I can guarantee you that I won't live long enough for either Tanto or the general to reach me. But I can also promise that I'll take care of Susan. I can send her out of the room because, ultimately, this just takes one person once she delivers the relay to me, so Tanto can reach

Susan in time. She'll be in the corridor. But I'll be dead by then."

"Why is that?"

Janet took another sip. "What do you know about computers?"

"Obviously not enough."

"All right, the first thing you have to know is that everything in a computer is related to everything else. No command, no impulse, nothing sparks inside a computer without leaving a trace in the network. There is no such thing as isolation. That's how Israel infected Iran's entire defense system through a thumb drive."

"I remember that," Roy grunted. "How'd they do that again?"

Janet shrugged, "Israel just waited until the guy went home and went to sleep. Then they slipped into his house and secretly planted a virus in his personal thumb drive. The next day, he took it back to work, plugged it into his work computer and the entire country's defense complex was infected within seconds. And, during that time, Iran was completely defenseless. Anybody could have launched anything against them and Iran couldn't have done a thing about it. Even their telephones and traffic lights were down."

For a moment Roy only stared. "So what does all that mean? That you're planning to crash the whole system? Don't you think that's a little obvious? And won't the place go into some kind of automatic lockdown if that happens? I mean, if our nuclear missile silos lose connection to Washington or Red Mountain, they automatically interpret that as an attack. And that means—"

"Yeah, that means that all silo personnel are required to carry out their fourth protocol and launch the missiles," Janet finished. "I know the protocols. And that's also why I know that this place won't go into automatic lockdown if I just reboot the security system. That is not some kind of tenth level mondo-emergency. This is just a reboot. But if it turns into a shutdown, then that would initiate a lockdown. Then nobody gets in, nobody gets out. Including us. So I'll have to stay behind and keep rebooting the system to make it look like a simple computer glitch. Now, I can guarantee you guys safe passage up and down that corridor for thirty minutes. But they'll find me at a half hour and kill me where I stand. Then it'll take them another fifteen minutes for them to secure the system and that will give you and your guys enough time to make a clean escape and get safe distance on that place. So you survive. Nobody knows it was us. Everybody goes home. Mission accomplished."

Scowling, Roy asked, "Do you really think I'm going to leave you behind or let something happen to you? Are you nuts?"

"Roy, this place has the best computer trackers in the world," said Janet. "I won't be able to throw them off for more than a half-hour even if I reboot the system through ten thousand encrypted satellites. But I can send Susan into the hall in the first minute so that Tanto and the general can grab her while I keep the computer in a loop."

"That's not a plan."

"I have to keep the computer occupied for as long as it takes you guys to get the job done. And this job could save the world. There's no other way."

"Well, we'll save the world but it ain't gonna happen like this." Roy shook his head grimly and solidly. "I'll find another way."

"You don't have a choice, Roy. We've only got one shot at this. And I seriously doubt that anybody will ever get another chance to try this stunt again. So we either succeed big or we lose big. And, if we go down, the rest of the world goes down because whatever creatures exist on the other side of that portal are going to kill everything in sight when they come through that gateway." She bowed her head. "Those damn fools are actually convinced that they can control what comes out of that portal. But what comes out of that portal is going to eat them alive. Then us. Then whoever gets in their way from one end of this universe to the next."

Roy released a moan like a suppressed laugh. "That's funny," he said quite soberly, "I thought you were a genius. And you think I would let you die in this? When you fell off the turnip truck, did you land on your head?"

Staring intently, Janet asked, "Do you believe in God, Roy?"

"As much as the next man, I guess," he grunted. "I sure as hell don't believe that whatever we saw in that picture is human. That narrows things down a bit. But whether it's a demon or an alien, whatever the difference is, I don't know. I know it's not of this world but that's a pretty vague thing. Meteorites aren't from this world. I've personally seen ships that I know are not from this world. I've even seen 'em on a submarine."

"Everybody knows about those," Janet replied, a dismissive gesture. "Anyway, I only ask because I do believe in God. And I am willing to die to make sure those things don't find a gateway into this world."

"That's fine with me," Roy nodded. "But you ain't gonna die on my watch. And I'm gonna tweak the plan to make sure that doesn't happen." He raised a hand as she opened her mouth. "No. You do exactly what you're planning to do. Leave the rest to me."

For a moment Janet blinked softly, then leaned forward, "But we're not just fighting for my life, Roy. We're fighting for the whole world."

"Good thing I'm a professional then." He took a deep breath, a nod. "That's what I'm good at. Just tell me, doc … It *is* doctor, isn't it?"

"Yes," Janet smiled. "I have a doctorate specializing in subatomic particle decay."

"Okay. Just tell me. What, exactly, did you mean when you said we might face opposition from a force that's not of this world?"

"I meant that that thing in the picture is no mistake and it's no illusion. This collider might be immoral, but it's very accurate." She blinked slowly. "If that creature is in this world as we speak, and it discovers you, it'll kill you if it can. It'll kill every one of you. So it's not the humans you have to worry about. It's the demons that have already come through that portal. Because I think they're still in that facility. I think they know what you're planning to do. And I think they're waiting for you."

A grim line hardened Roy's jaw. He said nothing, then set down the glass. He rose and walked to the door before pausing. "You do exactly what I say tomorrow. You set that thing offline at nine and keep it offline. That's all you need to know and all you need to do. Don't do another thing. You got me?"

Janet nodded, "Take care of Susan, okay?"

With a frown Roy turned away.

***

It was after midnight when Tanto answered the knock at his door. After he opened it, Roy slid inside and closed the panel.

"Jesus, man," said Tanto. "Now what?"

"We've got a change of plan and it stays between you and me, buddy," said Roy smartly. "Get the remotes. We're gonna cowboy a few things."

***

"That's our way in," said Isaiah.

Standing in solid darkness—Amanda had never seen such total darkness and so many stars in her life—she tightened her down jacket. She glanced at the snow-covered fir trees that thickened the slope like sentinels of ice. Then she asked, teeth chattering, "What did you say?"

"I said," Isaiah pointed, "that's our way in."

Amanda stared down at the road so far below. "An ambulance? You can't be serious! I mean, you're *not* serious!" A pause. "Are you serious?"

"Yeah."

"I'm not!" Amanda grunted as she straightened an arm, pointing. "How are we supposed to get inside an ambulance? And I thought you said we'd take a tour bus!"

"Change of plans. That's a private ambulance service. It's got priority and I've got its name. And I bet it's designated for use at this facility alone. It must be part of a detail that takes care of chemical or radiation accidents. They'd use something like that for this place. All we have to do is get inside it."

Amanda stared. "That's all? Well, that sounds simple enough. Get inside an ambulance reserved for radioactive disasters. And how do we do that?"

"No muss, no fuss."

"Until this moment I liked that phrase." Amanda fixed Isaiah with a stare. "You're crazy, you know that? In the first place your genetic memory or whatever it's called has driven you insane. Secondly, you carry a sword when swords went out of style a long time ago. Nowadays people kill each other in a more civilized manner. And, in the third place, how the hell are we gonna kidnap some EMTs and steal their ambulance?"

"I didn't say we were going to kidnap anybody. We just need to find out where they keep those things. They'll have a warehouse where they do maintenance, check the tires, put chains on it, whatever. But it won't be abandoned. It'll have some mechanics. We'll have to steal it out from under them."

Amanda lowered her chin into her coat. "So we're just gonna sneak into this warehouse and drive away with an ambulance? That the plan?"

"Well," Isaiah shrugged, "to be honest, I don't really plan in the conventional sense of the word."

"Ah, yeah, that's right. You like to make things up as you go."

"Something like that." Isaiah cocked his head. "But considering the rather skeletal intelligence you gave me before we started this fiasco, I didn't have a lot to work with. It's not like you gave me a playbook." He took a moment. "On the downside, I do have to say this is a rather desperate idea. Even for me. But desperate times …"

"We ain't *that* desperate. Even if we do make it inside that compound where are we going to hide all day until we get a shot at Blanchard?"

"All I know right now," Isaiah turned back into the fir trees, "is I don't wanna get killed standing on this ridge. Let's go."

"What time is it?"

"It's morning. Let's find a place to get some breakfast."

"Know any place called The Last Supper?"

***

"One thing about Switzerland," Amanda said as Isaiah swerved along the curving mountain road, "is that there is not a straight road in this country. And that includes whatever goat trail this is."

After a moment Amanda patted the dashboard of the rental car. "Why did you rent a car as soon as we landed?"

"Well, it's better to have one and not need it than—"

"Yeah, I know. Than to need one and not have it."

Isaiah laughed, "I always rent a car when I land in a new place. After grabbing my bag, it's the first thing I do.

The second thing I do is to rent a second car and stash it somewhere for an emergency."

"What kind of emergency?"

"Could be anything. But I do it in case I have to ditch the first car."

"You don't trust public transportation, huh?"

"Funny. No. I don't like to trust people with my own safety. Truth is, the first time I landed in Rome, the entire taxi world was on strike. Then, the second time I landed in Rome, the entire taxi world was on strike. Guess what was happening the third time I landed in Rome?"

"Yeah, I get the picture."

"Do you blame me?"

They cruised in silence before Amanda said, "Okay, you've told me the mechanics of how this collider works. But if you know so much, then why is it such a mystery to the rest of the world?"

"The Unread might call it a mystery," allowed Isaiah. "But anybody who knows anything about that collider knows that it was a dangerous idea from the beginning. The whole plot was corrupt and the people behind it were just plain evil or psychotic or power-mad. Whatever happens to people when they have a house full of gold and a graveyard for a soul. When these psychos conjured up the idea for this place a hundred years ago, they didn't care about the origins of the universe. But they did have an obsession for gold, political power, and whatever else cranked their tractor. So it goes without saying that they were more interested in power than truth. And the one thing people who crave power hate most of all are people who possess more power than they do."

"Who would have more power than a rich man?"

"Anyone who doesn't value riches."

"Why do you think that is?"

Isaiah shrugged slightly, "Because they can't control people who don't value gold, sex, violence, or political power. I mean, how do they control someone who values God more than gold? They can't. And they know it. And they can't stand people they can't control. Which puts people who hold spiritual values at the top of their list of things to destroy."

Hands cradling a thermos of espresso, Amanda mumbled, "Hundreds of years ago they were crucifying witches and warlocks. They were burning werewolves. They had the Salem Witch Trials. A ton of innocent people burned at the stake because of three psychotic children. Then, lest we forget, there were the Spanish Inquisitions that hung bodies from every tree they passed. And, after that, the entire world saw blatant religious persecution from Moscow to Beijing with hundreds of millions of Jews, Muslims, Hindus, Buddhists, Catholics, Christians burned alive, buried alive, hacked into pieces, or just shot dead. And let's remember to get a basket of fruit for The French Revolution and The Saint Bartholomew's Day Massacre. Why would anybody risk their life proclaiming something spiritual when virtually everyone on the planet was getting murdered for it? It's hard to understand what provoked that kind of persecution."

"The love for power is what provoked it," said Isaiah. "With power you get everything else. You get money, fame, sex, land, your own army. You decide who lives or dies. That's why the psychos you just mentioned killed all those innocent people. They were doing away with the competition. They wanted as little interference as possible, so anyone who got their attention also got his head wrapped in a bag of hungry rats or was flayed to death or got locked up in an iron maiden. None of them even lasted long enough to confess their sins. If they had any. But the Inquisitors weren't looking for confessions. They were looking for land and some spectacular headlines that would scare off the competition. And, of course, nobody touched the Rothschild lookalikes because their money financed half that murder in the first place. People who had faith in something beyond this world weren't just a target to them. It was their greatest enemy. People having faith in something greater than this world is what truly enraged them. Those are people that can't be controlled. Not even with death."

"So what does that say about these people we're dealing with?"

"Well, for one thing it says they're the offspring of a perverted race of despots." Glancing into the mirror, he added, "Yeah. I figured it'd come to this. But not so soon. We haven't actually done anything but change cars."

Amanda glanced backward between the seats.

"Don't do that," said Isaiah.

A white four-door car was following them.

Amanda asked quietly. "And now?"

"And now we'll have to lose them in such a way that they think it was their fault."

"How do we do that?"

"Play it by ear." Isaiah glanced into the mirror again. "You always have to remember that this is their country. If these guys can't keep up with us, they'll call the local police. And if that's not enough, they'll call the Swiss police. And if *that's* not enough they'll call out the Swiss army. Any way you look at it, we're in a net. That's why we have to make them think that they lost us by mistake. Otherwise, they'll just close the net and we won't even make it to the next hotel room."

"Are these the guys who make people disappear?"

"Probably."

"Are we ready for them?"

"The question is, are they ready for *us*?"

"Now I know why you keep your sword close."

Relaxing strangely, as if he were accustomed to this, Isaiah casually replied, "That's actually more of a habit. I've had the katana since I was six years old. I always find some way to keep it close. A guitar case. Luggage. A coat. I've thought of so many ways of concealing it I don't even put any effort into it, anymore."

"Deb was last year. Have you used it recently?"

"Why do you ask?"

"Are you staying in practice? It seems relevant right now."

"More than I wish. Cutting people up is one surefire way to get in trouble with the law and that's something I studiously avoid. And, interestingly enough, there's no such thing as a concealed carry permit for a katana. You can get a concealed carry permit all day long for a gun, but not a knife or sword."

"Why is that so interesting?"

"It's interesting that the most dangerous weapons are the most protected ones. I guarantee you that if everyone had to fight with a sword, or with sticks and stones, there'd be a lot less fighting. Not that I like weapons. Fact is, I don't. But if you have to fight, and in this world you have to fight way too often, then it's wise to stay ready for it." He released a deep breath. "I keep myself in shape not because I like training. Fact is, I don't like it that much. I hate hitting the weights and running and watching what I eat and the rest of it. But it's better than the alternative."

Amanda's face scrunched as she asked with what seemed to be genuine curiosity, "What's the alternative?"

"The alternative is getting killed by a Sicario, a Jihadist, or some punk with a twenty-five-dollar Raven who wants to take your shoes. Or even being set on fire by gutless junkies at a college who don't happen to love what you're saying. If you want to see the power of prejudice, try reasoning with some punk wearing a mask."

Amanda laughed out loud. "I happen to agree with you. But I'd add something."

"What's that?"

"I would say that the people who complain constantly about violence are the ones who use it the most. But that doesn't explain why you never leave your sword behind. Frankly, I think it gives you a sense of security. Or you're just flat-out superstitious."

"Well, it did get me out of Vietnam. It saved my life from some animals, human and otherwise, so I guess I am a little superstitious. And it did have a part in convincing Miruko to take me into his home, and train me, and feed me, and raise me with a classical education. I guess I consider it to be something like a good luck charm. Or a friend. Take your pick. It doesn't matter. Fact is, we've always been together and I guess I'm uncomfortable without it."

"I understand," Amanda said with a shrug, "I'm actually like that with a lot of things. Always have been. I don't think there's anything wrong with it. To be honest, I've been using the same hairbrush since I was a kid. I consider it a good luck charm. I even make sure I always tie my shoes the exact same way, left foot first. And there's the way I pack my purse, or luggage. The way I answer the door or study a person's body language. I think everybody has superstitions even if they don't admit it to themselves."

"Why are you hung up on body language?"

"Because I think everybody lies."

Isaiah laughed. "I have to agree." He paused. "So what does my body language tell you?"

"Oh, you're easy. Your body language says that you're very confident, but you make a conscious and consistent effort not to show it. It says that you truly do have nerves of steel." She sighed. "You look a person in the eye. You don't blink and you don't look away. You don't sweat. You don't slouch. You don't flinch. You keep your head up when you talk or walk or do anything else. But your machine-like control hints that you do have a temper and I think it scares you. That's why you keep yourself under such a tight rein. You're afraid that if you lose your temper, you'll kill somebody. And you're either not scared of dying or you just don't give a damn." She didn't glance back as she asked,

"You're not gonna let these goons follow us all the way to town, are you?"

"No," Isaiah frowned, "I'm gonna get a better look at them."

"How're we gonna do that?"

"I remember seeing a little store that ought to be open for breakfast. We'll stop there. See if they follow. They'll have to get out of the car to make it look legitimate."

"That's not bad," Amanda muttered, "for someone who doesn't plan."

Isaiah smiled, "I'm quick on my feet."

"Well, you've been pretty resourceful so far. But what if they have guns? And what if they really are the guys who make people disappear?"

"Now why would they make us disappear?" Isaiah glanced over. "All you did was ask Blanchard a few harmless questions, right?"

"Because he was lying to my face and he knows that I know it."

"You got all that from his body language?"

"As a matter of fact, I did. Just like I could tell that you weren't listening to him at all. You were studying his desk, his shelves, what you could see of the compound, the doors, the fence. I don't think you heard a word he said."

"I didn't need to listen to him when I saw a quotation framed on his wall."

"A picture told you he was lying?" Amanda stared. "How does that work?"

Isaiah sighed, "When someone keeps a quote that reads, 'Anything is better than lies and deceit,' I don't need to hear what he's got to say. It's a quote that seems harmless unless you know the story behind it."

"What's the story?"

"It's from *Anna Karenina*. Tolstoy."

"And that's important because …?"

"Because Anna Karenina kills herself, in the end, because she's been lied to so horribly."

"Oh, my God," Amanda said quietly. "How? Why?"

"She throws herself under a train after her husband has betrayed her. And her husband, on balance, wins out. His lies save him like they save most sociopaths. So that picture wasn't hung to condemn lies. It's to remind Blanchard that lies can save you if you don't care about who you destroy."

Amanda blinked slowly, staring out the windshield. "Well, I can tell you from personal experience that lies can kill you in a hundred ways. They can kill you emotionally and mentally, but they can also kill you physically. Betrayal is like death. And logic sure doesn't help you overcome it, so anybody who keeps such a horrible quote like that on their wall is some kind of monster." A pause. "You can tell how much a person hates you by how much they lie to you."

Silent, Isaiah nodded.

"I say we stick with instincts," Amanda said, turning her face to the window. "So what do your instincts tell you they're planning to do?"

Isaiah hesitated. "If you won't find it too alarming, honey, I think you're right."

"Meaning?"

"I think they're planning to kill us."

A small mom-and-pop store that was obviously not on the tourist list of things to do loomed on the right. Isaiah pulled smoothly into a space just to the right of the front door. He reached out and lifted the Honjo Masamune from its place alongside the door and slid it under the left side of his coat. Then he looked calmly at Amanda, "Just do what I do. We're just going to go inside and look around. This place is like a Cracker Barrel back home. There's plenty to see, so just act casual. After all, we're tourists."

"Where will you be?"

"Close. But I'll stay near the window to make sure they don't come near the car. You just browse. Check out the wines."

"How close will you be?"

"Twenty feet."

"Is that close enough?"

"Yeah. Just don't move when I move. I don't want to hit you by mistake."

"Got it."

Isaiah opened the door.

The white car pulled in beside them.

***

Inside, the store was shockingly opulent if one had judged it from the dull and frozen exterior. What seemed like a barn from the road looked like a Winter Wonderland inside with multitudinous wines of every varietal and size lining the walls.

The middle of the five-room log cabin-style shop was a collection of assorted foods, beverages, and tourist trinkets. Obviously, this was the local food outlet and breakfast stop so Amanda simply ordered bagels and coffee and began to stroll among the stand-up tables and wine racks, lifting one bottle and another.

Isaiah had taken a stand at the front of the store, apparently amazed at a dogsled with a well-worn leather harness. He asked the old clerk a few questions without removing his peripheral vision from either car.

After five minutes the clerk asked something in Swiss. Isaiah responded to her in German. "Probably," she said in English.

Amanda was compelled to walk over and whisper, "What did you tell her?"

"She said she didn't recognize the car and asked if we knew them. I said, no. Then I told her they were probably tourists and they'd be getting out in a minute."

"How do you know they'll be getting out?"

"Because we're not leaving until they do."

Five, ten, fifteen minutes passed and Amanda placed an armload of wine bottles on the counter, promising to pick out a few more. The old woman replied in fluent English, which surprised Amanda. But then she realized that you can't rightly operate a tourist-oriented wine store in Switzerland without speaking English.

A single door opened on the car and a man wearing a blue parka and cap stepped outside. He climbed the steps carefully and entered with a polite greeting. Then he began walking along the racks.

Isaiah never turned or glanced from the sled. His eyes were not fixed on the white car, but Amanda knew he was watching. Unconsciously she had eased away from the stranger but then realized she looked suspicious avoiding him and returned to the shelves, seemingly oblivious to his presence. With all the control she could muster she lifted and studied one label after another. And never had her knowledge of body language been more hypersensitive than it was in the moment.

The stranger's gestures were casual and unhurried, the masquerade of a connoisseur because his eyes didn't read the labels, so he wasn't here for the wine.

"Look at this!" Amanda said just loudly enough for the old woman to hear. "It's one of the rarest red wines from Rioja! Made from Tempranillo!" She turned. "How did you happen to get this Spanish wine? I've never seen a bottle in Switzerland."

The old woman gestured, "Wine is my husband's passion. We have traveled all over the world building our store, so we've been collecting wine for fifty-three years.

Yes, if my husband were here he would give you a real tour. He is the expert your 'experts' talk to before they go on TV."

"Oh, I wish he were here right now," Amanda smiled and glanced at the front window where the dogsled rested.

"He will be here shortly," she nodded.

Amanda turned to the front and her breath caught.

Isaiah was gone.

Amanda instantly took a step away from the stranger who was suddenly standing much too close for her; she smoothly rounded a counter to put something solid between them. Then a survival instinct prompted her to quickly cast a glance at the white car to confirm the second man's location.

He was gone, as well.

***

Isaiah violently pushed the man into the building far outside view of the front window. He had approached the driver and asked if he was interested in wines. Then, when the man began to reply, Isaiah struck him across the chin with an elbow and dragged him out of view of the clerk.

In the struggle, the stranger reached into his coat but Isaiah was faster and grabbed a semiautomatic pistol from the man's shoulder harness. Isaiah lifted the Glock ten millimeter to his face, laughing, "A Glock! A fourth generation ten millimeter with ten in the clip, one in the pipe. You like Austrian weapons, huh? Well, I never cared much for 'em, myself. They feel too much like a toy."

"What the hell do you want?" the stranger muttered, expressing no fear. "You're already in deep, pal. And, now, if you make a bonehead move against me or that idiot they teamed me up with, you'll have the entire Swiss army down on you and the little lady. It's already morning, but you won't live to see sunrise."

"Neither will you," Isaiah stated. "So what's the plan?"

"To tell that bitch to point her titties west and catch a train. You got a problem with that?"

"Just like that, huh?" Isaiah ejected the clip from the Glock. "So what do you need this little ol' thing for?"

"To kill you with?"

"Well, it'd sure do the job if I wasn't the one holding it." Isaiah whipped out the Honjo and the edge was instantly at the man's neck. "But this doesn't make as much noise."

Isaiah took one moment to search him, found a backup pistol on his belt, and tossed it into the snow.

The man spat, "You ain't gonna kill me, Isaiah! You'd have an entire army down on your head and you know it! You wouldn't even make it down the mountain! You sure as hell wouldn't make it home!"

"I'm not gonna kill you," Isaiah said calmly, "because you're gonna do exactly what I tell you."

"And what's that?"

"You're gonna take us back inside that compound."

The man gaped. "Are you crazy?"

"You're my passport."

"I'll blow the whistle on you and your girlfriend first chance I get because I don't think you're crazy enough to kill me when you've got a hundred rifles aimed at you." He frowned. "*And her.*"

"Trust me," Isaiah shook his head, "I truly don't care about living or dying. I've been living on borrowed time all my life and I never saw much worth living for in the first place. But I'm not in any hurry to die, either. So you need to get it through your head. I *will* blow your brains out if you alert the guards."

"You dropped the clip."

"We both know there's one in the chamber. And your friend will be in the back seat with my friend and she'll kill him, too. She's not afraid to die finding out what happened to her sister. But if you get us inside that compound, I'll let you go."

"Go ahead and kill me, tough guy. You think I'm gonna take you all the way back there just so you can blow my brains out?"

Isaiah almost laughed as he said, "I'm telling you the truth. Just take us back and I'll let you live." His eyes narrowed. "Trust me, man, if I wanted you dead, you'd be dead. No sound. No alarm. Nobody would know for a few days and we'd be back home by then. Is that any way for a hard case like you to die?"

Isaiah raised the man's hand and barely touched it with the edge of the Honjo; the blood flow was immediate. "You didn't even feel that, right? That means you'll still be trying to talk after your body goes one way and your head goes another. I know because I've seen it. It's actually fascinating. Makes you want to talk back to a severed head."

"You really don't know what kind of hardware they've got in that place, do you? Son, they've got thirty-millimeter miniguns covering every hallway and they're set with infrared detectors. They've got almost five hundred hired hands armed with everything from M4s to Benellis." He shook his head. "Isaiah, and I *do* admire your guts, hoss, but you and your girl won't get ten feet inside that place before you're vaporized. And make no mistake. There won't be any arrests. They'll throw you in that collider and vaporize you."

"Pardon me," Isaiah leaned close. "I have business inside the store."

"Whoa! There's no need for—"

Isaiah sharply brought the steel hilt of the katana down on the man's neck and he collapsed. Isaiah had knocked enough people unconscious to know whether it was real and this was real. This guy would only be out for five minutes but that was all Isaiah needed if he could keep Amanda under control.

He sheathed the sword and walked into the store knowing this would be the delicate part. He needed a distraction and Amanda would have to take it on the fly; there'd be no time for questions and answers. He walked up to her and said quietly, "Ask the old woman if she can show you what she's got in the back."

To her credit, Amanda simply turned without question to enthusiastically approach the old woman. After a brief conversation, the woman told Isaiah that she would be in the back of the store if he needed anything.

Isaiah turned into the second man who ripped out an exact duplicate of the Glock. But Isaiah was ready for it and swiped the Honjo out and down—two moves in two-tenths of a second—and the steel slide and polymer frame of the Glock sharply separated, one part clattering to the floor. For a moment the man raised half the ruined weapon to his face, then looked at Isaiah. "You gotta be kidding me!"

Isaiah placed the point of the katana at his neck and removed a backup Glock from his belt; he lifted it before the man's face. "I'll keep this one. Now you're going to take me and the woman back to the facility. And you'll do exactly what I say or I'll take you apart as quickly as I took apart your toy. Do you understand?"

The man's eyes darted to the white car.

"Where's Tony?" he asked.

"He's in the same situation you're in. Both of you are going to get me and her back into that compound. Then I'll decide what to do with you. Or you can both die right here. It'll take the police forever to identify two headless bodies with no IDs."

"Headless?"

"I always take the heads with me." Isaiah raised the gleaming tip of the Honjo to the man's chin. "And the IDs. And, in your case, I'll also unhook your GPS and use your car to initiate Plan B. So what do you want to do? Die or drive?"

"Hell," the man frowned, shaking his head, "you got a wild-ass plan that is not gonna work, honcho. That compound may not look like Fort Knox, but you better not step off the path without the right ID or it's your ass. And no place is safe for you or her once they start looking for you."

"I'll take those odds," Isaiah said quietly. Then he pushed the man toward the door. "Get in the back seat. I'll keep your gun. Your partner's, too. All you guys have to do is get us inside. If you do that, I'll let you live."

"You ain't gonna let us live! You can't! That'd blow your whole operation and I can tell right now that you ain't military so you ain't got no backup! You're some kind of lone wolf with a bone to pick and you've got a civilian girl tagging along!" He took a deep breath. "Man, you're in way over your head. You're playing with the big boys now. And they don't care who they kill to keep that place off the map." He gestured to everything around them. "Congressmen! Judges! Four-star generals! We've killed so many of your people we should rename this place Arlington National!"

"Move." Isaiah pushed him toward the door as he called out, "Amanda! We're leaving! Now!"

As Isaiah shoved the second man into the back seat, the first hitter was rising. Isaiah gave the Glock to Amanda and pointed to the back seat. "It's a Glock. There's no safety. Just point and pull the trigger."

"Got it," she said, concealing the gun in her coat. Then she locked a gaze on the guard in the back seat. "What's your name?" she asked mildly.

"Fred."

"Well, Fred, I *will* kill you. I just want you to know that in case you think I'm going to panic and scream like a little girl or do something stupid. The thing is, I won't. So if you make one move that I don't like, I'll shoot you until the gun is empty. I'll shoot you in the chest. I'll shoot you in the head. I'll shoot your dick off. I'll—"

"Yeah, yeah, lady, you'll shoot me dead. I got it."

"I just wanted you to understand me. I have no conscience. My doctor says I'm a psychopath."

"You should listen to him."

Isaiah came around the corner, the Honjo Masamune beneath his coat, his right hand in his coat pocket. "Get in," he said.

Amanda climbed into the back seat as Isaiah settled into the passenger seat after securing Tony behind the wheel. For a moment they just sat, and then Isaiah said slowly and carefully, "Okay. This is how it's going to work. I don't like either of you, so killing you won't bother me. But you've got something going for you despite how this looks."

As a man inured to danger, Tony stated, "I'd love to know what that is."

"The guards know you. When we get to the gate, you just tell them you have baggage. Or use whatever term you use for guests that are in your custody. Prisoners, if you will. I'm sure they'll understand. Then tell them that you have the situation under control, but you have to take us to meet the big dog. Then just drive through the gate like normal and go where I tell you to go. Is that clear?"

"Yep," nodded Tony.

"No problem," came from the back seat.

"There's just one more thing you should know," Isaiah stressed. "If I even sense that you are covertly signaling the guards or not going by this protocol, I will kill both of you before you can move one inch. Yes, Amanda and I will die, too. But we don't care. Do we, Amanda?"

"I don't care."

Without cause or provocation Amanda shot Fred in the leg.

Fred's howl of agony and his volcanic reaction rocked the vehicle for a long moment and solidified the air more than a hurricane. "Oh! Jesus!" he cried. "The bitch shot me in the leg!" He kept howling, "What the hell did you do that for? I didn't move!"

"Don't mess with me," Amanda stated, dead calm. "I'm psycho."

"Hell, yeah, you're psycho!" Fred screamed. "Oh, god! I can't believe you shot me! That was a damn hollow point! Jesus! Tony! Do something! Take this crazy bitch where she wants to go! I need a hospital!"

Tony looked at Isaiah and said without evident alarm. "Okay, sport, you win. I still don't believe you'd kill me like a dog, but I can't say the same for Anne Oakley back there. So what happens after I get you inside?"

After we conclude our business, you go your way, we go our way." Isaiah stared as Tony turned his head, gazing with incredulity at Fred groaning and twisting. Then Isaiah added, "*After* we conclude our business, so it's not that hard to believe." He shrugged, "We won't need you, anymore. And I don't hurt anybody I don't have to."

"Uh huh. What about Ms. Manners?"

"If you don't confuse her, she won't hurt you. But that's the only promise I can make. Just get us both where we want to go and you can get your act in the wind. That's the only deal on the table. Take it or leave it." Isaiah extended the moment. "Or get shot right here. Like Fred. It's up to you. All I have to do is look at her."

It was with amazing coordination that five white cars skidded to a stop directly behind the vehicle, and suddenly the expressions on the would-be cooperator's faces turned from stress to relief. Tony, the driver, simply turned a gaze to Isaiah as if to convey, '*You were saying*?'

From the backseat Isaiah heard Fred laugh angrily and with unconcealed contempt as Amanda turned in her seat. Then she looked at Isaiah as he said, "It's backup. They have three security cars from the compound and two national police."

Tony, still smiling, said, "You got balls for sure, dude, but you are one dumb son of a bitch." He shook his head as he casually took the Glock from Isaiah's hand. "They've had both of you on satellite since she landed at the airport. They been listening to her and watching her in the states for two weeks. They have her house wired, have her air. She hasn't made one move or had one conversation they haven't got on disc. And you thought you were just gonna walk in there and demand answers? God Almighty, man. You're lucky you're not already dead. They've killed more important people for a whole lot less than you sticking your nose where it don't belong."

Isaiah thrust his hand into his coat. "If you make the wrong move, I'll still cut your head off before they can stop me."

"I'm a professional," Tony stated. "I made a deal. I'll keep it."

An immaculately uniformed patrolman—the Swiss police really knew the impact of a sharp outfit—knocked with authority on Tony's window.

"Shut up, Fred," muttered Tony. "I'll handle this."

Fred bit down on his hand, stifling a moan.

Tony rolled down the window. "Yes, sir?"

"Are you gentlemen all right?" the police officer asked in English with an impressively diluted Swiss accent. "We heard there was trouble."

"Nah, man," Tony waved, "it's just business as usual with these tourists. They got lost so we're escorting them back to the compound. But thanks for the assistance."

"No problem."

Isaiah looked over the seat at Amanda. "Do *not* shoot him again unless I tell you to," he said sternly. "Do you understand me, Amanda?"

Amanda replied coldly, "I understand."

"So," Tony boomed heartily, "what's your big plan, hoss? Ask Blanchard how he lost seven physicists? Ask him questions he can't begin to answer? Hell, if you're that stupid, you might as well ask those old farts on the committee."

"What committee?" asked Isaiah.

"How would I know?" Tony shrugged. "But the committee is a lot bigger than Blanchard. He's just a paper pusher."

"Blanchard's not the boss?" asked Amanda.

"Oh, hell, no. Blanchard is like a second lieutenant or something. Barely has a commission. He's mid-level. The big man is the director-general. His name is Antonio Francois. And, if you ask me, he's French."

Amanda muttered, "That's a stretch."

"I didn't think the French had much to do with this place," said Isaiah. "It's not like they helped fund it."

"Who knows why the damn French are involved in this Satanic mess?" Tony was surprisingly talkative for someone that was supposed to be a high-dollar assassin. "Fact is, man, I don't think anybody knows who truly makes decisions for that place. It's all secret hush-hush stuff. Worse than the CIA. And it's been like that ever since I started working here. Even when they offered me a job, I said, 'What for?' They told me, 'We can't tell you.' I said, 'Does it involve killing?' They said, 'We can't tell you.' So I asked 'em, 'Well, where's it at?' They said, 'We can't tell you that, either.' So I finally said, 'Is there anything you *can* tell me?' They said, 'The money's good.' And that was it. So, quite obviously, paranoia is the name of the game with these guys. Even I don't know who cuts my check."

"Just tell me one thing," said Isaiah.

"Have I ever denied you anything?"

"Why are you taking us back to the compound when you said you'd rather die?"

"Ah, I knew you weren't gonna murder me, hoss. I read up on you. I got your file. I can even say I respect you. Of course, I can't say the same for Lizzie Borden back there."

"My file?" Isaiah asked. "Who'd you get my file from?"

"Hell, I have no idea who it was from. It was sanitized. And you know what that means, don't you?"

"Yeah," Isaiah noted. "It's government. My own."

"Son, you were betrayed before you packed a bag."

"All right. What does it say?"

Tony managed a minor shrug, "It said you don't kill people unless you have to. And you don't use a gun. You represent people for free. Do all that hero stuff. And it said you've racked up quite a body count with some kind of edged weapon."

"They know about the sword?"

"Well, I didn't know you had the katana until you drew it on me. I was actually re-thinking my lack of cooperation when you hit me on top of the head." His eyes widened. "Now, that got my undivided attention because I know for a fact that you've planted quite a few with that thing. Forty-seven to be exact. And mostly Spetsnaz. That is, if the CIA has improved its intelligence since Afghanistan. And, frankly, I didn't want to be another notch in your handle."

Isaiah leaned back, staring to the side before he asked, "Okay, you don't know who's ultimately in charge, so who gives you your orders?"

"Director-General Francois."

"Not Blanchard?"

"No, man," Tony grimaced. "Blanchard can't blow his nose without permission. Security details are handled by Francois. Like I said, he's on the committee. In fact, he's the only man here who can send us off the reservation. Blanchard may be an important man on the grass, but the committee members handle the rest of the world."

"That's all you know?"

"Yeah," Tony said, eyes wide. "Hey, man, I'm just a grocery clerk. You know the drill. They give me a name. I talk to somebody. Sometimes I have to do a little persuading. Rarely do I resort to violence because, fortunately, most people are smart enough to leave town when they're told point blank that a multibillion-dollar conglomerate as big as most nations has put a hefty price tag on their head. And then I tell them they can't call nobody for help because these cats have people everywhere including every tier of the United States intelligence services from the CIA to Customs." He hesitated. "And you two suicide cases made the list before you even left the States, if you want to know."

Isaiah was nonplussed. "Fair enough."

It was a dull, uneventful ride to the Large Hadron Supercollider Compound and it passed without conversation, then they were at the first gate.

"Is this place always so heavily guarded?" Isaiah asked.

"Not like this," Tony grunted. "But something real bad happened a little while back and security has been souped-up to the point where a fly can't get in. And it's gonna stay that way as long as the freaks who run this place are scared shitless like they are now."

Amanda spoke up, "Tony? Is that your real name?"

"Yes, ma'am."

"Bizarrely enough, Tony, and I wouldn't normally say something like this but it's a bit late to avoid drama. The truth is that you actually seem like a nice guy. It's hard for me to believe you were going to kill us."

"No," Tony shook his head with an aura of genuine honesty, "I didn't plan to kill you. I was just going to persuade you to leave town. Give you my speech. See you to a plane. I didn't see any need for violence."

"Why not?"

"For one thing, Francois didn't specifically tell me to kill you. He just told me to get rid of you. There's a difference. And, besides, I only kill people when I have to. It ain't personal."

"Killing someone is pretty personal, Tony."

"You don't understand," he said. "After Iraq I was essentially unemployable. There's not a lot that an ex-sniper is qualified to do. So, shamefully enough, this is how I whore myself out these days. And, to be honest, I did have the green light to make the call if it was necessary, but I've got reservations about killing other operators. I mean, it's just business, right? We're all just doing our job. So I see no reason to kill somebody just because they're working for Tom, Dick, or Harry. Hell, next week *I* might be working for those guys and *I* might be on the receiving end of this. But there's no cause to make this more violent than we have to. That, and I don't see any harm in you guys having a sit-down with Blanchard. You're not gonna get anything out of him, anyway, because he doesn't know anything. But Francois might know something. He's fairly high on the totem pole."

Isaiah asked, "How high?"

Tony shrugged, "I know he's on the committee and that's as high as it goes. You don't want any attention from him."

"You don't have any idea who's ultimately in charge of this place?" asked Amanda.

"Nah," Tony answered. "But I know that he, or she, ain't on this compound. Like all rich people, they don't do nuthin' themselves." He blinked in what seemed like amazement before, "Yeah, the committee members are scattered all over the world, man. And they meet like those guys in the old *Rollerball* movie, ya know? You remember that movie? They had this big committee that controlled everything in the world and they'd just meet on camera and decide who lives and who dies? They would just press a button that would said 'yea,' or 'nay,' and never say another word? Well, that's the way these guys work." He shook his head. "And they say *I'm* cold-blooded."

They drove across the compound toward the gigantic, circular, bronze-toned statue of Shiva that heralded the entrance to the Supercollider.

This was the main facility and was securely housed three hundred feet underneath the hard-frozen earth that protected it from both the radiation of stars and the prying eyes of spies. And it occurred to Isaiah in the moment that it would take more than an army to destroy the seventeen-mile-long supercollider that powered the blackness behind this evil—an evil he could feel. Suddenly every idea he'd possessed about solving the fate of Amanda's sister was answered in his soul. He had suspected but hadn't felt it with such certainty.

Instinct told him that Amanda's sister, Cynthia, was somewhere in the darkness separating the stars. But it was far, far, *far* too late to turn back from discovering the truth behind "why" and "how." It was too late for an apology. It was even too late to appeal to a higher authority who might judge this situation on legal ground because on this ground there was no such thing as a higher authority.

This place didn't take orders from the world; the world took orders from the wizards who ran this facility and for how long it had been like that was anyone's guess. It occurred to Isaiah, as they unloaded themselves from the car, that it might have been like this since the beginning of this dark dream, for whoever commanded the power a hundred years ago to construct a world-enveloping enterprise to turn back time, enslave the human race, open a space-time portal, reshape a universe with demonic powers, and perhaps even alter the galaxy itself, had more than enough power to control a few presidents.

"I'll take you downstairs to see Blanchard," said Tony, extending his hand. "But I think I'll have your pig-sticker first. No offense, Isaiah, but once you get in there and hear what you don't wanna hear you might start lopping off heads and we wouldn't want that, would we? Then I'd have to kill both of you. And I'd hate the hell out of that. And that's the truth."

Without protest Isaiah handed over the katana. He nodded once, "You take good care of that."

Tony's brow hardened as he studied the length of the sheathed blade. Then he unsheathed eighteen inches of it, staring. "I've seen a lot of these in my time," he commented, "but I've never seen one like this. What is it?"

"The Honjo Masamune," said Isaiah.

Tony sharply raised his face. "*The* Honjo Masamune?" He gazed down again. "Holy crap. This baby's been lost since World War II."

"Not quite."

Tony gently sheathed the blade, a nod. "Well, I'll take good care of it for you, hoss. I promise you that much." He sighed wistfully. "I hope you get this baby back, man. It's priceless. And they say it's magical. They say Masamune forged it so that it could cut a demon in half. But you already know that, don't you?"

"Yeah," grunted Isaiah. "I know."

"Okay. You guys follow me. No need for restrains. We're all friends here."

Tony walked past the idolized Shiva, waved at it vaguely.

"I hate that bitch," he muttered. "This whole place is filled with witches, warlocks, wizards, sorcerers, psychos and they're all *physicists*. And they've got all these weird symbols cut above all the doors. It's worse than Denver airport with that Masonic compass and miter all over the damn walls." He glanced at Isaiah. "You ever been there? To Denver airport? Ever noticed all that stuff on the walls and floor? That crap has been there since they opened the place. Just walking through it makes me feel like a Mason."

"Yeah," Isaiah responded, "I've seen it. But I don't think it means a whole lot."

"It means *something,* hoss. And I do know from my own eyes that Denver airport sits on top of the biggest underground survival shelter in the world. It's supposedly part of the president's last-ditch, last-stand location to survive Armageddon. But God only knows why they have a compass and miter and those Masonic signs of power, or whatever they are, engraved on the walls. I mean, I don't consider it spooky or anything. I deal with spooky stuff all the time, and Denver ain't one of 'em, but it's definitely weird. Even I don't know why the world's biggest survival shelter is located under a Masonic lodge."

Isaiah said, "As good as any other lodge, I guess. But why is this place located in these godforsaken mountains?"

"If you listen to the eggheads that run this whorehouse, it's because this particular piece of real estate is haunted. Or something like that." Tony took a crunching snow-step with a curse. "This damn snow. Anyway, I've heard it was built on top of some old temple that was used by the long-dead Greeks to worship some kind of heathen god named Apollo or something. I don't know. Don't ask me them weird questions, man. I just work here. I drive a car. I scare people. Sometimes I pull a trigger. But I ain't no witch or warlock or whatever the hell these people are. I'm just an everyday working stiff. I ain't got enough religious beliefs to fill a shot glass. Hell, that might be why they hired me. 'Cause I don't care what they do here. I just do my job, go home, and get drunk."

"Good job if you can live with yourself," said Amanda.

"*Live with myself*!" Tony barked a harsh laugh. "Girl? Why do you think I get drunk every night?"

Amanda's concern seemed genuine. "Then why do you work here, Tony? This isn't the only security job out there, is it?"

"You really wanna know?"

"Yeah, I really do."

"It's because the money's good and there's nothing to do. You just walk around and drink espresso and go home with a hooker." He glanced over his shoulder. "Yeah, hookers are basically legal in Switzerland. This place even has its own brothel, so it's real low stress. But then they lost a whole bunch of people about two weeks back and the uniforms began carrying every rifle they could get their hands on and I've been running my ass off since then putting out fires left and right."

Isaiah asked, "How did they lose people?"

"Time is short so let's just say it was a seriously fubar-ed situation and left a lot of people messed up in the head."

Isaiah was careful to keep it unforced. "Anything else been happening around here?"

"Ah," Tony motioned, "a lot of people have got lobbed off to the big Geneva asylum with nervous breakdowns. That kind of thing happens here more than any place I've ever seen. And I've seen war zones all over the world. But I've never seen so many people go insane at such a rapid rate in such a small place."

"How do you explain it?"

"Hell if I know, Musashi. We find people wandering around at night claiming they're seeing ghosts and demons and stuff. It'll be like that for weeks. And that's not even when they turn that collider up to full power, which they've only done twice, thank God." He shook his head. "When they do that, it's like *everybody* goes crazy around here. I've never seen anything like it. And they don't go crazy because of the stress because there's plenty of women and booze and every other kind of entertainment. No, man, people go crazy in this place saying they've been talking to dead people or some monster was raping them at night. It's weird as hell, man. And since they had this last accident with that collider, this freaking place has gone tee-totally insane with people seeing demons, talking to Satan, cutting the heads off their pets and sticking them on top of broomsticks. I'm tellin' ya, it's got bad around here, brother. Bad enough to even scare *me*."

Amanda asked, "Have *you* seen anything, Tony?"

"Nah," Tony waved, "I ain't got enough imagination to see anything. If I see something, I just write it off as bad whiskey. But plenty of others are claiming to see ghosts and goblins and skeletons in their rooms and hearing chains rattling in the walls and things goin' bump in the night. I had to respond to some emergency situations involving a few of the lab coats who were jabbering about how they'd rather die than meet whatever the hell is inside that collider. I managed to disarm two of them before they pulled the trigger, but the other one was too quick for me. He plastered his brains all over the wall with a .357 Magnum. But the thing is … well, it was even weirder than that. It was something about the last thing he said before he pulled the trigger."

"What did he say?" asked Isaiah.

"He said, '*He's here*,' and then blew his brains out." Tony released a sigh. "It was weird, man."

"He said, '*He's here*?'" Amanda asked. "What does that mean?"

"Hell if I know," Tony replied. "But I didn't like the sound of it."

***

Isaiah honestly didn't mind waiting a half-hour in the subtly illuminated office. Nor did he care to make an attempt to escape from the room even though they were not handcuffed to the chairs or bound by flex cuffs or ropes. And, considering their circumstances, handcuffs did seem redundant if not ridiculous.

He knew that Tony and more guards were alertly poised outside the door and additional backup was stationed at every corner, every corridor, every elevator and any other means of reaching the surface and that the herculean security system wasn't singly focused on Amanda and himself, either.

The guards were obviously afraid of something a lot more dangerous than them because it didn't require five hundred fully automatic rifles to watch one man and woman. This was the kind of firepower you dragged out to repel an invasion.

Isaiah was aware they were three hundred feet underground and—by his boldest estimate—less than fifty feet from the cement wall of the Large Hadron Supercollider. Although Isaiah half-expected to feel the slightest trembling or vibration or just an electric presence, there was nothing he could detect. It was like standing beside the outside wall of a centuries-old, unused subway. Unless a train was barreling down the track you might as well be standing outside a graveyard.

Amanda, conversely, was fidgeting and fuming and again asked, "Why do you think they haven't killed us already?"

After a moment Isaiah answered, "I suspect they want to find out what we know before they make a decision about what to do with us." He inhaled deeply, then added, "You know, Amanda, there's a fair chance they won't kill us. I'm not sure that there's any reason for you to get all worked up about this."

"Are you crazy!" She turned into him. "We are sitting on top of a demonic thermo-nuclear reactor that probably ate my sister alive and only God in Heaven knows whether they're going to throw *us* in there, too!" She slammed a hand on the chair. "Isaiah! How can you be so calm? And why did you let him take your sword? You didn't even put up a fight!"

"Because it got us in here, Amanda. And isn't that what you wanted?"

"To be held prisoner by these goons? *No!*" She looked in every direction. "I thought we were going to sneak back in here like Batman and Robin and make Blanchard tell us the truth! And now we're prisoners!"

Isaiah scoffed. "Amanda, everybody here is a prisoner. They think they're in control of this machine but they're not. They never have been, not even when it was just a bunch of blueprints. Whatever power is behind this machine is in control of both the machine and the people who think they're going to benefit from it because that's exactly what this entity wants them to think." His jawline tightened. "This entity wants them to think they're in charge. Then, when they can keep that portal open long enough, it's going to escape whatever dimension it's trapped in and kill everybody in this place."

"What will happen to the rest of the world?" asked Amanda.

Isaiah shrugged, "The rest of the world might eventually figure out how to beat it. I mean, if it comes into this world it has to take *some* kind of physical form. And I doubt that anything is dangerous without a head on its shoulders, so we can always kill it. But I doubt it's gonna be easy." A pause. "It'll probably be like trying to put a collar on an angry tiger. I wouldn't wanna be the first to lay hands on it."

"Sorry to keep you waiting."

The restful voice was preceded by the almost silent opening and closing of the door and Isaiah didn't have to glance to know that it was Assistant Director Blanchard who slowly came into view, then calmly settled behind his thick glass desk.

"Since we met yesterday, I've been briefed about you," Blanchard said as he leaned forward, hands calmly clasped. "Ms. Deker, why do you insist on taking such interest in us? I have assured you that your sister's death was accidental. And, in case you are unaware, there have been many accidents, and many deaths at this facility although, I might add, we do have a better record than those who built the Golden Gate Bridge that buried twenty-odd men at a time."

He squinted, adding, "The truth is that this is a very expensive, very complicated, and very dangerous machine. The construction was dangerous and the operation of this facility is even more dangerous. And I can assure you that there will always be a high incident rate of injuries in this facility just as there are high incident rates of injuries and deaths in any high-risk profession like being an electrical lineman, a police officer, a fireman, or a high-steel worker. Any number of occupations. But you seem to believe that something sinister surrounds your sister's tragic death and there is something evil or demonic behind it. Also, you seem to believe that we are attempting to conceal the matter."

Amanda was aware that she was simply staring, and gaping, as Isaiah said without noticeable emotion, "If you turn that supercollider up to full power again, you're gonna die, Blanchard."

The slow shift in gaze that Blanchard made from Amanda to Isaiah took fully three seconds before Blanchard froze. His tone dropped, distinctly irritated. "And just what do you know about a multibillion-dollar machine that was under construction before you were ever born, Isaiah?" He waited. "I'd rather be more civil and address you by your surname and not your Christian name but we have, in fact, found seventy-seven last names associated with you and I'm not sure which is accurate."

"Smith will do."

Blanchard smirked, "I'll just use Isaiah. At least that one is probably true. And truth seems to be a precious commodity with you two." Blanchard wiped his face, flicking away a bead of sweat. "You do realize the trouble that you've caused me, don't you?"

Amanda muttered, "I hope so."

With a grimace Blanchard added, "To begin, Ms. Deker, this facility is unlike any other that has ever existed and what we do here has never been done. Further, what we learn here is only shared with a privileged few, and that includes your government, as well. You see, the United States only knows what we decide they should know, and it's much the same with the member nations of our committee. It is even the same with the personnel who work here. The word for it is 'containment.' You only know what you are required to know in order to do your job."

Eyes widening, Amanda asked, "And you're telling us this because …?"

"What I am going to tell you will, of course, never leave this facility."

"Fat chance."

"No," Blanchard gestured, clearly indulgent. "What I mean, Ms. Deker, is the decision concerning your interference has been agreed upon."

"He's saying that someone above his pay grade has decided that we're never leaving this place," Isaiah commented. "I'm just curious, Blanchard, about why you're keeping us alive at all. It has something to do with Amanda, doesn't it?"

"How perceptive of you," Blanchard smiled. "You see, we've done a DNA analysis of the seven employees who disappeared during the last full-power test of the collider and we found, quite to our surprise, that they had something in common. And that included your sister."

Amanda's lips barely moved. "They were all Jews."

"Exactly," smiled Blanchard. "And so, in order to test our theory, we are going to turn on the supercollider again to full power and see if the surge duplicates the results of our last experiment, which took a regrettable turn." He gestured. "But that's what science is. You repeat the same experiment and if the end results are the same then you have what scientists quantify as a fact."

Rising, Blanchard strolled around the desk. "You see, until now we have only been able to keep the portal open for a nanosecond. But during the last experiment we kept it open for almost two tenths of a second. And the result was, well, shocking. In fact, we lost seven physicists, including your sister, to a phenomenon we still cannot explain. Nor do we have a clue why those who were taken were those who were predominately of Jewish origin. We only know what happened and so we must repeat the experiment and measure result against result. Of course, we are not telling those in the Observation Room who are of Jewish descent that they may very well meet their doom tomorrow morning. And since you are here, Ms. Deker, I see no reason to waste your life when you could distinctly help with the experiment."

"I can tell you why it's taking people of Jewish descent," said Isaiah in a bored monotone.

Blanchard's eyes widened. "And what would that be?"

"Because Jews are their closest ancestors."

The director tilted his head. "Ancestors?"

"The creatures trapped inside that dimension once walked this planet," Isaiah stated with bland certainty. "The Old Testament called them 'Nephilim.' They were giants. They were malignant. They were evil. And they were very seriously skilled in what seemed to be sorcery but it was just science. However, they did possess powers alien to normal human beings. They could shapeshift. They could read minds. They were far more intelligent than us. They were, in effect, the enemy of all mankind. And they were almost indestructible in battle. In fact, they would have conquered the world but for one man who made it a personal crusade to kill every last one of them."

"And who was this man of such renown?" laughed Blanchard.

"That doesn't matter. What matters is that these creatures wanted to destroy mankind and then retake their first estate. Or, to be more precise, they want to use the Earth as a staging area to launch attacks and take back their home. So, in the beginning, they had sex with the daughters of men and their children were predominately soldiers of Jewish DNA." Isaiah shrugged. "So all they're doing now is what they've done before. No one can say, 'Here is something new.' It's all been done. But they learned from their mistake. They didn't attack with enough men the first time, and they know it, so this time they'll attack with an army of *billions*. A force large enough to finish the fight. So right now they're preparing a deployment ten times larger than the first. They won't make the same mistake twice."

Blanchard laughed, "Nonsense!"

As Isaiah continued, "Right now they're just using the gateway to gain a foothold in this world because you have the weapon and they want to begin their attack. First, they need the portal so they can build an adequate army. That's why you've probably been losing people lately. You've had people disappearing, right? Well, that's because you've got one or more of these things running loose in your halls, genius. And if they've taken on flesh and blood, then they have to breath and they have to eat. So they're already here and that means they're getting some support staff in place on this planet."

Blanchard's face had frozen as Isaiah shrugged, "But since you opened that portal over two weeks ago, that's probably old news to you. Truth is, by now you should be accustomed to finding bodies with the arms and legs torn off, the heads missing. But there's no reason, yet, to panic. All they're doing right now is feeding, not recruiting." He paused. "When they start recruiting, *then* you can be afraid."

Blanchard's voice was croaked. "Why then?"

"Because, then, they'll begin infecting this world with their own bloodlines. And when they think they've got enough of a half-human army for their purpose, they'll use the full power of that supercollider to open a portal back to where they were created. And you can choose to be a soldier or you can choose to be a slave. But you won't be some sorcerer-supreme commanding millions of super soldiers. You won't be building an empire to the stars because the firmament they're after isn't corporal. It's something higher. It was created first, and it was once their home. But they were cast out. Now, their big plan is to go back with an army powerful enough to take it by force."

Amanda tilted her head at Blanchard's silence. She expected laughter or even some kind of rebuke toward Isaiah for being so "shallow" and "unscientific," but Blanchard had suddenly become visibly nervous. He was motionless. He was sweating. And Amanda could almost see his pulse pounding in his neck.

He wiped his forehead in the coolness of the room.

Amanda stated, "You don't seem all that surprised about Isaiah's analysis, Mr. Blanchard." She stared as Blanchard fixed her with a vacant stare. "What else has happened since my sister vanished? Why are all those men in the pavilion carrying machineguns? Why is everyone so nervous?"

Blanchard sighed, hands relaxing flat on his see-through desk. "To be honest, Ms. Deker, I don't believe it will hurt to tell you that we have indeed had a series of … events, you might call them … since the incident involving your sister."

"How many more have been killed?" asked Isaiah.

Blanchard responded with a nebulous gesture, "As with any industry, we have industrial accidents. Some are wounded. Some are killed. We take extensive safety precautions, but accidents in a facility this large and powerful are inevitable. And, then, some of our people have simply gone missing."

"*Missing*?" asked Amanda. "They went missing without their arms and legs? Missing without their heads? Did their heads go looking for their legs?"

"We haven't found all of them." Blanchard inhaled deeply, released it. "But, in truth, we're missing two guards, three mechanics, and two electricians."

Isaiah said, "So this power that you arrogantly think you can control didn't just take away a few of your folks when you opened that portal, right? It left you with one or more of its own?" He shook his head. "Your arrogance is gonna get you killed, Blanchard. Your death is walking the corridors of this place right now."

"Your myopic view of power is the only arrogance I see, Isaiah." Blanchard made no effort to conceal his contempt. "You obviously view everything according to historically and scientifically disproven superstitions and vague presuppositions of what is real and what is not. Presuppositions, I might add, that have been empirically invalidated over the past hundred years by repeated scientific research, and so your conceptions are worse than arrogant. They are ignorant."

He lifted an arm to the thick window behind him that allowed a distant glimpse of the supercollider. "Here we deal in nothing but pure science, Isaiah, and not black-and-white Sunday School lessons taught by retired, blue-haired English teachers who wouldn't know the difference between a neutrino passing through a Higgs boson field and a worm crawling through a black lagoon."

"Captured anything disturbing on your security monitors?" Isaiah asked mildly. "Like anyone being torn to pieces just for the hell of it?"

"*No*," Blanchard sneered. "And our central command sees every move inside this facility. So if there were an intruder, human or otherwise, he would be captured or dead." He straightened his collar. "I don't mind telling you that our guards are also bonded agents of the Swiss government and have the authority to use deadly force at their discretion. There is not a more secure facility in the world."

"But the collider hasn't been turned on again since what you refer to as 'the incident?'" asked Isaiah. "Right?"

"That is correct because we have spent the last few weeks strengthening the insulation," Blanchard remarked. "It's simply part of our normal maintenance procedures, something planned more than ten years ago and had nothing to do with the power surge that temporarily overloaded the ATLAS and the pipes."

"The pipes?" Amanda asked.

Blanchard gestured obscurely, "That's what we call the tunnel that accelerates the particles to ninety-nine percent of the speed of light so that the collisions will yield the results ATLAS is designed to measure."

"The pipes," Amanda muttered, pursing her lips. "That's a rather benign phrase for something so deviant. But I guess it should suffice for the witches and megalomaniacs who deserve the electric chair for the danger they've unleashed here."

"*Anything* is dangerous in the hands of a fool," Blanchard retorted. "You don't give a knife to a child. You don't give a pistol to a blind man. And you don't give control of the most powerful machine in the world to a bunch of superstitious old fools who don't understand they hold the past and the future in their hands."

Blanchard leaned forward. "We are not, Ms. Deker, a bunch of irresponsible cowboys. We are a group of highly disciplined scientists who adhere to a decades-old plan that has been examined by the keenest minds. Do you think this shutdown was a result of the accident?" He laughed. "This shutdown was planned fifty years ago! And so was the startup tomorrow morning! You see, we have timed our rotations, our startups, and our maintenance to a cosmological clock, Ms. Deker, so we know exactly what we're doing. A cosmological clock, by the way, that your sister sharpened. So the primary objective at this time is to repeat the results of the last collision. But if everyone of Jewish descent is also taken, as your sister was, then we have what scientists call confirmation. However, until we understand exactly why such things are occurring, we merely have an event and not a reason or cause. And facts can only be determined when we understand both cause and effect." He glanced at Isaiah. "And we may leave ignorant kindergarten stories of gods and devils where they belong. In a lockbox. In the attic. With the rest of the antiquated superstitions of the Old World that will soon be replaced by the New World."

Blanchard rose and strolled to the window behind the desk, hands clasped at his back. "Did you know, Ms. Deker, that Robert Oppenheimer and Edward Teller had no idea what would happen when they created the first atomic explosion in the Manhattan Project? Yes, it's true, all of them held genuine concern that an atomic explosion would create a chain reaction of nuclear explosions that would destroy the world."

He turned back. "You see? Those great, philanthropic leaders of the scientific world had no idea what would happen when they pulled the trigger, so to speak. But they did it, anyway, in the name of science. And, of course, winning the war. But, then again, Germany had already surrendered, so we had already won the war. The last holdout was Japan and whether it was necessary to nuke them into surrender or starve them into submission remains an unending debate. But let me be concise. The salient point is that we now have endless electricity." He raised an arm to the outside world. "Because of twin nuclear reactors an aircraft carrier can travel at full speed for twenty-three years before it needs refueling. The old things have passed away. This is the day of new things, of a new world, and all because some very educated men took a very calculated risk in the name of progress."

"So this weapons' program is for the good of all mankind?" asked Isaiah.

Blanchard laughed, "This is not a weapons program, you idiot! Everything we have done here has been in the cause of preserving life!"

"Of course it's a weapons' program," Isaiah laughed, equally amused. "The fools who came before you didn't conjure this ten-billion-dollar facility so they could discover the origins of the universe." He shook his head. "No, Blanchard, they built this machine so they could access a power that would allow them to control the universe. And that's the most dangerous weapons' program in the history of the world. More dangerous than any hydrogen bomb. More dangerous than any chimera. And more tragic than any graveyard of regrets. And now, in the name of progress, you've got seven dead physicists and seven dead support personnel. And let's not forget that you've got a creature running loose in your so-called secure facility that probably has the strength to kill everyone inside these halls."

"This imaginary creature that you continue to refer to is a figment of your ignorance," Blanchard frowned. "Just as your superstitions of gods and devils and demons running loose in this facility."

Blanchard sat and leaned back, idly running fingers across the glass desk. "In my detached opinion it will be morally justifiable if Director Francois chose to make both of you disappear because you have caused this facility such dangerous inconveniences. I shouldn't need to tell you that requesting the assistance of the Swiss Police to apprehend you was something we simply do not do." A pause. "We are expected to handle our own security matters and it is considered imposing, insulting, and even somewhat dangerous to ask for help. That is the unwritten contract we have with this government, and an agreement we have very thoroughly maintained."

Suddenly a light began blinking on Blanchard's desk and his face froze and whitened in the same moment. He had risen even before the door opened and Tony stepped in holding what Isaiah identified as a Heckler & Koch MR55.

"Where?" Blanchard whispered.

"Mile 13, Section B," Tony stated, succinct. "We lost three more maintenance guys. And they're … still there."

"Did you seal the section?"

"We shut the sub-doors leading upstairs, but we've got nothing on radar and there's nothing moving on the monitors or infrared." Tony glanced at Isaiah, shook his head. "As always, it doesn't register on anything electronic."

"Who found the maintenance workers?"

"An electrician."

After a pause Blanchard said with obvious disappointment, "Very well. Notify the Director-General. Put the electrician in isolation. Insure that he talks to no one by radio or phone. And clean up the scene immediately.

Report back to me as soon as it's done. Also, secure these two in the same room and post guards at the door. They are to have no human contact. Refer all inquiries to me."

All business, Tony shut the door and Blanchard's gaze fixed again on the light still silently blinking.

Amanda's voice held no sympathy. "So the little purple light means that you're up the creek without a paddle again?"

"It's magenta," said Isaiah blandly. "It's the same alarm system used on off-shore oil rigs. Different colored alarms mean different things. Red is for fire. Yellow means poisonous gas. But a magenta alarm means that Jesus has returned and it's every man for himself." He focused on Blanchard, who had not moved. "How biblical did this just get, Mr. Blanchard?"

With unconcealed—in fact, *unconcealable* hostility—Blanchard shifted his gaze as the door opened once more and three guards in black BDUs stepped inside. One guard spoke with formal courtesy, "Ms. Deker? Mr. Isaiah? Would you please allow us to escort you to your quarters?"

Isaiah stood. "Of course."

"I'll be glad to change company," Amanda rose, hoisting her purse. "Good luck hunting your make-believe demon, Mr. Blanchard. And my condolences to the very real families of the very real victims."

***

It wasn't quite six in the morning when Tanto led Janet and Susan into an underground tunnel leading into a World War II bomb shelter located less than two miles from the CERN compound.

They had traveled part of the way by river taxi, switched to a street taxi, entered six underground parking garages and left in six different vehicles, sometimes together, sometimes separate, and once in the trunk of a car, before finishing a two-hour ordeal that would have been a ten-minute trip as the crow flies.

Janet knew the answer, but didn't stop herself from asking, "So this is how you Delta guys sanitize yourself before you meet somebody? You drive all over creation, jump off a few trains, swim a river or two and then show up soaking wet with fish in your hair and bugs stuck to your teeth?"

"Yeah," Tanto muttered. "It's a pain in the ass. You gotta drive a hundred miles to go twenty. You gotta switch boats and cars a dozen times. You gotta go into restricted air space so they can't track you by chopper. You can only lose satellite surveillance in parking garages and you can only do that if you've already disabled the cameras. These goons have satellites, bank cameras, hotel cameras, ATM cameras, and traffic cameras under their control every minute of the day. They got eyeballs, man, I'm tellin' ya. They can find you in the outhouse of a whorehouse."

Moments later Janet was genuinely surprised when they entered what must have served as a well-fortified World War II bunker. The gigantic underground structure had withstood the test of time with impressive integrity although it was worth considering that it had never been used as a bomb shelter because no nation ever bombed Switzerland. Still, the Swiss had prepared for the worst.

Large lunchroom tables on the lowest level were all loaded with military gear and, although Janet was no expert, it seemed like enough weapons and gear to supply a battalion instead of four Delta commandos and two computer geeks.

"Wow," Susan said to Tanto. "Do you guys always prepare like this?"

"Always," Tanto said very seriously. "We are *never* outgunned. Come on. Let's eat. The food here ain't bad. I'd try one of them ham and cheese bagels. They're pretty good. Ol' Jackman ate about six of 'em this morning, the greedy bastard. I didn't think I was gonna get one for *myself*."

General Jackman walked forward decked out in black-and-white BDUs and as heavily armed as any grunt Janet had ever seen. Whatever else the general might be, he was no coward. Clearly, he was going to lead his men to victory or the grave. And, either way, he would lead from the front.

"Morning, ladies," Jackman smiled. "Want something to warm you up? These Swiss boys know how to make good coffee; I'll give 'em that. It's over here."

Munching on a bagel, Roy smiled as Janet approached. He saluted her with a large cup of coffee.

"Yeah, good morning to you, too." Janet smiled. "So what's all this? We don't even show up for our jobs for another two hours and the compound is probably only ten minutes from here."

"Well," Roy shrugged, "I'm not sending you in there defenseless so we need to go over a few things."

"Roy, I've told you; there's no way to get a weapon through security. There are two metal detectors and then they X-ray you before they let you enter the elevator that goes down to the collider. Then you have to go through the same process again to get into the Observation Room. I couldn't get searched better if I got butt naked which, by the way, I would be glad to do to avoid all that crap."

Roy shook his head as he resumed eating. "I'm not stupid enough to send you in there with a gun, honey. But we've got stuff we can load you up with that will give you and Susan a good chance to make tracks if we can't reach you. But, hell, eat up first. Have some coffee. Damn, this is good stuff. Wish we had coffee like this at Bragg. The coffee we get at Bragg can stand up without a cup."

Susan took a seat at the wooden lunch table and didn't hesitate at the food or anything else as Janet took a place beside Roy. After glancing around the warehouse-sized bunker, she asked, "So what's with all the weapons? Are we not going with our plan? You seemed pretty sure about it last night. Or this morning. I forget. All this James Bond stuff is making me lose time."

"Don't worry," mumbled Roy. "We're still going with the original plan. But, to be honest, I'm not a big fan of plans because my best-laid plans all turned into my greatest regrets. Beginning with my one and only marriage." He paused. "I guess you could say I'm more of an improvise and overcome kind of guy. I like to prepare for anything and everything, which is why I got you girls up early. I'm not gonna send you in there without a couple of cards up your sleeve in case you have to play them. But they're simple tricks, and we got time." He motioned. "Go ahead. Eat up. You're gonna need your strength. Believe me."

***

Amanda awoke in their "cell" and felt she'd slept for at least three hours. She vaguely wondered if they had slipped something into her last meal the previous evening but dismissed it as irrelevant. After all, they were going to die, anyway.

Thankfully, they'd secured Isaiah and her in something like an underground hotel room with two beds, a kitchen, sink, and bathroom so they'd passed yesterday and last night in relative comfort and, the best part, they hadn't seen Blanchard again.

She turned as the door opened and a man entered.

He was aristocratic and aquiline and Amanda effortlessly identified him as French. There was simply something about the high forehead and his jet-black hair that refused to admit his age, as well as the patrician cut of his suit. He was a bit taller than Isaiah, but less muscular, and spoke with an undisguised accent.

"Ms. Deker," he smiled. He stretched out a hand to Isaiah, "And I've been told that Isaiah is your only name, but that's fine with me. I like a man who likes to keep a secret. Would you mind if we shared a few words?"

"Not at all," said Isaiah without obvious hostility.

Amanda glanced down the corridor where guards were bearing three stretchers like those used on a battlefield. They were canvas, flat, and hand carried. She was vaguely surprised they weren't green like those she'd seen in war photographs.

A bloody arm suddenly fell from one of the stretchers.

And when it fell, it's not like it dangled from the stretcher. Rather, it *fell* completely unattached to the floor and, in the long-lasting moment, Amanda got a wide-eyed look at the dismembered, bloody corpse that lay beneath a cheap blue tarp like her daddy had used to cover the lawnmower. She saw a bloody head beside a shoulder and an unattached arm laid across its chest. She glimpsed, barely, that the left leg had been stripped of flesh to the surprisingly white bone.

"Hold up!" the rear guard called and the other turned.

"Damn!" the second guard exclaimed. "Cover him up, man! If anybody sees this, we'll be chasing down nervous breakdowns all day!"

The tall man standing in the opening of the room calmly closed the door, shutting away the scene, as well. "I am sorry," he stated benignly. "Tragic accidents do sometimes occur at facilities that use vast amounts of electrical energy. Even the smallest mistake can cost a human life."

"And you would be Monsieur Francois?" asked Isaiah.

Francois beamed. "At your service."

"I heard you lost three more people," Isaiah continued. "That would make seventeen in total, wouldn't it? *Ad astra per aspera*?"

"Yes," Director Francois agreed. "A rough road leads to the stars."

"Indeed. It appears you're racking up quite a body count in your quest."

Director Francois seemed to sigh yet his wide chest barely lifted. Then he said, "It's true that we've recently had a rash of very unusual accidents. Today we lost three good men. Yesterday we lost a track worker who wandered off his detail. But we are presently reviewing safety procedures and we're quite confident that any imperfect measures will be addressed. But, as with any cutting-edge scientific endeavor, the sword devours one side as well as the other. And, as you know, there is no science without experimentation and experimentation always involves a level of risk, so accidents sometimes happen."

"When you intentionally allow a demonic entity to run loose, it's not an accidental death," said Isaiah. "It's conspiracy to commit murder." He stared. "You opened a portal to another dimension, but it left one of its own to open the portal from this side if its demonic brethren can't open it from their side. So this creature has been here with you since you lost your physicists. And you've known that it was here, and that makes you guilty of conspiracy because it has to eat, and that's why you've been losing people to it. In fact, that's why you've been sacrificing people to it." He paused. "I expect that it's developed quite a taste for human flesh by now."

Francois acted as if Isaiah had said nothing as he continued, "Ms. Deker, I have been notified that Interpol is very much aware of your presence here. But I must advise you before you decide to speak with them. It might be extremely inconvenient for all of us if the agents were made aware of your recent hostilities toward our personnel, including gravely wounding one of them in the leg. In fact, crippling him and ruining his chance for a pension, which opens you to what is guaranteed to be a very substantial civil settlement that I do not believe you are capable of paying."

"And how is my dear Fred doing since I shot him in the leg?" asked Amanda.

"He's in the infirmary in stable condition, thank you for asking."

"Believe me, it was nothing."

Francois strolled forward and stopped as if there were an invisible wall separating himself from anything less than himself, which was everything. "I only mention the incident because the rather private fellowship that manages this facility wishes to avoid any third-party intrusions upon our restricted activities. But if we are forced to report your use of a firearm to maim one of our security personnel then we will have no choice but to enjoin full criminal and civil actions against you. And that is something we very much wish to avoid. So I ask you plainly. What do you want to do about the situation?"

"It was his gun and he threatened my life," stated Amanda. "I'm sure Interpol would be glad to hear your side of the story as well as ours."

"We trust you'll handle the situation most tastefully," Isaiah said forcefully to Francois. "We'll just take the money and run."

"That would be wise," Francois murmured as he walked away a single step before stopping in place to turn. "And so you two would be content to return home despite misgivings about your sister's tragic death?"

"I need a better explanation than what you've provided," said Amanda.

Isaiah said emphatically, "*No*. We don't need any more explanations."

"I want to see her body."

"I'm afraid your sister's body was tragically destroyed in the accident, so there is no body to examine," Francois answered coolly. "I understand both your grief and frustration, Ms. Deker, and although I am accustomed to bearing tragic news to inconsolable loved ones of those lost in both the construction and the maintenance of this facility, I have concluded that there is simply no painless way to convey these events. Nor is there anything I can say to ease your suffering, so I will not attempt what is not possible."

Francois watched them before he asked, "Would you like to see your sister's workstation? Then I can more completely explain to you what happened. I assure you that there was nothing nefarious afoot. We are hiding nothing, nor are we betraying anything by revealing certain aspects of this facility that we would prefer to remain private. Your loss certainly privileges you to such knowledge. And I do not wish to indulge your good friend's imaginative thoughts of demons and creatures from alternate dimensions running amok and killing us at their leisure, so he is also welcome to come."

He waited while Amanda held his gaze. Then he added, "I'm sure that when you see the dangers that your sister obliged to undertake in her very important job you will view her tragic death in another light. You will see her as the hero of science that she really was, and not the meaningless victim of an arrogant and heartless bureaucratic machine. I will not say that I am offended by Mr. Isaiah's imputations, but I will defend myself by opening the doors of this institution so you may judge freely, for yourself, whether your sister's sacrifice was in vain or whether it assisted science in reaching a bold new frontier."

"We'll just take the money and go home," said Isaiah.

"I believe you owe your sister this much respect," said Francois as if Isaiah hadn't spoken. "And … and I never wish to make these matters more painful than necessary, but I personally knew your sister, Ms. Decker."

Amanda's eyes narrowed. "You knew Cynthia?"

Francois grimaced as he continued, "Yes, I knew her. I also knew she required special assistance and I was diligent to make certain arrangements to accommodate her. And, tragically, I was not unaware of the many rumors, innuendos, conspiracy theories, accusations, and outright lies that have sullied your sister's great contribution to this institution's priorities, which have *nothing* to do with the occult or other such drivel. Those are all meaningless lies parlayed by a myopic academia that will never understand scientific progress until they need it to save their meaningless lives. Indeed, your sister was a scientist, Ms. Decker, and a proud scientist. She was even a great scientist despite her handicap, which I, personally, never considered a handicap at all, but, rather, a gift from God. And her work was not in vain. So, please, allow me to show you what your sister achieved before you drag both Cynthia's name and her contribution through the mire of an investigation that will do neither Cynthia nor this facility any justice."

"That's good enough for us," said Isaiah, nodding at Amanda.

Amanda's brow hardened as she glanced at Isaiah.

He minutely shook his head.

"Or," Francois added placidly as he lifted a phone, "I will call Interpol's Geneva station and their agents could be here within the hour." He paused. "Yes. I can do that. Or you can simply take one hour to see what your sister achieved. And, after that, if you wish to further pursue this avenue, I will not impede you. Even now, you are free to leave or stay. The choice is yours."

"If we're free to go, then why did Blanchard imprison us in this room all day yesterday and last night?" asked Amanda bitterly.

"Mr. Blanchard's limited authority, and his use of it, are one example of why he does not possess additional authority," said Francois apologetically. "The fact is that Mr. Blanchard is in charge of the day-to-day management of the compound, but he has no authority in matters of experimentation or scheduling or security or anything else that might be critical to operations of this facility. And, in moments of crisis, he sometimes makes decisions that he is unqualified, and unauthorized, to make." He bowed minutely. "That is why I was informed of this situation and why I have intervened. First, I did not want you to be accidentally injured in Mr. Blanchard's zeal. Secondly, well, we have nothing to hide, Ms. Decker. And if you will allow me to show you, I believe you will agree. And then you will understand that your sister's death was only an unfortunate accident and I will personally insure your safe passage to the airport."

"This is *nothing* like Blanchard told us when we talked to him earlier," Amanda shook her head. "And something tells me he was *not* lying." She cast Isaiah a glance; he held her stare and silently mouthed, "*Take … the … deal.*"

"I think," said Amanda at last, "that we'll take our chances with Interpol, Mr. Francois." She nodded at the phone. "Make the call."

Isaiah bowed his head.

"What?" Amanda exclaimed. "Isaiah! What is it?"

Francois stared down with the most angrily cloaked aura of disappointment Amanda had ever sensed. "A pity," he smiled tightly. Then he picked up the phone and, after a moment, said, "Would you please escort Ms. Decker and her bodyguard to the collider corridor? Yes, in full restraints. Thank you."

With that, Francois walked past them and out the door, closing it quietly.

Isaiah's voice was dismal. "I hate to be the kind of guy to say I told you so …"

"*I heard you!*" Amanda gritted. "Hey! I told him to call Interpol, didn't I? What else did you expect me to do? Call 'em *myself*? We're prisoners! And that phone didn't even work when we got here! I know! I checked! Why did he even go through that masquerade in the first place? Why didn't they just throw us under the train to begin with? Like *Anna Karenina*! I'm gonna read that book! Why waste time like this?"

Isaiah blinked slowly and answered even more slowly, "He was trying to get this institution out of a very uncomfortable situation without killing us because that will certainly bring about an investigation by both Interpol and the FBI. So he would have gladly given you five million bucks. He would have gladly flown us home first class. He would have happily provided Cynthia, body or not, with any old-world mausoleum near your home so you could visit her. There is nothing he wouldn't have done to make you happy so you'd forget this whole thing."

"So what was all that crap about calling Interpol?"

"You don't understand," answered Isaiah. "He was willing to do anything *but* call Interpol. That's why he was hoping you would go with him to the Observation Room. Then they would run some kind of harmless experiment past you and you'd see that there's nothing more dangerous about this place than any nuclear facility. After that, they'd give us a car and let us go—unharmed, mind you—down the road with our unprovable accusations. It would be nothing Interpol hasn't heard a thousand times and Interpol would do nothing because we would be alive and you would be rich. And this place could continue like they've continued for the last one hundred years."

"And now?" Amanda asked, wide-eyed. "Now they're gonna kill us?"

Isaiah nodded.

"*Jesus, Isaiah!*" Amanda stomped a foot and lifted her hands. "How did you get us into this mess? I thought you were good at this stuff! This isn't what Deborah told me about you! I'll tell ya that!"

Isaiah rolled his gaze across the ceiling.

"Why didn't you just *tell* me to take the deal or they were going to kill us?" Amanda continued. "You could have told me plainly, ya know? Everything doesn't have to be cryptic! But all you said was, we'll take the deal! Hell! I'm not going to just take the deal! Not when I think that this place killed my sister! Christ! Talk about phone tag from Hell!"

Isaiah spoke calmly, "If I had told you that they were going to kill us if you didn't take the deal, then Francois would have known we were onto his game and playing him, instead. But you insisted on bringing Interpol into this, which is something they do indeed dread. And now, if Interpol is going to get drawn to this regardless whether we're dead or alive, they would certainly prefer it if we're dead. Now, there's no reason for them not to see if the gateway takes you like it took Cynthia. Then they'll just kill me, too. Interpol will poke around, find nothing, and this place will continue with business as usual."

"Well I didn't figure all that out!" Amanda protested. "Couldn't you have signaled me or something?"

"Forget it." Isaiah twisted as if to adjust his webbed belt. "Give me a minute and I might get us out of this. Just do me a favor."

"What?"

"Shut up."

"Ha. You're hilarious."

The door opened and armed guards entered with heaps of chains and cloth restrains. It took them five minutes and when they were finally done Amanda felt like a death row prisoner. She had cuffs on both wrists, a chain around her waist, and a chain leading from her waist to her ankles, which were also cuffed. And, last, they placed a bag over her head after gagging her so that she couldn't make a sound.

She could only assume Isaiah got the same treatment.

"Let's go," said a guard, grasping her elbow.

Amanda shuffled down the deathly quiet corridor.

***

"Okay," said Janet, removing the hairpin from her ponytail. "Let's go through this again because I don't want to kill myself."

Roy nodded, "Go ahead."

Janet held the long hairpin to a light bulb. "This thing is all-the-way solid, right? Like any other hairpin?"

"Yep," Roy nodded.

"So it doesn't hold any kind of liquid?

"Nope."

"But one touch of the tapered end of this thing will instantly disable anybody who gets in my way no matter how big he is?"

"Right."

"Instantly?"

"Instantly."

"Well," Janet paused, "what if I accidentally stick *myself*?"

"In its very diluted form, which this *isn't*, propofol induces unconsciousness and stops you from breathing. It's the same thing a surgeon gives you when he tells you to count backward from a hundred and you only make it to ninety-nine. Just remember: If you touch someone with the sharp end of that thing, it will put them down. But if you *stick* someone, you'll kill them." He stared. "Permanently."

Janet grunted, "Well, I've never heard of someone *im*permanently killed."

"My point is: Don't stick yourself."

"Good safety tip."

"So? You ready?"

"You guys are ridiculously dangerous, you know that?" asked Janet. "Anything else I should know?"

"That's it. Just don't stick yourself." Roy sniffed, gazed around the inside of the disguised utility van that had transported them from the warehouse to the CERN facility. "Okay," he added. "We're almost there. Once we drop you off at the gate, make your way to your station and we'll make our way to one of the 'D' escape tunnels that lead from the collider. We'll silently take out the guards and wait for you to scramble the alarm system. After that, you and Susan just stick to the plan. Roger that?"

"Roger that," Janet nodded.

"Check your watch again."

Janet turned her wrist. "I've got exactly eight o'clock. *Now.*"

"Perfect." Roy clicked his watch. "And what time do you make your move?"

"At nine. Straight up."

"And then?"

"Stick to the plan."

"That's right," said Roy sternly. "*Stick to the plan.*"

Janet nodded slowly, "So I just stay in my seat and keep the computer offline until the final ten minutes. But, before that, Susan makes a run for it." She pointed to a large crate in the sharply swaying van. "May I ask what that is?"

Roy said, "That, Ms. Computer Genius, is an experimental one-hundred-megaton, triple-stage hydrogen fission weapon that we're going to send through the portal if we can't blow the helium and nitrogen tanks and destroy the collider." He shrugged, "I doubt that it's enough to vaporize whatever dimension is on the other side but it might kill a handful and make them think twice about coming through again."

"Did you say one hundred megatons?" asked Janet.

"Yeah."

"That's several hundred thousand times Hiroshima."

"Approximately, yeah."

Janet scowled, "That doesn't track. A one-hundred-megaton, triple-stage fission weapon would weigh at least ten tons. I don't see how a van could carry it."

"Not this one," Roy shook his head. "This one is loaded with some kind of new nuclear fuel they've never used." He stared at the bomb. "I hear the formula's been on the books for fifty years but they were too scared to make it. 'Bout like they were scared to develop the first atomic bomb. But when they perfected a process, they did it."

"Is it radioactive?"

"Not inside the case."

"What kind of nuclear fuel we talking?"

Roy shrugged, "I got briefed on what little I'm cleared to know, but I hardly understood a word. All I got is that it's a very highly irradiated mix of plutonium and uranium and a new, very volatile compound that's only been a theory until now. They practically created a new element for it."

Tanto chimed in, "And it ain't light, neither. The son of a bitch weighs five hundred pounds."

"But you're not going to use it unless you have to?"

"Right."

"Well," Janet hesitated, "why would you have to?"

"Because we don't know what kind of new maintenance they've done to this collider," stated Roy. "If the satchels aren't enough to blow the helium and nitrogen tanks and bury this thing, then we use the bomb."

"And destroy a very large portion of this dimension and that dimension at the same time, right?" Janet stared. "And we all die?"

"Consider it a last resort."

Janet leaned forward. "Let's make sure it doesn't come to that."

"You just cut the alarms to that escape hatch and I promise that I'll get you and Susan out of there before anything happens." Roy glanced to Tanto. "We hot?"

Tanto nodded, "We're hot."

"But if you don't use the bomb, what do we do with it if we succeed?" asked Janet. "I mean, this is seriously classified technology. We can't leave it behind. And we're not going to take it with us, are we? We'll be running for our lives. And we can't run real fast hauling a five-hundred-pound bomb."

Roy stated clinically. "If I don't type in the code, it won't go nuclear. But after we blow the gateway, I'll set the bomb on self-destruct and we'll have plenty of time to get clear of the blast."

"What about radiation?"

"The self-destruct mechanism is just a charge of C-4 and the corridor will contain the detonation and radiation so that we don't kill every heathen in Switzerland. But the first thing I'm gonna do is get you out of that Observation Room. Understand?"

She smiled faintly. "Don't be late."

Roy frowned.

"Not on your life."

***

The agonizingly long walk "down the plank," as Amanda regarded it, seemed awfully cold and strangely quiet and it occurred to her how much slower everything seemed to happen when you didn't actually like what was indeed happening.

The thought irritated Amanda because she sensed she should be making peace with God or thinking of something far more profound. But here she was, in her final minutes, thinking of how she should have had more fun.

Finally a door clanged shut behind them and the bag was ripped off Amanda's head. Then the gag was removed and she gasped for a moment before watching them remove the bag and gag from Isaiah.

Director-General Francois stood watching impassively. "I see no reason to keep you blind and mute," he smiled. "But, unfortunately, I cannot remove your restraints. The ATLAS is a finely calibrated machine and we cannot allow tampering."

Amanda tried her cuffs. She wasn't going anywhere. "Is this what you did to my sister?" she grated.

"No," Francois said plainly. "Your sister was securely housed in the Observation Room like the others when the incident occurred. You alone will have the experience of witnessing this phenomenon face to face. I almost envy you."

"You're welcome to take my place," Amanda muttered with unconcealed spite. "I'd love to see you meet your god."

With a humorless laugh Francois motioned to the guards, who retreated to either side of the door. "Feel free to express yourself if you must, Ms. Deker," He glanced at the Observation Room's window so far above their heads.

"In here," he added, "no one can hear you scream."

With that, Francois turned and walked out the door.

The guards followed.

As the panel was locked, Amanda yelled, "Isaiah! I'm sorry I got you into this! This is all my fault! I'm sorry I yelled at you! I'm sorry for everything! I'm sorry!"

Wordless, Isaiah was twisting ferociously against the handcuffs, contorting his body with quick, violent movements. His teeth were clenched. His eyes were shut tight.

"Isaiah!" Amanda pleaded. "Just accept it! We should die with dignity if this is how we're gonna die! Stop struggling! Look! Isaiah! If this is it, I just want to tell you that I know I was falling in love with—"

"*Got it*!" Isaiah shouted as he ripped one hand free of a cuff; he merely seemed to touch the other cuff and both hands were clear. He undid the chain at his waist and the cuffs around his ankles and walked to Amanda, sweating profusely.

"What the hell!" Amanda gaped. "You let me say all that and you could have got us free any time you wanted?" She started angrily squirming and twisting against the cuffs as Isaiah freed her. "You're a bastard! You know that? I can't believe I was about to tell you that I was—"

Isaiah hurled her chains aside.

"How did you do that!" Amanda managed.

"I keep handcuff keys hidden in my sleeve. Come on!"

Amanda was hauled from her feet, fairly flying, and then they were at the steel door. Isaiah violently twisted the circular handle but it didn't budge. Then he twisted, if it were possible, with even more force but it was obviously locked. For a moment Isaiah spun his head gazing up and down the collider. It was an awesomely gray, silent space humming with a force that made Amanda's hair stand up.

"Now what?" she whispered.

Isaiah frowned, "I don't know. If we can't get out of here, we're gonna have to stop this machine."

"How are we gonna do that?"

Isaiah grimaced as he fiercely searched the scope of the ATLAS. It was at least four stories high with cement and lead and steel combinations of construction protecting it from within and without. Whatever held it together was as carefully sealed as any secret ever buried by science or sorcery. Indeed, it seemed like a living, enormous thing, this steel, scaled serpent that vanished in both directions.

"What are you staring at?" Amanda whispered although she couldn't understand why and didn't try. "Do you see something?"

Isaiah pointed angrily at a gigantic white tubular connector that could encapsulate a freight train. "The ATLAS," he said breathlessly. "That's where the particles collide. That's what we've got to disable."

"But how!" Amanda spun in the same manner. "We don't know how this thing works! Even *they* don't know how it works!"

Isaiah said in a quiet, deadly voice, "It works the same way anything else works. Like dominoes. One domino at a time. All you have to do is take out a few and you'll crash the whole system."

He quickly climbed the steps leading to a small platform located beneath the ATLAS. He rushed to the white cylinder and began pushing and pulling on every handle within view, but nothing happened. No doors opened. No circuitry was exposed. The machine was locked as tightly as a vault.

Suddenly the entire collider roared to life and the cement beneath Amanda's feet began trembling. It was like the foreboding of an earthquake. Timidly, Amanda placed a hand against the wall to feel it trembling, as well, and heard someone say fearfully, "Isaiah? We need to get out of here …"

Frantically twisting a handle, Isaiah didn't answer.

Slowly Amanda turned her head to see lights in the far distance of the pipeline as they abruptly begin blinking with the strange, alarming magenta coloring. Then a siren erupted as an inhuman roar thundered in the tunnel.

Amanda whispered …

"Oh, God, no …"

***

So far, their entry into the main corridor had been routine.

Janet and Susan had been exposed to three rather invasive searches, X-ray machines, metal detectors, and an array of cameras that registered every physical tic, including sweating, before being led, as before, to the Observation Room.

Janet glanced up from her computer terminal to see the rotating lights meant to warn maintenance personnel of the impending test scheduled for this morning and, according to new protocols, she was not authorized to leave her station unless granted permission by the supervisor. And today the supervisor was Director-General Francois himself and he was not moving although the Assistant Director William Blanchard, was shifting nervously as he stared at the ATLAS.

"Steady, people," Francois said with pacific calm. "This is what we've trained you to do." He glanced to the side. "What is the power level?"

Janet had already been introduced to Margaret.

"It's at sixty percent," answered Margaret, fingers cautiously poised over the keyboard. "And climbing."

"Very well," Francois nodded. "Do not be anxious, my friends. Remember your new protocols. We use the alarms to warn maintenance personnel to get clear of the corridor, so just man your stations. We are all professionals here."

Susan was at her terminal, face down, fingers flying.

Janet knew that her colleague was working feverishly to finish stringing together a pattern of foreign and domestic satellites, each with encrypted passwords, which she had been secretly collecting for the past two days. When Susan's string was complete, she would forward the connection to Janet and Janet would put the internal security system off-line. At that moment Susan would have exactly twenty minutes to escape, but Janet knew, despite her promise to Roy, that she wouldn't be able to leave her terminal at all without some kind of violence. She would have to stay at her station and continue putting the computer offline or the guards would locate the Delta commandos.

She had already told Susan what was going to happen and, after the anticipated argument, Susan finally agreed to simply rise and walk out of the room for any reason that required a bathroom, something that even the supervisor could not prevent. Then Janet's terminal began blinking and she opened a new window. Janet read the satellite connection, locked it down, and began calling up relays.

A hideous scream echoed in the tunnel outside the door even as Susan rose from her seat and stopped in place.

Guards posted near the door rushed to the entrance, glaring in the direction of the cries. They bent as if peering into a pipeline then straightened with violent shouts and raised rifles, firing simultaneously.

At the burst of gunfire, Francois whirled.

"What are you doing!" he demanded as he launched himself to the door. He passed Susan without heed and she looked at Janet as if asking for direction; the entire plan had gone to hell. That fast.

On Janet's screen the security code began blinking.

Inviting.

Daring ...

More screams in the corridor.

"*If I die,*" Janet whispered, "*you die.*"

She shut it down.

***

"It's down," whispered Tanto.

Tanto was first to the door of the escape tunnel and placed a charge against the outside lock; the explosion was loud enough to carry for miles in these alpine hills, but it would also be hard to locate because sound carries further in the cold and no one would be able to determine how many miles away it originated.

He and Roy were in the tunnel together and running forward as the air around them thickened with the sound of an enormous, unearthly roar followed by a series of clearly human howls of horror and agony. But they didn't—*couldn't* hesitate now that they had begun and reached the collider inside two minutes as Jake, Picket, and General Jackman came up hauling the weapon.

Although Jake and Picket were naturally quiet and stoic, they were without question the physically strongest members of any Delta squad. Each man was built thick and low, like a bison, with over-muscular chests and arms and stout legs like professional weightlifters. In truth, they were almost as herculean as the general, which was impressive in itself. Together they had little trouble, with Jackman's seemingly ageless might, hauling the weapon through the tunnel almost as quickly as Roy negotiated it without any burden at all.

Tanto spun to Roy. "Go get the girls, major. I got this."

He hurled a duffel bag to Roy, who caught it and threw it to General Jackman. "Change of plans, general. The charges are set for forty-five minutes. Let's do it."

Jackman caught the duffel full of charges and, to Jackman's credit, he didn't react with any emotion whatsoever. Unlike movies, elite commandos do not raise their voice in the heat of combat. If they cannot talk to a fellow soldier in a normal voice, they use hand signals. Shouting in combat was considered bad form and earned serious disrespect. All screaming did was heighten fear and confusion and there was always too much of both.

Jackman said in a normal tone, "What happened to thirty minutes?"

"It's a change of plans to protect the girls, general," said Tanto. "Let's get her done, sir. I think we best move smooth."

"Smooth is fast," muttered Jackman.

He loped to one of the ubiquitous all-terrain vehicles, leaped into the seat with the duffel, and raced past Roy as the Delta commando crouched beside a steel door.

Somewhere there was the sound of an enormous fight involving gunfire and the enraged roar of some great beast as Roy twisted away and to the side, flattening himself against the wall. One second later an explosion disintegrated the door and Roy's rage smashed the remnant out of his way.

He was inside.

* * *

Francois had frozen in the door obviously shocked and staring in the same direction as the guards as they continued firing and the howl of some enormous beast continued to advance on the Observation Room. Then Janet heard the Director-General vehemently shout, "*Damn it*! *Not now*!"

Spinning, Francois was back and bearing down over Margaret. "How much longer before we hit one hundred percent?"

Margaret snapped, "Two minutes!"

"*Two minutes*!" Francois whirled, alternately glaring between the door and the window. Then, with a violent effort, managed to calm his voice as he stated, "Get ready to engage FS-One. Are you ready?"

"Yes."

"Engage."

"Engaged."

"FS-Two."

Margaret glanced in the direction of the hideous screams. "Engaged!"

"FS-Three!"

"Engaged!" Margaret shouted. "Detectors at maximum!"

Blanchard—Janet noticed—had moved deeper into the Observation Room, separating himself from the entrance. He glanced nervously to either side as if searching for an exit, but there was no exit. There was one way in, one way out. And the only way out was filled with two guards firing fully automatic weapons. Then Janet saw that Susan had quietly retaken her seat and was merely watching the frenzied activity, head low.

There was no escape, and she knew it.

Janet was prepared to die. But she knew Susan wasn't.

Janet's computer terminal blinked; they had almost traced the interruption back to her terminal. She shut it down again and stood, walking toward Susan. When she reached her, she grabbed Susan's hand and moved toward the door.

"Where are you going?" shouted Blanchard, causing Francois to turn.

"*Stop her*!" commanded Francois.

One of the guards at the door turned and stepped forward as Janet ripped out the hairpin. It was only a slice of a movement, but she touched his face and was amazed that he went down before she'd even drawn back her hand.

He hit the floor with a muffled thud. Only his rifle made a clattering that sounded benign compared to the explosive atmosphere now thick with sulfur and smoke. But even before he fully settled, Janet stepped into the door and instinctively turned to stare in the direction of the remaining guard's gunfire.

Her breath caught.

A gigantic, black, manlike shape was grappling with a dozen armed guards in the far distance of the tunnel and it was clear, even at this range, that the guards were quickly losing the battle and that the beast had intentions of approaching the Observation Room with a rage unlike anything Janet had ever witnessed.

It was an animal but it was an animal battling with the intelligence and intent of a human being. And, clearly, it would win, in the end.

"What the hell is that!" Janet involuntarily shouted; she was shocked beyond any attempt at control.

"Get out of here!" yelled the guard. "Get to the elevator!"

"No!" bellowed Francois. "We must finish this!"

"To hell with this!" one physicist shouted as he leaped up and ran for the door. And that was all it took for the entire room to erupt to their feet and suddenly everyone was flying toward the guard, who stepped forward, giving them room.

"Hold the elevator for me!" shouted the guard as he quick-changed clips in his rifle. "Don't leave without me!"

Janet, still frozen, suddenly broke from her trance and was running toward the elevator with Susan in tow. Whatever the Delta team planned to do they better do it quick because whatever was coming up this hall was not going to stop with the Observation Room. It was going to open the ATLAS permanently to let that thing's entire dimension enter this world and then it was going to kill everyone in this facility.

Before it began with the universe ...

***

Amanda found herself staring at the gray granite walls, now visibly shaking.

She had been listening to the sound of battle for minutes and still couldn't decide who or what was fighting who or what.

One part of the battle was obviously some kind of animal. That much was clear. The other part was human with the expected sounds of explosions and machinegun fire. But there was yet another sound that was growing beneath Amanda's feet—a sound almost like the thunderous entrance of some otherworldly force—and she mutely turned in place as Isaiah raced up, breathing hard.

"I can't get the door open to disable the ATLAS!" he gasped and suddenly raised his face, staring into the tunnel. His eyes narrowed, curious and angry, and Amanda followed the direction of his gaze.

In the distance a gigantic black silhouette of a manlike beast was loping toward them on tree-trunk legs, appearing beneath a magenta alarm and then disappearing into a space of darkness before appearing again beneath another magenta alarm and—as it closed in—so did Amanda's horror.

She clutched Isaiah's hand but couldn't speak. Her mouth moved to form words but no words emerged.

Then she screamed.

***

"Hold the door!" Janet shouted.

She was the last in the elevator and slammed her hand against the panel that was already closing. "The guard told us to wait!"

"To hell with him!" someone shouted.

"No!" screamed Janet. "We wait!"

A black shape violently appeared in the elevator door and Janet yelled as she leaped backward into Susan.

"*Roy!*" Janet cried and violently pushed the others aside to leap out of the elevator, pointing down the corridor. "It's coming! I don't know what it is!"

"It's what you said it'd be!" said Roy, holding the door. He hit the red button to stop the elevator, then glared at the terrified inhabitants. "If any of you touch that button, I swear to god I'll kill you like a dog."

He kissed Janet quickly and turned toward the hallway. He pulled open a thick tubular chute slung on the lower half of his rifle and inserted what Janet knew from movies was a hand grenade. Then he slammed it shut and began walking forward before he stopped, staring at the ceiling.

"Janet?" he said.

"Yes?"

Roy pointed to the far side of the elevator.

"Is that one of the vaults?"

"*Yeah! They're some kind of titanium!*"

"No need to yell, honey. Calm down. Can you close them?"

With effort, Janet swallowed, trying to calm down. Then she said, "I would have to close all of them at the same time, Roy. They're built into the facility and they're all on the same trigger. It's everything or nothing."

"How do you close them?"

"I can do it from my terminal in the Observation Room."

"Let's go."

Janet didn't question him; she never had and never would—she knew that in an instant. And then she was running beside him as they rapidly approached the guard at the Observation Room door. Just as they reached him, he threw down his smoking rifle and turned into them as if to retreat.

"What the—" he began.

"Get out of the way," Roy muttered and didn't wait for the guard to obey; Roy threw him against the wall as Janet raced to her terminal and began typing as fast as her hands could move. She slammed every command to initiate a total lockdown and raised her face as a smothered roar emanated from the ceiling and floors and one clang after another echoed in the corridor.

Margaret's abandoned computer sounded off, "*Power level is at one hundred percent … Velocity is at one hundred percent … Power level is at one hundred percent … Velocity is at one hundred percent …*"

Janet screamed, "Shut up!"

She didn't even try to stop herself from rushing forward to bend over Margaret's desk where she instantly began shutting down power that was feeding the ATLAS chamber and pipeline. "It's over!" Janet snarled, jaws tightening. "No one's coming through! No one's going home!"

She pushed the last button and turned to the power grid and began slamming off every breaker and everything switch marked with a red "Do Not Touch" label or button. It only took her seconds to completely cut power to the collider and then the vibration within the ceiling and floor stopped at once.

Janet lifted a gaze to the door.

Roy was gone.

***

"Run!" shouted Isaiah.

Amanda was already running along the concrete floor of the collision corridor as the shout reverberated across the shell surrounding them. She didn't look back because she knew that thing was still coming and she didn't know where she was going but it didn't matter as long as it wasn't here.

Maybe it was the adrenaline or maybe Amanda was just in better shape than she had thought before all this began because they ran full-out for at least five minutes before Isaiah, who was in great shape, pulled up breathless.

"There!" he gasped.

A single door stood open, framed in magenta and black; the horribly mangled corpse of a worker laid across the threshold. Obviously, the thing chasing them had already passed this way and not everyone had reached containment quickly enough.

Isaiah shoved Amanda through the door before dragging the body into the chamber and then he was inside, as well, cursing with the strain it took to pull the huge door shut behind them. He spun the circular handle, a handle not unlike those used on submarines, until it stopped. Then Isaiah turned in every direction before he leaped to a wall.

He shouted, "Get back!"

Amanda had already moved as Isaiah kicked a glass enclosure on the wall. He smashed the broken fragments aside with his bare hand and reached into it to haul out a long iron rod and a steel fire ax. In the same split-second he slid the crowbar and steel ax into the door handle and jammed them both against the door jam, sealing it. Even with a quick glance Amanda knew it would take a bulldozer to turn that handle.

The door was struck.

An angry bellow thundered through the steel.

The impression of a human fist violently dented the heavy slab and Isaiah and Amanda stepped back together, watching. Then there was another impact and another image of a fist was smashed into the door, and another, and another, and another until … silence.

An angry roar erupted in the corridor.

Green blood seeped from a small fissure in the door.

Amanda pointed and whispered, "Look!"

Silently stepping forward, Isaiah raised a hand and gently pressed it against one of the impressions smashed into the thick, steel, submarine door. Then he said, "So you *do* have limits." Isaiah leaned against the panel, head bent as if to catch his breath, as he gasped, "You can't do anything you want, can you, sport?"

Amanda didn't know if she took a moment because she needed to pull herself together, or because she was giving Isaiah time to do the same. It didn't really matter. The only thing that mattered was that they were safe—at least temporarily.

"We gotta keep moving," Isaiah said quietly as he turned into her and drew her close in his arms. Then he gazed down into her eyes and kissed her. He leaned back before he smiled and nodded.

"I think I'm falling in love with you, too."

Amanda gaped, "Hey! I thought we were gonna die! People say crazy things when they think they're gonna—"

"Let's go."

Grasping Amanda's hand, Isaiah led her into the hallway, leaving this impression of a decompression chamber behind them. They emerged into what was an iridescent-colored corridor that appeared to run parallel to the collider; it was as if this entire facility was laid out with circle upon circle; everything ran parallel to another circle like an image of "6" laid atop another slightly off-angled "6."

"Which way?" asked Amanda finally.

"It doesn't matter," said Isaiah and led to the right. "But I'm gonna burn this place down before I leave."

"We'll be in big trouble," said Amanda, linking her fate to his without hesitation until it was said and, even then, without regret. "I'd say we're *already* in big trouble. If these guys don't get us, Interpol is coming after us. Or it's gonna be the United States or the Soviet Union or God-only-knows."

"They can sue me," said Isaiah. "This place is history."

***

Janet finally found Roy a hundred feet down the corridor leaning against the flat, gray wall. "God!" she gasped and stopped running. "I thought I'd lost you!"

"No," Roy shook his head tiredly as he lifted a phone. "I had to find a phone. And they have these emergency phones in the wall at set intervals."

"I know. I'm the one that told you about them."

"Just saying …"

Janet waited until she heard Tanto's voice emerge and Roy said instantly, "Abort. I repeat: Abort. Abort. Abort. We have *two*. I repeat, we have two tangos inside the perimeter. I've got the girls but you come to me at the control room. And watch yourself. They're big and it'll take heavy ordinance to put one down. Go loud."

Janet wasn't sure what Tanto said but Roy hung up and turned to her. "They're going to come to us. But we can't stay here. That thing is somewhere on the other side of these doors. Let's get back to the Observation Room." He shook his head. "I don't think that door will hold it long but it's all we've got."

As they began walking with a strange slowness toward the Observation Room, Janet remarked, "You know we can't use the elevator now, don't you? When I put this place into lockdown, it shut down the elevators, too."

Roy nodded, "Yeah, I figured. That's standard procedure. But we can't open this place up, either. Not with these things running around. They might get topside and then the casualties will be totally unacceptable."

"So what do we do?"

"First we try to locate them."

"How do you know there's two of them?"

Roy said grimly, "On my way up."

"What do you mean?"

"I came up a stairway north of this part of the corridor." He sighed. "I came over a lot of dead bodies. At least twenty. But that stairway is north of where that second creature was seen. So if it had passed the Observation Room from the north, it wouldn't have been way down there in that south section of the corridor. It would have been in the room where you work. So I know there's at least two of them." He shook his head. "Why can't we see these sons 'a bitches on the cameras?"

Janet's ponytail flew left to right. "All I know is that it doesn't register. I don't know why. It might have something to do with how it had to change on a molecular level to have substance in this world … I mean, whatever negative energy is enabling it must have been neutralized on a subatomic level, so there's a problem reading its light spectrum."

Roy answered, "Well, we might not be able to see it on camera, but we can see whatever it knocks down, so maybe we can track it like that." He smoothed back his sweat slick hair. "First thing we have to do is maintain some kind of barrier between us and whatever the hell that thing is so we can figure this out. But, just to be sure, my boys can't get out through the escape tunnel now, right?"

"No," Janet denied, "there's no way out of here until I take us out of lockdown. Until then, every corridor is sealed, every escape tunnel is sealed, every elevator is shut down, all outside power is shut off. Right now we're on batteries. There's no way in and no way out. Not for us or that thing."

"And the collider?"

"It's shut down, too."

"Good," Roy nodded. "At least we don't have to worry about any more of those things coming through." He took a moment. "Hell, these two are gonna be hard enough to put down."

"You think there's only two of them?"

"I pray to God there's only two," Roy said more slowly. "I don't even know if we've got enough ordinance to put these two down."

"It's not positively or negatively charged or it would register on camera, and that means it operates in some kind of unknown light spectrum with an unknown energy source," Janet continued. "But it's still flesh and bone. And it doesn't have unlimited strength or it would have just vaporized those guards. You think it's strong enough to smash down a vault?"

"Whoever planned this place is an idiot," Roy mumbled.

"What do you mean?"

"These vaults are made of a titanium alloy. But the problem with titanium is that it's brittle. Titanium can take flat pressure better than steel and it's half as heavy. But the edges are a lot more easily cracked than something made of steel. That's why a steel door might hold that thing. But titanium won't last long if they can splinter it."

"Could you translate that?" Janet asked.

Roy enunciated more slowly. "When this thing figures out that it can crack this vault by attacking it from the edges, it'll start smashing down these doors like bowling pins. And that will mean we're out of time. We'll either have to kill both of them or bury this place under a billion tons of ice and stone."

"The bomb?"

"If we have to."

"Can you blow it from the Observation Room?"

"No. The cement and steel will block the signal. But I can remote detonate it if I can get inside the collider tunnel."

"Any plan you've got is good enough for me," Janet muttered, and meant it. "*Any* kind of death would be better than falling into the hands of that *thing*."

Roy nodded tiredly, "That ranch is starting to look pretty good right now."

"Yeah," Janet raked hair from her face. "I'm in if you still want the company."

"It's an open invitation."

"I accept."

They walked a while in silence before Roy glanced over his shoulder, waited, then spoke more slowly as if to calm her. "You know, I've actually got a pretty nice place. It's just south of Laredo. Not too far out in the country. Not too close to town. Sort of the perfect distance. I inherited it from my daddy, who inherited it from my granddaddy. They were both ranchers."

Janet tried to slow down her mind that she was still electrified. "How big?" she smiled wanly. "I'm not gonna shack up with a poor rancher."

Roy laughed, "It's about ten thousand acres. But in Texas they call anything less than half a million acres a garden. And it's got a nice colonial house. It needs a little fixing up but it's got style. And it's solid. And I've saved enough to start with maybe a thousand head. Then I'll just work it and see what happens."

"I've had enough of the CIA, anyway."

"You can make up your mind just like that?"

"I made up my mind when I realized you'd changed the plans without telling me and you were coming for me before anything bad could happen." Janet smiled broadly. "I told you I liked cowboys."

"But not heroes."

"Yeah, well, maybe I can live with both."

***

"Good Lord!" Amanda gasped as she turned away from yet another titanium vault that had very solidly cut the corridor in half. She whispered tiredly, "Isaiah? How many of these stupid damn doors do they have in this place?"

"I don't know," Isaiah sighed as he returned from the door's control panel—the first he'd failed to bypass. He grimaced as he drew a deep breath. "All the tunnels are probably like this—a vault every couple hundred yards. But we have one thing going for us."

"I'd love to hear what that is."

"Somebody put this place in lockdown. I don't know who, but I'm grateful. Because, otherwise, we'd be dead."

"Because you couldn't stop the collider?"

"I wasn't even worried about the collider, anymore," stated Isaiah. "After I saw that thing coming down the corridor, I forgot all about it. Anyway, the collider was shut up tighter than a bank vault. And I honestly don't know if that's to protect the collider or the people outside it." He kicked debris from their path. "My guess is that it's meant to protect the collider. I don't think the people that run this place give a damn about what happens to whoever's close when they turn it on. The only thing they care about is opening that portal. And if they have to kill someone to do it, they're not gonna shed any tears."

"I agree," said Amanda, and noticed she was shuffling. "This thing goes on and on. We're never gonna get out of here. What do you say we come up with another plan? How about we access an air duct and crawl out like they do in the movies?"

Isaiah muttered, "These corridors *are* the air ducts. That's why they interlock. Everything here goes around in circles—the air, the electricity, the bacteria. Everything is constantly moving in a circle in series of sixes or zeros laid on top of each other. All we can do is keep going until we find a way out."

Amanda hesitated in place. "Well, pardon me, but walking around in a circle doesn't sound like much of a plan."

"I'm wide open to ideas."

"Why don't we go back to where we started and follow that big tunnel until we reach some kind of maintenance station?" Amanda stared up. "I mean, even subways have maintenance stations, don't they? With ladders that lead to the street? Why don't we find one of those ladders?"

"That's a good idea," Isaiah said evenly. "Except for one thing."

"What?"

"Do you really want to go back into that collider tunnel where that thing almost ran us down?"

"Well," Amanda hesitated, "no. But maybe it's gone now. I mean, it didn't look stupid to *me*. And if there's a way out, I bet that thing found it. Anyway, we're sure not going anywhere fast in here. I mean, I don't know who built this place but they sure didn't have much of an imagination. Any fool can build a place that looks like a donut."

Isaiah stopped and was staring over the corridor, the ceiling, the walls, the floor, as if searching.

"Do you see something?" Amanda asked.

Isaiah continued to stare. "Maybe."

Amanda gazed up. "Feel free to share."

"Maybe a way out."

Amanda didn't remove her eyes from the ceiling.

"Through the ceiling? How we gonna get up there?"

"You go first."

"Ha!" Amanda bent as she clasped a hand over her chest in laughter. "And then I'll pull your two hundred and something pounds up behind me? Yeah! I'd like to see that!" She fanned her face. "Whew! I thought you actually had a doable escape plan for a second. I got sort of excited."

Isaiah steadily stared over her.

Amanda stopped laughing.

"You can't be serious," she muttered.

"I can lift you up there. What's wrong with the idea?"

"It's *not* an idea! I can't pull you up there! And you sure can't jump up there! And what am I gonna do if that thing is up there when I get up there? What am I gonna do with you down here and me up there while I'm getting molested or raped by some demonic thing from another planet? *Holler at you?*"

Isaiah tilted back, face at the ceiling. "Honey, in the first place, there's a good chance that there's nothing up there. Now, my idea is this: I give you a boost and you take a look and tell me if there's some kind of construction tunnel above this ceiling. There might be electrical access panels—anything that we can crawl into and get out of this corridor. Which is going no place. Fast."

Amada looked from Isaiah to the ceiling.

"Just take a look?" she asked. "That's it?"

"That's it."

She dusted off her clothes. "Well, okay. I mean, I don't suppose anything can go wrong with a quick peek. But don't go anywhere."

"Go anywhere?" Isaiah gestured to the ceiling. "How am I going to go anywhere? I'll be holding you up there."

"All right, all right, let's do this."

Isaiah bent and cradled his hands and she stepped into them. She bounced once, twice, three times before shouting, "Go!"

Isaiah straightened and Amanda grabbed the grate above their heads. As Isaiah staggered to find balance, her fingers tightened on the mesh and then stabilized. Finally, Amanda pulled down; the grate didn't give. She pushed, and it lifted easily.

"Okay!" she gasped. "A little higher!"

With a groan Isaiah pushed her until she could look over the edge of the duct and saw nothing but gray wiring and white rectangular tubes. She called down, "There's nothing but a bunch of wires and breaker boxes and vents! I don't know!" A pause. "There sure is a whole bunch of wires! I don't think it's safe up here!"

"Like it is *here*?" gasped Isaiah. "All right! Climb up! Look around!"

Amanda heard a herculean crash in the corridor below and she was literally thrown into the overhead crawl space. She scrambled quickly to look down through the access duct and saw Isaiah backing away. Already frantic, Amanda whispered, "What was that crash?"

"Something knocked down one of the vaults," said Isaiah quietly. "Look around up there. Do it fast."

Amanda was scanning. "What am I looking for?" she whispered. "A rope or something?"

"Yes!" Isaiah's voice was nervous. "Looks for some unused wire! Anything like that! Then tie it off and throw me the rest!"

"Here's a wire!"

Amanda picked a wire at random and pulled hard and more of it emerged from the wall. "Good grief! This is a lot of wire!" She continued pulling. "Isaiah?" she said more loudly.

"Are you still down there?"

"Where am I gonna go?" was the response. "Hurry!"

Somewhere in the depths of the corridor beneath her, Amanda heard a howl unlike anything she had ever heard before. It was not like a wolf or a dog or even a man. It was as if the darkness had taken shape and was announcing its presence. Finally Amanda flung the wire down the opening and shouted, "That's it! Get up here!"

She didn't need to say it twice because Isaiah was already climbing. He was through the duct within seconds, pulled up the wire, and then grabbed the mesh covering and slammed it back into place as a shadow appeared on the floor of the corridor.

A shape slowly approached.

Even from her limited view through the wire mesh, Amanda was horrified as the creature came into view. It was at least seven feet tall and black and was wearing some kind of bizarre armor. It was grotesquely over-muscular and atop its mountainous, sloped shoulders, its head was unnaturally elongated vaguely reminding Amanda of skulls she had once seen of Aztec artifacts.

Crystal skulls, they called them.

The beast had stopped directly beneath the duct and Amanda realized she had stopped breathing.

Very slowly, it turned. It gazed at the walls, at the door that led downward to the collider. It stood a long time in place, staring at everything, before it moved and was lost from view as it descended the stairs.

Isaiah had not moved, had not even attempted to catch a glimpse of it. He waited until Amanda raised her face. Even she couldn't hear her muted whisper as she nodded, "It took the stairs."

Isaiah leaned forward, staring down. And he stared a long time. Then he looked close into Amanda's eyes as he said, "Whatever happens, don't open this duct. Stay here until I tell you to come down."

Amanda's breath was faint. "Wait! What are you gonna do?"

"I'm going to lock it out of this tunnel."

"Are you crazy?" Amanda's frantic whisper abruptly rose in volume. "It'll kill you! You didn't see it! It's big! I mean, like, gorilla-big! If it sees you or hears you it will tear your balls off!"

"Don't encouragement me. I can do this."

"Don't get killed!"

Isaiah was staring down at the magenta-lit stairway that descended into darkness. He inhaled once, twice, like a man preparing to dive into the ocean, then he wrapped a hand around the wire as he looked up at Amanda, "Don't move at all. I'll be—"

"How can this wire hold your weight?"

"It's bolted to the wall."

"Okay, okay, be careful."

"Don't touch anything until I—"

Isaiah stopped, staring down narrowly, moving only his eyes.

Beneath them, the creature had reentered the corridor and was staring at where it had been. But now the mesh covering that had concealed the air duct was removed and Isaiah was clearly in view if the creature raised its face.

Then they would be dead—simple as that.

And, probably, just as fast.

Amanda couldn't breathe. She barely realized her chest was moving, but no air was felt in or out. She was horrified beyond the capacity for feeling or moving or rational thought and only dimly realized that Isaiah was much the same because he hadn't moved a muscle either. Only his gaze had shifted ever so slightly so that he could see the thing from the corner of his eye.

The creature swayed in place and seemed to sniff the air. Then its mouth opened and Amanda almost screamed as she beheld sharp jaws—fangs like a shark's teeth all lined in rows—widening as if to taste their fear.

Amanda's scream stopped in her throat.

Another long moment passed as it stood in place.

Then it raised its face.

Amanda stared into the coal-black eyes.

It roared.

***

Roy stopped in place, lifting his face.

"What is it?" asked Janet, also stopping.

Raising a hand, Roy lowered his head as if he were listening to something faint and far away. He stood like that for a long time before he said, "Get me back to the Observation Room and call up every monitor."

"But we just talked about it," Janet mildly objected. "The monitors can't read either of them."

"The monitors can tell us if all the security vaults are still standing." Roy began moving at a normal pace. "I think that thing just did something massive."

"You think it knocked down a vault?"

Janet hustled to keep up.

"Yeah. I do."

"What does that mean? That it's time to make a run for it?"

"Not yet."

"So what do we do?"

They rushed into the Observation Room and Janet frantically typed codes into the computer to call up every security monitor inside the underground portion of the facility. Suddenly every monitor in the chamber was alive with utterly motionless images of empty corridors and seemingly impervious titanium vaults until …

"Oh, hell," expressed Roy. "Look." He pointed at a screen. "Can you tell me where that broken vault is?"

"Yeah. It's … Oh, no! That's only twenty-two vaults north of this room!" She raised her face to Roy. "Do you think the second one turned north instead of south and that's why it didn't get to us first?"

"That's exactly what I think," Roy said without expression.

Janet straightened, "And now it's doubling back to this section of tunnel?"

"Or using the unsecured sub-hatches to follow the collider tunnel. Or a combination of both. It doesn't matter." Roy's teeth were bared as he said, "Now that it knows how to break titanium, it's gonna cover ground a lot faster."

"How fast?"

"I don't know," Roy shook his head, blinking tiredly. "It depends on how smart it is or maybe … what we can throw at it."

"Why don't we just bury this place, Roy!" Janet grabbed his arm with both hands. "We can't let that thing reach the surface!"

"If it comes to that, I'll blow the bomb," Roy stated coldly. "Not even that thing can survive a ground zero detonation of one hundred megatons. I don't care *what* it's made of. But we ain't there yet. You said that you can't control these vaults on an individual basis?"

Janet found herself searching the console. "I'm not saying it can't be done. I just mean that I can't do it because I don't have the encryption codes and, with these resources, it'd take me forever to break them. Maybe General Francois could do it. He can do everything else down here."

"Where is he?"

Janet searched the Observation Room before realizing she half-expected him to still be there. Then she glanced at the door, lifting a hand. "I guess he's at the elevator with the others." She raked ragged bangs from her eyes. "Or he might have used an unknown door to escape this place. Hell, I don't know. And Blanchard is gone, too. I guess they made tracks at the same time." She clicked a switch. "Let's see."

A screen came alive with a view of very still personnel crowded at the elevator. It appeared as if no one had moved an inch since Janet left. She saw Susan standing in the door and staring down the corridor.

"Neither of them are at the elevator," she stated. "They must have escaped through an unsecured door. No surprise. And I can't access topside cameras. I can only see what's going on down here." She taped in a code. "Security cameras for the offices are off-air. I guess Francois didn't want a record of whatever he's doing."

Roy grunted, "He's going down with his ship whether he wants to or not. He's going down with it even if I have to go down with him."

Janet turned a gaze to Roy.

"That's what I like about you," she said.

"What's that?"

"You're so old-fashioned. You say what you mean, mean what you say. You lead from the front and cover your own ground. You don't leave anybody behind. You don't quit. And if you die, you die. No fear. No regret." Janet lowered her head. "It makes me doubt *myself* since I'm scared to death."

"Ah, hell," Roy muttered, "if you ain't scared, I sure don't want to share a house with you."

"Why not?"

"Because if you ain't scared—like me—you're crazy."

***

The beast had torn its way halfway into the ceiling, ripping shreds of steel and hurling them aside like wet paper, before Amanda realized she was scrambling back screaming.

Amanda recognized what was a monstrous abomination of black claws and black fangs and huge arms tearing and shredding and lashing out at her and coming closer and closer with each pass and then Isaiah was there, too.

With a roar Isaiah leaped forward holding something in his hand and suddenly the entire ceiling above the corridor was lit with an electric blue, soundless light both blinding and stunning and Amanda became aware that she was *flying* before she smashed painfully into a wall and fell across something hard.

Beneath her, the corridor reverberated with a wounded animal cry before the sound retreated into what seemed like the stairway. "Wait!" Amanda screamed and reached out with a single hand as Isaiah dropped through the hole torn through the ceiling.

She scrambled forward, staring down, as Isaiah repeated the procedure he had executed on the first door. He ripped a fire ax from a box and spun the wheel of the door until it stopped. Then he slammed in the fire ax and a steel crowbar and forced them against the iron jam of the door before he stepped back, hands on knees, gasping.

"Are you okay?" gasped Amanda. "Isaiah! Can you hear me?"

Isaiah managed to raise a hand and his voice rose to her, as well. "Don't move one inch, Amanda."

Her face twisted. "What? No! I'm coming down!"

"No!" Isaiah said angrily as he straightened and pointed at her face. "Stay exactly where you're at! Do *not* move!"

Amanda wiped away a tear. "Why are you telling me this?"

Isaiah wagged his finger, still obviously trying to catch his breath, before he said brokenly, "Because ... there's a bare wire up there ... that I used to knock the hell out of that thing ... and it's carrying enough voltage to kill you." He bent, laboring for breath, then stepped forward, squinting up.

"Okay," he gasped, and swallowed, "can you see what's around you?"

Barely moving her eyes, Amanda gazed at the wires and ceiling.

"Yeah," she said uncertainly.

"Okay. That's good. Now, can you drop through that hole without touching any wires?"

Amanda crept forward an inch, carefully searching for anything that seemed dangerous although she wasn't sure what that would be. "I don't think so," she managed. "What wire did you use to shock it?"

"Look for a naked wire," Isaiah replied. "It's copper. It's not white like the others. This wire doesn't have any insulation. It's just a bare wire and it's copper or brown in color. Can you see it?"

Amanda peered closer in the half-light of the ceiling and thought she perceived a brown-colored strip of wire on the far side of the rent opening.

"I think I see it," she whispered. "Is that it over there?"

"Yes," Isaiah nodded. "That's it. Now, move without touching it. Just drop through the hole. I'll catch you."

Amanda found herself staring down but she had been through too much horror to hesitate. She curled into a seated position on the edge of the ravaged ceiling and crossed her arms on her chest as she slid off the steel panel.

She screamed as Isaiah caught her in a steel grip.

"Oh, God," she whispered, burying her face into Isaiah's chest. "Oh, my God. How did you hurt that thing?"

"I told you," Isaiah said quietly. "I hit it with enough voltage to knock down an elephant. I think it was a line of four-forty. It was big. And, when it hit, it went blue like a bolt of lightning. And that was too much for it."

"Is it gone?" Amanda asked. "I mean, for good?"

"No," Isaiah shook his head. "Once it realizes what happened, it'll be back. And pissed. And I doubt the same trick will work twice. We've got to get out of this part of the tunnel."

"How are we gonna do that?"

"If I'm right, it knocked down a vault somewhere along this corridor. We'll have to go down that way, past the vault, and hope for good luck." Isaiah gently lowered Amanda to her feet, her arms still wrapped around his neck. "Hell," he added with a glance down the hall, "*any* kind of luck would be better than what we've had so far."

Beside them, a fist struck the steel door.

And again.

But this time it was different. Rather, it wasn't as strong or as insistent as the original battering the door to the collider corridor had withstood. In fact, this battering seemed weak and even hesitant compared to the incommensurate force that had almost torn the first sub-hatch off the steel hinges.

The door was hit again.

And, again, it was weaker.

"So," Isaiah said with curiosity and contempt, "you're not the anchor man." He continued to stare at the panel as the battering continued. "Some of you are stronger than others." He nodded. "I figured."

Amanda was slowly finding her voice and, thank god, some control.

"You figured what?" she asked evenly.

"I figured that what the old Jewish scholars wrote about these entities was, more or less, fairly close to the truth," said Isaiah. "From what I remember, demons are limited to the strength that was imputed in them when they were created, so what they were when they were created is all they'll ever be. They can't gain strength or lose strength. They just are what they are. It's almost like predestined damnation. But I guess God knows what he's doing." He frowned, "Some were created with the strength of sergeants, and some were created with the powers of a prince. And there was one created with the strength and wisdom of a king and I don't see any door stopping *him*. But as long as they keep that collider down, we might be safe."

"So you're saying that thing can't knock down this door?" Amanda was gazing up. "But it knocked down that big vault. How can it be strong enough to knock down that vault and not strong enough to knock down this door?"

"The big one knocked the door down. This one isn't strong enough."

Amanda's eyes widened and she held up her arms as far as she could reach. "That thing was big as a house! It's bigger than a gorilla!"

Isaiah gently grasped her hand and turned.

"Yeah, well, obviously they do come bigger."

****

"Hold it!"

Roy had already whirled and leveled his machinegun—Janet still didn't know what kind of gun it was and didn't care—at a shape that silently appeared at the door of the Observation Room.

"General!" Roy shouted as he rushed forward.

Jackman fairly collapsed into a chair, gasping as Tanto quickly backed into room keeping his rifle trained on the corridor. "Jesus Christ," whispered Tanto as he ripped a black balaclava from his head and swiped a forearm across his face. "God Almighty, major," he shook his head at Roy, "we almost bought the farm, man."

"What happened?" Roy bent over the general. "General?" Roy snatched a large water bottle and thrust it in his hand. "General. Drink this."

Roy straightened, staring at Tanto.

"Tanto? What happened?"

Tanto slowly shook his head, "We ran into one of them, boss." He took a few moments trying to breath. "And it just …"

Tanto's words fell away—with his expression—as Roy stepped to the door, glaring in both directions of the corridor. He turned back.

"Tanto?" Roy stated more sternly. "Listen to me."

Eyes tight, Tanto moaned, "Jesus Christ!"

"Tanto! Look at me!"

"That thing killed Jake like—"

"*LIEUTENANT!*"

Tanto's eyes snapped open. He took a moment, gazing about the room, before he focused on Roy and quietly asked, "Sir?"

"Where are Jake and Picket?"

Tanto clutched his vest with a bloody hand. "They're dead, sir." He took a moment to wipe sweat from his face. "They got killed when it ambushed us." He stared widely and vacantly at the wall as he whispered, "I ain't *never* see nuthin' like that. It came out of nowhere and killed Picket before we even knew it was there. Then Jake got off a shot before it turned into him and ripped out his heart. And I mean it ripped out his heart through his vest! Then I hit it point blank with a grenade and blew its ass all the way down the stairs and we managed to seal the door before it climbed up to us again but damn, man. What the hell have these people done down here? That thing is the Devil!"

Leaning back against the wall, Roy raised his face. Then he lowered it and shook his head before gazing steadily at Janet.

"Check on the vaults," Roy said without emotion. "See which ones are still standing."

Janet typed quickly and lifted her eyes to see Roy staring patiently and with perfect composure. He was not breathing heavy and his gaze was steady and clearly analyzing their vividly alarming situation without revealing any undue alarm.

"Thirteen vaults are down," she said clinically. "It looks like …"

"The big one," stated Roy.

"Yeah," she agreed. "It looks like the most powerful one is inside this corridor and the vaults aren't strong enough to stop him. From what I can discern from a pattern, it looks like it's just searching at random. But sooner or later it's going to knock down the right door and find us. And if you don't have enough ordinance to put it down …"

She didn't finish.

She didn't have to.

Roy lifted the rifle, resting the stock on his hip.

He bowed his head.

"Yeah," he said somberly.

***

Isaiah stood over another shattered vault. He knelt and seemed to measure the claw marks, and finally nodded.

"These impressions are a lot more distinct than they were at the last vault," he murmured.

Amanda asked, "And that's important?"

"Yeah."

"Why?"

"Because now we have proof that the first one we saw didn't do this," Isaiah stated coldly. "There's obviously two of them. And the biggest one—the most powerful one—did this. Then it let the other one hunt us down while it went its way." He raised his face to the corridor. "They seem to work in coordination. Like people. But one doesn't necessarily know where the other one is or what it's doing, so they're not telepathic. Still, they seem to work in unison. Maybe they have some kind of language."

"You think they can *talk*?"

"Why not? People can talk. Why not aliens or whatever they are?" He nodded, "Yeah, I think they can talk. And they can plan. But even though they work together, one doesn't always know what his buddy is doing, so they don't have the same brain. And, like I said, they're not telepathic."

"But how can we know that for sure?" Amanda asked. She couldn't remove her eyes from the horrendous impact marks driven into the titanium vault. "I mean, what makes you say they can talk and communicate verbally but not telepathically?"

"Because the other one would have already called for his big brother to rescue him from that stairway. And if his buddy had freed him, we would have run into him by now. He'd be hunting us down out of sheer revenge because I'm beginning to think that electrical line hurt him worse than I thought. So, obviously, they can't check status with each other any better than we can. We have to talk to each other, so I'm thinking that they do, too. So we don't know where it's at, and it doesn't know where we're at. We're both just wandering through this maze and we could bump into each at any time … or never."

"I like 'never' better," said Amanda. "Come on, Isaiah. You're a genius at this stuff, remember? Finding ancient books? Getting out of tight spots? You're resourceful and brilliant? So how about getting us out of this particular tight spot?"

Isaiah shook his head, "The only thing we can do right now is keep moving and hope we come across something useful. We're not getting anything done here."

"I'm with you," Amanda strode forward matching him step for step. "Did I tell you that I work for free?"

Isaiah laughed, "You don't mind working for me?"

Amanda considered before she admitted, "Well, no offense, but your place could use a woman's touch. Or, maybe, we'll move up in the world and live like real people. Hey! That's an idea! You ever lived in a real house with doors and windows and closets and stuff?" She laughed. "Maybe a wraparound porch? A little greenhouse? We can have a garden! Don't you like to eat healthy food? I do!"

Isaiah hadn't smiled in a long time and remembered how sorrow was better than happiness, how mourning was better than gaiety.

It occurred to him how everything he had ever learned seemed a bit tedious as Amanda genuinely lifted his spirit, and his spirit had been in a canyon for as long as Isaiah could remember. So, whatever this was, he wasn't going to walk away from a potentially precious thing. That is, if he could get them out of here.

"Actually," he said, "I've never had a garden."

"Oh, really? Why not?"

"Never cared to have one."

"You don't like healthy food?"

"Gardens die. Everything dies."

Amanda paused. "That's sad, Isaiah. Is everything in your life so expendable? Don't you have anything you really care about? Something you love?"

"I care about staying alive. Never had much of anything else."

"Now you do," said Amanda, her hand tightening on his.

It was a long moment before Isaiah replied.

"We'll see," he said.

Isaiah had counted steps between vaults and knew the doors were shut every few hundred yards. And with almost eighteen miles of tunnel, that added up to a lot of vaults. And he hadn't managed to bypass a single one, so unless they literally came across an open door, which was highly unlikely, this was a walk to anything but freedom.

Still, with Amanda tightly clutching his hand, he said nothing.

"Can I ask you something weird?" Amanda began.

"I ain't goin' no place."

"Was that thing wearing armor?"

Isaiah paused. "I've been wondering that myself."

"It happened so fast, I'm not sure."

"I'm fairly certain that it was."

"An ape wearing armor?"

"Well, it's not an ape. It's actually a pretty intelligent entity. More intelligent than us, even. And if we're smart enough to wear armor, I guarantee you it's gonna be smart enough to wear armor."

"That makes it tougher to kill, doesn't it?"

"It makes it a lot tougher."

"Great." Amanda paused. "Well, at least I've got you. Like you said."

Isaiah shook his head with a laugh.

"Lucky me."

***

Tanto had recovered with remarkable swiftness and was leaning against the frame of the open Observation Room door staring alertly into the corridor, glancing this direction and that, a finger on the trigger of his rifle.

General Jackman was finally beginning to collect himself and was gazing over the various monitors as if searching for something specific. But he had said nothing, and Janet felt compelled to ask, "General? Can I help you?"

"Huh?" Jackman raised his gaze. "Uh, no, thank you. I was just trying to see if there was some way to blow those Semtex charges and survive the catastrophe." He paused. "So far, I don't see any." He sighed. "Nobody down here lives if we blow those tanks. And you said there was no way out?"

"Not unless I take this place out of lockdown. But, if I do that, then this creature escapes into the world. And I don't think you want that."

"No," Jackman shook his head with new energy. "It's not. If we have to blow those charges, or the bomb itself, and bury this place under a billion tons of ice and dirt, then we'll blow it to keep those bastards down here."

"Did you guys manage to set all the satchels?" she asked and was abruptly surprised that she hadn't asked before now; she realized that absolute horror rather effectively overcame more pedestrian faculties like "reason."

Jackman slowly nodded, "Yeah, but we still have one satchel." He shrugged. "We always hold one back in case we need it for an emergency. And six of those Semtex charges are enough to destroy that collider, anyway."

"Is it true they can't be disarmed once they're initiated?" asked Janet to make small talk; the truth is, she really didn't care. She simply wanted to talk about something besides the horror stalking them through these corridors.

"If someone has enough time, sure." Jackman gasped as he shook his head. "But it'd take a U-Haul full of circuit breakers and two weeks of planning. So with the time and resources they have down here? Nah. They can't defuse them."

"How about the demons? Can they defuse them?"

"Personally I don't think those bastards are any smarter than we are."

"Just asking, but is there some other way to turn them off?"

"Sure," Jackman nodded. "Every satchel has a code that will turn it off right up to the last second." He heaved a deep breath. "But I learned this morning that Roy and Tanto encrypted the codes last night making it ten times harder to turn 'em on or shut 'em down."

"Why did he do that?"

"So that nobody, including any American intelligence source, could remote detonate them to make sure we do the job their way."

"But isn't that violating orders?"

"Yeah," Jackman grunted. "But in this gone to hell situation you gotta improvise. Anyway, he told Tanto that if he wasn't back with both you girls in thirty minutes to go ahead and blow the place and all of us could die together." He laughed, "But, then, that's Roy. He's a cowboy. He wasn't about to leave you behind. Neither of you. None of us, neither. And I admire that. I truly do."

Janet laughed.

"Yeah," she said quietly, "I do, too."

"Look!" Jackman violently pointed at a monitor. "That must be the crew Whitaker warned us about. That's Amanda Deker and that guy, Isaiah. How the hell did those two idgets get down here?" He stood, leaning heavily on the desk. "Those stupid flatfoots! Like we ain't got enough problems down here!"

Janet looked up as Jackman finished and saw a medium-sized, muscular man accompanied by a petite woman in a black dress walking slowly up a corridor. She checked the readout as she shouted, "Roy! Get over here!"

Roy was across the room.

"What is it?" he asked, dead calm.

"Those are two innocent people," Janet said with renewed energy. "That guy is this woman's bodyguard and she's here trying to find out how her sister got killed. You remember them from the file, right?"

He nodded once.

"We can't let leave them out there, Roy."

"Any way to reach them without raising the vaults?"

"No."

"Damn it."

"What do we do?"

Roy released a deep breath, jaw tightening.

"Where are they now?"

"They're four vaults down to the south and they're about to reach a dead end. There's no access panels. No electrical ports. And that vault is still standing. When they get to that wall, there's no place to go."

Roy's lips moved silently before he murmured, "Four vaults. If the spacing remains the same, which it always *doesn't*, that's probably about half a mile. So that's five minutes down there, five back. And I'm betting those things can move faster than we can. Is there any way to lure those creatures away from this section of tunnel?"

Janet started at the screens before saying, "I can probably lure them away with light. Give them a taste of the outside. That's where they want to go, anyway, isn't it? Then I can shut the doors again after you get back here with these guys."

"The creatures can't get out through the escape tunnels?"

Janet shook her head, "Absolutely not. The tunnels are closed by blocks of steel that can theoretically withstand a ground-zero detonation of a nuclear blast."

Roy straightened.

"Use the lights," he nodded. "Lure them toward the escape tunnels."

"You're going after these guys?"

Roy lifted the heavy ballistic vest over his head and laid it on the desk. "Tanto's in no shape. But before you begin opening the vaults between me and them, shut off the lights in this section of tunnel for a couple miles in either direction. But leave the lights on for whatever section contains me. And I'll be moving fast, so keep up."

"Got it."

Janet began tripping lights as Roy removed extra clips, his bandoleer of grenades, his helmet and, finally, his kneepads. When he was finished, he looked like a modern ninja minus his equipment.

"Reducing your weight for speed?" she asked.

"Uh huh."

"I think you're missing something."

"Won't be the first time," Roy muttered. "What now?"

Janet took a moment before she said, "What if speed doesn't work and you run slap into one of them without your rifle and grenades?"

Roy shrugged, "If I run into it, I'll do my best. They spend a million dollars training us to not feel fear."

"Wow. Does it work?"

Roy raised his face.

"Nope."

***

Amanda, remarkable, had recovered her powers of reason.

"Tell me this," she said. "What, exactly, are we looking for?"

Isaiah was gazing along the floor and walls as they slowly strolled as if searching for signs that the creature might be close.

Isaiah responded, "What?"

"I *said*," Amanda repeated, "*what* are we looking for?"

"Oh, well, we're looking for unlocked doors, that's for sure. And we're looking for any sign that it might be close to us."

"Like what kind of sign?"

"Blood." Isaiah shrugged. "Do you remember how blood seeped through that crack in the door leading from the collider? It hurt itself. It's bleeding." He nodded, "Yeah, this thing's a lot stronger than us but it's limited. Just like us."

Amanda glanced nervously aside. "It ain't *that* limited."

"But it's still limited," Isaiah repeated. "It finally found a way to get through these titanium vaults, but I bet it pays a price." He took a moment. "It's like beating your head against a wall. You can do it but it's gonna cost you. Same with this thing."

Amanda nodded, finding herself also gazing around at absolutely nothing. "And if we *do* see blood?"

"Then it's probably right beside us. Or in front of us. Or behind us. Either way, it's not gonna be pretty."

"Can't you say *anything* good?"

Isaiah stopped and turned into her, wrapping his arms gently over her shoulders. He stared down. "We're not dead, yet."

She tilted her head, then buried her face into his chest.

"Oh, come on," Isaiah pushed back her bangs. "It's not that bad, honey. If there's a way in, there's a way out. We just have to find it."

"You make it sound simple," she murmured. "But I'm not an idiot, Isaiah." She leaned back, gazing up. "And I know this. If these people are no longer in control of their secrets, they'll make sure that everything down here stays buried till the end of time." She blinked, as if remembering.

"Did you ever read the old Edgar Allen Poe short story, 'The House of Usher'? It wasn't actually a book."

"I've read it."

"Remember how Usher's sister was alive in her grave and she had to claw her way out of that coffin? Or tomb? Or whatever it was?" She gazed along the walls. "That's how I feel right now. I feel like we're covered in blood wandering the halls of some cursed mansion. Or clawing our way out of a grave."

Isaiah said nothing as Amanda continued, "Do you remember how his sister suddenly appeared at Usher's library door, all bloody and torn up just before the place got nuked by the Wrath of God?"

Isaiah laughed, "I didn't know you had a photographic memory."

"A story about a young girl being buried alive makes a very strong impression on a young girl. But what I'm saying is that they have put a hundred billion dollars into this place to make sure nobody ever emerges in the case of a worst-possible scenario. And this *is* a worst possible scenario. I mean, good God, this is even worse than 'The House of Usher' with a dead girl roaming the halls."

"She wasn't actually dead."

"She was close enough!" Amanda glanced along the walls. "What I'm trying to say is that I don't think there's any way out of here because these people will nuke this place themselves before they let their secrets get out. And I want you to know it's okay. I think you did a really great job in a very bad situation." She paused. "And if I have to trust my life to anybody, I'll trust my life to you."

With a faint smile, Isaiah asked, "Did you tell me the truth earlier?"

"About what?"

"You'd really work for free?"

Amanda laughed, "Do you have full medical?"

"I'll get it."

"What about visual and dental?"

"I'll get that, too."

"And equal profit sharing? Just you and me? Faith in each other?"

"I'm game if you are."

She smiled. "We'll see."

***

Roy had reached the first vault.

It was shut like an anvil and the vaguest thought of how that animal could knock this barrier to the ground was simply stultifying. Roy didn't even try and imagine what else it might be able to do. This was bad enough.

He had left his vest, his arsenal of grenades, his rifle— everything but the .45 caliber pistol—in the Observation Room. And he wasn't even sure why he'd brought his sidearm but, standing in the vault like an Olympic runner set to begin a race, he didn't care. He only knew something in him didn't want to die without putting up some kind of fight, however futile.

For a split-second Roy had a hideous vision of some Unnamable *It* stalking 'round the far corner of the world laughing with its empty skull sockets glowing red and a single skeletal hand holding a dagger dripping with blood whispering his name …

Roy muttered, "You guys better be ready to haul ass." He keyed the mic. "Okay, Janet, open the first vault and watch me closely. Open the vaults one by one as I get to them. And close the last vault as I pass through it. Don't let that thing come up behind me."

The vault opened with a steady but slow speed and Roy rolled under the base before it was two feet above the floor and then he was running but not full out. He knew he had a few hundred yards before reaching the next barrier and an unequal distance to each wall before he reached the civilians; he paced himself at what he knew he could maintain and not much more because he didn't fail to remember that it was a long way down there and a long way back. And he wasn't about to lock up before he made it back.

He covered the distance, not even bothering to scan connecting corridors for dead bodies or living creatures. He knew that almost all maintenance personnel had abandoned this place at the first magenta alarm and anyone that stayed behind was dead. In fact, the only reason he involuntarily glanced into connecting tunnels at all was because he was horrified that he might see the gigantic bestial thing loping toward him, claws clutching …

Roy estimated he would get off a few shots, but the end would be the same.

The second vault was open when he reached it and he kept his stride to the third vault and then …

Roy stopped in a single stride and thumbed back the hammer of the .45 to take a dead aim. He didn't shout a warning.

Isaiah and Amanda Deker stared at him in open shock.

Roy waved sharply. "Come on!"

No questions.

Isaiah reached Roy easily even after he snatched up the woman, who was gasping and clutching her chest. Roy sternly pointed up the corridor.

"Go as fast as you can!" he demanded.

Roy turned and was running, half-expecting the man to fall back a stride but the man matched his pace as if the woman were weightless. With every glance over his shoulder Roy confirmed that the man still held her tight in his arms, almost flush against him in every way, her arms folded across her chest, her face flat against his chest.

"Keep running!" the man shouted.

Roy needed no encouragement; he increased his pace to all he could maintain for the remaining distance and when they cleared the last vault to the Observation Room the man had only fallen back a dozen paces. Then, when the two of them cleared the portal, Roy raised the radio again, "Lock the vaults! Lock the vaults! Lock the vaults!"

Immediately the closest vault slid from the ceiling and three seconds later it shut with the sound of a vacuum. Then, and only then, did Roy allow himself a moment. He fell back against the wall and bent, hands on knees, heaving air. He wiped sweat from his face and could not have cared less about the identities of the man and woman. His chest was a blast furnace, each breath boiling in his throat. He dimly realized he had his hand on the .45 but there was no sensation.

He knew he was alive although he only knew that because. he could see that he was still standing. Nothing in his body—or, rather, no *feeling* confirmed it. Finally Roy managed to gasp, "How … how the hell did you guys get in here?"

The man slowly settled the woman to her feet as she leaned into him. "We were shanghaied." He took a moment. "They were going to sacrifice us to those things."

"How'd you know there's two of them?"

"We ran into one of them. We saw evidence of the other one." The man named Isaiah gazed across the ceiling. "What's the body count down here?"

"There's ten or so alive in the control room. I'd guess that anyone who didn't get out of here before the shutdown is dead. And we're next if we don't hit the road." He raised the radio. "Janet? Do you copy?"

The response was instant: *"Great job! I watched every step! I think you covered that last half-mile in, like, three minutes! That's gotta be some kind of record!"*

"Tell Tanto not to shoot the first thing he sees coming down this hall because it's gonna be me. We're headed your way." Roy took a deep breath. "Can you guys go a little further?"

"Lead the way," said the man.

"What's your name, anyway?"

"Isaiah. This is Amanda."

Roy gasped, "Yeah, I thought so. Just wanted to make sure." He glanced at Amanda. "Nice to meet you."

"Hi," said Amanda.

"We just have a little ways to go, guys. Then we got food and water for you. Sure you can make it? We can take a break if you need one."

"I can make it," gasped Amanda.

The man nodded.

Roy spoke into the mic, "Janet? Open the doors one by one and keep everything behind us on a monitor. Make sure that thing doesn't sneak up on us."

Isaiah gazed down at Amanda. "You sure?"

"Yeah, I'm sure."

With an irritated groan Roy pushed off the wall and began walking down the hall with a faint wave. "Cheer up, guys. A couple hundred yards and you can rest." He inhaled deeply. "We're hoping to get out of here."

"Thank God," whispered Amanda.

Isaiah glanced back at the vault.

"That vault won't hold it," he stated.

"We know," said Roy.

"So what's the plan?"

Head bowed, Roy simply shuffled forward. His voice, when it reached back, seemed weak and defeated. "Hell, I just said we're hoping to get out of here. And hope ain't nothing like a plan."

***

As Isaiah rested, head bowed, on a desk, Amanda began with rapid-fire questions after she drank a bottle of water. Then she pointed to a monitor focused on the elevator.

"I know that guy!" She leaped forward. "Isaiah! Come over here and look at this monitor! That's Tony and the guards! And Tony's still got your Honjo Masamune! And a machinegun!"

Tanto lifted his head. "*The* Honjo Masamune? The demon sword?"

"Yeah," Amanda replied with a smile. "It's Isaiah's sword." She peered closer. "Why don't they leave? Why don't they go up to the surface?"

"Because all the elevators are on lockdown," said Janet. "And until I decide to take this place off lockdown, nobody's going anywhere. Not us. Not the scientists. Not the guards. And not those things."

Amanda stared before she leaned back in the chair, one foot hoisted. Her voice, when she spoke, was hoarse and coarse. "Yeah. I got it. You're not going to unlock this place until those things are dead."

"Good and dead," elaborated Tanto.

Janet didn't reply as Amanda stated without hesitation, "I think Isaiah and I have a right to know exactly what those things are." She paused. "We've already been introduced to them. And my sister is probably dead because of one, or both, of them. We have a right to be here and we have a right to know some things."

Janet asked, "My personal opinion? They're demons."

"That's what I think, too," Amanda muttered. "Oh, happy days."

"I'm sorry about your sister," offered Tanto with what seemed like true empathy. "I lost a couple of brothers to them, too."

Amanda turned, "May I ask your name?"

"Tanto."

"Thanks, Tanto. I'm Amanda. This is Isaiah."

"Yeah," he nodded. "We got briefed on you guys. I was afraid you'd work your way down here and get involved in this fiasco. But, as it turns out, it's all hands on deck, anyway. We need all the help we can get."

A very tired smile cracked Amanda's face.

"On a more somber note," Tanto continued, "some of us think they're demonic but we don't know. All I know for sure is they're the most dangerous things I've ever seen. And I thought I'd seen it all."

"I'm Major Roy Burris," said the commando who met them in the corridor. "I'm glad you guys survived this long but you need to prepare yourselves. We're here to destroy those things, so this ain't over by a damn side. Still, if there's a way out of here, we need to find it. And after we kill those things, we'll use it."

"And if we can't kill them?" asked Amanda.

Roy focused on her. "Then we have a bomb big enough to bury this place for the next ten thousand years." He frowned. "And nobody goes home."

Silence.

"What unit are you guys?" asked Isaiah.

"Delta," said Roy.

"Thanks for your help, major."

"Just call me Roy. We were sent here to destroy the collider but that plan went the way of all flesh right off the bat."

"Who briefed you on us?" asked Isaiah.

Jackman waved. "I did. I'm General Atol Jackman."

"That's four whole stars," commented Tanto.

Jackman laughed. "Your file came from the White House. Don't ask me where they got it."

"Thanks, general," Isaiah nodded. "Yeah, we've come to understand that the only secret here is this place itself."

"It ain't a secret no more," muttered Jackman. "If all the survivors are running around topside screaming about being chased by monsters down here, the word is out. I wouldn't doubt that the Swiss military has already set up a perimeter."

"We were hoping you guys wouldn't show up," Roy stated. "But then we saw you on a monitor and decided we couldn't let you die, so we took a chance. Went after you."

"You guys risked your lives to save us," said Amanda.

Roy stared in his coffee cup. "Ah, if I can help it, I ain't gonna let nobody get killed by those things. Wouldn't be decent."

"Thank you, major."

Roy simply nodded.

Janet said blankly, "Well, no worries. We're temporarily safe. But I think one of those things heard something and came after you guys. I saw a table get tossed aside in a conference room about ten miles down the tunnel. But it hasn't registered since then. Or not that I'm aware of. It's not like I can actually see them." She blew out a hard breath. "My best guess is that they're trying to access an electrical tunnel or crawl space or maybe a maintenance walkway. Something that will allow them to bypass the vaults."

Isaiah commented, "These things know more than you think."

Roy turned. "Why do you say that?"

"It's an intelligent entity," Isaiah said without hesitation. "What it really wants is to access this control room. It's far more intelligent than man, so it should be able to solve the problems you haven't been able to solve in no time. And you've already hooked up the collider with enough power to make its plan work." He paused. "It's looking for this room. And when it finds this place, it's going to carry out its orders."

Roy frowned, "Orders?"

"Both of these entities are soldiers," said Isaiah. "In their dimension they have majors, colonels, generals. About the same as our world. And then there's a king. And, ultimately, that's who gave them their marching orders."

"How do you know this?" asked Janet.

Isaiah shrugged, "Well, so far, everything in Jewish legend has turned out to be true. So if I'm right, that thing is what we would instinctively call a demon. Now, 'demon' is just a convenient word. In reality, it's just a creature from another dimension. But it's a creature with a far different nature. It's a creature of chaos and cruelty and it has its own obscene reasons for why it does things. But if Jewish legend is right, then these things have a hierarchy, and I think these two are soldiers. That's why I think they're gonna try and use that portal to bring the rest of their army into this dimension."

Roy was silent, then, "What, exactly, is their big plan once they get here?"

"My best guess is that they want to turn this planet into a slave colony. And once they get a big enough army, they'll attack who they've been waiting to attack for millions of years. But they'll have to get here and get organized first."

"Organized?" asked Roy. "To attack who?"

Isaiah didn't blink.

"God."

***

The conversation took the wind out of the room. Everyone spent a good five minutes simply staring at walls or computer screens or their feet. Then Janet asked, "How do you know all this? I mean, I'm not an idiot. I've read up on this stuff. But you sound like some kind of rabbi and I'm not absolutely convinced this is demonic. First, I'm formally a scientist, so I like proof. And I know that there are at least eleven dimensions and these creatures could have come from any of them. So there's no empirical evidence that they come from what Christian mythology calls Hell. They could be from Mars. They could be from a dimension in one of my fingernails."

"For practical purposes, and considering our current situation, it makes no difference where they come from," Isaiah answered. "We know they're physically and intellectually superior. And I wouldn't doubt that they're superior to us in warfare. So any thoughts you harbor of fighting them with conventional weapons is more than likely doomed. You might wound or kill a few million of them but I think there's *billions*. There's nine billion people on the Earth. Why can't there be nine billion in their dimension? So they'll eventually overrun and enslave us and no wall can stop them." He frowned. "You think these two expendable soldiers are dangerous? Let me educate you. These two are probably peons compared to their master. And when he gets here, it's over. There's only one power in *any* dimension strong enough to stop him. And, unfortunately, that power isn't here to take care of this."

There was a pensive moment.

"I don't know," muttered Roy. "I don't know if I buy into the religious part of this. But something is for damn sure going on. Ghosts. Demons. Aliens. I really don't care what you call them. I don't care what they are. All I know is that we have to stop them."

"Huh," grunted Tanto. "Well, it sure looked like a demon to *me*. It sure acted like a demon and it damn sure killed like a demon. And if something walks like a duck and quacks like a duck … it ain't no damn giraffe, man."

***

It was a short, silent walk to the elevator and Susan was clearly overjoyed to see Janet alive. She leaped forward as Janet rounded the corner and didn't lessen the bear hug until Janet managed, "Okay! Okay! It's good to see you, too!"

Susan separated and smiled, joyously holding up a hairpin. She laughed, "They think it's poison. I told them one touch would kill them."

"Did you have to knock anybody out?"

"No," Susan shook her head. "Actually, the guards were a big help. Especially the one named Tony. He's, like, their boss."

Tony stepped up to Isaiah, extending an arm.

He held the Honjo Masamune horizontally, still sheathed.

"I took good care of it," Tony nodded. "But this is the hour of darkness, hoss, so it's time to give it back to you and it's time for you to use it." He gazed along the sheathed blade. "I hope all that legend stuff is true and this thing really can cut a demon in half."

Isaiah glanced to the men behind Tony. "This all we got?"

"Yep," Tony stated. "We're all that's left. We had about a hundred men down here but half were killed outright and the others escaped to the surface. I guess it don't matter. This is our foxhole, now, and we're manning it."

With a half-turn Tony lifted an arm and virtually every guard nodded politely to the Observation Room group. "These guys know that something from the far side came through that collider and it's killing people like there's no tomorrow, so they're with me and I'm with you. So whatever call you make, we'll back you up." He focused on Roy. "They sent in a strike team, huh?"

"Delta," said Roy. "We came here to blow this place. But those things sort of derailed our plan. I think they knew what we were gonna do and didn't want it done."

Tony scowled, "They?"

"There's two of them," said Isaiah. "At least. And they're working together."

After a long pause Tony muttered, "Well, hell. Are these things from another planet or what?"

"They're from another dimension."

Tony stared. "Is that *possible*?"

"Do you know anything about neutrinos?" asked Janet.

Tony hesitated. "I know that the guys who build hydrogen weapons talk about neutrinos a lot and I don't like the sound of it."

"Well, these things are made of antimatter neutrinos that have somehow managed to assume the form of matter in this world because they carry no electrical charge whatsoever. Or that's the only theory we've got. But it's almost as if they can absorb the electrical charge of whatever environment they inhabit and alter it into some kind of hybrid charge that we've never encountered. That might account for their survivability. And ours, too, or this place would have been blown to smithereens."

"They survive because they're so freaking strong," Tony muttered.

Janet sighed, "Tony? Is that your name?"

"Yeah."

"Tony, these things have survived for millions, if not billions, of years in their dimension. They are made of a substance that comprises the essence of electrons, something so subatomic that we cannot even begin to fathom what it is. But in this world they're flesh and bone because that's what comprises an entity in this world. So they have the power to forsake their first estate and assume the shape of whatever world they choose. But they're not unlimited in what they can do. When they came into this world, they also took on the limitations of this world. I mean, they do have powers that are way beyond human, but molecules are still molecules, so they're limited. Just like we are."

"You're saying they're flesh and bone?"

"Yes. That's the point I'm trying to make. So don't panic."

Tony point to a surveillance camera. "But if they're flesh and bone, then how do they avoid every camera in this place? We've been trying for weeks to get them on camera but it's like they're invisible."

"Their signature is probably the same as the open air," said Janet. "Cameras or radar give you a signal because the electromagnetic waves bounce off something made of matter. But these things *absorb* radar and light just like antimatter would do. They absorb the electrical current of this world without any blowback. And that's why no signal bounces back to you. That's why you can't see them electronically by radar or camera."

Tony turned his head. "I figured I would end up in this kind of hell. God knows I deserve it."

"We need to get back to the Observation Room," said Isaiah. "That room is its ultimate objective because if it gains control over the collider, and opens the portal, it's over." He scanned faces. "For all of us."

"Yeah," Roy muttered, and chambered his rifle. "Lock and load, boys. If it wants anything from here, it's gonna have to live it out with us."

***

In what seemed like a surreal and strange calm, every physicist that had been cowering within the elevator resumed their stations in the Observation Room with only the faintest minutiae of fear. Their eyes darted to mark the slightest fluctuation and yet they said nothing as each seemed to accept the situation with remarkable resolution now that they were relatively safe—at least for a while.

No one had spoken for half an hour as the seventeen CERN guards worked alongside the Delta commandos, all of them having taking orders without a single question or a split-second's hesitation to do exactly what they were told. And within that half-hour they had erected what seemed like a formidable barrier of desks, consoles, chairs, file cabinets, and anything they could tear from the walls, further barricading the south corridor.

Leaning against a wall, staring impassively with Amanda beside him, Isaiah watched as Roy walked up, wiping sweat. He spoke as he tried to catch a breath, "All of that won't slow it down more for than a few seconds. But it's giving them something to do. I'd rather have an angry soldier than a scared one."

Isaiah glanced at the ATLAS; Roy followed the gaze.

"Now what?" Roy asked.

"So we can't destroy the ATLAS, huh?" asked Isaiah. "Not without killing everyone down here?"

"Nope." Roy wiped the back of his neck. "Can't be done. Not without freezing this place along with the collider because the corridors run parallel to each other and the wall separating them isn't thick enough to contain the blast."

"We need another idea."

"Then you'd better think of one because I'm fresh out."

"Janet," stated Isaiah.

She raised her face. "Yeah?"

"Who in this room knows the most about this collider?"

A woman stood at a console. She was brown-haired, middle aged, and her brunette hair must have once been beautiful, but now looked like a ragged wig torn and blown by the wind. Her face was pale beneath tear-streaked makeup.

"I'm Margaret," she stated, all business. "I know more about this place than anybody except Francois."

"Can you turn on that collider?" Isaiah asked.

Margaret blinked. "Why would you want to do that?"

More slowly, Isaiah asked, "Can you ... *open* ... the collider?"

Margaret paused. "Yes."

"To the very same portal these things came from?"

"Yes." Margaret hesitated. "I can."

"And you can close it?"

"Yes."

"On command?"

Margaret's head tilted. "That's a strange question. We've never been able to keep it open for more than a nanosecond. The only way I know how to shut it down intentionally would be to pull the plug." She paused, face half-turning, as her eyes grew suspicious. Or even frightened. "What are you thinking?"

Isaiah's gaze locked on the ATLAS.

"Can you open two dimensions at the same time?"

Margaret leaned sharply on the console. "*What*?"

"Can you make two dimensions collide?" Isaiah asked again.

Everyone was staring at the exchange.

Margaret's gaze aimlessly roamed as if searching for someone to help. "We *might* be able to do that. I mean, that's all neutrinos are, theoretically. They're particles that can be from anywhere. So, yeah, I think it's possible. But it's never been done. There's no formula for it. I don't even think it's been contemplated. Why are you asking?"

"Yeah," Roy asked quietly. "What are you thinking?"

Isaiah abruptly pushed off the wall and walked toward Margaret and she didn't move until Isaiah stood before her and leaned down. Then Isaiah asked distinctly, "What happens to a human being standing inside the ATLAS when the particles collide and it opens a portal to another dimension?"

Margaret's mouth opened but no words emerged. Finally she managed, "Are you thinking about getting *inside* the ATLAS and then opening a portal to several dimensions at full power?"

"*That's insane!*" Roy shouted, angrily stepping forward. "What good is it going to do to die inside that thing? That'd be like exposing yourself to the core of a nuclear reactor! It'll fry your shadow to the wall!"

"Margaret, I'm not your enemy," Isaiah said calmly. "Whatever comes out of that ATLAS is the enemy. And they're not taking prisoners. I don't care what they've told you here. I don't care what kind of Shiva drivel they've driven into your head or how much money they've paid you to pretend you believe in that nonsense." He didn't blink. "I need your help to make two dimensions meet with this dimension."

For a long moment Margaret simply blinked. "You're telling me that you want *two* dimensions to collide with *this* dimension? At the same time?" She gazed at the console. "Uh … I think the machine is capable of it, but there's no procedure. We would have to just take our best guess." She raised a gaze. "Why would we do that? It might result in an explosion that could level this planet. God only knows."

Isaiah turned has face to the door as a distant crash rumbled in the tunnel. He looked at Roy as the major said, "Janet, check the screens."

A moment later Janet remarked, "It just knocked down the furthest vault. That's … um … twenty vaults away. But I don't think that's the big one." She hit another button to watch "playback," and clicked it forward. "It took it almost a half hour, but it finally cracked the titanium. The stronger one did it a lot faster." She looked at Roy. "I guess his big brother gave him some tips and now this one has figured out where the Observation Room is and it's coming as fast as it can."

Amanda dryly commented, "It knows where we're at because it's already looked everywhere else. God, that thing is dumb."

"How long do we have?" asked Roy.

Janet's lips moved silently. "I'd estimate six hours more or less. I don't think the vaults are going to slow it down more than that." She gestured to the screen. "It may have taken it a half hour to tear down one vault but it succeeded, so it'll succeed with the rest of them."

Roy moved to Tony. "What kind of ordinance do you have?"

Tony dismally responded, "Major, all we got are these Bushmaster M4A3s. Some of us have Benelli M4s." He shook his head. "We're only equipped to handle a civilian attack. We are not equipped with RPGs or Dragons or even a damn .50 caliber that might stop a Leo 2A4, a Merkava IV, or an M1A1 Abrams. We don't have *anything* that will hit with 300-millimeter armor penetration, so hitting that thing with these slingshots will be like throwing popcorn at it from a 747."

"Good grief," Roy muttered. "So much for safeguarding the most dangerous machine in the world." He added, "Tanto? Rig that last Semtex for remote detonation on my command. No delay."

Tanto's chin dropped a fraction. "Are you sure, major?"

"Yeah."

Roy took the daypack—the last satchel—and knelt, removing a remarkably small timing machine connected by multicolored wires to a transparent cellophane bag that contained—what looked to Amanda—like pink toothpaste.

Amanda was staring with fascination and noticed Janet was much the same as Tanto began pulling wires from the timer and twisting them together. He stuck two naked wires through the cellophane covering of the bag and began adjusting a series of dials so small that Amanda could only read dots.

"What are you planning to do?" asked Janet.

"Yeah," chimed Amanda. "What are you guys gonna do?"

Roy muttered, "If I can figure out some way to channel the blast, we're going to ambush it with this satchel. But we have to focus the force of the explosion or we'll bust open the collider."

Isaiah was hovering over the device, staring down.

"Use the vault," he said.

Roy stopped moving. Then he gazed about the room. "I don't think we have anything tough enough to knock a hole in that titanium, man. And I'd have to place this *inside* that vault at the point furthest from the wall. But ten feet of niobium-titanium vault plus this much cement and steel might be enough to soften the blast so that it doesn't crack the wall and bust open the collider." He paused. "And kill us all."

"A laser beam," said Margaret hesitantly. "Would that work?"

Roy scowled, "This place has a laser beam?"

"There's one upstairs," she nodded. "Maybe the laser could carve out a hole in the vault just big enough to hold the satchel."

Roy lifted his face to the ceiling. "Upstairs?" He gazed on her again. "What good does that do us? We're not taking this place out of lockdown. Not even to grab a laser."

Amanda stepped forward. "We might have time," she said quietly. "It's still twenty vaults away. It won't be here for hours."

"We *might* have time, yeah," Roy nodded. "But we don't know what other doors might open besides the vaults, and then that thing could reach the surface." His tone softened. "I took the risk once but I ain't taking it again. What's your name? Amanda?"

She nodded.

"Don't get me wrong. It's a good suggestion, Amanda." The commando smiled. "Sorry if I'm coming across a little short. I appreciate your ideas. But I'm not willing to take this place out of lockdown."

"There's a way to get upstairs while we're still in lockdown," said Margaret, "I'm privy to it because I was briefed by Director Francois. It's the same way he escaped."

A physicist in the room erupted to her feet glaring at Margaret. "You bitch!" she screamed. "Why didn't we use it to escape!"

Margaret replied dully, "You knew the risks when you signed up, Jennifer." She focused on Roy. "Francois used a door that's not on the blueprints. Just like those sub-doors aren't on any blueprints and they're hidden from the public."

Roy looked at Margaret. "Where's this door?"

"It's halfway down the hall on the left. It looks like a solid wall but there's a temperature control module that's actually a keypad and it opens the door."

"Where's the laser?"

"It's a few feet down the hall topside. It looks like a utility room."

"What's the code for the escape door?"

"Only the director knows."

"I'll bypass it," Roy grunted. "What about the code for the utility room?"

"I don't know."

"We'll deal with it when we get to it." He turned to Isaiah. "How do you wanna do this? I'm going after the laser. Do you want to come or do you want to stay?" He gestured. "I'd offer you a gun, but I see you've got your own way of doing things."

"I'll stay here," stated Isaiah. "Take at least ten of the strongest guards with you. This isn't Star Trek and I don't think this is a laser. And if I'm right, it weighs a ton."

"All right," Roy nodded, "you handle it down here. They're more scared than they look so they could use you."

"What makes you say that?"

"Word gets around. They respect you."

Isaiah's frown revealed nothing more.

Roy turned to the guards. "We're going after this laser. But everybody is coming back here. And if any man tries to go over the hill, I'll kill you. I need ten strong men. No bad backs. We ain't got time."

All of them stepped forward and Roy selected a team, beginning with the biggest. Last, Roy placed his hand on Tanto's shoulder and said, "Now, for you gentlemen staying behind, I am placing Tanto in command. And Tanto has killed more men than cancer so you should be safe. Got it?"

Nods.

With an arm elaborately decorated with violent red, black, and green tattoos, Tanto lifted his heavy black rifle, settling the stock on his hip.

He didn't smile.

"This is where we hold the line, boys."

***

After Roy's crew disappeared, Janet found some military-style Meals Ready to Eat in a cabinet and microwaved them. As everyone finished up their preferred cuisine, Amanda remarked, "Only the military could spend a million dollars in research and come up with something that tastes just like SpaghettiOs."

Isaiah tossed his uneaten meal into a trashcan and turned to Janet. "Do these creatures have any kind of electromagnetic signature at all?"

"No more than sunshine or your reflection in a mirror," Janet shook her head. "It seems like they absorb light, radar, electrons, whatever we've got. I'm becoming convinced that's how they've managed to exist in this dimension in the first place."

Isaiah straightened. "Thanks."

He entered the corridor and saw that Tanto had assumed a position behind all the CERN guards. It was almost as if Tanto had taken a post where he would shoot the first man to mutiny. Isaiah simply stood, staring at the barrier.

Isaiah's mind wandered to when the creature had smashed blow after blow into that submarine hatch. He wasn't certain but he estimated that that hatch was designed to resist hundreds of thousands of pounds of pressure per square inch, which was probably the only reason it had withstood the onslaught. But that was taking very little from the beast. It had done enough damage to the steel to convince Isaiah that it would have prevailed if it had continued. And with the thought Isaiah tried get a rough estimate of the beast's limitations.

Yeah, Isaiah calculated quickly enough, it was phenomenally strong, but the fact that it was limited at all meant that it was ultimately vulnerable and ultimately killable. The only question was whether they could survive long enough to take it apart piece by piece. He assessed its main advantages—strength, speed, durability, intelligence, and training. And its determination and emotional character, a combination of ambition, hate, and rage had helped propel it from one galaxy to another so its advantage in sheer will power was quite simply off the map.

But it did have two disadvantages: It was practically alone and it *was* ultimately vulnerable. So if they could trap it where they could hit it with enough ordinance to bleed it to death drop by drop, then it would fall, in the end. But that brought Isaiah back to the question of whether they could survive long enough to do enough damage fast enough and that was a serious wild card.

Isaiah spoke without looking directly at Tanto, "You guys operate in small teams, don't you, Tanto?"

With a frown he nodded, "Yep."

"What do they teach you to do if you're outmatched in every way?"

"They teach us to run," Tanto stated with no hesitation. "Or EVAC. Or hide. Or escape. To disappear. To get the hell out of there. Know what I mean?" He shook his head. "We ain't regular Army, man. We don't operate at battalion strength. We don't have artillery. We usually don't even have air support. So if we're outmatched, we do what damage we can and then we hit the water, the woods, urban areas or slums, whatever we got. We do a tactical retreat and reposition to fight another day."

"And if retreat is impossible?"

"Then we set up a defensive ambush." Tanto shrugged. "An ambush can be a game-changer, but an ambush is a gamble because an ambush can work both ways and usually does. It can put you in a position where you absolutely have to win or you're gonna die and it makes retreat, if it doesn't work, a thousand times more difficult." He regarded Isaiah with a curious gaze. "You're wondering how we can turn the tables on these bastards because they have every advantage, right?"

"Yeah, pretty much."

"Good luck with that one," Tanto laughed harshly. "We can't retreat. There's no high ground for an ambush. There's not even any solid cover. This is what we call a standup fight and it's gonna be won by whoever has the will to win it." He shook his head. "Ain't no school for it. Never was."

Isaiah paused. "No," he said. "Never was."

They stood shoulder to shoulder like two scarred and hardened veterans facing execution. Neither revealed any weakness, fear, nor regret. It was as they had lived their whole lives in this arena by choice or by fate and neither was surprised that it had come to this, nor would they have changed a thing.

Slowly Isaiah nodded, "Yeah." He paused. "All right. I'll be in the Observation Room. I'll let you know if we see anything."

"Good enough."

Inside the chamber, Janet was staring with obvious confusion at six monitors as if they were dedicated to a single task. Amanda was behind her, arms crossed, also staring, and they were muttering to one another. Isaiah walked up and watched, but what he saw would have confused anyone with less than a doctorate in physics—it was a truly dazzling display of incomprehensible symbols.

He saw that every other physicist was gazing at the same set of screens. Then he noticed Margaret standing on an elevated platform surrounded by a semicircle of monitors blinking with every color of light and exhaustive equations filling page after page only to be replaced by more equations as the last ones blinked out.

Slowly Isaiah mounted the steps and stood beside Margaret to ask, "How's the math coming?"

Margaret didn't glance up.

"Oh, it's just hunky-dory."

After a pause, staring with unsuccessful calculation at the screen, Isaiah gave up and asked, "What's your best guess?"

"Of making particles from two separate dimensions collide at the speed of light inside the ATLAS at the same time?" Margaret freely laughed. "Until now we've only been able to detect particles from one dimension. But since we know the equation that opened the portal that vomited these things out, we're back-engineering to see if we can simultaneously open an opposing portal. It's actually not as complicated as it sounds. That is, mathematically. But there's no way to confirm my calculations. I can't guarantee what's going to happen if we pull the trigger on this."

Amanda appeared at Isaiah's side. "Pardon me, but this is insane. And how will any of this … this interdimensional hopscotch … get us out of here?"

"Getting out of here is not the priority, anymore," Isaiah said quietly. "We have to do something to close this portal or everybody on this planet's gonna die." He turned to Amanda. "I'm sorry, Amanda, but I can't make any promises about Cynthia. I'm going inside the ATLAS to detonate the bomb in their dimension and seal this portal if I can. But if that doesn't work, you'll have to destroy the portal from this side. And that means all of you will die, too. Either way, it's unlikely any of us are getting out of here alive. So, ultimately, there's no reason why I *shouldn't* try. It sure can't get any worse."

Amanda's voice was faint. "Yeah … I know. Cynthia is dead. I've accepted that. But this seems like a real bad idea for you." She paused. "For everybody else, too."

Margaret sighed and raised her face. "Amanda, I'm sorry about your sister. I knew Cynthia. I really liked her. But bad ideas are all we have left. What will happen when we bring all three dimensions together? Who knows? Each dimension, if everything goes as planned, will be on a subatomic level equal to the level of antimatter particles that existed before this universe was created. What I'm trying to do is calculate the last moment before the Big Bang. And Isaiah, I do believe, plans to alter that moment so that these portals don't come into existence in *any* timeline—including this one." She raised a gaze to Amanda. "In other words Isaiah is going to try and alter the course of every galaxy in existence by altering the chain reaction created by the original Big Bang."

Isaiah muttered, "It's got potential."

"So does suicide," Margaret said without hesitation. "Do you have any idea what might happen to you if you're inside that machine when I hit the switch?"

Isaiah's voice was dull. "A short history of time?"

"You could get yourself dead at the speed of light." Margaret pointed to numbers on the largest screen. "That equation is the place where these things come from. But we've also located another … well, *area* … that has the opposite readout as this dimension. And if we can smash these diametrically opposite neutrinos together, we might be able to make all three dimensions converge before the Big Bang and then you can set off that bomb, trigger a new Big Bang, and recreate everything that exists. If it works, you might do away with these creatures completely. You'll make it so they've never existed." She blinked, a dead stare. "Isaiah, you do know you could also wipe out the Earth, don't you?"

Isaiah frowned, "I don't believe timelines are that malleable. Throwing a rock in the Mississippi River isn't going to change the course of the river."

"Okay. That's possible. But have you also considered that you could be beamed into nothing but outer space and die on arrival?"

"You agreed that the idea has potential."

Margaret placed a hand on her chest. "Why are you listening to *me*? What do I know? This isn't physics! This is just a Persian bazaar guessing game and I have no idea what's going to happen! To put it mildly, you're *truly* going where no man has gone before!" She gestured to the screen. "I mean, sure! There's a chance that the opposite electrical charges and the matter, antimatter collision from these dimensions will open a gateway and then you can destroy this alien dimension with a nuclear weapon but I can't promise that! You're talking about smashing one irresistible force into another irresistible force! And now we're talking *real* butterfly effects! I'm talking about the kind of butterfly effects that might destroy the matrix of everything that has ever existed anywhere in any galaxy in the history of everything!"

Janet had stepped into the room with the last words. She focused on Isaiah. "You're taking the bomb with you inside the ATLAS?"

Isaiah cast a glance. "I'm setting off the bomb and closing the portal from the other side if I can. Maybe it will even destroy that dimension."

Janet: "What about *this* dimension? What about this timeline?"

"If Margaret is right, the explosion will be contained in the moment that existed before the Big Bang. And if you want to get theoretical about it, this has all happened before and what we're doing is just another repeat of the event that created the Big Bang in the first place. It's like a time loop." He paused. "Safe to say we're in uncharted waters."

"Without a paddle," muttered Margaret.

Janet turned and walked from the Observation Room.

Margaret slowly turned in her chair, gazing up with a fatal stare. "Isaiah? You know, of course, that anybody who pretends to understand this time paradox is a fool? And that includes me." Her lips tightened. "And what you are proposing has never been imagined by the craziest science fiction writer that ever lived. It has—*for certain*—never been calculated by any physicist because this is *beyond* the place where the map ends! In this event we are lost at sea with no stars, no sky, no sun and no moon to show us the way home. All we've got is dead reckoning in the darkest night. This is *The* Unknown." A pause. "Here, there be dragons. And you're going to land right in its mouth."

***

A wall panel soundlessly opened.

Roy gazed up the white, spiraling stairs leading toward the surface and turned to Janet who had suddenly arrived, breathless and staring up.

"You stay here," Roy stated sternly. "I'm going up to grab this French fry. Then I'll get back with him and the laser."

"Wait a minute!" Janet gasped, grabbing his arm. "Did you know that Isaiah is taking the bomb with him into the ATLAS?"

"Yeah," Roy nodded curtly. "We talked about it. Why not?"

"Because he could blow us all up!"

"We're gonna get blown up, anyway, if we don't do something!" Roy stared as Janet lowered her gaze. Then he added more quietly, "It'll be all right. Just stay here. I'm going up. C'mon, guys. On me."

"You might need me up there!" stated Janet.

"They've got more problems down here than I'll have up there," Roy muttered. "I can handle this psychopath. And these boys can carry this laser, or whatever it is, down here. But you've got to help Margaret and Amanda keep an eye on those monitors." He paused, staring back. "Can you do that for me?"

Janet blinked, "Yeah. Okay."

Roy nodded.

"See you on the range."

***

Leaning back, Margaret muttered, "Ya know, when you asked me if a human being could survive being inside the ATLAS with particles from three dimensions colliding at the same time … I mean, it was so crazy, I didn't really take you seriously." Her gaze was empty. "But, seriously, are you serious?"

Isaiah mumbled, "You sure make it sound like I'm serious."

"Yeah," she nodded, "I've thought of suicide once or twice myself. But I want to say that your survival, even if you can beat that explosion out the gateway of this demonic dimension or whatever it is, is very unlikely. Now, I honestly don't believe there's a crippling level of radiation inside the ATLAS, but we don't know what unknown radiation these alternate dimensions are made of."

Isaiah stated precisely, "I just want to know if you can you keep the portal open long enough for me to detonate the bomb inside that dimension and escape the blast by retreating into this dimension."

Briefly nodding, Margaret said, "If the power isn't interrupted. If the collider can handle more than a hundred trillion volts of electricity for that long. If some twenty-dollar chip doesn't burn up and the whole thing melts. On balance ... I'd say the odds are eighty-twenty."

"Eighty that I make it?"

"The opposite."

Isaiah gazed at the ceiling. "I already know this is probably a one-way trip, so just do what you can and I'll do what I can to beat the explosion out the door." He was quiet. "At this point I don't think it's up to you and me."

"It never was," muttered Margaret. "But what if the bomb doesn't even affect that dimension? What if they're just, like, spirits that can't be destroyed by force?"

"Then you blow the collider from this side."

Margaret brushed her hair back. "I knew I should have taken that job at the South Pole. At least it would have been boring."

Isaiah stated, "I just want to be perfectly clear. You said that once I'm inside the collider, and these particles smash into each other, everything inside that ATLAS will be outside space and time? I won't be on Earth, right? I'll be at whatever existed a few moments before the Big Bang?"

Margaret closed her eyes before replying steadily, "As far as I calculate, that is mathematically correct. You will be outside space and time. You will be in the heart of the power that created everything that exists and there is not a time when it was *not*. You will supposedly be at the heart of the Big Bang a few moments before it went boom." She shook her head as if to shake off fog. "Good lord. You could be right. For all we know, this has already happened. This might be the event that triggered the Big Bang in the first place."

Isaiah hesitated a moment, and his voice was fatal. "How much longer do you need to check your numbers?"

"I just have to double-check things."

"Be careful to keep the collider down until we need it. Then program what you did when Cynthia was taken."

"Isaiah? One more thing you should think about."

"Yeah?"

"Have you thought of the possibility that they might be waiting for you on the other side? I mean, you're here. You're prepared, yeah. But what about them? They might be prepared, too, and they're ready to kick your ass on arrival."

Isaiah sniffed. "Have you also considered that whatever I do on the other side is just going to bring me back here again? Have you considered that you and I are destined to do this over and over until the end of time?"

Margaret's dismal stare revealed her mind.

"I try not to consider everything."

***

Antonio Francois gasped as Roy's hand tightened on his throat.

The Delta commando had lifted the larger Frenchman from the ground with a single arm to slam him against the wall and leaned close.

"Where's the laser?"

Francois's face twisted as he gasped, "What laser!" He grabbed Roy's wrist to no effect. "We don't have a laser!"

Roy dropped him to the floor, enunciating each word as he drew his pistol. "Then I ain't got no use for you."

"Wait!" Francois plaintively lifted both hands. "Wait a second! Why do you need a laser?"

"To cut a hole in the titanium."

"Who told you we could do that?"

"One of your people." Roy thumbed back the hammer on the forty-five. "You'd better produce something or you're a dead man."

"We do have something that they use for cutting titanium!" Francois retorted. "But I don't know what it is! All I know is that maintenance uses it! It's in the closet down the hall!"

Roy half-turned his head and the ten security team members that had been dispatched by Tony, who had become a *very* loyal supporter of this endeavor, were out the door. As they exited, Roy shoved the director into the hall and, when they reached the closet, found it was locked with a code module.

"What's the code?" asked Roy.

"How would I know?" sputtered Francois. "I'm not in maintenance! I just run the facility!"

"Fire in the hole," Roy said as he pulled out a small block from his belt and slammed it against the lock. He turned aside as he pushed a detonator and the explosion shredded the lock, frame, and wall so that the door freely swung open.

Behind it were three steel canisters connected by multicolored tubes.

Roy looked at Francois and the physicist's eyes widened with apparent alarm as he gestured wildly, "Don't ask me!"

A security guard stepped forward, then bent and seemed to gaze along the gauges and dials. He turned to Roy. "I think it's a plasma arc welder, major."

Roy squinted. "What's that?"

"It's a welding machine, sir. It's similar to oxy-acetylene welders used by high-steel workers. But this thing uses ionized gas, electrodes, and a plasma arc that heats up to fifty-thousand degrees Fahrenheit." The guard stared at the machine. "This thing, when it's lit, it does look like a laser beam so I understand their confusion. But it's not a laser beam. It's just ionized gas."

Roy pointed. "Do you know how to use it?"

"I know the procedures on paper," the guard nodded. "I learned the basics in trade school. I was going to be a welder for CAT. But this thing is tricky. It's not oxygen-based welding. And a lot can go wrong."

"What do you mean?"

"Well, sir, a normal welder will hit maybe ten thousand degrees with the right mix. But this uses very explosive gases in an atomized plasma arc. And if you get the wrong mix going, it could blow us all to hell."

"What gases?" asked Roy.

"Hydrogen, helium, oxygen, nitrogen; that's what's in these canisters."

"Can it melt that slab?"

"Sir, this welder can melt *dirt*," the guard answered. "It can easily melt niobium-titanium, which is what those slabs are made of." He cautiously placed a hand on the machine. "This thing, if you set it to the right mix, it gets as hot as the center of the sun. It can melt a hole through *anything*."

Roy slung his rifle.

"Let's get it downstairs."

***

"What is that!" Janet shouted.

Everyone was instantly at Janet's monitoring station staring at a screen as one of the titanium shields virtually disintegrated at what seemed like the impact of a cannon blast. One second later, dust and debris began to settle and for one split-second a shape could be seen covered in white dust.

Amanda hit "stop" on the keyboard and froze the image.

"That's it!" Amanda shouted, pointing. "That's the one that chased me and Isaiah in the collider tunnel!"

Margaret muttered, "So that's a demon, huh?" A corner of her mouth quirked. "Well, I know this sounds childish, but just how strong is that thing? I mean, in animal terms?"

"If I'm right," Isaiah answered, "some are stronger than others. They all have different purposes so they all have different strengths. I'd say that one is at least as strong as a gorilla."

"And you say this one's a soldier?"

"That's my guess."

"You seriously think this is a demon?" Margaret pressed. "Like an Old Testament demon? That kind of demon?"

Isaiah sighed before, "The word, 'demon,' is just a word we use to describe what we don't understand. No matter how good someone's imagination is, nobody can imagine what a god or a demon or a ghost or an angel is truly like or where it's from. But that creature is definitely not from this world. And if this task is important, and I think it is, then I imagine his boss sent his best man, so he's probably as strong as they get."

Janet asked hesitantly, "I hate to even ask what sounds like such a simpleton question, but are you implying that the Biblical Satan is this thing's boss?"

"I guess it's as good as any other theory."

"So this a bonified card-carrying demon, huh?"

"Well, he ain't no Mormon." Isaiah leaned on the desk, staring at the screen. "A belief in these bizarre entities is older than recorded history. Even today, it's a concept that's prevalent in every culture on the planet. Some kind of monster that comes for you at night. Steals your children. Terrorizes you. Kills your family. And every culture has a different name for them. They're called demons, asuras, tzitzimimeh, shayatin, shedim, daevas, djinn, or alu. And every culture has a different name for their dimension. Some call it Hell. Others call it Sheol, Xibalba, Narakam, Diyu, Tartaros, Kuzimo, Vffern, Peklo, Hades, or Hellheim. It's a thousand names for the same creature, a thousand titles for the same place, but the whole world believes that there's *something* out there. So since the entire world holds the same concept, I am inclined to believe that *some* kind of entity meets our crude definition of a demon. And that one fits the bill for me."

Amanda asked, "But didn't you tell me that knowing a demon's name was the secret to controlling it? And that using a demon's name was something that even Jesus did?

So knowing its name would give us power over it." She stared. "Wouldn't it?"

"That's just Jewish folklore."

"But you said all the other folklore had proven true."

"Well, maybe that part is true, too. But since I don't know its name, it's a moot point."

"At least it's honest about its intentions," muttered Margaret. "It wants to kill every one of us."

"Take the worst part of yourself and imagine what you'd be like," Isaiah nodded. "That's what you're looking at."

"You have a very poor opinion of the human race," said Margaret. "Although after two divorces I tend to agree."

"That thing is just more honest about its evil," said Isaiah. "Everybody lies. Everybody steals. Everybody even kills in their own way. It's just a matter of how. The only difference between that thing and us is that it comes from another place and it makes no pretensions about being anything other than what we classify as pure evil."

Amanda said quietly, "That's a really dismal attitude, Isaiah."

"In this world the strong feed on the weak in a thousand ways. If they can't use you, they destroy you. So you're either a prince, a slave, or an outlaw." Isaiah pointed at the ghostly image encapsulated in white dust. "That one's a gladiator. And he's hungry."

Janet asked, "And the other one?"

There was an uncertain gesture before Isaiah said, "I guess they always work two by two. Like a master and his disciple. That's not something Jesus invented. It goes back a few thousand years before him. I wouldn't be surprised that other galaxies came up with the same idea. It's just logical to send out a group of people to accomplish something instead of a single person. I don't think the earth has a monopoly on reason."

Everyone was silent before a voice groaned in the corridor.

"A little help here!"

Isaiah led them out the door to see Roy in front of ten guards straining to carry a huge, gray metallic machine attached to gigantic steel cylinders. Each man was glistening with sweat and each was visibly bent with faces contorted and moaning, in various languages, what sounded like heartfelt curses.

Roy gasped, "This son of a bitch weighs a ton!" He hauled a few breaths. "You idiots gonna just stand there or what!"

Tony and the rest of the guards rushed forward, each lending a hand in the lifting and carrying as Janet broke into a laugh. As the burden was removed from Roy, he collapsed against the wall, bent with hands on knees. His head was lifting slightly with every breath as Janet walked forward and placed a hand on his shoulder. "You still wanna be a cattle rancher? It's hard work."

"Not now," gasped Roy. He turned to the other guards who were, to a man, in a disinclined posture. "Is everybody still alive?"

Heads nodded and Janet heard a few harsh utterances in what sounded like German or Swiss or a very irritated mix of both. Then Janet noticed Director-General Francois at the rear of the crowd with both hands behind his back. She didn't know if his hands were cuffed or tied or if that was merely his attempt at a dignified repose, but his face clearly revealed livid indignation.

Roy slapped a small semiautomatic in Janet's hand and pointed at Francois, "Make this ugly bastard open the first two vaults so we can set up this gear at the third door!" He removed a Colt Commander Model .45 from his belt—Isaiah knew the gun from his background—and aimed at Francois. "If you do not do exactly what she tells you to do I will blow your head clean off and thank you for giving me an excuse. Do you understand?"

Janet had already moved, not caring one whit about what Francois had to say. She grabbed his arm, noticed that his wrists were indeed handcuffed, and pulled him toward the Observation Room saying, "I can't open just one vault. But you can. So you're going to open those next two vaults south of here, *and only those*. And you'll keep them open until I tell you to close them."

Francois began to speak.

"Save it!" Janet snapped and chambered the semiauto. "I never worked for you, anyway. I'm with the Central Intelligence Agency."

Francois's face twisted. "All of you are liars! The CIA! Your president swore he wouldn't let you interfere!"

"That was the *last* president, you pervert." Janet pushed the director into a seat. "America has a new sheriff and he only gives psychopaths like you one chance. *You* can destroy this place or he'll destroy it for you. Now, open those vaults. And *only* those vaults."

"You're all going to die," muttered Francois and began typing a code Janet had never seen. If she was back at MIT, she would have assumed that it was a fragment of a virus aimed at overriding the continental power grid.

One vault, then the second vault rose out of view.

"Now fix it so I can override the lockdown and turn the power on for the collider. And don't get cute. I'm catching every keystroke. And whether you believe it or not, I'm a genius." Janet placed the barrel of a pistol to his head. "Now."

Francois typed in a long command and finally swiveled the chair. "There. You have what you want. Now what?"

"Roy!" she called, but when she turned Roy was already close and took the steel cuffs. He pushed Francois's chair violently to the wall and hooked one cuff to a pipe. Then he spun the director in the chair and leaned close. "I don't care what that thing is. But you need to get something straight.

That thing is here to kill us. All of us. So if you wanna get out of here alive, you'll cooperate."

Stepping back, Roy turned to Janet, who stepped forward to support him. "Look," she said lightly. "Take a seat. You need to eat."

Roy grimaced in pain, "What about you guys?"

"We already ate."

"Where'd you find food?"

Janet opened a cabinet and pulled out a bag. "In here. I think it's what you Army guys eat in the field. What do you call them?"

"MREs?"

"Yeah. They have an emergency supply down here. Give me one minute. I'll heat up a bag of cardboard lasagna and then you can set the Semtex." She glanced at the screen. "They've reached the third vault. Is that where you're gonna put it?"

Roy nodded with what seemed perilous exhaustion, "Yeah." He lifted the radio. "Tanto?" A moment. "Tanto? Do you copy?" He waited. "Tanto!"

A strained reply: "*Copy, major.*"

"Make sure that guard only burns a hole halfway through that vault. Make it just big enough for the satchel and not an inch more." Roy paused for breath. "Do *not* let him burn through that door. Make sure he knows that. And watch him. Stop him just as soon as it's big enough to hold the satchel. Roger that?"

"*Roger that, major.*"

Dropping his arm to his side, still holding the radio, Roy simply rested, saying nothing. He was breathing more deeply and steadily as Janet removed the bag from the microwave and laid it on the desk with a fork.

"Come on, Roy. This ain't over yet."

"This is hell and gone from over," he shook his head. "Those things are coming like freight trains and I'm not sure if we have enough ordinance to even put one of them down." He grimaced. "If that satchel doesn't at least wound it, we're gonna have a helluva close quarter battle session. But if we're going down, so are they. I swear to you."

Janet put a fork in his hand. "Eat. There's time to talk. And they've already started on the vault." She peered at the screen. "Wow. A laser beam."

Roy mechanically began shoveling food. "It's not a laser," he mumbled. "It's something else. But it'll get the job done."

"Yeah, well, it looks like a laser beam." Janet glanced at Francois. "My, how the mighty fall," she said with no semblance of compassion. "And where are your friends now? They could have easily flown you out of here when you were upstairs. What? They didn't take your call?" She laughed. "So, they've thrown you under the bus to save their ass and institution. I bet, when this is over, they'll say that this whole fiasco was your fault. They'll talk about how you exceeded the limits of your authority with unauthorized tests. They'll publish papers about how you violated protocol. How does it feel to be alone?"

"I am not alone, you cretin!"

Janet laughed, "You're going to die in a maximum-security prison with your dream unrealized, so you can drop the masquerade. That is, if you don't get eaten alive first. Or shot dead by Roy. Or me." She paused. "I've never actually killed a man but, in your case, I don't think it would bother me a whole lot."

"Neither the United States, nor Switzerland, nor France has jurisdiction here," Francois muttered. "CERN is a legally recognized institution bordering two nations and neither of them will cooperate with your nation or even the United Nations! Why do you think we choose this location in the first place?" He sneered, "Do you think we're fools? We planned for this contingency!"

"You didn't build here for diplomatic or security reasons, director. You perverts chose to build here because this place stands on the temple of one of your gods—Apollonia to be exact. But none of that matters because I'm not arresting you by the authority of France or Switzerland or the United Nations. Hell, those guys are in league with you. So they're not even going to know we have you. And neither will any other country that bankrolls this obscenity." Janet smiled. "We're keeping you to ourselves."

Francois fixed her with a sullen stare. "Your authority stops at your borders and you have vowed to execute your duty without prejudice and only within your jurisdiction. What makes you think you can arrest me?"

"Oh, I'm well within my authority, Francois, because I'm a bonded federal officer sworn to protect my country's secrets anywhere in the world and I'm arresting you for *spying* on the United States. And spies have no right to a trial by jury, no right to a judge and no right to legal counsel."

"You can't prove I'm guilty of spying!"

"When I get through with your computers, I'll prove it. Do you even know what being a spy means?" Janet stared. "Well, I'll tell you. It means you have no civilian, military, or international rights whatsoever. And you are not protected by the Accords of the Geneva Conventions, either, which only respects uniformed soldiers. It means, basically, Mr. Director, that the United States can legally hold you for the rest of your life without trial or even human contact. As far as the world is concerned, you'll be dead. Leavenworth does have a pretty good library, though. You can always read about how miserably all of you failed to remake this world in the image of your whore."

Francois muttered, "Your own people will crucify you." He trembled with each word. "We have people inside your government, too, you fool! How do you think we've managed to operate without interference for so long? This won't end with my imprisonment! It will end with yours!"

"I hate all this legalese," Roy shook his head. "If he doesn't cooperate, kill him. It don't make no difference to me."

Francois's lips barely moved. "You're a barbarian." He stared at Janet. "You have no idea who or what you've challenged. All your great leaders have been behind this effort since it began. Even your own people will kill you for this. And whether we succeed here or with another supercollider, we *will* open the portal. The hour has come. This is the last generation of mankind's arrogance. And fire unleashed by your so-called God will not destroy this world. But it *will* be destroyed and remade in the image of a goddess that will make your pathetic Yahweh into a slave. And then you will see true power."

"It's a shame *you* won't be around to see it," muttered Roy. "But you're too crazy to appreciate a good light show, anyway."

Francois's voice rose in pitch, "The age of science has been surpassed by a greater age! A far greater age! We have opened a portal that is beyond human knowledge! A portal that makes our greatest scientific achievements look like the skull and bones voodoo of some ignorant savage!" He leaned forward. "All of you will die! And we will live according to how Shiva decides we will live! The hour of the dragon is upon you."

Janet laughed, "Battling mythologies. I see you've chosen your side. But you're not only insane, Francois, you're insanely ignorant. You don't even know the mythologies that you hate and despise." She raked back her hair. "For someone who so murderously hates what other people believe, you're amazingly ignorant about what other people actually *do* believe, Francois. All you have is your pride and prejudice. And neither of them is worth a damn."

"Any movement on those screens?" asked Roy.

Janet shook her head. "There's nothing." She blinked. "It could just be standing there. Or communicating. Or waiting. Or planning. The mind of an interdimensional Jeffrey Dahmer is beyond me."

Roy slid the bag aside. "All right. That was good. Thanks."

"May we share many more cardboard MREs."

"Let's hope not," Roy wiped his mouth. "So how many vaults stand between that thing and the satchel?"

"It has to go through four more vaults before it reaches the welders," said Janet. "Then we'll close the last two doors separating us from the explosion and, if you time it right, you'll blow it up while we're safe in here."

Roy shook his head, "No. I'll have to set off the satchel by remote transmission and a microwave signal won't travel through those vaults. We'll have to leave the doors open between us and that thing until I detonate the bomb and hope for the best."

"But won't the explosion—"

"No," Roy shook his head. "Shrapnel can't turn corners, so if you stay in here, you're safe. And the concussion doesn't have this far of a radius. But there's no guarantee that the explosion will kill that thing, either, so as soon as we blow the vault, we'll have to close on it fast and make sure it's finished." He paused. "We'll see."

Standing, Roy lifted the rifle and glanced out the window of the Observation Room where Margaret and Isaiah stood on the platform of the ATLAS.

"Oh, hell," he muttered. "Now what?"

***

Roy sprang onto the ATLAS platform with energy that would have seemed impossible fifteen minutes ago and asked, "What are you doing out here without some guards, man?" He pointed toward the Observation Window. "We don't know for certain that that thing is in the corridor. It could be in this tunnel."

"Just taking a look," said Isaiah. "Can your men squeeze that hydrogen bomb into this cylinder without damaging these magnets?"

Roy glanced into the ATLAS. "Yeah. There's enough room. But I don't know whether that nuke isn't gonna go active the second those particles start colliding in here. It could go nuclear as soon as Margaret hits the switch."

"Doesn't it have fail safes?"

"It's got seven fail safes. But who knows what's gonna happen when a bunch of protons start hitting it at the speed of light?"

"Understood. I just wanted to know if this chamber is big enough to hold that nuke without damaging any of these magnets," Isaiah continued. "This ATLAS is calibrated with a laser micrometer. If it's off one thousandth of an inch, it won't work."

Roy was glaring nervously at both ends of corridor.

"I think it's good but hurry it up," he said shortly. "This ain't a good defensive position."

"I've seen enough," Isaiah stepped back. "Now I know why I couldn't open this door when Amanda and I were trapped in the corridor. It can only be opened from the control room. Like a bank vault. And Janet didn't know we were down here." He nodded. "Let's get back and prepare a last chance suicide run."

***

Roy carefully stuffed the satchel in the crevice carved into the titanium vault by the plasma arc welder and slowly, silently stepped back. All of them stared down as if it would explode at any second.

"Well," said Roy, "that's the best we can do."

"How big will it be?" asked Isaiah.

"Equal to about five hundred pounds of TNT," Roy answered. "And if that thing has torn its way halfway through this vault when I blow it, he should get the full force. This alloy isn't made to resist that kind of pressure and the walls will amplify the concussion." His gaze flowed across the walls. "The concussion alone might kill it."

"And if it doesn't?" asked Janet.

Roy shrugged, "Then we close on it and try to finish it with regular ordinance. Bullets and grenades. If that thing's made of flesh and blood, it bleeds."

There was a pause.

"Some things can bleed an awful long time," Isaiah observed.

Roy's grunted, "Yeah. I know. I saw a saltwater crocodile bleed for three weeks after it lost a leg. It killed six more villagers before we put it down." He sniffed. "If it bleeds, sure, we can kill it. But some things can bleed long enough to kill you and your whole hometown before it goes down."

"Have you ordered Janet to close the last two vaults once you and the guys lock horns with it?" asked Isaiah.

"Yeah."

"To keep it from reaching the Observation Room in case it kills all of you?"

"Uh huh." Roy placed the stock of the rifle on his hip. "If Delta doesn't kill it in this free-for-all, then there's no more Delta. No more guards. Simple as that. You guys will be on your own. And I hate to say it, but at that point you might as well launch your suicide run. You won't have anything to lose, that's for sure."

For a moment Roy gazed at the ceiling. "But if it does kill me, and you guys somehow manage to finish it, don't be too fast to rush into the light of day. You're gonna have to use a lot of caution if you don't want to get shot dead."

"Why is that?"

"Because I guarantee you that the Swiss army has already set up a perimeter around this mountain. So if this demon, or that collider, doesn't kill you, I can promise you that they will. They'll think you're infected or not even human or some damn thing. To be honest, they're not gonna be looking for a good reason. They'll be scared and there will be a quarantine in place. Standard procedure."

Isaiah nodded, "In the unlikely event any of us survive, I'll remember."

Standing beside Tony, General Jackman stated, "Well, I gotta be honest. This ain't the first suicide mission I've been volunteered for but this is the proverbial end of days mission for sure. Still, if we're gonna die, let's make sure we take those things with us."

Unexpectedly Tony mumbled, "If we're doomed to cash it in, I'd appreciate a chance to pay up some of my debts, if that's even possible." He slowly shook his head. "Christ, I done seen so much war I gave up believing in good and evil a long time ago. But there ain't no contest here, boy. *Hell, no*. This is evil like I ain't never seen evil in thirty years of looking evil dead in the face. And that's saying something."

Margaret's voice emerged from a radio.

"It's one vault away."

Roy pressed the mic.

"We're on our way."

***

As they gathered in the Observation Room Isaiah stood alone in the corridor staring at the vault a half-mile away but he didn't plan to be standing here when that satchel exploded. It didn't take much calculating to know the chances of anything standing within a half-mile of the oncoming detonation, especially when that shrapnel would be channeled down this corridor like machinegun fire.

Roy stuck his head out the door. "C'mon, man! It's on the other side of the vault!"

Isaiah entered the portal and shut it, swiveling the handle.

"Don't do that," said Roy "I need a line of sight."

"What? You have to be standing in the corridor?"

Roy shook his head, "I don't like it, either. That blast is gonna fill that corridor with enough debris to demolish a tank. And as soon as the satchel detonates, we all have to charge down on that thing whether the corridor is on fire or not. We'll just have to take our chances on whether it's wounded."

"How could it *not* be wounded?"

"Hell if I know. They don't train us to fight demons."

Isaiah picked up a spare rifle.

"Forget that," Roy stated. "If we can't stop that thing, we'll only have two chances left to finish this. That's when you initiate your plan and, if you don't succeed, the general blows the satchels on the collider and kills everybody. I only have one question."

"What's that?"

"If you're bound and determined to do this astral travel thing, why don't you go ahead and go? Let us finish these things by ourselves."

Isaiah shook his head. "I can't leave until I know that we've put these two down."

"Why?"

"Because it'll be one less factor I have to calculate on the other side. And the less I have to consider, the better."

"If you go, I want some kind of signal to know whether you've even made it to the other side. Because if you don't make it, we blow the collider. But I am not sending you into Hell's Gate and then kill myself and everyone else in this place when there's a *slim* chance you might actually pull this off."

Everyone stared at Isaiah.

Amanda stepped forward. "I have an idea."

Isaiah turned to her. "No."

"It's the only way!"

"If you go with me, you'll die."

Amanda scanned the room. "What are you talking about? We're probably gonna die, anyway! At least if I go with you, I can bounce back through the gateway and tell Roy that you made it and we still have a chance."

Roy asked tiredly, "Did you just say, 'bounce back through the gateway?'"

"It's a portal!" Amanda raised her hand at the ATLAS. "It's the same thing as a door! And a door swings both ways! If we can go into that dimension through that portal then I can come back through it as long as the collider is still alive! But if you blow up the collider, then Isaiah won't have any way to escape the bomb!"

No one spoke until Margaret stated, "Amanda is right. She can return through the ATLAS as long as the collider is up and running. But she'll only know if Isaiah has made it to the final conflict. She won't know the outcome."

On the wall, a monitor flickered and a fragment was torn from the third vault, the only vault separating them from the creature.

Roy snatched up his rifle. "Lock and load!" He focused on Isaiah. "If we can't put this one down, you try your suicide run. And as soon as Amanda comes back through the portal you got exactly one hour to finish it on the other side." He held up a finger. "You'll have exactly one hour, Ronin, to finish the fight and escape the biggest nuclear blast any dimension has ever seen. Got that?"

Isaiah nodded.

Amanda closed her eyes.

"Talk about a chance in hell," she whispered.

"Whoa!" Janet spun with the word. "It's almost through the vault!"

Roy slammed both hands down on the console before he snatched up the detonator and ran to the door. "Everybody get behind something solid!"

He stuck his arm out the door and pressed the button.

***

Strangely, Amanda heard nothing and within a moment found herself staring at the open door where Roy had disappeared and there was nothing but white light. The air surrounding her was almost solid with a weight that prevented her from even moving her head. But she could also not look away from the door. Then she saw Roy's body fall limply to the floor; he had been pressed against the wall as if by an invisible hand.

Then a roar filled the tunnel and the Observation Room was a liquid thing—as solid as a flood—completely condensing inside the chamber with an invisible mass thundering over her body and inside her head. Then Amanda was screaming as she suddenly found the ability to slam both hands over her ears. And she kept screaming, realizing somehow that it was helping her equalize the pressure inside her body as the last of the explosive effect was gone and there was nothing but silence.

Roy's voice boomed from the door.

"On me!"

He charged into the corridor.

Every man with a weapon scrambled out the door and Amanda raised her gaze to a screen to see a titanic humanoid shape rising from ragged rubble completely sheathed in white debris and dust.

Whether it was wounded or not was impossible to determine but it moved slowly before it staggered and fell. Heavily coated in ash, it was horrifyingly visible and Amanda confirmed what she'd suspected earlier: It seemed to be wearing armor. She didn't know how long she stared before Isaiah snatched up a rifle and ran toward the door.

"*No!*" Margaret screamed. "If you get killed we won't have a chance to close the portal from the other side!"

Isaiah shouted over his shoulder.

"They need all the guns they can get!"

Shots erupted in the corridor as Amanda and Margaret leaped back. And, after a moment, Amanda heard someone say in her voice …

"I thought you didn't like guns …"

***

By the time Isaiah reached the conflict, a holocaust of firepower was focused on a black-and-white shape shattering walls and he knew in a heartbeat that it was the same beast that had attacked them earlier. This time, however, it seemed far greater in scope and Isaiah was certain that it was wearing armor.

It was more than half again the size of the largest grizzly and seemed to be made of stone instead of flesh. Already half a dozen guards lay dead at its feet and it was only beginning to recover from the blast.

It lashed out with a single arm that no one could have anticipated and took a guard's head off at the neck before swiping the half-closed hand back through empty air. Roy bellowed at the wholesale carnage and fired a grenade.

The grenade must have hit the creature dead center but Isaiah didn't know for certain because he was in the air—air thick and blinding with smoke—before he painfully crashed into debris that he didn't take time to identify. He chambered his weapon and struggled to his feet, instantly aiming at the beast.

He held down on the trigger for a long, concentrated blast at what seemed like center-mass of the creature and even in the swirling white dust saw where the bullets were defeated by whatever armor it wore over its torso and head. Isaiah raised aim at its face and kept the trigger pressed and the beast took a series of steps backward, flinging up a single arm as if to ward off the fusillade.

Rifle fire was converging on it from every direction and from every survivor, but the beast would clearly survive the carnage to kill all of them unless they could somehow defeat its armor.

"Get down!" roared Roy, lifting something to his shoulder.

Isaiah knew what it was and dove behind a barely visible bulk of wall large enough to shield him from the detonation of the Javelin—a Light Anti-tank Weapon—and was deafened at the resulting explosion. Isaiah had no idea if anyone else had survived the blast, but he leaped to his feet staggering.

The beast slowly rose.

The blast had knocked it backward and to the floor but didn't kill it. Still, the armored chest revealed a slash of black and green that Isaiah quickly calculated as flesh and blood and it had lost its helmet. Now it's face and head were exposed.

In the speed of the moment Isaiah couldn't be sure, but he saw other rifles erupt with fire and vaguely realized he was not the only survivor.

The beast roared with what could be described as human rage as it charged into a trio of guards, and even though they never ceased firing they didn't live long enough to do any damage. But in the rush of the conflict Isaiah was certain that its armor was not any more impervious to ordinance than steel. Yeah, it could repel bullets and grenades for a time but not forever; they had to pour down on it until they reduced its armor to shreds.

"Son of a bitch!" shouted Roy as he scrambled across the debris and snatched up a fallen rifle. He didn't even rise as he rolled and centered his fire at the gap in its armor that should have been visible to all by now.

The beast protectively closed a hand flat over its chest and raised its other arm across its face as it angrily staggered backward. Then it flung out both arms and bent forward to roar and Isaiah got the first clear glimpse of its face.

Above gaping jaws its eyes were liquid black. But somehow Isaiah saw, or sensed, an end to it—a place where intelligence and strength glassed out like a glade reduced to charcoaled nothingness by a consuming blaze.

They were wearing it down.

"Aim high!" Roy bellowed above the din of gunfire and scrambled across a space, snatching up another Javelin.

Isaiah took a solid stance, pulling the stock of the rifle tight into his shoulder, and aimed for its right eye. He fired a single shot and the beast wrenched back and screamed, grabbing its face with its right hand as Isaiah fired a bullet into its left eye, causing the same reaction. It staggered almost to the point of the demolished vault clearly wounded but still a long way from going down if its rage was any indication of its endurance.

The image of a retreat, however slight, encouraged the surviving guard to instantly close on it unleashing full clips and changing clips without report.

It stepped beyond the ragged remnants of the vault.

Roy fired the second Javelin.

This time Isaiah didn't have time to dive behind cover and instinctively lifted a single arm over his head as he half-turned to evade the furnace of fire that engulfed the monstrosity. Isaiah was not aware of how much time passed before he staggered, deafened and stunned, to his feet, and to his vague astonishment he heard a bestial howl.

With difficulty Isaiah managed to focus and saw that the creature did appear to be gravely wounded this time; its chest was clearly visible with gaps of bright green almost as glowing as the distant emergency light still working in the corridor. Indeed, most of the walls and ceiling were torn and demolished by the explosions and gunfire, but enough light remained for Isaiah to see Tony hurl his rifle aside and leap forward, snatching up one of the two remaining Javelins.

With what would have been considered a suicidal rush, Tony advanced in front of the raging gunfire. Then charged over rubble with broken steps to where he was actually on a level equal to the beast's chest and head. And it was clear that Tony knew the simple process for readying and firing the Javelin.

He raised it to his shoulder, took two seconds to poise, then leaped outward and down, landing solidly on the beast's chest as he shoved the Javelin into its chest.

"*Eat this*!" was all Isaiah heard before the encompassing explosion—an explosion amplified in strength by the enclosing walls—fully lifted Isaiah and hurled him down the corridor. But this time Isaiah was slower reaching his feet, stunned again by the detonation, and realized that anyone who had stood close to the perimeter of the blast was dead.

Quickly Isaiah glimpsed a black shape rising and recognized Roy.

For a moment the Delta operator stared at the red and green carnage on the far side of the broken wall and then dropped a clip before angrily slamming in another, walking forward. He ruthlessly shoved Tony's dead body aside and pointed the rifle straight down into what remained of the creature's head.

He pulled the trigger and held it down until the clip was empty. Then he dropped that clip without a word and inserted another, plunging the barrel inside its torn chest and he pulled the trigger again, emptying another clip. And, last, Roy shouted over his shoulder to whoever was crawling through the debris, "*Fire in the hole*!"

Isaiah ducked behind rubble but not before he saw Roy shove his hand inside the beast's chest and ever so strangely in that superhuman acuity that only comes in a life-and-death situation, Isaiah also saw the pin from the grenade spinning like silver through the dusty white air. Then he saw Roy turn and dive behind a thick sheet of titanium as the grenade exploded inside the beast's chest.

The blast was not deafening because Isaiah was already deafened from the explosions and gunfire. Afterward, with difficulty, he rose from his prone position, first to gain balance, then to reflexively check the status of his weapon, and finally to raise his face to see nothing but an ocean of gore on the far side of the vault. He did note Tony's motionless body and knew he was dead but that was all the strength he possessed to realize anything at all.

Isaiah inhaled deeply, taking his time, blinking sweat and blood from his eyes, and then swiped a forearm across his face. He only barely paid attention to Roy as he rose and stared down at what remained of the creature.

Yeah, it was dead. Or whatever molecular blueprint it had used to construct this monstrous image was dead.

Roy muttered some indistinct curse that Isaiah couldn't have heard if he were standing beside him. Then Roy changed clips like a machine—the perfect soldier reacting by instinct, skill, reflex, training, and base courage—and turned back to Isaiah. He helped to lift the three remaining guards to their feet and ushered them forward as he made his way to Isaiah. And when Roy reached him, he didn't even lift his face.

"Looks like demons ain't bulletproof," he said.

****

After they reached the Observation Room there was no joy or relief expressed by survivors. They simply drank water or poured it over their heads and sat. They were emotionless on the exterior although expletives were gasped.

The three surviving guards were stunned but not severely injured.

Only Isaiah and Roy were bleeding badly.

Isaiah discovered that his wound was the most extensive and required immediate attention, which Amanda and Margaret were quick to apply. Roy's injury was a long cut down his face to his neck that he tended himself with a Swiss bandage. After pressing it to his cut, Roy pulled it off and stared down.

"Sulfur?" he gaped. "They haven't used sulfur since World War II." He paused. "The Swiss didn't even fight in World War II."

"Well," said Margaret as she used scissors to cut open Isaiah's pants leg, "it seems like the maniacs who built this place raided an old Swiss bunker to stock their secondary medical units because they have enough food and water and medical supplies for a dozen world wars. The Swiss must have felt left out during the big one."

"This *is* the big one," said Roy, placing the bandage back on his face.

Janet tightly grasped a shard of titanium and fiercely ripped it from Isaiah's thigh as Isaiah's jaw clamped tight. Then they stuffed and clotted the wound with dressing and wrapped his leg in bandages and tape; the bandages did nothing to leaven the pain, but pain was the last thing Isaiah was concerned about. He reached out to Janet, gasping, "Give me the radio! I have to talk to the general!"

She immediately handed it over and Isaiah spoke, "General! Are you there?"

A pause.

"*Is that you, major?*"

"It's Isaiah. The major is wounded, but he'll be all right. Have you loaded the bomb into the ATLAS?"

"*We're doing it.*"

"Remember what I told you," Isaiah continued. "Be careful not to touch any of the magnets. I'll be down in a minute."

"*Roger that. Did you get both tangos?*"

"No," Isaiah responded wearily. "We got the small one. The big one is still running around." He paused. "And be advised. The one we killed was wearing armor. I repeat; they are wearing armor. It'll take all the ordinance you've got to put down the second one but they *are* vulnerable. If you engage it, just fire everything you've got. It will go down."

"*Roger that. Over.*"

"Over." Isaiah dropped the microphone as he mumbled through mashed lips, "And this ain't even the hard part ..."

Margaret sharply lifted her face from bandaging, "You're right. Your fight hasn't even started, chief. You still have to execute your suicide plan. And if your plan doesn't work, which it probably won't, then you have to blow the bomb. And God only knows what will happen when you do that. I don't even know what will happen when I start the collider. That thing could detonate when I flick the switch. *That* would solve our problems."

Isaiah managed, "What's the power level?"

"Janet used Francois's personal ID to bypass the electrical shutdown for the collider so it's close enough."

"Close enough for what?"

Margaret stood, smoothing out the last piece of tape. "To be precise, it's at ninety percent. If I open up one more substation, it jumps to one hundred percent and you're going to see particle collision heaven. And I won't tell you again that this has never been tried. It's never even been contemplated, so this is where science ends and God begins."

Isaiah somehow managed to reject horrific doomsday images as he asked, "Have you calculated a collision between these opposing dimensions so they'll simultaneously collide with our dimension?"

"Yes, yes, yes, *Hell yes*."

Isaiah leaned close. "Are you sure?"

Margaret extended both arms before she let them fall. "Isaiah?" Her eyes were wide and searching. "Are you seriously asking me if I'm absolutely certain whether I've coordinated a needle fired from a cannon in the Antarctic, a needle fired from Jupiter, and another needle fired from Saturn to collide in the same one-thousandth of a second inside a one-inch crater on the moon? How the hell can I be sure? It's never been done! You're asking me to calculate the speed and trajectory for a Mars landing with my cell phone! I can promise you that you'll end up *somewhere* if this works at all!" She gasped faintly. "If it doesn't work, then we're *all* going to end up in another dimension."

"Just give me a yes or no, please."

"*Yes*," Margaret nodded. "Yes, I think I've got the math right. Numbers are just numbers, no matter how crazy everything else in the world gets. Like this. In fact, math is the only thing *I am* certain of anymore. But do you have any idea what kind of nightmare dimensions you could be smashing together? With you in the center of it?" She briefly raised a hand at Amanda. "And with Amanda, God bless her heart, right beside you? God, I can't believe she's going with you just so she can leap back—if she can—and tell us that you've engaged the most powerful being in the universe in some kind of godawful final conflict. Which is exactly what this is going to be."

"If I don't shut this portal from the other side," Isaiah said, "somebody in Japan, or Russia, or China will open it again. And I believe the next time will be the last time. Whoever opens this door again will leave it open. And that'll be the end for all of us. And when I say for all of us, I mean—"

"Yes, I know what you mean," said Margaret. "You think I don't know all this? You think I'm not intimately familiar with the Many-Worlds Interpretation? The String Theory? The Quantum Theory? Or how the Acting-World Theory can predict the behavior of nanoscopic objects? Do you think I don't know the sheer, unbelievable power it takes to generate forty Tera-Electron-Volts inside this machine? Do you think I'm not aware of every conceivable risk involved in this experiment?" She stood, arms at her side. "Do you know that the K'iche' Maya called Hell, 'Xibalba'? Do you know what that means?"

Isaiah shook his head.

"It means 'place of fear.'" Margaret stared. "Even the bloody Mayan Empire—and we're talking about base savages who cut the hearts out of living people just for the hell of it!—were terrified of this place. So don't get me wrong. I'm not worried about whether I can send you to Hell, Isaiah. I'm worried about whether you won't go insane once you get there and not do your job! And to imagine you going head-to-head with Satan or Lucifer or Shiva or whatever the hell it calls itself is way beyond human comprehension. It's not that I don't have faith in you. I do. I've seen you in action. You've got guts and you've got brains. But even angels won't take a stand against this guy."

"He's just another creature," said Isaiah.

"He's probably the *first* creature!" Margaret replied fiercely. "And he's probably the most powerful creature!" She blinked slowly, bent forward, and spoke more quietly, "I *have* read the Bible, Isaiah. I'm not a complete heathen. Have you ever read the book of Jude? Because there's a scene in it where Satan is confronted by Michael—one of the most powerful of all angels—and even Michael wouldn't fight Satan. The only thing Michael does is say, 'The Lord rebukes you.' And that's it. Even Michael, as powerful as he has to be because Michael is 'Commander of the Armies of God,' wouldn't lock horns with Satan over who would claim the body of Moses, so we're talking about one tough son of a bitch! This guy probably wiped out the dinosaurs!"

She turned and walked away.

Isaiah was having trouble concentrating. He took a series of sharp breaths as rhythmic as the second hand on a clock, trying to recover, before he cast a narrow glance at Amanda; she was standing, arms folded. He didn't need to see more.

She was scared to death.

About like him.

***

It was only a few minutes before Roy and Isaiah joined General Jackman on the altar-like stand outside the ATLAS as they loaded the one-hundred-megaton bomb into the cylinder. The contorting effort required them to carry it an inch at a time and, when it was done, they fell back against the walls or to their knees, breathless.

"How can …" Tanto gasped, "something so small … weigh so much? I mean … I thought that welder was heavy! But this thing weighs a ton!"

Roy wiped away sweat. "Again, buddy, it's a new mix of fuel. They haven't even found a safe way to test it, but they say it works. And I don't think they can even measure its yield. Saying that it has a one hundred megaton yield is just a wild-ass guess. As far as they know, this damn thing could yield a thousand megatons. They have no idea how big this is gonna blow."

"It's gonna blow *big*," groaned Tanto.

Slowly Roy straightened and arched his back before leaning forward again. "Man alive, I'm getting too old for this." He gently laid a hand on the bomb. "Give 'em hell."

Isaiah walked toward the exit.

"Let's do this," he said, suddenly hesitating. "And don't forget that we've still got one of these things running around. If we don't kill it in a standup fight, you'll have to blow this collider, anyway, and destroy everything down here."

"What are the odds of you pulling this off?" asked Roy. "I mean, you're gonna try to capture Satan in a place outside of space and time and then drop a nuke on his head? What are the odds?"

Isaiah revealed nothing.

"I wouldn't bet the farm."

***

Isaiah was too beat up to immediately enter the ATLAS. He needed a few minutes to collect himself, tend his wounds, and rehydrate. He didn't know what he would be facing on the other side and he didn't need to be in a weakened condition when he did.

It didn't matter who had the idea they should eat and drink before they began, but when they got to the Observation Room there were a dozen MREs prepared and Susan had broken out a new case of bottled water.

They had sent the rest of the Observation Room physicists with plenty of food and water to the elevator where they had, with admirable ingenuity, set up a makeshift MASH unit. They had collected everything even remotely related to survival from every storage room and were, from all appearances, making themselves comfortable. And Roy had ordered the surviving crew and guards to the elevator but left Francois chained to his chair in the Observation Room; it was if Roy didn't want Francois out of his sight.

The only other people remaining in the Observation Room were those critical to the last two stages of this gambit.

By reflex Isaiah searched the computer screens, but the remaining vaults were in place. And there was nothing moving on the monitors but, of course, that meant nothing. He vaguely noticed how Janet wasn't eating, and her expression was beyond worried.

It was alarming.

"You okay?" asked Isaiah.

"Huh?" Janet glanced toward him. "Uh, no, I'm still worried about your plan. I'm scared about going all the way back to the Big Bang and changing history. I just don't think it's a good idea. That's all. I can't get over it."

Jackman grunted, "Why not?"

"Because you're changing the timeline, general. I told you once before. The butterfly effect."

General Jackman took a moment, gazing about, before adding, "But didn't one of you say time is like the Mississippi River? And throwing a rock in the Mississippi River ain't gonna change the course of the river, right? So the consequences of changing that dimension should just stick with that dimension." He stared. "Have I got that right?"

"I was referring to 'minor' changes," answered Janet. "This is not a minor change. This is a move to trigger the Big Bang in a new way. And even the Mississippi River begins *somewhere*. If you go all the way back to its source and drop a nuclear bomb, who knows what would happen to the river? I mean, I do hate to repeat myself but this is no 'minor' butterfly effect. This is, forgive me, the father of the mother of all butterfly effects."

Margaret stated, "But it only involves two dimensions, Janet. Our dimension won't be involved. It will be outside the space and time of our dimension. There's a fair chance there will be no consequences in this dimension at all."

"That's impossible to know," said Janet. "But I guess it doesn't matter. It's the only plan we've got. It's like Roy says. We're all going to die, anyway, if we don't do something radical. And this is radical by all that is holy."

Jackman resumed eating. "To tell the truth, I don't give a damn no more. We gotta do something and this is all we've got, so let's do it. We sure won't be any worse off if it *don't* work, that's for sure. And, by the way, have you figured out yet why we can't see these things on camera?"

Janet sighed, brushed back her hair, and said, "Once again, general, we can't see them because there's a very large light spectrum and this thing's composition isn't in the spectrum that we can read with these electronics." She paused, then added, "A satellite station might have something for it, but not this place."

"Can't you see a ghost on infrared?" asked Tanto.

Janet groaned, "I've heard that question a thousand times, Tanto, and the answer is always 'no.'" She shook her head. "TV shows have been lying to people for years telling them they can see paranormal activity with an infrared camera. That is pure rubbish. Infrared just reads heat and it often gives you a false-positive of something that was there an hour ago. Like, a raccoon might have crawled across a tree and left a silhouette that looks like a ghost. So infrared is the *least* reliable means of seeing something paranormal or from another dimension although people make millions telling people that it can."

Tanto glanced around the table before asking, "So what's the best way to detect something supernatural?"

"Tanto, these creatures aren't supernatural any more than we are. They're perfectly natural. They're just from another place and made of different stuff. In many ways, we're superior to them. In other ways, we're inferior. But, to answer your question, the best way to see something from their dimension is to get our hands on a machine that can read the light common to their dimension."

Everyone had begun staring at her.

Gesturing with a fork, Janet added, "Everyone thinks the absence of any color is white, right? Well, the opposite is true. The absence of any color is black. Isaac Newton proved that before his manuscript on light got burned up. And it's the same with antimatter. The reason we can't see it is not the absence of light. It's the presence of *too much light*."

Janet waited. No one spoke.

Finally she set down her fork and said more slowly, "Okay. Listen. Have you guys ever looked up at night to see all those billions and billions of stars? Yeah? Okay, then imagine all those billions of stars smashed together into a space as small as a grain of sand. That's what antimatter is. Imagine how condensed, how complex, how mysterious that is. And now try to imagine all the power of the electromagnetic spectrum of light that would be thrown out of such a concentration of antimatter. It would be invisible to us because that fantastic spectrum of light would simply be off the chart.

"Now, these creatures obviously have the power to alter their physical forms and they have absorbed the neutrinos of this dimension to produce themselves in the physical shape of monsters, but they're still a hybrid mix of matter and neutrally charged antimatter." She waved vaguely. "Yeah, yeah, I know. You guys have watched *Star Trek*. You know that matter and antimatter don't mix. And, usually, they don't. But that only means that these things know how to neutralize the electrons comprising their original substance to join the positively charged electrons of our universe on a subatomic level."

"I don't follow that," said Jackman. "If they can look like whatever they want to on some kind of subatomic level, then why don't they look like angels? Why don't they look like God or something? If they can look like anything, why look like a damn gorilla?"

"First," Janet stated, "because they wouldn't be able to hunt us, herd us, or kill us if they're ghosts or shadows or some foggy image of a raccoon. That's another reason why they have literally absorbed the neutrinos and molecules of this dimension. They have to be able to touch human beings. But I think this transformation also permanently alters their composition. In other words, it makes them vulnerable."

"How does that work?" asked Jackman.

Janet didn't skip a beat. "When they forsake their original form to assume the form of flesh and bone, they can't change back. They are, in a sense, flesh and blood. And it makes them vulnerable. It's, like, someone can choose to have their legs amputated, right? Okay. That's easy. Just chop 'em off. Well, that's exactly what these things do when they come here. They forsake their first estate. They get their legs chopped off. But we can't just simply choose to have our legs put back on. What's done is done. And it's the same with them. Once they forsake their original form and absorb the molecules of this world on a subatomic level, they can't undo it. I mean, everybody with a brain is aware that it's a lot easier to absorb radiation than it is to get rid of it, right? You can absorb it in two seconds. But it might take you a century to get rid of it. And that's what they've done. They've absorbed the radiation particular to this universe and it's pretty much permanent. Which is both good and bad."

Roy was acutely studying a monitor as he morosely stated, "I can guess the bad part. What's the good?"

"The good part is that once they absorb the radiation of this dimension so that they can physically touch us, they're limited," said Janet with a glance. "The bad part is that they're in this to the death. They know they can't go back, so they're like those gladiators of old times who would tie their foot to a stake and make a last stand against an entire army in the middle of nowhere with no retreat, no surrender. Because they know they're in this to the death, you're going to have to kill every one of them. And, as we've all seen, these things don't exactly die easily.

"But to answer your real question: Why do they look like monsters? *Because they want to.*" Janet gestured to the wall. "They could choose to be invisible. They obviously have the power to choose invisibility just like they have the power to look like angels or demons. And, so, why do they choose to look like monsters instead of gods? The answer to that is simple. It's because they want to subdue and overcome this world by fear. That's why they assume a mask they think is most frightening to us. A mask that makes us afraid of them. So they *do* have the power to construct whatever form they want in this dimension. But they're still flesh and bone, which means that if they can touch us, we can touch them, too. And *all* flesh and bone has a limit to what it can take." She glanced at faces. 'It's complicated."

"No kidding," mumbled Roy. He went back to eating. "Well, I know they ain't bulletproof. That's good enough for me."

Janet signed, "Yeah, they're not bulletproof, which might mean they're vulnerable to everything we are. But you should remember that you're only fighting a puppet made out of hijacked molecules. And whatever spirit or soul or unknown power energizes this thing probably *is* indestructible." She pointed lightly. "What you killed in the hall was just an irradiated suit of clothes."

"You mean that that thing is still alive?" Jackman gaped. "Are you saying that blowing his ass into smithereens didn't kill the bastard?"

"Oh, you destroyed its molecular suit," Janet answered. "But I don't know if it's dead because I don't know if it was electrical in nature or if it was energized by some kind of bizarre, unknown power." Her gaze roamed over the ceiling. "And, now, that power could just be floating around up there waiting to inhabit something else. To tell you the truth, I have no idea. We're in the twilight zone in every way with this one."

With what seemed to Isaiah an amazing revelation, Tanto said blandly, "Maybe that explains ghosts, poltergeists, demonic possessions, and all that crap. These things can't really be killed because what keeps them alive ain't the same thing that keeps us alive. All you can do is drive it out or kill the body it's possessing. But, then, it'll just go into another body. And round and round we go. Where it ends, nobody knows."

With readable nervousness, every face at the table turned toward Isaiah who was, remarkably enough, dead calm.

Finally Janet said, "Isaiah, you know, of course, that whatever shape you encounter on the far side of that portal is probably going to be its true form, don't you? It's more powerful that way. To shape-shift has to drain its power and I don't think it will do that unless it has to. And I don't know for certain, but I don't believe it would have any reason to conceal its face from you in its own dimension. So, in its true form, it could be a thousand feet tall. It could be as bright as the sun. You might go blind just looking at it."

Roy muttered, "You're in No Man's Land on this one, son." He sniffed, cocked his head. "Not to be cold about it but … better you than me." He chewed, then, "Of course, you can always just push the button and we'll all go see God together. If there is one. Which I'm beginning to believe on a whole new level."

Wiping sweat from her face, Amanda stated, "I can't see how you *don't* believe in God after killing that thing in the tunnel. I wasn't even there but my only thought was that that thing has to be straight out of Hell."

Roy eyebrows rose as he replied, "Crossed my mind, too."

General Jackman had been unusually silent with his face turned toward the Observation Room window. Then he seemed to ask no one in particular, "What would happen if we brought back any of the people who have already been snatched up? Someone who's been to the other side? Could they help us?"

"We can't do that," said Janet instantly and turned a gaze to Amanda. "If they've been in that dimension for longer than a few hours, Amanda, then they're irradiated. There's no way around that. They might even be weaponized."

Jackman grunted, "Weaponized?"

"They may have been molecularly altered into hybrid creatures that these interdimensional maniacs need in order to do whatever it is they want to do. And I have no idea what that is."

"They want to go home," said Isaiah flatly. "And their penultimate master wants to take what he's always been denied." His jaw tightened in a frown. "Because man possesses what he will never possess."

Roy was staring. "What's that?"

"A spirit," stated Isaiah simply. "He wants what God gave to man. And he'll destroy everyone on this planet because of it." He grunted. "That's the dull thing about Satan. Since he was created, he hasn't changed. He still wants what doesn't belong to him. And if he can't have it, nobody will."

Leaning into it, Amanda asked slowly, "So you're saying that these abominations are doing this just because they don't have a spirit? Are you serious?"

Isaiah shook his head sadly. "Satan wants what every creature wants but none of them are powerful enough to fight for it."

"What would that be?" asked Roy.

Isaiah fixed him with a steady gaze.

"He wants to be the Crux of Power."

Amanda whispered, "Someone already won that crown." She bowed her head. "And his throne is forever."

"Huh," grunted Roy. "If you ask me, I'd say that machine out there is the crux of power. But, then, I'm not a spiritual guy. Or I didn't used to be. I'm getting closer every minute."

With an angry scowl Jackman rumbled, "Well, I've got a question that might even be more important than this miserable situation." He stared around them. "Why haven't we seen the other one yet? The big one?"

"General," said Roy, "with all due respect, sir, I don't want to hear that explanation again. We haven't seen it, sir, because it's outside our eyeballs somehow."

Jackman shook his head. "That's not what I'm talking about, son. I mean, why hasn't the big one attacked us already? Do you think it even knows that its little buddy got his stupid ass shot off?" He stared at them. "Maybe it doesn't even want a fight. Maybe it just wants to prowl around the two hundred miles of tunnel they got down here and wait until it can escape into the world. This ain't the only supercollider in the world, you know. Maybe it's planning to leapfrog up to Russia where they're building a collider that's more than fifty miles long. When that damn thing is operational, they'll be able to transport Moscow itself back to the Stone Age."

No one offered an answer.

"There's no way to know what it's thinking," said Margaret, not bothering to conceal her fatigue. "We only know that this species is smarter than we are. If we can think of it, they can think of it. They've probably already thought of it. I'd say they've been ahead of us for millions of years."

"What makes you say that?" asked Jackman.

"Because these creatures have been sending us very complex formulas through the ATLAS, general, that are way beyond our knowledge. That's how I know they're much smarter than we are." Margaret tiredly pointed to the ATLAS. "Since we opened that portal, we have been on the receiving end of equations so complex that no mathematician on the planet has even imagined them. So these things possess the knowledge to build a supercollider that's ten times stronger. That's why they've been trying to help us improve this one. They want us to build a bigger and better one." She shook her head. "And that kind of intellectual achievement takes hundreds of thousands, if not millions of years. So they've been at this a lot longer than we have."

"If these things are so smart, why don't they build their own damn collider?" asked Jackman.

Janet answered, "Obviously, general, because some kind of superpower has forbidden them from doing it." An empty gesture. "I mean, let's face it; they have the intelligence and they absolutely have the raw material. Every gram of antimatter is equal to all the visible matter in this galaxy so it's not from a lack of intelligence and it's not from a lack of resources. Or even a lack of desire. We know they want one. They just can't build it."

"Then why does this superpower let *us* do it?" Jackman pressed.

"I don't know," said Janet frankly. "I guess this superpower has decided that putting this kind of power into their hands is putting it in the wrong hands."

"Ha!" Jackman gustily slammed a hand down on the table. "Like we're the right hands? I think we've proven that our hands are the wrong hands, doc! Maybe this superpower ain't that smart!"

Janet shrugged, "Or, maybe, it's just that the rules that limit us are not the same rules that limit them. We have the freedom to build this. But they don't. And they're not free to leave that prison, either." She tapped her chest. "*We* have to open the portal for them. They can't do it, and they know it. That's why they've been covertly working with these people for a hundred years. That's why they've given favor to the witches who built this pitch-black cauldron of spite. That's why they've insinuated themselves into the necessary halls of political power. But when that portal is permanently open and they no longer need us? Look out, man, and color me gone, baby. I will not stay in *any* dimension inhabited by those things." She leaned forward, staring at Roy. "You promise you'll take care of that, right?"

Without looking up, Roy mumbled, "Let's not get ahead of ourselves. Getting killed down here is easy enough."

A space of seconds, and Jackman looked at Isaiah, "What are you going to do if whatever has command and authority in this … this place you're going … doesn't give a damn about that nuclear warhead?"

Isaiah knew his face didn't express much. "I guess I'll just push the button and see what happens." He turned his gaze toward the ATLAS. "There won't be anything left to do."

The silence lasted.

"You're a brave man," Jackman nodded. "You're a soldier."

Blinking tiredly, Isaiah grimaced.

"In a war without a truce," he said.

* * *

Ten minutes later Roy said, "Okay, I think we've got as ready as we're gonna get. What's the first move, professor?" He looked at Isaiah. "I'd say you're captain of this ship until your hour is up or that ATLAS explodes in a holocaust that's gonna make Switzerland look like Death Valley."

Isaiah asked Margaret, "You're sure the explosion won't reach this dimension?"

"Yeah," said Margaret, emotions dried up. "If we shut down power to the collider, we'll close the portal and the effects of the bomb will remain … wherever it's at. Or *when*. Whatever. But if I shut down the power you can't dive out the window after you push the button. You'll be on top of the explosion." She locked a gaze on Amanda. "So will you."

Isaiah bent forward in his chair, elbows on knees, hands clasped as he looked to her again. "Is there any way to remove Amanda from the equation?"

Amanda's mouth opened.

"Communication might be possible," Margaret replied. "I mean, it's *theoretically* possible and that would remove Amanda from the equation."

"Explain that."

"Well, radio waves travel forever through space, don't they? As long as the portal stays open, there's a slim chance we can still communicate by low frequency radio waves and that means Amanda doesn't have to go. But let me stress: We don't know if that will work. Amanda should go with you only because I'm actually more certain that Amanda can step back through the portal than I am about whether radio waves can reach us from a place that is probably hell and gone beyond space and time."

"Hey!" said Amanda, standing and staring at Isaiah. "I'm going! That thing took my sister! And you need me as backup, anyway! What if radio waves can't reach this place? But if I can go through the portal then I know I can come back! It's like going out a door and coming back in again! But this radio thing is just a theory! Are you gonna bet all our lives on a theory?"

Tanto muttered, "We've been doing that since we started."

After a long moment Isaiah signed, "We'll do both. Amanda comes back the second we make it through the portal. She's in and out. But I'll stay and try to shut down the gate from the other side." He locked on Margaret. "If I tell you to, how fast can you shut down the collider to keep the explosion from reaching this world?"

"I can shut down the collider in a split-second," stated Margaret. "All I have to do is pull the plug. But it's like I said. Pulling the plug will also shut down communications and your war-mongering ass doesn't get home. And the rest of us don't go home, either. Because, if you fail, then General Jackman, here, blows us all to hell to destroy the collider. So you either win big or every single one of us loses big. There's no in-between." She paused. "Soldier."

"I admit that ain't much of a plan," Jackman muttered. "I don't mind dying for my country, but I'd rather see that thing die for his. And I don't want to see any of you hurt worse than you already are."

"*There*!" Amanda shouted as she pointed at a screen.

Roy was at the console staring up. "Where!"

"There!" Amanda touched the screen. "I saw something!"

"It can't be!" grated Margaret. "That's inside this section of the corridor! What'd you see, Amanda?"

Amanda stared a long moment before shaking her head. "It was, like, dust on the floor shifted. Like a shadow, or something, was moving through it. I'm not sure! But something did move! I know it!"

With a grimace Roy looked toward Isaiah. "If she's right, it's found a way past the last two vaults and into this section, which gives us about two minutes before we're in a standup fight." He took a deep breath. "If you're gonna go, go."

Isaiah rose, walking forward. "Give me the detonator and radio."

Roy pulled a small black remote from his vest and Isaiah accepted it. Absently dropping the radio in his coat, Isaiah stared at the detonator in his suddenly sweating grip. "Just flip the lid? Press down? That's it?"

Roy nodded. "There's a thirty-second delay on the nuke but, yeah, that's it. Just flip the lid and press. After that, there's no turning back and not even one of those things can stop it. It's too complex. Even for them." His frown deepened. "It'd take them a month to figure it out and they ain't got a month. They're gonna have exactly thirty seconds. Same as you." He nodded curtly, "Good luck, brother."

"Yeah," Isaiah muttered as he slid the remote into his pants pocket. He lifted the Honjo Masamune from the table where he had laid it; it was never far from his side now and wouldn't be until this was finished.

"I guess we're ready," he said to Amanda. "But as soon as I establish communication with Margaret, you come back through the portal."

Margaret muttered, "So much for a cigarette."

"For dust you are," Roy said as he slung his rifle, "and to dust you shall return."

Isaiah stepped into Margaret. "If you don't hear from me immediately after Amanda returns, destroy the collider.

Because if I can't shut down the portal from the far end, I'm detonating the bomb."

"I'm ready," muttered Margaret. "Are you?"

Jackman picked up a rifle. "Holy God. If I make it out of here, I'm gonna blow up every one of these damn things in the world, orders or no orders."

Amanda was at Isaiah's side as he walked toward the door.

And the Beast blocked out the light.

***

It was pure instinct that made Isaiah throw himself backward into Amanda as she screamed and a gigantic armored arm swept through the air obliterating the concrete doorframe to send a slicing storm of white shards through the chamber.

Sprawling clumsily across the floor with Amanda howling beneath him, Isaiah twisted to rip the katana from its sheath as he simultaneously hurled the sheath aside. Even in the moment Isaiah knew he'd never need the sheath again.

This creature was much larger than the one they'd already killed. It was at least ten feet tall and as wide as the door itself and was armored in what resembled black iron. It had a thick helmet and breastplate with hulking forearm bosses and greaves covering both shins.

With a glance at Margaret, it bent forward roaring.

"*You've come!*" bellowed Francois. "*I told the fools that you would come!*"

Suddenly it looked to the side to focus on Francois chained to his chair gazing up with the purest expression of worship. And as Francois opened his mouth to speak again, the beast casually reached down to wrap a gigantic hand around the director's head. Then it closed the hand into a fist, liquifying Francois's skull.

With a shout Roy unloaded to throw thirty rounds directly into its chest and it didn't even turn its head into the attack. Rather, it lifted its face again, higher, and seemed to study the screens aligning the wall before it stalked forward like a colossus risen from some age-old throne of granite.

Isaiah leaped aside and swung the katana to hit it solidly in the knee and the beast staggered a half-step before it roared again and struck down toward Isaiah, but Isaiah had anticipated that and had already flung himself beyond its reach, rolling across the floor as Roy shouted, "Grenade!"

Isaiah took an extra tenth of a second to see Margaret cleanly leap a high computer console and Amanda fling herself behind a wooden desk before he ducked, too.

Isaiah didn't know where the grenade impacted the beast, but he knew it struck true because, when he looked up, he saw the creature staggering backward, its armored chest on fire with flames that flowed like white water over its blue-black face.

Finally it turned into Roy and screamed.

The Delta commander raised his rifle. "Grenade!"

"Grenade!" shouted Tanto.

There was no decision to make; Isaiah saw it bleeding from the knee where the katana had sliced deeply through its leg despite how substantial it had become. And the grenades were sending splinters of armor spiraling like knives through the air.

This was the last stand.

Isaiah ducked as the dual explosions of the grenades laced the room with white-hot shrapnel that cut through steel and flesh alike. Then he raised his face in time to see the beast recovering like a boxer trying to rise from a colossal blow; it was off-balance and staggered before it slammed a fist into the wall. As it raised its face to focus fully on Roy, Isaiah claimed the first clear view of its countenance.

It looked like Cro-Magnon man would have looked like if he had been born from a union of a gorilla and a demon; its brow was broad and low; its eyes were utter black holes with not even the faintest trace of light reflected in their obsidian core; its chin was square and blocked to match the rest of its body lending it the image of a gargantuan beast that ruled by strength and strength alone. And its teeth were not fanged but square and thick to give it, on the whole, the impression of pure brute strength.

If God had meant to send forth a creature of nothing but main strength, he could not have created a more perfect vessel.

"Go!" cried Roy. *"Get to the ATLAS!"*

Isaiah knew he still held the katana as he scrambled across the floor and grabbed Amanda's hand, hauling her out the door. Then they ran to the stairway that led downward to the ATLAS. Isaiah only hoped someone would still be alive when they reached it because the gateway could only be opened from the Observation Room.

More explosions sounded in the corridor.

Then the roar of an unearthly beast chasing them …

As the ATLAS opened …

***

As Isaiah, dragging Amanda, reached the dais beneath the ATLAS, he spun in place at a sudden silence. It descended from the Observation Room like a flood of horror. Then a voice cried, *"Get in the damn machine!"*

Isaiah shoved Amanda before him and hurled himself into the chamber scrambling over the cylindrical hydrogen weapon as he heard the beast erupt into the collider corridor and it began to climb the stairs to the ATLAS. Then the entire chamber exploded in a blue light that engulfed them both with electric tendrils stretching straight as a highway toward an unending blue-green sheen …

Isaiah turned his gaze to see the bestial image poised in the door of the ATLAS.

It roared as everything was engulfed in …

Light.

***

Where they were going took more than a few moments because Isaiah was aware of traveling along a long blue ribbon of green and blue light that sliced through bands of what seemed like stars and the journey continued and continued and continued until …

They stopped.

Isaiah took a moment to see a white orb suspended behind them and he twisted to grab Amanda who was somehow floating face down like someone drowning in an invisible flood. He violently twisted her upright as Amanda awoke with a start and stared first at him and then at the azure infinity surrounding them.

"Oh, shit!" Amanda exclaimed. "Okay! I've seen it! Make us proud! I'm outta here!"

"You can't go back yet!" said Isaiah. "That thing was almost inside the ATLAS! I have to make sure it's safe."

Blinking rapidly, Amanda gasped, "Is this the Big Bang?"

"I don't think so," said Isaiah. He pulled the radio from his coat. "Roy! Margaret! Do you read me?"

A moment.

Static.

"*I've got you!*" came Margaret's voice. "*Are both of you okay?*"

"Yes!" Isaiah answered firmly as he continued to spin, glaring across every blue-black, crimson, endless landscape. "I don't know where we're at but we're somewhere! Has that thing left the ATLAS? Can I send Amanda back?"

"We're not sure! We can't see it! Keep her there another minute!"

Isaiah suddenly realized they weren't floating; rather, they were standing on a substance that seemed like some kind of vaporous white firmament. He instinctively knelt, feeling through the faint sheen that half-covered his feet.

His hand rose, lifting what merely seemed like … white sand. He lifted it to his face and sensed nothing familiar. It wasn't a beach. It wasn't the remnants of an ancient volcano. It was simply … void … as if it existed only for itself.

"Huh," Isaiah grunted and saw the hydrogen bomb resting beside his right leg; he didn't straighten as his brow hardened. "Well, we're standing on something so that means we're … lost in space."

"Oh, no," Amanda moaned, a hand on her forehead. "Margaret's math sucks." Then, slowly, she lifted her face and whispered, "Isaiah? What is that?"

Isaiah searched.

Where the sky had been crimson and azure, it was quickly blackening in a single consuming thundercloud that cast the abyss into the deepest melancholy shadow Isaiah had ever seen or imagined. At once the landscape vanished and the white firmament was transformed like a grave from morning to midnight and the air within their lungs and upon their skin seemed to solidify with a darkness that could be felt.

Isaiah's grip tightened on Amanda's hand.

"Don't move," he said.

"I thought I was supposed to go back."

Isaiah glanced to see the snow-white portal increasingly surrounded by a vicious red ring; the ring had tentacles like those of an enraged serpent and they were lashing out to strike mist from this mysterious ground.

Anything they hit would be killed.

"I don't think that's a good idea yet," he said.

Strangely Isaiah could still clearly see Amanda for it seemed they stood within an arena of light effortlessly defying this deepest canyon of black.

"What is this place?" Amanda whispered. "Isaiah?"

"He's here," said Isaiah.

"What?" Amanda turned her face, searching. "*What* is here?"

A black silhouette appeared from the gloom as if taking substance from the night. It stood before them, a single forearm behind its back, like a gentleman, and it was very obviously a man. And for a moment no one moved or spoke.

"Whom do you seek?" asked the figure.

"Oh, my God," croaked Amanda. "It talks."

Isaiah studied the form as he realized that no king would go himself to meet anything less than another king and so he answered, "I seek no one. I've brought you a gift."

The silhouette's face did not move but a voice did distinctly emanate from within it. "We know of your gift." It laughed. "Fire to destroy fire. How piquant."

"A demon with a sense of humor," Isaiah muttered. "How piquant." He glanced to confirm the bomb was still near as he added, "I'm not here to talk to a slave."

"Everything you believe is wrong," it said, slowly approaching. "These many dimensions were not created by what you understand to be God. They were created by a being that was very much like you when he began so many billions of years ago—as you understand years. But your species is not advanced enough, yet, to comprehend the infinite vastness and measureless age of the cosmos. Nor do you have need of your weapons. You have no enemies here."

There was something about the words that left Isaiah confused. Was it saying that God did not exist and *this* was eternity? That this was man's destiny? Is this the world that the human soul eventually comes to after so many resurrections and rebirths and reincarnations? Was life truly an unending, evolutionary ladder to this place? Or was a man indeed fated to live and die once?

Cautiously Isaiah asked, "All right. Where's your master?"

"He is here." It lifted an arm. "Speak, and he will answer."

Isaiah glanced above, beyond.

"But he won't reveal himself?"

"Isaiah?" Amanda stated hesitantly. "*Look …*"

Barely turning his head, Isaiah saw the object of her concern; the spherical gateway behind them was now violently enclosed by the crimson holocaust that had encircled it as if to destroy it. But the sphere somehow endured as Isaiah again focused on the silhouette.

"You're trying to destroy the portal," he stated.

"You will not be returning to your world," the silhouette said. "We will make you like us, knowing good and evil."

"The first temptation," said Isaiah. "So I guess this is the right place. Except you've already used temptation and it's not going to work again. So why is your master afraid? Has he not stood before God? What can man do to him?"

The figure said plainly, "Why would man do anything to us? We are your friends, and you have no enemies in this pasture, or any pasture. And you would be surprised at how many there are. So, no, you are not alone in the universe. You are simply one of many millions of life forms, and all of them are like you, and all of them are your friends." He pointed to the hydrogen warhead. "Why would you bring a weapon to the house of a friend? Here, we are all priests. We are all perfect. We are all free."

"Only God is free," said Isaiah. "And you're no priest."

"Why do you say I am not a priest?"

"Any priest that worships himself is nothing but a fool."

"But is that not what the God of your understanding holds? Is that not his highest commandment? *Thou shalt honor the Lord thy God*? Is that not the corrupted commandment of your deity?"

Isaiah grimaced, "I'm not a religious man. Never have been. But talking to you inspires me to believe in anything *but* you."

"Now this is your home."

"Let the woman return to her world."

It laughed. "*This* is her world now." It took another step forward. "What is done cannot be undone. No one can violate time as you have so arrogantly done and escape." It scoffed, "Did you really think you and your pitiful weapon could remake creation?"

Isaiah took a step to his right, instinctively circling.

"So you can see into our world?" he asked.

"Yes."

"Can you interfere in our world?"

"When we find a suitable soul to possess."

Isaiah nodded slowly, "So you have to use a human body to affect our world. That's why you need the gateway. You can't physically do it yourself. You can't cross over without the portal."

It began to circle counter to Isaiah as if preparing for battle. "You understand the power that fuels the universe and yet you do not understand yourselves. Your arrogance blinds you. That's why it's my favorite sin. There is no need to tempt the proud. Their doom is within them. Or haven't you heard? Only the humble will see the face of God?"

If you know its name, you can control it …

But Isaiah knew it was useless to ask this creature's name. It would never surrender its name unless it was defeated. And with that thought Isaiah used his right thumb to subtly unlock the katana from the scabbard but the scabbard was no longer there; he had flung it aside when he battled the creature in the Observation Room. Even then Isaiah had decided he'd never need it again. And he'd been right.

"Where are those you took from our world?" he asked.

It stretched out an arm.

Out of nowhere—Isaiah had not even glimpsed a movement in the dark—seven black silhouettes stood in single file. They were all similar in shape to this creature and it took Amanda only a moment to recognize the one who had been her sister.

Cynthia Deker was sheathed in a blood-black sheen as absent of light as the obsidian curve of her unblinking eyes. There was nothing human left within the image of a corpse that stood in that black funeral shroud.

Amanda cried out loud, "*God! … Oh, no! Cynthia!*"

Isaiah's hand tightened on the hilt of the katana.

Whatever Cynthia had been on earth had been horrifically transfigured to duplicate the demonic shape of these denizens of Hell. Her eyes were utterly black spheres and her face was as expressionless as her military stance. And after Isaiah scanned her gaze to see if any thread of humanity or even life yet remained beneath the image of death, he saw nothing at all. Whatever they had transformed her into was subatomic.

Amanda stepped toward the messenger. "Damn you! What did you do to her?"

"Now she is like God," it said coldly, "knowing both good and evil. She is free."

"That isn't freedom!" Amanda pointed and took several steps forward; Isaiah thought of grabbing her but didn't. She deserved her rage. "That's death! You killed her! You're not a God! You're a monster!"

Isaiah glimpsed Amanda's hand clench in a fist. She took another step and then she stopped from instinct. Isaiah knew it had to be instinct because that was the only power that could have broken her tidal wave of rage.

Amanda grabbed Isaiah's arm. "Let's get out of here!"

"Foolish woman," it laughed. "You are destroyed from lack of knowledge. You have always been destroyed from lack of knowledge. The truth is that Isaiah can take you nowhere. We can close the portal any moment we choose. Or send you anywhere we choose."

Eyes narrowing, Isaiah asked, "You know me?"

It stated, "We listen to your world. We watch your world. So, yes, we know you by name."

"But you can't read our minds, can you?"

The pitch-black silhouette revealed nothing. Isaiah glanced at Amanda, at Cynthia's heartbreaking form, and then again at the massive, muscular silhouette.

Measuring it.

Isaiah stepped further to the right, and forward, as he said, "I know you can't be killed. But I'm going to take your pride because of what you've done to that innocent woman. I'm going to take your head … in your own temple … in your Holy of Holies … and before the throne of your master."

The black density of the creature solidified.

"You will fail," it said and lifted an arm.

Isaiah glanced over his shoulder to see the blazing red ring surrounding the portal triple in size and intensity like a circle of liquid lava closing in upon a single cell of living light that was the last hope of the universe.

The silhouette seemed unable to withhold anger from its tone, "The circle shall not endure. You will not return to warn your world."

"They already know you're coming," frowned Isaiah. "But you won't be coming today."

The expressionless face turned hard on Isaiah.

"Why?" it asked.

"Because I'm in *your* world today," said Isaiah. "And it will take you a long time to get up from what I'm gonna do to you."

It's face tilted forward. "How arrogant. Do you know who I am?"

Isaiah's frown deepened as he swung the katana in a tight circle, settling on his grip. "Who you are doesn't matter," he said. "Shiva. Jinn. Lilith. Baal. Caesar. A thousand names for a thousand tombstones. Each equally meaningless."

"What purpose will it serve to slaughter you?"

"I didn't come here to talk," said Isaiah. "This is your ground. You have every advantage, so I have an idea." He lifted the katana. "You kill me."

"Serve me and I will give you the world," it said.

Amanda screamed, "You *are* afraid!"

It shook its head. "*Fool.*"

"*Kill him*!" she shouted.

Isaiah didn't remove his eyes from the creature.

"Count on it."

It growled, "I will destroy you."

Isaiah took a slightly angled stance, the katana in his outstretched right hand.

Isaiah's teeth gleamed as he whispered …

"*Come on …*"

***

Utterly numb, Janet frantically crawled from beneath what seemed to have been some kind of computer console now demolished into a tangle of wires and broken shards of screen and plastic knives before Roy reached her side, hurling off debris as it were weightless. In a second, she was clear.

"You all right?" he gasped, glancing at the door.

Janet moaned, "Not even close. Where did it go?"

"It's somewhere in the corridor," Roy replied. "We don't have a visual on it, but it's not finished. It won't be finished until it gains control of this machine."

Janet glanced at a screen.

"The power's still on! How is that possible?" She looked to the dais and saw Margaret scrambling to punch in codes to a variety of massive computers and rushed up the stairs. "What are you doing?"

With a grimace Margaret shouted, "I'm trying to keep the power on! That thing tore down a substation! I managed to reroute the circuits but there's only eleven substations and we need at least nine to keep the portal open! Isaiah and Amanda have to return now!"

"We have to kill that thing first or they're walking into a massacre," replied Roy calmly. "Where's the substation that it tore up?"

"The substation is wasted! It's dead! It's shit!"

"Where's the *next* substation!"

"It's three hundred yards down the corridor!" Margaret swept sweat from her face. "It's three hundred yards," she repeated, as if uncertain whether she'd already said it. "You're right. That's where it's going. It has to be. Destroying the power is the only way it can close the portal. But why it wants to close the portal is beyond me! I thought it wanted to *open* the portal."

"Change of plans," Roy said as he changed clips in his rifle. "Its plan was to seize control and then open the gateway. But that plan is off the tracks. Now it's going to shut down this facility, kill us, and wait for a repair crew that doesn't know it's down here. Then it'll start over." He grimaced. "The damn thing is persistent, I'll give it that."

Margaret looked up. "You've gotta stop it, major! If you don't, we'll have to blow the entire collider. We won't have any choice! We can't let another crew come down here and turn this thing on again."

Roy turned.

"Let's go, Tanto."

Hefting the last Javelin, Tanto followed.

Jackman stepped up. "What about me?"

Roy shook his head. "You gotta stay here, general. And keep that detonator close. If it gets past us, you have to blow the pipes." A furtive glance. "Or if anything else comes through that machine, blow everything. No hesitation. No regrets."

They were gone.

***

The creature circled to Isaiah's left when suddenly, and clearly by sorcery, a duplicate katana appeared in its right hand. But the demon's katana was as deep black as dark energy and as dense as the depth separating stars.

"Man has fallen far," it continued.

Isaiah calmly continued to circle right, matching it step for slow step. "So you need those fools on earth to open the portal for you," Isaiah said calmly. "Did you also tell them how to build it?"

"Yes."

"Why?"

"They cannot worship what they cannot see."

Isaiah stopped and lowered the katana to his right, angling it from his body. "So you're the one," he said. "You're him."

It did not reply.

"Yeah," Isaiah frowned, "I figured it would come to this. In my world this is what we call a stand-up fight. It'll be won by whoever has the will to win it."

For a moment it seemed to gather itself. It raised the long blade in its left hand, staring balefully. "So be it," it rasped.

The night-black katana slashed left to right in a horizontal blow that would have sundered an oak tree as Isaiah leaped back; the blade cut the cloth of his coat leaving a coldness and Isaiah knew by the quickest instinct that one touch of that blade was death.

In the same flash Isaiah also lashed out with a duplicate horizontal strike and it ducked with the skill of a seasoned warrior as the katana passed over its head. Then it did what

Isaiah expected because Isaiah had already half-turned to block its backhand blow; the katanas struck and rebounded and Isaiah quick-stepped back with a glance at his blade.

The Honjo Masamune had defied the impact and that should have amazed Isaiah but he had no time for amazement or anything else; this was strength and skill and something unknown and there was no more time for thought.

It shrieked as it leaped holding the katana with both hands and stabbing straight for Isaiah's chest and Isaiah violently brought the Honjo katana up with a power blow that would have broken a lesser blade. The impact was tremendous and blasted the black katana, with the creature holding it, to Isaiah's left.

It was in range.

Isaiah bridged the gap before any consciousness of his movement registered in his mind to slash again, this time aiming for its ribs and he struck through it and continued with the blow, cleaving through what constituted its flesh.

With a roar the creature arched its back and swung blindly in a backhand attempt to hit Isaiah, but Isaiah had already, almost casually, stepped outside range and the beast's blade cut through empty air. Only then did Isaiah realize that this confrontation was inside a stark arena of white light descending from a powerful source.

Beyond this, all was darkness floating over the face of the deep. But here they stood in a circle—no, a land of light as bright as the morning. But that was all the time Isaiah had for a conscious thought as it attacked again.

Isaiah had its timing and deflected blow after blow while equally returning them as he retreated and the light followed. But neither of them struck the other. Every blow had been evaded or blocked or parried or had simply passed without a touch. And yet with each collision of blades Isaiah registered the creature's enormous strength and was constantly stunned that the Honjo Masamune katana did not shatter but absorbed every hit without damage while perfectly returning the same.

If ever a blade was forged for killing mortal or immortal …

Isaiah held it in his strong right hand.

***

Staring in horror at the conflict, Amanda lifted an arm across her chest.

It was fire and ice.

The demon screamed and whirled and slashed with blinding fury in a flurry of cuts that were so fast and complex Amanda couldn't truly see if the sweeping black blade was even moving and yet Isaiah blocked blow after blow before countering with his own attacks that the demon evaded by the faintest, flashing margin.

Howling in fury, the demon redoubled the blurring flurry of so many blows far faster than the eye could follow and yet Isaiah said nothing as he blocked, parried, slid, ducked, or evaded with a perfect step of pure ice. And, through it all, the arena of light kept them separated, alone, and highlighted, effortlessly defying the night.

The entire world had been split into darkness and light so that there was just this.

Demon and Man.

Fire and Ice.

To the end.

***

This fight had already broken every rule of kendo Isaiah knew because fights with katanas never lasted more than seconds. In kendo, the first blow struck was death and that was almost always the first blow thrown so they had already advanced beyond anything Isaiah had ever experienced. In every other fight, every other training session Isaiah had ever endured, this conflict would be over by now.

While the creature's blade *was* death to the touch, the Honjo katana was not less. It seemed vibrant, fulfilling a purpose. Never since Isaiah had held it, and he had held it all his life, had he more vividly felt the life of the blade.

They each leaped, blades colliding edge to edge and holding. Each fighter was close enough to kiss and yet neither could move without risking a lightning-fast blow he could not avoid at this close range. They were frozen like a statue saluting the shadow world in a world of shadow.

Isaiah had an impression in the back of his consciousness that it did possess a face beneath the obscure sheen that clothed its features. Beneath the funeral veil of darkness Isaiah glimpsed black orbs like eyes and the grim line of its mouth.

The creature bent into its stance, pushing.

Isaiah's jaw tightened and he pushed against it.

This was the most dangerous position one could hold against another katana. Neither could retreat, neither could strike, neither could shift even a fraction of an inch without losing control of the opponent's blade.

It roared, "*You can't defeat me!*"

Isaiah's lips drew back in a snarl.

"You've *been* defeated!"

***

Staring down from the Observation Room, Janet saw Roy and Tanto hit the collider corridor floor in a full run. They mounted the ATLAS and searched before Roy lifted his mic: "*Confirmed! They're gone! The bomb, too! I'm gonna give him his one hour! General, if you don't hear from us in an hour, blow it!*"

Jackman: "One hour. Roger that."

Janet looked at her watch. Then she turned and mounted the dais to where Margaret was shifting between computers. The older physicist moved with the alacrity of someone half her age as she shifted power platforms.

Margaret slammed in a command and lifted her face blackened by the smoke and soot of explosions. In the ghastly florescent light that had inexplicably survived the chaos; her eyes made her look like a zombie with a hideously white stare.

"Is it gonna hold?" gasped Janet.

"I don't know!" Margaret bowed her head, catching her breath. "It tore out a substation and I don't know how it did that without getting killed! There's enough electricity in that substation to kill a thousand people! How could it do that without getting killed?"

Janet shifted. "I don't know. Maybe it's operating on some other kind of power we don't understand."

"Like what!"

"I don't know!" Janet repeated. "Maybe it's the secret behind dark energy! Maybe it's the power that created dark energy! How would I know?"

Margaret hurled a tablet across the room.

"*Damn this place!*"

***

Roy leaped a shattered steel cylinder, landing silently.

He was crouching as Tanto came down beside him. With a glance Roy assured himself that Tanto was holding up—not an easy thing considering the beating they'd endured. For a split-second Roy was grateful for the agony of Delta training. It never ended, and *was* Hell, but always gave you an edge that carried you through.

"It's gone for the next one," Tanto gasped. "But it's going slow. Isaiah hurt it bad with that sword, man."

"Yeah," said Roy. "Okay. Police up. What we got?"

"I got two full clips, four frags, and the last Javelin."

"It'll have to do."

They breathed deep, centering.

"A quarter-mile pace?" asked Roy. "Can you handle it?"

"Still in the fight, sir."

"Then let's put this down before it puts us down."

They were running as they rose.

***

"*Whoa!*" shouted Janet as her hands leaped off a keyboard. "*What happened!*"

"Oh, no!" Margaret flung her chair across the dais to magically stop in front of another computer. She began typing, gazing at the screen. "That thing took out another substation! The computers can't even function if we lose another one!"

Janet cried, "Is the portal down?"

"*Yes!*"

"Reroute the power!"

"I'm trying!"

Fumbling frantically, Janet lifted a phone and dialed; she knew every phone in the corridor would simultaneously begin ringing and Roy should answer. If he didn't, she would go after him demon or no demon.

Almost immediately, Roy picked up.

"I know!" he said. "It hit another station! We're on it!"

"What's it doing!"

"It's trying to shut down the collider!"

"Why now?"

"Something must have happened in Isaiah's dimension because now it's willing to shut down the collider and hide in this place for as long as it takes for them to repair it! And that thing can wait a thousand years! It's got time on its side! We don't!"

"Then go get it!"

Janet jerked her head back as the slam of a phone struck her like a slap in the face. She took a deep breath and turned to Margaret. "Any luck getting the portal back up?"

"Not yet!"

"Does this mean Isaiah and Amanda can't return?"

"They can't come back with the portal down!"

"How far is the next—"

"It's three hundred yards just like the last one!"

"Shit!" Janet grabbed a desk. "Can I do anything?"

"No!" said Margaret angrily. "You don't know the system!"

"I'm taking the ATV!"

Snatching up a fallen rifle, Janet ran from the room.

***

"I got you!" Roy shouted as he erupted from behind a pylon.

As the beast began ripping wire from the third substation the bullets again rebounded from its armor to no apparent effect, but the impacts did push it off balance and Roy immediately saw why—the blood-soaked leg revealed bone.

As Roy dropped the clip, it charged.

Tanto fired a grenade into its chest.

The blast was magnified by the cement cylinder and Roy bellowed as he staggered; he noticed Tanto had done the same and even the beast had reacted similarly; they were all hit with the same concussion and suffered the same effect.

Roy's teeth gleamed.

"You're going down!"

Even before the shock wave lifted, Roy saw one of the satchels positioned inside the cylinder far above his head.

Too far to reach but not too far to shoot.

Roy slammed in a clip and instantly lifted aim, unleashing a full clip into the satchel and was actually amazed when he lowered the rifle to see the satchel still plainly in place as if it hadn't been touched by a single round. Then the beast was on top of them and Roy leaped to the left to avoid the thunderous fist that shattered the cement floor. As he rolled to his feet Roy saw Tanto also rising, pulling out a machete.

"*No!*" Roy shouted but Tanto had leaped forward to violently strike sparks from the beast's armor. Then the creature's return blow ended the fight as it struck with a single arm, taking off Tanto's head. Roy watched as Tanto's body took a single, staggering step before it fell forward and the beast turned into Roy once more.

Roy's training returned to him; no, Semtex won't detonate if it's exposed to bullets or pressure. It was designed to deny any cause of outside ignition. But if Roy could set off a blasting cap *inside* the satchel …

Spinning, Roy saw a portable walkway against the wall.

No time!

He ducked frantically and rolled under the collider pipes as the cement where he stood was pulverized in a sandstorm of jagged shards.

Either the beast did not possess enough remaining strength to destroy the collider itself or that was not part of its plan. It leaped atop the pipes with shocking agility, considering its leg wound, and descended beside Roy.

It inhaled once, deeply.

The battle was won.

Roy saw victory in its eyes, so it was in no hurry to finish off this human that stood before it and its final triumph. There were no more soldiers, no more guns, and no one was left to rescue Roy from its grasp. So, now it could finish the power grid at its leisure without destroying the pipes themselves, furthering its purpose.

It was as if it had known this ending from the beginning.

Staring up, Roy frowned revealing no fear, no regret. Then he glimpsed movement far to the side and flung out an arm, "*No!*"

Janet fired Tanto's grenade launcher that she had lifted from the floor and Roy was already rolling beneath the pipes to put something solid between himself and the blast as the grenade hit the abomination in the back.

The concussion was exactly like before and Roy staggered to the far wall groaning, trying to reduce the pressure in his head. He didn't even need to look to know that Janet was on her back in agony, torpedoed by the unexpected sonic impact.

As he violently came off the wall, Roy tried to get a reading on the beast and saw the thing pushing itself up from the floor, its armor on fire. With a roar the creature reached over a shoulder and snatched the white-hot iron plate from its back, flinging it aside. Then the breastplate simple fell to the floor. Last, it removed its ragged helmet that had been dented and torn by grenade after grenade.

Now it had no armor.

Roy saw the Javelin close.

Leaping forward, Roy snatched it up as Janet raised her head to see the beast poised upon the collider. Crouching on the pipe, its apelike face lazily swung between herself and Roy as she screamed, "*Shoot the damn thing!*"

Roy raised the Javelin as the creature bent.

Staring up, Roy aimed between its eyes.

It laughed.

"*Go to Hell,*" whispered Roy.

He pulled the trigger.

The Javelin struck it in the face and disappeared into the square image of might and the beast arched backward, howling with both hands at its head for a split-second before the detonation liquefied the grotesque head and chest in a mushroom of vaporized flesh. Yet, still, it stood, half the colossal body swaying backward and forward again until it pitched toward Roy, a single arm uplifted, and crashed to the floor.

Roy pushed up from the floor and by reflex evaluated his hearing, his balance, his wounds and—and this was the wildest guess—how much fight he had left in him. With a groan he gained a knee, rising.

"*Still in the fight,*" he whispered.

Janet hadn't risen from the floor and was moaning as she rolled from side to side. She had probably never been exposed to such an enclosed concussion and Roy was both relieved and stunned that she was alive at all because more people were killed by the sonic force of a blast than from shrapnel or flame. As Roy reached her side, he gently raised her to a sitting position and her gaze centered on the gargantuan beast lying in the corridor.

It wasn't moving.

Half its hulking body had been liquefied.

Janet gasped, "Get me inside the substation!"

***

This could not endure.

Isaiah was determined that he would not be the first to move. He would let *it* decide its blow when it stepped back or struck, and his counter would have to be instantaneous and would probably end this.

Suddenly the creature was transformed into a blood-drenched demonic form with glaring eyes of black that shrieked in Isaiah's face.

Isaiah revealed nothing—no fear, no concern; he did not waver in his resistance or shift more than what was needed as they slowly continued to circle, still maintaining their position chest to chest, blade to blade.

It shrieked again and lifted the blade a fraction.

Isaiah shouted as he brought down the Honjo Masamune slashing its forearm to sever the appendage and the demon's sword and hand fell toward the ground. But before the arm even hit the white surface Isaiah reversed the katana and brought the blade up to sever its other arm. And, with that move, Isaiah stepped directly before it, the katana uplifted.

Isaiah roared as he struck.

The Honjo Masamune hit the crest of its head and continued though its neck and chest and the rest of its body until the tip of the katana struck the unearthly ground behind it. But that was not enough as Isaiah screamed, whirling in place to swing around with the katana clutched in his right hand, and his right hand alone, to cut the abomination in half at the hips, the hardest part of its body, in a one-armed, backhanded blow—a swordsman's most difficult cut—to sever it into six fragments; the white steel katana continued into the gleaming white air leaving a wake of blood so that when it was done Isaiah stood face to face with it, so close and glaring, as the beast slowly slid apart, and fell.

Breathing heavily, teeth bared, Isaiah stood for a moment with the katana raised. But another blow was not needed. Then he viciously flung blood from the steel and stepped back as a shadow gathered over the corpse, condensing around the creature and, vaguely, Isaiah could discern faint movement within the congealing, occult depth.

It gave the impression of reconstitution empowered by a cosmic force that was once vibrant but now oozed over this shadow substance like black oil, and, in that moment, Isaiah knew that, no, it could not be destroyed by any weapon forged by man.

The form it inhabited could be destroyed, but the dark energy that gave life to the heart of it was destined to die a different death.

Cloaked in black even within the arena of light, the demonic shape slowly rose from the floor. It was imperfectly reconstituted and Isaiah knew it would need time to repair the damage it was suffering. But it was healing.

It laughed.

"I only wanted to see how deeply your arrogance runs," it said.

"No," said Isaiah, "you didn't. You wanted to kill me. And you failed. Like you've always failed. I wish I could have seen you thrown down." His eyes were fierce. "Someone said you looked like lightning falling from Heaven."

"The battle isn't over," it sneered.

With a frown Isaiah lowered the katana.

"It is today."

Without removing his eyes from the grotesque obsidian form that shuffled forward matching Isaiah stride for stride, Isaiah backed slowly toward Amanda's trembling form to gently grasp her right hand.

A narrow glance confirmed to Isaiah that the tiny red light on the nuclear weapon was still functioning. He raised his gaze to the beast.

"Are you going to tell me your name?" asked Isaiah.

It laughed, "My name is Baal. No … Forgive me … My name is Moloch. It is Belial. No, I forget. Yes, now I remember. It is Pazuzu. No, it is Charun. Gremory. Krampus. Naamah. Sitri. Tannin. Valac. Zagan. Rahab. Do you wish to know more?"

Isaiah reached out to flick up the lid covering the trigger to the mega-bomb. Once he flipped the switch there would be no stopping the explosion, so he looked over to see Amanda standing inches from the almost dead portal. Even though the gateway retained a thin veneer of light, Isaiah knew that they had lost power on the other end.

"There's one name you failed to mention," said Isaiah, looking back at the ravaged figure.

It stopped in place.

"Oh," it said, "that one."

"Why not claim what's rightfully yours?"

"What belongs to me was stolen by a tyrant."

Isaiah tilted his head. "For a king, you sure lose a lot."

"The truth deceived me."

"I guess you didn't understand the truth."

"The truth," it said bitterly, "is that there are many gods." Abruptly, it laughed. "Did you know that by my power I created what your world calls all things supernatural? What they call miracles and sorcery and magic? But there was one God who forbid me from receiving what was rightfully mine … for he is a jealous God."

"What was rightfully yours?"

"Worship."

Isaiah once more raised the tip of the katana. It glanced at the point of the sword poised at the trigger and paused. Then it raised a gaze.

"It will profit you nothing," it said.

"Well," Isaiah allowed, "it ain't gonna do you any good, either."

Isaiah flicked the switch.

"Holy God!" screamed Amanda.

Isaiah spun to see her with hands uplifted at where the portal once existed but now there was only a ring of fire filled with dark matter swirling like an angry shark beneath black water; there was no place to go, no escape. There were trapped in this dimension with a nuclear bomb ticking off the last thirty seconds.

Amanda whirled to Isaiah.

"What do we do!" she shouted.

Isaiah looked at the creature.

"You've made your choice," it said.

***

Janet had raced around the substation throwing multitudinous switches and looked up and down, abruptly motionless, as if searching for a ghost. Her rage couldn't be contained to physical action.

"What the hell is wrong with this thing? Why isn't it kicking in?" Janet pointed viciously. "There! Roy! Get up there and throw that big red switch on my signal! *But wait for my signal*!"

Roy leaped over the debris of a fence and was instantly on top of the huge steel conduction box where he saw a red switch pointing straight up. He knew enough about breakers to know it had to connect. As he laid a hand on it, he twisted to see Janet poised beside a series of white switches, holding one in each hand.

"On my signal!" she screamed and rapidly began throwing a series of switches up and then down until she almost immediately covered the distance of the substation. As she slammed the last switch, she spun.

"*HIT IT*!"

Roy threw the switch.

***

As a sun blazing at noonday the portal suddenly reopened before them disintegrating the blazing crimson ring so that it showered across them red rain and Isaiah didn't hesitate as he grabbed Amanda's hand and leaped into the gateway; he wasn't going to give it another chance to disappear without them.

He heard the voice behind them.

"*Isaiah*! *I'm coming for you*!"

As they were engulfed by the portal Isaiah glanced back to see the last seconds erased on the timer of the mega-bomb and then everything was overcome by a soundless white that followed them into but not through the portal as whatever was visible in this alternate world vanished in the white heat of the purest power.

***

"Is it working?" Roy shouted.

Janet staggered back, hands at the sides of her head. "I don't know!"

"Dammit! Is it working, Janet?"

"I don't know, Roy!"

"How can you know?"

Flinging arms out, Janet shook her head.

"We have to get back fast!"

Roy grabbed her hand, dragging her over debris. Then, together, they leaped into the ATV and in seconds were flying toward the nearby Observation Room.

***

Margaret's hands jumped from the computer like she'd been shocked as Roy, his arm slung over Janet's shoulders, staggered into the control chamber.

"Whoa!" Margaret shouted. "What was that!"

Janet groaned, "Did you get the power on?"

"No!" Margaret gasped. "I didn't! What happened?"

"Is it *working*?" shouted Roy.

Margaret scanned every screen. "The machine might be working but the computers have to reboot! It takes a minute!"

The floor trembled and the walls visibly quaked as every light surrounding the collider suddenly came alive and they turned together to see the ATLAS door open even though Margaret didn't command it. Face twisting in regret, General Jackman pointed the detonator at the machine as he groaned, "I'm sorry, guys."

"*Wait*!" shouted Janet, dragging Roy forward.

Blazing blue light had erupted from the open door of the ATLAS sheathing the Observation Room window in a cobalt-azure haze as two figures emerged from the cylinder, each leaning on the other, one holding a shining white katana.

"It's them!" Janet laughed hoarsely. "They're back!"

Raising his gaze, Roy dropped his head again. His word was the very last word of a man spent with exhaustion, "*Yeah …*"

Jackman dropped his hand to his side. Then he bowed his head and slowly shook it for a long moment. "By God," he muttered, "I'm going to make this deathtrap a controversy until the day Jesus tears the sky apart and comes down, and I hope he lands graveyard dead on top of this place and judgment starts right here."

Upon the solid platform, Amanda and Isaiah embraced.

Roy laughed, "Make the most of it." He tightened his arm around Janet. "You ready to go home?"

Janet rested her forehead into his chest.

"Yeah," she whispered, "take me home, cowboy …"

***

It was three months before Isaiah found himself moving inside his bookshop without being in agony. That butcher-knife sized shard had done more damage to his leg than he'd realized at the time and, even now, he was amazed he'd managed the duel against whatever that thing was. But he no longer pondered, in his more honest reflections, what it was.

It was a demon or worse. And with that thought Isaiah glanced at the aluminum case holding the Honjo Masamune; it was leaning against the wall behind the counter of the bookshop, always close.

The international debacle following the final conflict within the collider was almost as spectacular as the battle itself. Only the overtly theatrical saber-rattling of a United Nations Peacekeeping Force insured their safe passage from Switzerland after the U.S. threatened to withdraw all funding for the UN if they did not intervene. And, in the end, all charges were dismissed, early retirements were arranged and no one was sentenced to prison on the continent or anywhere else. And CERN continued searching mask after mask for a power they would never understand. A power that was a living thing and would come to them only at its appointed time.

No. It wasn't the perfect ending.

But what is?

Amanda walked into the aisle with an armload of books. She studiously began placing them on a shelf before she glanced toward Isaiah standing without working or seeming to work. Her brow hardened.

"Hey," she asked quietly. "You all right?"

Isaiah blinked, "Yeah."

"Is it your leg?"

"No," Isaiah shook his head, and glanced at his rapidly expanding theological section, which was newly bracketed by multitudinous books on evolution, creationism, time, physics, space, and light as well as every theoretical beginning and every theoretical ending of the universe, scientific or not. In fact, his store had become something of a specialty shop and a place for intensely intellectual, but civil, discussions over coffee and beer and sandwiches—an unexpected benefit over Isaiah's past, unimpressive prosperity that he and Amanda had translated into the luxury of a real home not far away. No, it wasn't a big thing. But Isaiah had learned to appreciate the day of small things.

"You're in pain," Amanda said as she laid the books aside and gently placed a hand on his shoulder. "Do you need one of your meds?"

Isaiah smiled and glanced high at what he didn't truly understand and never would. He didn't know how they had won the day. All he knew was that the day had been won and a force beyond them all had opened that portal three seconds before the purest power engulfed that entire dimension. And although he had never considered himself a spiritual man, Isaiah found himself inclined more and more to such thoughts these days.

Where would it end?

Who knows?

"Isaiah?" whispered Amanda. "Are you okay?"

"Yeah," Isaiah nodded. "Did you get the new seeds for our garden?"

"What? I didn't think you cared about the garden."

With a smile Isaiah slid a book onto the shelf and turned. He gently laid arms over her shoulders and leaned close. He gazed down into her eyes until Amanda laughed.

His own words were the truest Isaiah had ever known.

"I'm beginning to care about a lot of things."

THE END

For More News About James Byron Huggins, Signup For Our Newsletter:

http://wbp.bz/newsletter

Word-of-mouth is critical to an author's long-term success. If you appreciated this book please leave a review on the Amazon sales page:

http://wbp.bz/cruxa

**AVAILABLE FROM JAMES BYRON
HUGGINS AND WILDBLUE PRESS!**

DARK VISIONS by JAMES BYRON HUGGINS

http://wbp.bz/darkvisionsa

Read A Sample Next

ONE

Sitting upon a bough, the raven watched.

In the dying of the light the little boy swung slowly from the tree, his body broken, a noose around his neck. And at the edge of the forest a car burned and the raven watched as flame rose from the heat like hate rising from the heart of the sun.

The raven and the boy were together as the fire burned and burned and began to fade in the last of the day but still the raven did not move. It stayed upon the bough and did not leave the boy alone until the sun had descended and was gone.

The raven watched as the boy was claimed by the darkness of the night. It watched as the fire smoldered and the smoke vanished in the evening gray that overcame the day. It watched and it watched and it watched and it watched until something else had begun to burn in the dying of the light …

Fire rose in the raven's eyes.

* * *

Joe Mac felt the gray November cold more completely than he'd ever felt it before because he could no longer see the leaves fade from rust to gold or gaze upon the skeletal silhouettes of trees etched against the gray November sky.

Now he lived in the world of the blind, so feeling the cold was all that remained. The rest was darkness and he would inhabit this darkness until the day he died and they buried him in the dirt and this darkness.

The raven came as it always came; it descended with the sound of enormous wings to land with a thunderclap on the home Joe Mac had built for it.

Three years ago they met as Joe Mac was first learning to live in the world of the blind. The raven had come to him every day as he sat alone in the back of the barn, and Joe Mac named him "Poe" after the old poem. And every evening they would sit together in the back of the barn in Joe Mac's eternal night.

Poe did not rise or even seem to notice the familiar Mrs. Clemens as she approached, but then Poe rarely flew away when someone came close. Rather, he seemed to know the exact distance for danger and ignored anything else.

Mrs. Clemens brought Joe Mac his supper – an act Joe Mac reckoned to her uncommon human kindness – and spent a moment to inquire about his health. But Joe Mac sensed something different in Mrs. Clemens tonight. Her steps were halting and seemed to wander before she laid a hand on his shoulder.

Lifting his face, Joe Mac asked, "What is it, Mrs. Clemens?"

Mrs. Clemens shuffled, and Joe Mac felt the strength lessen in the hand; it was not much of a change, it was true, but a hand with little strength is even more revealing when what little strength it possesses is diminished ever more.

Joe Mac repeated more sternly, "What is it, Mrs. Clemens?"

"Oh," moaned Mrs. Clemens, "it's horrible, Mr. Joe Mac. Just horrible. Oh, god, I don't know how to tell you."

"Just say it."

She faltered, "It's about your grandson, Mr. Joe Mac. It's about Aaron. The poor thing disappeared from daycare today."

Joe Mac's left hand tightened on the arm of the chair. "How could they lose a four-year-old boy? Have they called the police?"

"Your poor daughter has called everyone! We're all scared to death something terrible has happened!"

With a shrill cry Poe erupted into the night sky as Joe Mac stood pulling his wool coat more tightly across his chest; he snapped his cane to length. "Why didn't someone tell me about this earlier?" he demanded.

"They've been too busy searching for him, Mr. Joe Mac! They've looked everywhere! And you can't even …"

She let the sentence die.

"Take me to my daughter," said Joe Mac. "And compose yourself, Mrs. Clemens. We don't know that anything terrible has happened. Compose yourself! Stay calm. And take me to my daughter."

TWO

"Here's the case file on that little kid."

Jodi Strong raised her eyes as the file was laid upon her desk. The veteran New York City detective, Thomas Grimes, who delivered the file pulled up a chair and leaned back, folding hands on his chest.

"What do you want with this thing, Jodi?" Grimes asked and didn't attempt to conceal either his curiosity or confusion. "There's already a million cops on this, and we got twenty cases of our own to work."

"I took the original call last week when I was in uniform," said Jodi. "I interviewed the daycare workers, the mother, the father. And then they found the little kid but he was already dead. Just like the others."

Grimes spoke in a weary monotone, "Jodi, it was your case when you were in uniform. It was your case when you took the missing person report. But you got promoted to detective three days ago, and it ain't your case no more. It belongs to the task force and you ain't on the task force, neither. So what are you doing?"

Jodi shook her head, "Grimes, I know it's always a mistake to get personally involved in a case but –"

"Then don't."

"But that scene at the house really shook me up," Jodi continued. "I saw the little boy's room. I saw his picture. I felt like I knew him. And then he ends up … like he ended up." She slapped the file. "I'm tired of this psycho!"

Grimes sighed, "Jodi, the FBI has a thousand people on this. We've got about a million. One more cop ain't gonna make no difference in this. And we need you *here*."

Jodi made a slight sound as she sucked breath through her teeth. Then she said, "He's made a mistake, Grimes. They're just not finding it. Nobody's perfect."

"Well, this psycho is pretty close to perfect because right now the task force guys tell me they don't have a clue. One of 'em told me they're no closer to catching him now than they were four years ago."

Jodi opened the file and leaned back; "Aaron Roberts. Four years old. Abducted from the playground of his daycare. His body was found one hour after sunset –"

"Same as the rest of 'em."

Jodi continued reading as Grimes stood and leaned over her desk.

"Jodi," he began in a patient tone, "listen to me; I'm glad you made detective. I think you're a natural. But you're wasting your time. Whatever mistake this guy made ain't gonna be in no file. There's no fibers, no hairs, no prints, no DNA. There's no witnesses, no video, no tracks." He pointed toward the door. "This guy has killed twenty-four people, and he could walk through that door right now and confess to everything we've got and we wouldn't be able to pin him to a single thing. He doesn't take anything. He doesn't leave anything. He has no motive. He has no face. He has no name. *He's a ghost.*"

"Excuse me."

Jodi lifted her face to see an exceeding large man standing on the far side of her desk at the same moment she realized he was blind.

The man was slightly less than six feet but built like a brick. His body seemed one uniform size from his linebacker shoulders down through his barrel chest to his waist and weightlifter legs. His head was a square granite block set on a short neck. His white hair was standard military high-and-tight. His arms were heavy and the hand holding the cane was thick with strong-looking fingers although he held the shaft with a fisherman's touch.

Jodi was instantly curious why the man's presence gave her a palpitation of alarm. There was certainly nothing obviously threatening about him. And yet an aura of doom seemed to cloak him even more than the knee-length undertaker coat or the impenetrable black glasses; it occurred to Jodi that his appearance could not have been more unsettling if he'd been wearing a black funeral veil over his face. In all he reminded Jodi of a Texas tombstone she'd once seen that read, "*As you are, I once was. As I am, you will be…*"

Jodi whispered, "Good god …"

Grimes turned, gaped, and grabbed one of the man's blacksmith arms. "Joe Mac Blake! I haven't seen you in years, Joe! How ya been, man?"

"You're lookin' at it," said Joe Mac. "They still got you in robbery, Grimes?"

"Same 'ol same." Grimes theatrically lifted a hand toward Jodi as she rolled her eyes; *he's blind, you dolt.* "Jodi, this is ex-homicide detective Joe Mac Blake. Joe is a legend! Joe, this is Detective Jodi Strong. She's the newest member of the team." A laugh. "Well, this is a blast from the past, buddy. What are you doing downtown, man?"

Joe Mac lightly tapped the desk with his cane. "Got a seat for me?"

"Sure." Grimes pulled up a rolling chair. "Sit down."

Joe Mac felt, found the chair, and sat. He turned his face toward Jodi, "Nice to meet you, Jodi. Grimes is a good man. He'll help you get the lay of the land around here, but it won't take you too long." He paused. "Can one of you tell me who's handling the Aaron Roberts case? He was the little boy that got killed last week."

"Officially that case belongs to the task force," said Jodi. "He's another victim of a serial killer we've been trying to catch for a long time."

"The Hangman?"

Jodi stared, then, "We've been ordered from on-high not to use that phrase, but, yeah, it was 'The Hangman.'" She glanced at the file. "But as it happens, Joe, I've got a copy of the file right here."

Joe Mac lifted his face. "Have you had a chance to look at it?"

"No. I just got it. What can I do for you, Joe?"

"Aaron was my grandson." Joe Mac's face was stone. "I know I can't contribute to the forensics, but if you have any personal questions about Aaron, maybe I could help you out a little bit."

Jodi stared. "I'm sorry for your loss, Joe."

"Appreciate it."

After expelling a long breath Jodi said, "Look, Joe, they've got a task force briefing in about twenty minutes. Why don't you come with me? The FBI will be there along with Captain Brightbarton. He's in charge."

"I don't have a badge anymore."

"You're with me. You'll be okay."

Joe Mac rose, his hand moving his cane.

"Let's go."

* * *

Joe Mac knew he was seated in the third row from the back, the second chair from the right side of the room. He'd been here many times during his thirty-five-year career as a New York City uniform patrol officer and then as a gold shield homicide investigator, and he knew every line of this place.

He also knew that the front few rows would be filled with investigators and uniform patrol supervisors. The next rows would contain FBI personnel. And the last few rows would be filled with forensics experts, psychologists, and people like himself.

Captain Steve Brightbarton announced, "All right, gentlemen, you've all had a chance to review the forensics on four-year-old Aaron Roberts. As of this moment we can confirm that Aaron was killed inside that warehouse. The suspect used blunt force trauma to break all his bones – the same thing he did to the other victims – and then he hung him by a noose around his neck. Same as the rest. Forensics says the tool used in the attack was a club coated in bronze, so keep your eyes open for a plain-view search. Crime Scene didn't recover any DNA. No hairs. No fibers. No prints. Not even any touch-DNA. We don't have him on video. We have no witnesses. The car was stolen from a police impound lot, and that's all we got. At this time I'll turn it over to FBI Special Agent Jack Rollins."

There was little to hear besides the rustling of clothing as Jack Rollins stood and Brightbarton took a chair.

"Afternoon," Rollins began, "you all know me. But for the uninitiated my name is Jack Rollins, and I am the Special Agent in charge of the FBI task force. Everything Captain Brightbarton just told you is accurate. I'll only add that the murder of Aaron Roberts is consistent with the twenty-three murders preceding this, so confidence is high that we're dealing with the same suspect. As usual, the suspect left nothing behind. The rope he used was standard clothesline that you can purchase at any hardware store. He torched the vehicle with a half-gallon of gasoline inside a one gallon milk jug armed with a two-dollar, off-the-shelf egg timer so we have no prints, no fibers, and no DNA.

"We have nothing further on a description. We know he uses disguises, and we have him on traffic cameras as an old man, a young man, a poor man, a rich man. The only thing we know for sure is that it's a man. We have isolated no salient physical characteristics that would make him easier to identify. He could be me. He could be you. All we can tell you is that we believe he's a white male in his mid-thirties. He's about six foot, 180 pounds. He very, very strong physically, and we believe he has a superior IQ. So our strategy is for the NYPD to continue their stop and frisk strategy of any and every person of interest. We want you to continue priority patrols and stakeouts of secular daycares, church daycares, schools, malls, playgrounds, parks. Meanwhile, we at the FBI will continue to work forensics and continue our enhanced surveillance of every name the computer spits out. Now, we do not know if this psychopath is armed but, of course, you know to approach him as if he is." He paused. "I know I certainly will. And now I'll turn this over to Dr. Marvin Mason. He's assistant senior anthropologist for New York's American Museum of Natural History. He also has a doctorate in archeology, and he is continuing to work with our Division of Behavioral Science to keep an up-to-date profile on this guy. So, Dr. Mason? Would you, please?"

The chamber was subdued, which allowed Joe Mac to hear Dr. Mason's soft steps and then the microphone was turned, apparently to accommodate his height.

"Thank you," said Mason.

Imperceptibly Joe Mac nodded; yeah, from the depth of his voice Mason wasn't big, but he wasn't a lightweight, either. Joe Mac estimated him at a few inches less than six feet, about 170 pounds. His accent was native Long Island.

"All I can tell you is what I've already told you," Dr. Mason began. "As you know, this subject takes the time to break every bone in a victim's body, and then he hangs them by the neck from a tree. We've done extensive research, and we have found this manner of human sacrifice, or punishment, to be so prevalent in ancient cultures that we can't isolate any specific cult or religion or sect or civilization as the primary instigator. He could have taken it from the Jews or the Gaelic tribes or the Vikings or various Asiatic cultures. All we can say is that we believe you're looking for an individual who kills in this highly methodical manner because he is motivated by some kind of pathological religious psychosis." He paused. "We know you guys are working hard, and all of us at the museum want to help. But that's all we've been able to come up with.

There's just nothing exotic enough about what's he doing to narrow it down to any one culture or religion. It's barbaric and savage. But it's not exotic. Throughout recorded history it's something that's been done by almost everybody."

Jodi said, "Dr. Mason?"

Mason paused. "Yes?"

Beside Joe Mac, Jodi stood; she was leaning on the chair before them. "Doctor, how long is he going to keep this up?"

"We believe he's going to keep it up until you catch him or kill him."

"Why do you say that?"

"Just like we don't know what kind of obsession is motivating him, we can't say with any certainty when this obsession will be fulfilled," Mason answered. "I think it's safe to say that you're dealing with someone who is very smart and very cautious but also completely insane and I see no reason why he will stop doing what he's doing."

"History doesn't suggest a motive?" Jodi asked.

Mason sighed; "The closest thing we've found to a motive are rituals used in turn-of-the-century Europe to destroy werewolves." He cleared his throat. "In Europe, when they caught someone they suspected of being a werewolf, they would put them on a rack, break their bones, hang them, and set them on fire. They did the same thing to people suspected of witchcraft. Even in this century. Even in this *country*. But we don't think he's doing all this because he suspects someone of being a werewolf or a witch. We think he's doing it because he's afflicted with a bizarre religious psychosis that is totally beyond the understanding of any sane person and probably beyond his understanding, too. We don't think even he knows why he's doing what he's doing. He doesn't know why he's doing it, but he can't stop himself. That's how crazy we think he is."

"But why do you insist it's a religious psychosis?" Jodi pressed.

"Because breaking someone's bones and hanging them from a tree are traditional religious punishments. Both of them are in the Bible. Both of them are in the Koran. Both of them are in the Torah. In a nutshell, they're universal religious means of punishment for someone breaking a religious law regardless whether that law comes from Yahweh or Allah or Shiva. Does that answer your question?"

Jodi nodded, "Yes, thank you."

FBI Special Agent Jack Rollins stood – Joe Mac heard the scrape of chair legs – and asked, "I'm sorry but I don't know your name Detective –?"

"Detective Jodi Strong, sir."

"Are you on the task force?"

"No," Jodi answered firmly. "I worked the original missing person call on Aaron Roberts when I was in uniform."

Hesitation.

"I see," said Rollins. "Well, the fact is that we don't know any more about who killed Aaron Roberts than we know who killed the rest of the victims, detective. We know this guy's methods. We have no idea who he is or why he's doing this."

"I understand," said Jodi.

She sat.

Joe Mac followed Mason to his chair on the back of the dais and listened as Brightbarton approached the podium.

"That's it, gentlemen," said Brightbarton. "Check your boxes at the end of shift for any updates. And remember: Approach this guy with the most extreme caution. And that means approach him with your gun *out* and shoot him graveyard dead if he even *looks* at you funny. Be careful out there. Dismissed."

Joe Mac didn't move as everyone rose and began filing out the three doors. He lost contact with any presence on the podium in the mulling of footsteps and conversation like one might lose sight of an eagle against the sun. He did know that Jodi hadn't moved. Neither had she opened the file she'd brought from the office. He would have heard the rustling of paper, and there wasn't any.

"I checked up on you," said Jodi.

Joe Mac's voice was a soft growl; "When'd you have time to do that?"

"When I went to the bathroom. You're a legend."

Joe Mac revealed nothing.

"The lady in the bathroom told me that you solved over a thousand homicides. She said you were a detective first grade with a gold shield, and you were one of those real guys always out there, always hunting. Then you lost your eyesight when you rescued that little boy from that house fire. And I know it sucks – I mean, don't get me wrong; I would never say I know *how much* it sucks – but you did save that little boy's life. And I bet you're still a great detective."

Joe Mac lifted his chin. He seemed to hear better that way; he didn't know why. He didn't care. It worked, and if anything worked at this stage of his life, it was good enough. "Are you thinking you could use some help?" he asked.

By the scraping in her seat Joe Mac knew she turned. "Well, Joe, you knew Aaron. And I've already talked to your daughter. She's in no shape to help me or anybody else right now. So what do you say we ride out to that daycare center and take a look around?" She stood. "Anyway, the daycare's right down the road from your daughter's house. And you live close by, don't you?"

"I live in the barn out back," said Joe Mac. "They sort of turned it into an apartment." He shrugged. "It's good enough."

"Then let's take a ride, Joe. If nothing else, I'll take you home."

Joe Mac stood.

"Bring what you got on this case."

* * *

Joe Mac didn't need eyes to know exactly where they were at any moment. His soul knew this terrain by neurological imprint. He imagined that he might have driven much of it by himself even now.

"I don't know if I told you how sorry I am about Aaron," Jodi said – the first time she'd spoken in her squad car. "I know that nothing is fair in this world but this truly wasn't fair in an ungodly, horrible way that should be damned to Hell."

Someone once said the greatest sound is silence, but Joe Mac couldn't remember who it was. He only knew he had nothing to say until Jodi finally turned the squad car slowly to the left and announced, "Here we are, Joe."

She parked and Joe Mac could feel her stare.

"You ready for this?" she asked.

Joe Mac nodded and opened the door.

"Let's do it," he said.

He extended his cane though he hardly needed it; he could remember every inch of this daycare since he'd seen if often enough when he could still see; it was a compact one-story building with three wings like a *T*. There was a playground with brightly colored plastic equipment out back. It was surrounded by mesh fence about four feet high that had a gate leading into the building. There was one exterior gate on the left. The entire facility was a half-acre surrounded by pines.

Joe Mac had already moved to the front of Jodi's car as she walked up and said, "Do you remember the layout?"

"Yeah."

"Wanna go up to the fence?"

"All right."

Joe Mac had no problem negotiating the sparsely occupied parking lot. He felt the curb with his cane and stepped up knowing the feel of grass beneath his feet; it was a half-inch deep with dry ground beneath. He estimated three steps to the fence, and he was right. He placed a hand on the top of the steel mesh and lifted his chin.

He became aware that he was waiting for … something ….

"Those pine trees back there," said Jodi. "Do you think he could have come in through those? They would have hidden him from view until he came right up to the fence."

"He could have." Joe Mac turned his face toward the back acreage as if he could still see. His voice was faint. "Still green up top. Thick enough. Dead pine needles don't make a sound when you walk on 'em … Yeah. Let's go back there. I know the crime scene boys went over it but it won't hurt to do it again."

"I'm game," Jodi said, and they turned to walk along the fence line.

The front easement had been mowed up to the steel mesh, so Joe Mac didn't have to worry about weeds. Then he felt Jodi's hand at his left elbow, guiding him gently, and he wasn't offended. Guiding a blind man by a light touch at an elbow was something people just seemed to do by instinct.

Joe Mac was accustomed to the drag of his cane on grass; it was much different than the steady, balanced, light touch he used on concrete. He had to lift it higher and touch more quickly; it was more like stabbing fish than the smooth side-to-side he normally used.

Joe Mac estimated twenty steps to the end of this fence line, and he was right. They turned to the left and resumed walking when Jodi said, "I think he used this side. The other side faces the road, and I don't think he'd use that. He'd have to stop his car on the road, jump out, run up to the fence and try to grab one of them. And the kids would have probably run away from him, screamed for their teacher, and they would have called for a unit. He would have never been able to get out of the area before one of us caught up to him. I think he knew that."

"You're right," said Joe Mac. "He wouldn't do that."

"This guy doesn't leave anything to chance." Jodi's voice took a tinge of impatience. "Sometimes it amazes me how crazy people can be so smart when it comes to killing other people. It's almost … cosmic."

They reached the section furthest from the building, and Joe Mac said, "Stop here. What do you see?"

Jodi said, "Well, this is the farthest point of the fence, and they don't mow the grass back here. It's about waist high right up to the playground. But it's been stomped down a little by the search party."

"How big was the search party?"

"It wasn't all that big. There wasn't enough time to organize a big search party or even get the word out. Aaron was reported missing at three in the afternoon, and they found his body at seven-thirty." A pause. "If he'd been missing for a whole day I'm sure we'd have had thousands of people walking the woods out here. But all they had that day was a few cops and some neighbors. Then they found Aaron's body beside that warehouse, and there was no more reason to look."

"Keep moving," Joe Mac motioned. "Keep looking down. Tell me what you see. It doesn't matter what it is."

They strolled and Jodi began "Looks like we got one rabbit hole … Rabbit tracks … There's a fresh mole hill … A coke can … "

"Bag it."

"Got it."

They continued.

"We got another mole hill … A blue leaflet … Bagging it … A candy bar wrapper … Bagging it …. I don't know why those guys didn't bag all this stuff … Amateurs … I should have come back here myself, but I was at your daughter's house …"

"I appreciate it. Keep looking."

"I don't think this is going anywhere, Joe … This coke can and candy bar wrapper look really old … I don't think they have anything to do with what happened …"

"Never assume anything, kid. Keep going."

"Okay … Well, there's some kind of dead thing … Looks like it used to be a bird …There's a piece of white string …"

Joe Mac stopped. "What?"

"What?" Jodi repeated.

"A what?"

"A string?"

"Did you say 'white string?'"

"Yeah. It's white."

"You wearing your gloves?"

"Yeah."

"Pick it up."

Jodi led him to the wood line, bent, and straightened. After a pause, she said, "It's just an ordinary piece of white string, Joe."

"Follow it."

After a moment, Joe Mac felt a tug on his arm. "This is kind of tricky, Joe. Stick close to me. It …" They took several steps, "… it leads into the woods."

"Just follow it."

Jodi suddenly stooped and stayed low for a long time. "That's it," she said. "That's the end of it. It doesn't go any further."

"What's beyond this wood line?" he asked. "Can you see?"

"Yeah. Way back there. There's a field."

"Take me to it."

By Joe Mac's count it was thirty-seven steps to the field – his entire life existed now in how many steps it was from anything here to anything there. They stood for a long time and Joe Mac knew they were in the open because the trees no longer shielded him from the wind and he could feel the sun on his face.

"Anything?" he asked.

"Joe," she said with noticeable consternation, "what am I supposed to be looking for in an empty field?"

"Just tell me what you see."

"Well," he heard her hands slap her thighs, "I don't see anything but grass, Joe. And … whoa. I can see your daughter's house from here. It's about a half-mile away. Maybe a little more. Hey, is that your little green barn back there?"

"I reckon. Unless they got two barns."

"It's cute." Jodi took a moment. "Okay, the only other thing I see back here are some crows circling something on the other side of the field. Something must have died over there. Probably a coyote or a rabbit. Nothing else would –"

"Crows?" asked Joe Mac.

"Yeah. They look like crows."

"Take me over there."

They began across the high grass, and Joe Mac got the hang of it pretty quick; he'd do fine unless he stepped in a hole. Otherwise he could move as easily as Jodi seemed able, and then Jodi grabbed his arm; "Hold it, Joe. Yeah. I can see what it is."

"Is it a dead animal?" asked Joe Mac.

"Looks like it."

"A dead cat?"

Silence.

"Joe? How could you *possibly* know that it's –"

"Is it a dead kitten?"

"God Almighty. Yeah, it looks like it used to be … a kitten."

"How long has it been dead?"

"Uh … well, I'm not really an expert at decomposition, Joe, but it looks to me like it's been dead about a week. I don't know what those crows think they're eating, but there's not much left."

"So why are they circling?"

Jodi paused. "It looks to me like this really big crow is getting the rest of them all worked up over the bones. He's, like, herding them. Or something."

"Bait," Joe Mac stated with a bitter frown. "The string. A kitten. Aaron didn't go to the fence to see a man. He was taught to run from strangers. He walked over to see a kitty cat tied to the end of a string. The man was hiding in the grass. Then, once Aaron was distracted, this guy rushed up, snatched him over the fence, and ran off with him. Quick as that. He snatched the cat up, too, but threw it down after he was clear. He probably didn't think it was important enough to take the cat. He didn't think anybody would put it together. Or maybe Aaron was putting up a good fight, and he needed both hands." His teeth gleamed. "Yeah. That was probably it. He would have taken the cat, too, but Aaron was putting up a good fight and so he killed the cat. Broke its neck. Tossed it."

"Why didn't he just leave the cat at the daycare?"

"It's too obvious. And it's probably a trick he's used more than once. If it got in the papers he'd have one less trick."

Silence and sadness seemed to overlay them, and Joe Mac could faintly hear Jodi's movements. He knew she was standing with arms crossed, staring. He didn't feel like saying anything, either, as she whispered, "How horrible."

"Yes."

Her shriek cut the air, and Joe Mac heard her jump back. She gasped before she exclaimed, "That crow flew right over my head!"

She reached down as if to pick up a rock.

"Wait," said Joe Mac.

"What!"

"Is it a big crow?"

"Biggest crow I ever saw, that's for sure! God bless! That thing scared me to death! It could have parted my hair."

Joe Mac took a slow half-turn toward the tree line. He simply stood until he heard the familiar caw and he nodded. "And you say the crows led you here?"

"What?"

"The crows? They led you to the bones?"

"Actually, it was just that really big one. The one that scared me. He was circling around the bones real high, sort of herding the other crows down over the cat. I think he's like … their leader. I mean, if crows have 'leaders.'" Suddenly she jumped back. "Look out, Joe!"

Joe Mac heard the familiar, powerful wings as Poe soared over him low enough to touch and listened until Poe was gone. Then he started forward.

"Look for some foot prints."

* * *

"Yeah!" shouted Captain Steve Brightbarton as he swung a fist through the air. "The psycho finally made a mistake!"

Jodi turned at the edge of the roped-off crime scene to see Joe Mac standing like a black harbinger of death in the middle of the field; the gigantic crow rested on the ground beside him like a faithful servant. She turned and walked forward, and when she reached Joe Mac she was curious that the crow didn't fly away.

It simply stood where it stood.

Staring at her.

"They've made casts of two shoe prints," she said. "They're way outside the earlier search grid. That's why the neighbors didn't find them, although I don't think they would have put it together anyway. They say the crow led them back to where he musta' parked his car." She hesitated. "Now that we've got a footprint, we might be able to trace the brand of shoe. If we're lucky, it's exotic. If not, we'll just run down everybody wearing Nikes. We might be looking at a billion suspects, but we'll know he's *one* of them."

"What are the prints like?" asked Joe Mac.

Jodi expelled a long breath. "They look to me like some kind of tennis shoe. Maybe a size ten or eleven. Like I say, the guys don't know what brand, yet, but they'll know by tonight." She looked at the crow, which was placidly staring back at her with almost-human ambivalence. "Do you two know each other?"

"You mean Poe?"

"It has a name?"

"Doesn't the Bible say everything has a name?"

"I don't know," said Jodi. "I don't read it, anymore."

"Maybe you should." Joe Mac paused. "Maybe we both should."

"He sure is the biggest crow I've ever seen."

"He's a raven. They're bigger than crows."

"He's almost as big as an *eagle*."

"That's what my daughter says."

Jodi knew she was scowling; it was fascinating how the thing held her gaze like a cat might do – never blinking, never looking away. It seemed to know she was curious about it and was returning the sentiment.

"He looks like the devil," she said.

"My daughter says that, too."

"Is he a pet?"

"Just a friend."

"He's a strange friend."

"Old men have strange friends."

Jodi turned toward the crime scene, arms crossed. "Well, like I said; he must be their king or something because he was herding the others over the bones of the kitten. I would have never looked over there if it hadn't been for him."

Joe Mac turned stiffly from the scene. "Take me home, if you would. Crime Scene can handle this without us. I want to check on Pamela before it gets too late."

"Sure."

As Joe Mac turned, the raven lifted off, and Jodi kept glancing up to see it circling them as they meandered across the field and through the woods and into the parking lot. And when they reached her vehicle, the raven came down with a formidable, utterly unafraid descent to land solidly on the roof of the squad car.

For the first time since she'd met him, Jodi saw Joe Mac smile. He reached up with his free left hand, and the enormous raven took two fearless steps toward him and hopped onto his forearm with a steel-vice grip. It bent its fearsome head – its hooked beak seemed sharp as black iron and much more frightening up close – and Joe Mac affectionately smoothed the glossy blue-black feathers.

"Go on," said Joe Mac.

At the words the gigantic raven erupted into the sky with a grace and fearlessness that struck Jodi with instinctive amazement. She had never seen such a powerful creature explode upward with such utter confidence and grace. She muttered, "You two really are friends, aren't you?" She realized she was gaping. "Did you say he's a wild raven?"

"He comes when he wants. Goes when he wants. Seems pretty wild to me."

"And he's not scared of people?"

Joe Mac opened his door. "Why would he be scared of people? You can't even get close to him unless he lets you."

With a grunt, Jodi opened the door.

"Yeah. I wouldn't be scared of anything, either."

* * *

Jodi waited at the entrance of Joe Mac's humble barn as he tapped a path back from his daughter's house. She wasn't surprised that the crow – wait, it was a raven – had circled over Joe Mac all the way over there and all the way back. What surprised her was that the raven seemed to have identified her individual car and could determine the difference between her squad car and all the other squad cars cruising to and from the crime scene.

Joe Mac stopped at the door and turned.

Jodi asked, "How's she doing?"

"She's been sleeping. It's gonna take her a long time." He felt for the lock using his forefinger as a key-guide. "They say you don't ever get over it. One day you just get up and start moving. But when you bury a child a part of your heart crawls down in that grave with 'em and stays there."

"Yeah," Jodi responded. "I lost a brother. But I know it's not the same. Not even close. Nothing compares to losing a child."

"Sorry about your brother."

"So am I. Drugs. We let him down, I guess. The whole family."

Joe Mac opened the barn door. "Come on. I'll make you some coffee. I learned how to do all that stuff where they rehab blind people."

"Fancy."

"Nuthin' but the good life."

Entering what was obviously a revamped barn Jodi saw – with a single glance – a recliner, a double bed, a plate of food on a small kitchen table, and Joe Mac's entire wardrobe strung along the far wall; it was a typical barn layout with added shelves and a bathroom slapped onto the back.

"You like to keep things simple, huh?" she asked.

"I got a roof. I got food. I got a bed. What more do I need?"

He began to clang around in his kitchenette as Jodi lifted and opened a lawn chair. She didn't feel the need to inform him that he only had one recliner. He knew, anyway, so she could deal with it if he could. She asked, "How come you were never assigned to this case? Seems like you would have been chief investigator for a serial killer like this."

"He wasn't killing people back then," Joe Mac called. "I retired six years ago. Back then he wasn't even a blip on the screen. It was only after I got hurt and put out to pasture that he started racking up a body count." He pulled two cups off a plywood board. "You bring the file in from the car?"

"It's right here."

"I want you to read it to me."

"The whole thing?"

"The whole thing."

"So you're gonna lend me a hand, Joe?"

He turned. Stared. "I guess that's up to you. I want to find who killed my grandson. And I can't do it by myself." Jodi saw a deep pain solidify his face. "I don't think nobody else would have me, no way."

Jodi felt a grimace. "Well, I think you've still got a few good moves left in you – you and your buddy. What's his name?"

"Poe."

http://wbp.bz/darkvisionsa

**AVAILABLE FROM JAMES BYRON
HUGGINS AND WILDBLUE PRESS!**

HUNTER by JAMES BYRON HUGGINS

http://wbp.bz/huntera

Read A Sample Next

Chapter 1

"Vicious little beasts, aren't they?"

The words, spoken with ominous disaster, came from a white-haired old man in a white lab coat. Seated patiently, he watched as a host of red army ants, some as large as his thumb, attacked what he had dispassionately dropped into the aquarium. The ants overwhelmed the rat in seconds, killing it almost instantly with venom, then devouring it. In three minutes a haggard skeleton was all that remained.

Dr. Angus Tipler clicked a stopwatch, staring down. "Yes," he frowned, "utterly vicious."

He turned to others in the laboratory of the Tipler Institute, the leading crypto-zoological foundation in the world. His face portrayed consternation. "What are we to do with them?" he asked, almost to himself. "They kill with venom long before they dismember their prey." He looked back. "Yes, and so we must therefore devise some type of ... serum, if for no other reason so that people will stop bothering us all the time. Has anyone concluded the molecular weight of the poison?"

A woman bent over an enormous electron microscope positioned neatly in the center of the room muttered in reply. "Not yet, Doctor. I need another minute."

Dr. Tipler said nothing as he turned back to the aquarium where the ants were safely—very safely—contained. The rest of the laboratory was filled with virtually every poisonous animal in the world, insect and mammal and reptile. There were black scorpions, Indian cobras, adders and stonefish, brown recluse spiders and the lethal Sydney funnel web, the most dangerous spider in the world. A single unfelt bite from the tiny arachnid would kill a full-grown man within a day. It was Tipler himself who had created the anti-venom.

"It seems this venom is neuromuscular in nature," he said in a raspy, harsh voice into a recorder. He waved off the video technician who had recorded the grisly episode. "The venom, no matter the location of injection, seems to infiltrate the ligamentum denticulatum, thereby bridging the pons Varolii to decussate the involuntary respiratory abilities of the medulla oblongata. Now, if we can—"

"Dr. Tipler?"

Tipler raised bushy white eyebrows as he turned, seeing a young woman scientist with long black hair. The Asian woman was obviously apprehensive at the intrusion, despite the old man's well-known patient nature.

"Yes, Gina?" His voice was gentle. "What is it?"

"There are some men to see you, sir."

Tipler laughed, waving a hand as he turned away. "There are always men to see me, lass. Tell them to wait. The commissary should still be open. They serve an excellent roast chicken. It is my best recommendation."

"I don't think these men will wait, sir." She stepped closer, lowering her voice. Her eyes widened slightly. "There are three of them, and they're wearing uniforms."

Tipler barked a short laugh. "Uniforms! What sort of uniforms?"

"Army uniforms, sir."

Tipler laughed again and shook his head as he rose. "All right, Gina. Assist Rebecca in discovering the molecular weight of this venom. And, also, if you would be so kind, extract venom from, oh ... let's say fifty of these infernal creatures. Just sedate them with chloroform and use the electroshock method—the same procedure we use for the black widows." He removed his glasses with a sigh and stood up. "And I will deal with these impatient men in uniforms."

"Yes, sir. They're waiting in the observation room."

"Thank you, lass."

Upon seeing the three, Dr. Tipler stopped short. He had been told often enough that, upon first impression, he was not an imposing figure, so he had no illusions. At seventy-two years of age he was short and thick with a wide brow and snowy hair laid back from the forehead. But he knew that his eyes, blue like Arctic ice, distinguished him from other men both with their startling color and their equally startling intelligence. And equally their quickness to perceive the heart of a mystery. And it was that perceptiveness, a blending of art, science and intuition that had made the world's eminent paleontologist and crypto-zoologist.

Crypto-zoology was in itself an almost unknown area of biological expertise. Fewer than a dozen distinguished scientists in the world practiced it with any measure of dedication. And, for the most part, few scientists realized that it was practiced at all. But, in essence, it was a systematic and highly rigid system of investigation designed to determine whether species thought to be extinct still inhabited the planet.

Tipler had known significant success in various stages of his career, discovering the last surviving Atacama condors in the Andes Mountains of Chile in 1983, and later discovering a species identified as the blind stone-fish, off the northern coast of Greenland. The deep-water fish had been thought extinct since the Paleolithic Period, but Tipler had pieced together a theory that they still existed in the south-flowing East Greenland Current, which drew directly from the Arctic Sea. He held even further suspicions that the fish existed higher in the Arctic Circle, protected by the vast ice caps of the pole. But a lack of funding had prevented further exploration.

However, his startling discoveries had earned him a modest measure of global recognition, which consequently delivered the attention of several wealthy philanthropists who deemed his unique nonprofit enterprise worthy of endorsement. So, with significant funding and a larger, better-trained staff, he had founded the Tipler Institute. Now, a decade later, he was recognized universally as the world's leading expert on unknown species, and their extinction or survival. Along the way he had also gained significant exposure to deadly snakes, fish, and spiders and discovered, to his own surprise, that he had a remarkable acumen for pinpointing the molecular characteristics of each type of venom.

Studying venom was, at first, simply a means of aiding those few medical institutions already overwhelmed trying to keep apace with the new strains of poison. But through a working relationship with the Centers for Disease Control, Tipler also joined the crusade, synthesizing over a dozen effective anti-venoms over the past decade. Nor did he find it distracting. Although he was an increasingly sought-after author, lecturer, and researcher, his greatest pleasure remained the simple pursuit of biological science.

From time to time, however, agencies not academic had sought his aid. And he had assisted. Once the Central Intelligence Agency had requested that he do what their physicists could not; develop a counteracting agent for a deadly poison in use by Middle Eastern countries. Tipler had succeeded and consequently heard no more of it. And last, the U.S. Army had asked him, rather sternly, if he could not identify a substance in their own anti-germ warfare serums that tended to incapacitate soldiers. In this, too, Tipler was successful, and modifications were made in the synthesis of the serums. Again, he heard no more of it. Yet he knew they would return, as they had.

A thin smile creased his squared face.

Before him, he knew from his World War II days as an infantryman, was an army lieutenant colonel, whose rank he identified from the silver oak leaves on his uniform. There was another man in uniform, a major, and an unknown representative who wore nondescript civilian clothes. But, as always, it was the man in civilian clothes who commanded Tipler's attention, for he was accustomed to subterfuge. Tipler greeted them as the man in the rear silently lit a cigarette, settling into a chair.

"Dr. Tipler, I'm Lieutenant Colonel Bob Maddox," the short, gray-haired man said distinctly. "This is Major Preston Westcott. And that "— the colonel gestured vaguely—" is Mr. Dixon. He's a liaison with the Department of the Interior."

Tipler smiled as he weighed the colonel; the army officer carried himself with an air of indisputable authority, as if his self-worth relied upon his rank. His insignia were so highly polished they couldn't be overlooked, even by civilians. His face was slightly pudgy and his stomach strained against his uniform. He held his hands behind his back as he spoke. "Thank you for seeing us on such short notice, Doctor. I assure you that we won't take up too much of your time."

Something in the voice intimated to Dr. Tipler that he had no choice in the matter, but he revealed nothing as he moved to sit at a table directly opposite the mysterious Mr. Dixon. "Oh, I am always ready to assist the military, Colonel," he said with exacting courtesy. "In fact, as you are probably aware, I just finished working with an army research team to design new protocols for Arctic survival. So please, continue."

Maddox was obviously in charge, Tipler realized, and Prescott was present to verify the meeting or take mental notes. He hadn't yet concluded a purpose for Dixon.

"That's part of the reason we're here—your experience in the Arctic. We also understand that you're the world's leading authority on crypto-zoology." Maddox strolled before the table. "So we hoped you'd be able to help us with ... a situation."

Tipler decided to play their game for now. He did not look at Mr. Dixon. "Perhaps," he replied casually.

Clearly, Maddox was proceeding with caution. "Doctor, we would like to ask you some questions about species of predators found in the Arctic Circle. Specifically, species that inhabit the deep interior of Alaska and the North Face region." He stepped forward, almost delicately. "Recently we lost several members of an elite military training squad to an animal. They were killed. And we want to determine what manner of animal it was."

Tipler absorbed it without expression.

"Surely," Tipler said finally, "Alaskan wildlife officials can be of more use to you than an old gaffer such as myself. And I am not certain in what aspect my credentials in crypto-zoology are related. Crypto-zoology is the study of animals long presumed to be extinct but which are, in fact, not. Such as some of the marine reptiles like the one the Japanese fishing vessel, the Zuiyo Mam, snagged on a line nine hundred feet below the surface of the Pacific near Christchurch, New Zealand, in 1977. Or," Tipler could not resist adding, "perhaps like the beast of unknown species that attacked the U.S.S. Stern in the early 'eighties, disabling its sonar system with hundreds of teeth driven deeply in the steel. It was documented with the Department of the Navy and the ship was examined by the Naval Oceans Center. They reached the fascinating conclusion that damage to the sonar was caused by the attack of a large and unknown ocean-dwelling species."

Maddox stood in silence. His face tightened. "Yes, Doctor. We are aware of those incidents. It is certainly verification of...something. But those cases are not why we have come."

"I presumed." Tipler smiled. "So, shall we get to the reason? I am a bit overwhelmed by my work."

Gravely, even apprehensively, Maddox laid a gory series of full-sized color photographs on the table. And Tipler precisely set glasses on his nose, leaning on broad hands to examine them. So total was his concentration, it was as if, in seconds, he had physically removed himself from the room.

The old man made no sound as he studied the photographs, but his brow hardened frame by frame. His lips pursed slightly and he began to take more time with each, returning often to the first, beginning over. Finally he lifted a single eight-by-ten and studied it inches from his face, peering at the details. "Colonel," he said, casting a slow gaze over the massacred bodies. "These wounds, were they all inflicted by the same creature?"

There was no hesitation. "Yes."

"You are certain of this?"

"Yes, Doctor, we are certain."

"And how can you be certain? In science, certainty is determined by exceedingly strict criteria."

Maddox grimaced slightly. "There were obscured video images. Nothing too revealing, but it gave us glimpses of whatever this was. We couldn't make out the species. And, despite what I said earlier, we can't be, uh, absolutely certain on whether it was one or two of them. It's just that the evidence, except for some of these photographs, seems to indicate that."

Without reply, Tipler shifted several of the photographs of massacred soldiers until he had the most vivid, the ghastliest. He placed a hand on it and touched the image of wounds as delicately as if the soldier were before him. Finally, he mumbled, "This is not the work of Ursus arctos horribilis."

Clearly, Maddox was trying to be patient. "Could you be more specific, Doctor?"

"This is not the work of a ... a Grizzly." Tipler was again staring at the photo he had lifted, a close-up image of tracks leading across hard sand. The elongated footprints moved in a straight run down a strand to disappear in the distance, but some of the tracks were disjointed, as far as three feet to the side. It was not a straight line of tracks, though clearly the creature had been running straight. Rocks littered the stream.

"Now ... " the old man continued in a genuine tone of confusion, "this is somewhat curious."

"What?" Maddox asked.

"The way that the tracks are broken."

"That's what our own trackers said, Doctor. I mean, despite the cameras, we want to know about this. Do you think there could be two of them?"

Tipler took a long time to consider. "I am not an expert in tracking, Colonel Maddox. I cannot say. But I do not think that there were two creatures involved in this ... this catastrophe."

"Then how do you explain the way some tracks are so far to the side from others?"

"As I said, sir, I cannot explain such a phenomenon."

Maddox concentrated. "You're certain this isn't the work of a Grizzly, Doctor? Or maybe a polar bear? A tiger, maybe?"

"No, not a Grizzly, nor a brown bear," the professor expounded in a low tone. "For one matter, a Grizzly has five claws. And whatever did this had four predominant claws, and a smaller one. But the paw print is distinctly ...humanoid. Now this," he paused, "is damn peculiar." A long silence lengthened. "No, gentlemen, not a bear of any kind. Perhaps a tiger could have caused this much carnage to your team, but the tracks are ... just ... they just appear to me to be somewhat too manlike. In fact, *far* too manlike."

"But clearly no human being could do something like this, Doctor." Dixon spoke for the first time.

Tipler raised his eyes, gazing over bifocals. "I would not make a determination of any fact until I had obtained the information necessary to make the determination of that fact, Mr. Dixon." He smiled. "That is the discipline of science."

Dixon leaned back, smoked in silence.

The army officials were, indeed, leaning forward as Tipler raised a magnifying glass from his pocket, studying the photograph more closely. Finally he lowered it with the glass, but continued to stare profoundly. His voice was quiet. "These tracks ... how far did your men follow them, gentlemen?"

"Why?" Maddox asked.

"Because they do not 'register.' "

"Register?" the colonel asked. "What does that mean?"

"They ... they are not in line." The scientist gestured. "A tiger, which is the only terrestrial beast that could have struck with such fury, registers when it walks or runs. Which is to say that both paws on the left side are in a line, as they are on the right. There should be two paw prints set closely together, in a straight line, left side and right side. And, clearly, they are not the tracks of a Grizzly, though they resemble one in size."

"Yes," Maddox said. "Our military trackers told us that. But they lost the trail when it moved to high ground. They said no one can track across rock. This animal seemed to know it was being hunted."

"Most creatures are more intelligent than we presume, Colonel," Tipler replied, casting a narrow glance at Dixon, who was smoking quietly. "No," Tipler added finally. "It was not a tiger. The fury of the attack is commensurate with a tiger, but it is not feline or canine. Nor is a larger species of Ursus. No. Whatever did this ... was distinctly bipedal."

They waited, but the old man merely placed his glasses back in his lab coat pocket. Then he bridged his fingers, capping them, allowing them to continue the conversation.

"Bipedal?" Dixon asked without friendliness. "Does that mean what I think it means?"

"Quite probably," Tipler smiled. "It means that whatever killed your men walks on two legs, Mr. Dixon."

"That's preposterous." Dixon leaned back again. "Humans are the only animal that walks on two legs, Doctor. What do you suggest left these tracks? *Bigfoot*? This thing must have been registering! It's just that the tracks are too difficult to read."

"Difficult, yes," Tipler scowled. "But not impossible. Is that why you called me here? Because your men have already told you that they know of no creature that could have done this? And now you wish to know if, perhaps, there is an undiscovered species?"

"To be honest, I'll admit it occurred to us," Maddox replied. "And let me add that this is a situation of some seriousness, Doctor. We've got dead soldiers near secure facilities and we want to know how they died. We want to know why they died."

Tipler gazed over the photos of carnage. "I cannot give you the answer, gentlemen," he said finally. "There were species of beasts that are presumed to have been exterminated hundreds of thousands of years ago, yet we still find evidence of their continuing existence. But I am not familiar with this paw print, or footprint." He paused and strolled a short distance away before turning back. "In order to answer your question—to even attempt to answer your question—we would need a scientific expedition, saliva samples, blood samples, plaster casts of the prints, hair samples, video surveillance records. If you are willing to fund an expedi-"

"We can't do that." Dixon stood up. "There are factors which preclude that option. We just wanted your best opinion, Doctor." He paused for effect. "We still do."

Tipler held the stare.

"My best opinion, Mr. Dixon, is that whatever did this has the strength of a Grizzly, the speed of a Siberian tiger and, quite probably, the stalking skills of a tiger. Which happens to be the most skilled predator on Earth. Further, if it managed to evade the initial pursuit of your military, I would confidently surmise that it has unnatural intelligence."

"So," Maddox asked, asserting some kind of vague authority, "what do you think it is? I want your best guess."

Tipler sighed once more and glanced at a photo of the tracks. "Your best guess will be revealed by these tracks, Mr. Dixon. But I don't understand why some of them"—he pointed at several—"are so far to the left of these others. It makes no sense that I can see."

They exchanged glances as the old man stared over them. Then, after a moment, they began wordlessly gathering papers.

"Will you be hunting this beast again?" the scientist asked, interested.

"Yes," Maddox replied solidly. "We will."

"Then I suggest you find a man who can possibly track it," said Tipler.

He hesitated, as if scientific passion and personal loyalty were competing with something more hidden, staring at the photograph.

"I know the man," he said softly, "who could do this? If anyone could. But I do not know if he will cooperate. He has his own reasons ... for why he does things."

Maddox stepped forward. "Who is he?"

Tipler stared slightly to the side, brow furrowed.

"His name," he said finally, "is Nathaniel Hunter."

Chapter 2

The sunset breeze carried a sweet tang of mountain laurel. Nathaniel Hunter was emptying his simple leather pack onto the table. The door of his cabin was wide open, allowing the green sound of rushing water to move over him. And yet it wasn't sound, but a sudden silence, that made him lift his head.

Where there had been a communicative chorus of bird surrounding his backwoods home, there was now an unnatural quiet. He turned to stare out the door, listened, and heard a car coming slowly up the one-lane dirt road. It was still a mile away.

It took them more than ten minutes to arrive. He met them on the porch wearing old blue jeans, a leather shirt, and knee-high moccasins.

One of the contingent—a portly army colonel—spoke first. But it was the man in civilian clothes, standing in the rear that drew Hunter's sullen attention. Quiet but close, the man was dressed in a suit you would have forgotten without even trying, and dark sunglasses protected his eyes from any probing. Hands clasped behind him, he followed the others like a schoolteacher ensuring that the students perform the assigned task. It was clear who was truly in charge.

"I am Lieutenant Colonel Maddox of the United States Army," said the man in uniform. "We would like to speak with Nathaniel Hunter, if that's possible."

"I'm Hunter," he said, his voice low.

"Well." The colonel stepped forward, an ingratiating smile on his lips.

"We'd just like to get your opinion on some photographs, if you don't mind. Of course, if there is a problem, we can arrange a more formal appointment."

Hunter took his time before turning toward the door, motioning vaguely. "Come into the cabin," he said.

It took only a few minutes for them to recount their story of blood and death in the snow. Then they displayed a series of photographs on the cabin's crude wooden table. They wanted his best guess as to what the killer was, they said, and they wanted to know if there was more than one of them. Hunter bent over the photographs and studied them for a moment. His eyes narrowed as he examined the tracks, as well as the terrain.

Maddox began, "We want to know why these tracks here are so far from the others."

"Wind," Hunter said simply.

Hunter heard the man introduced as Dixon step forward. But Maddox only stared as he said, "Excuse me, did you say 'wind'?"

"Yeah." Hunter had expected this confusion. "These tracks to the side were in a straight line with these others. But the wind moved them, inch by inch. The other tracks weren't moved because they were shielded from the northeastern breeze by this boulder."

Maddox seemed astounded. "Wind can do that?"

Hunter pointed to the tracks. "These to the side were originally over here, like the others. You can see the gap that was left when they were moved. The wind just edged them to where they are here." He shrugged, gave the picture to Maddox. "It's a common phenomenon on sand like this. Is that what you wanted to know?"

"Uh." Maddox started. "Uh, actually, no. We wanted you to—"

A sudden, silent atmospheric change in the cabin stopped him short. It was as if the room had been instantly charged with a primal force, something utterly savage. Hunter watched as Maddox slowly turned his head. He almost smiled at the nervous expression on Dixon's face as he began to sense what was behind him. Slowly, moving only his head, Dixon managed to look down stiffly. Hunter saw sweat glisten suddenly on his forehead.

Massive and menacing, Ghost stood less than a foot behind Dixon and Maddox, slightly to the side. The gigantic wolf was almost entirely black, touched with gray only on his flanks.

Ghost's jet-black eyes seemed to possess a primal and predatory glow. Black claws clicked on the wooden floor as he took a single pace forward, head low, again unmoving. Ghost's uncanny silence seemed more terrifying than a roar.

Hunter made them suffer for only a moment. With a slight smile he snapped his fingers.

"Ghost," he said.

The wolf glided innocently through the men and sat beside Hunter.

Hunter spoke politely. "You were saying, Colonel?"

Maddox had trouble speaking. "I, uh, I was saying that... uh, we wanted you to help us with ... with ... something."

Hunter smiled at the trembling tone and noticed that Major Prescott's fists were clenched. All of them were sweating, and Maddox's face was pasty, whitening by the moment. He knew this would take all day with Ghost in the room. He looked down, speaking so low that none of the others could catch the word.

"Outside," he said.

Treading with an air of shocking animal might, the wolf moved fearlessly through the three of them. Then it reached the door and angled away, disappearing with haunting silence and grace. The air silently trembled with the wildness, the power, the very scent of it as it was gone. But Hunter knew Ghost would remain close, just as he knew they wouldn't see the wolf again—not ever—unless it wanted them to.

"Good Lord," whispered Maddox as he took out a handkerchief, wiping his face. "Is that ... is that your dog?"

"He's a wolf."

"Yes ... yes, of course." The colonel cast a nervous eye to the doorway and involuntarily backed up. "But ... but what does it do?"

Hunter stared, almost laughed, but suppressed it; there was no need to mock them, even incidentally. They weren't at home in his world, though he had managed to become both prosperous and respected in theirs. He added, "He does whatever he wants to do, I guess. He comes, he goes."

"I mean, do you own him?" Maddox added. "Is he trained? Does he always come and go like that?" All three of the men had repositioned themselves so they could keep an eye on the door.

Hunter half-shrugged. "No, he's not trained, Colonel. And nobody owns him. He comes when he wants. Goes when he wants."

"But ... but how much does the thing weigh?" Maddox asked. "I didn't think wolves got so ... so huge."

"That depends on bloodline," Hunter answered, continuing to unpack. "Most male wolves go a hundred or so. Ghost is about a hundred and fifty, more or less. He won't get much bigger."

Maddox began to recover degree by degree and Hunter tried to move it along. He knew they were still dancing around the central issue. He continued quietly. "Now, gentlemen, if you're ready to talk, maybe we can get down to why you wanted to see me. What do you want?"

Fortifying himself, Maddox stepped forward. He pointed at the photographs of slaughtered soldiers.

"We want to know," Maddox said in a stronger tone, "what kind of creature could have done this? What kind of creature could have walked through an entire platoon like this, killing such heavily armed men?"

Frowning slightly, Hunter shifted the photos and finally shook his head. "Maybe a Grizzly," he muttered, but with obvious uncertainty. "But I doubt it."

"Why do you doubt it?"

"Because a Grizzly will usually maul its victim," Hunter answered, more certain. "It'll hit over and over, tear off your scalp, your face. And whatever did this struck once, maybe twice, with each kill." He pointed at a photo. "This man was killed with one blow. So whatever did this didn't attack out of fear or rage." He paused, eyes narrowing. "Whatever did this ...had a reason."

"But what animal would ... I mean, what animal could do something like this for a reason?"

Hunter shook his head. "I don't know."

"But aren't you supposed to be an expert on—"

"Colonel," Hunter cut him off, "I don't consider myself an expert in anything at all. I just do what I do, the best way I can do it. And I don't think I can help you. I can't tell you what killed your men." He waited; they were stoically silent. "I can say, however, that whatever killed these men didn't kill for food. It didn't kill out of defense. And it didn't kill to defend territory."

"Like a tiger might have done?"

"It's not a tiger."

"But how can you be certain?" Maddox was openly disturbed. "You just said that you're not certain what did this."

"Because these men were attacked on level ground with open field all around them." Hunter was relaxed and certain. "Tigers don't do that. They'll attack from an elevated position or from ambush. A tiger will never put itself in a position where it might have to chase prey. They don't chase."

"Tigers won't chase prey? Why?"

Hunter shrugged, went back to removing equipment from his pack. "No one knows. Instinct, maybe. Maybe because they're so heavy. But if a tiger doesn't catch you within three or four bounds, you're probably a free man."

Struck by a stray thought, he pointed vaguely to a grainy photo. "See these tracks?" he continued. "This ... thing ... was moving fast, and in a straight line. It's as if ... I don't know ... as if it was trying to reach something." Drawn to direction of his own words, Hunter studied several photos, quickly arranging them in a new order. "Do you see this? All of these men went down in sequence. It moved through them, killing quick and moving to the next, always headed in the same direction." For a long time he paused. When he spoke again, his voice was flat. "I'm not sure that this is an animal."

Slowly Dixon stepped forward, almost indulgent. "Mr. Hunter, this has got to be an animal. Certainly, and this should go without saying, no human being could have done this."

"Believe what you want." Hunter was unaffected. "But I've never seen an animal that killed like this. Animals have reasons, like fear or rage or defense, when they kill. And there's no evidence of that here. Not that I can see. It didn't maul, which would indicate anger. It didn't eat. It just killed and moved on to the next victim." With a faintly fatigued sign, he stood back. "You wanted my best guess, gentlemen. That's it."

"What about the tracks?" Dixon pressed. "You're certain they're not bear tracks?"

"No, they're not bear tracks. They're not even close. Your own people can tell you that." Hunter stared at him. "In fact, if I had to make a determination, I'd say they were human."

Dixon blinked. "Have you ever seen an animal leave tracks like this?"

"No."

"Never?"

"No."

Dixon seemed slightly agitated, but cast a quick glance to the door. "Look, Mr. Hunter," he began, "we were told that you're an expert at tracking. And please don't tell me you're not. We've checked you out."

Hunter laughed soundlessly.

"Yeah, we do that with everyone," Dixon continued, as if he'd seen the expression a thousand times. "Nathaniel Hunter. Grew up in the wilds of Wyoming. Your father died before you were born and an old trapper and a Sioux Indian woman raised you. The trapper taught you to track when you were just a kid, and you're supposed to be the best in the world. Some kind of legend. They say you can track a ghost through fog, and you've been used by police departments to find kids lost in wilderness areas when everyone else has failed. And that you've located animals so on the brink of extermination that there were only a handful left. Then, when you were twenty, you found a tree in the Amazon that provided a better treatment for spinal meningitis. You sold it to a pharmaceutical company for about twenty million. And since then you've discovered a dozen plants that provide antibodies against various bacterial infections. Yeah, and I know this old shack isn't your only place. You have a penthouse in New York filled with about twenty million in art and rare books, a place in Paris that rivals the Smithsonian for rare artifacts. You go wherever you want, do whatever you want. Got a private jet on standby at JFK Airport and high friends in high places in both government and private business. You're the money behind the Tipler Institute." Dixon shook his head.

"You're a kick in the head, Hunter. You've got all that damn money and you hardly spend a dime on yourself. All those luxury spots of yours sit empty while you spend most of your time at this old shack." He grunted. "You're an interesting guy, all right, but the one thing everybody agrees about is that you're some kind of wilderness guru. So surely you have some clue of what this might be. Even if it's just a suspicion."

Hunter held Dixon's stare, not bothering to look friendly. "I've already studied them, Dixon," he said. "They're vaguely like a bear but the tracks are badly marred and mulled, so it's hard to tell. And then this thing is bipedal, so it doesn't move like a bear when it's either running or loping or walking. This thing, whatever it is, probably weighs about three hundred, and it's right-handed. It looks to the right a lot and pauses about every fifty feet. It's hunched when it moves, as if it's stalking. And when it turns it pivots both feet at the same time. When it kills it tends to strike from right to left, placing its weight on its left front leg, like a boxer."

A stunned silence.

Maddox was the first to speak. "You can tell all that from those photographs?"

Hunter nodded.

"But ... how?"

Hunter waved a hand at the photos. "Sideheading, dulling and compression, pressure release marks, wave and pitch, curving. Simple things, Colonel."

"But our pathfinders, our trackers ...they couldn't tell us all that."

Hunter sighed. "Well, I'm sure that your people are good, Colonel. But that's what I see. You can take it or leave it."

Maddox said nothing for a moment, turning and strolling across the room, cupping his chin. He seemed to be pondering. After a moment he looked at Dixon. "Mr. Dixon, I'd like a word with you," he said. "In private."

Dixon, black glasses concealing his eyes even here, held Hunter's stare for a long moment before he turned away, walking across the room. Hunter leaned against the table and watched them whisper. He didn't know what they were discussing but he had an idea. He had no plans to cooperate.

"Mr. Hunter." Maddox walked back slowly. Clearly, he was attempting to phrase his words carefully. "I would like to make a request, and I would like for you to genuinely consider it before you reply." He lifted his face, honest for all Hunter could tell.

He nodded. "Go ahead."

"This, uh, this situation," Maddox continued, "is not exactly what it seems. I'm sure you consider it to be a tragedy that our soldiers were killed. And remember, these were all good men. Men with families. But there is more to it than that."

Hunter said nothing.

"In truth, Mr. Hunter, this creature, whatever it is, has killed many times in the past three days—mostly military personnel, bodies that we can conceal, in a sense. But it seems to be headed south. And soon, if it continues on its current course, it will reach a populated civilian area."

"Why can't you find this creature by triangulating infrared signatures from satellite?" Hunter asked. "The technology exists for a hunt like this through the global imaging system. Seems like you could isolate its heat signature."

"We're not fools, Mr. Hunter. We've tried that. But there is an abundance—an overabundance—of large animal life in that area. There's moose, bear, elk, wolf, so many creatures that tracking by heat signature is futile. What we need is someone who can track this one, specific creature. Because if it reaches a populated civilian area, I am not certain how successful we will be in containing it. Tens, perhaps hundreds of people would die." Maddox raised his hands, almost plaintively. "Now, I realize that you're not under, nor have you ever submitted to, military command. Nor, should you decline, can I compel you against your will to assist. But I am asking you as a man—as an honorable man—to help us. I am asking you to help us track this thing down. I'm asking you ... to help us kill it."

Hunter absorbed it awhile in silence.

"Your people aren't sufficient?" he asked.

"No," Maddox replied flatly. They've already tried and they failed. In fact, they died. The results were ...discouraging, to say the least."

Hunter stared at nothing, said nothing for a long time.

"We have a killing team assembled," the colonel continued. "You need not be involved in that aspect. If you can only track this creature through those mountains, somehow give our people an opportunity to confront it, then your job will be done. You will be present as an observer. And the team that we have assembled is extremely proficient. You will be quite safe. In fact, it may be the safest action you've undertaken in some time. One other thing we learned was that you are a man prone to taking risks."

Hunter rose slowly, turned away.

He stared out the window and searched the surrounding tree-line, already dark. And he half-scanned for Ghost but knew the wolf would remain invisible unless he wanted to be seen. Yet he would be there, un-moving, waiting, listening to every word. And if Hunter were attacked, the great black image of pure animal fury would roar into the cabin like a storm with flashing fangs and claws, and God help anything mortal that got in his way. Somehow Hunter knew he had already made the decision but he waited, sensing something that troubled him.

"All right," he said finally. "But for this I'll need Ghost."

A pause.

"Whatever you want," Maddox said, nervousness entering his voice at the mere mention of the wolf.

"And I won't submit to military command or authority." Hunter turned back with the words. "If I lead the track, then I'm the one that leads. Nobody countermands my decisions or my methods. This is gonna be hard enough as it is. I don't want someone who doesn't understand what I do trying to give me orders."

"Of course not. I will ensure your authority in certain areas. This ...this support team will be present only for the confrontation."

Hunter turned away again, staring into a slowly gathering dark. He could tell from the air that a cold front was coming, rain not far behind. But there was something else, something that continued to hover over him—a premonition.

He felt it, but couldn't identify it. Yet he had made his decision, realizing that, if innocent lives were truly compromised by a creature as obviously powerful as this, there was really no choice.

"Set it up," he said, low. "Let me know."

Maddox swayed. "Good. Just be aware this is going to happen soon. Perhaps as early as tomorrow."

"That's fine," Hunter said, glancing at Dixon one last time.

Utterly concealed, Dixon's eyes were reflectionless pools of black, revealing nothing. And Hunter sensed rather than read the faintest apparition of a smile on the haggard face. And he knew that whatever disturbed him was hidden in that darkness.

Chapter 3

It's where the map ends; an unforgiving, heavily forested frontier of permafrost, tundra, glacier and air that froze skin at the touch. Hunter had been here once before, and knew it was an easy place to die.

Countless hikers, adventurers, and even native Alaskans had lost their lives in the merciless terrain of the Brooks Range. And Hunter didn't underestimate its brutality. He knew that it was through respect and caution that a man stayed alive in these mountains. And a lack of either would have only one outcome; the land was littered with legends of those who failed to heed advice and went unprepared into the high country, never to be seen again.

Hunter knew what equipment was essential for the average trapper or camper: a large-caliber scoped rifle, a shotgun, plenty of ammunition for both, an oversupply of preserved food, an ax, hatchet, sheath knife and a smaller folding blade for skinning, a tent, topographical map of the areas with federal emergency stations marked, a compass, rope, rain slick, matches and flint for making fires, a ball of leather twine, emergency medical equipment, grain for two pack mules and a horse, and a radio.

But Hunter traveled light, trusting his life to his skills. He never challenged the forces of nature, he respected them. But he knew he could effortlessly live off the land for weeks at a time and could improvise shelter in even the most hostile weather. So he carried all he needed in a compact belt rig that rested at the small of his back. He also had a pouch on a leather strap that went over a shoulder in the style of ancient Apaches. Inside it he carried air-dried beef jerky, herbal pastes for either cooking or wounds, a compass and map, and lesser-known tricks of the trade for tracking—chalk, a marking stick, pebbles.

He had a single canteen on his right side, though he rarely used it because he would drink at almost every stream, knowing dehydration was a lightning-fast killer this high. A large, finely-honed Bowie knife and hatchet were on his belt and he carried extra cartridges on the strap of the un-scoped Marlin 45.70 lever-action rifle that he carried over his shoulder.

He wore wool pants, a leather shirt and jacket, and knee-high moccasins lined with goose down, and carried no other clothes. The extra insulation in the moccasins would protect his feet against the cold, dry quickly, and allow him to move soundlessly. And he always wore leather while tracking because, unlike polyester or cotton, it made almost no sound when it scraped branches or leaves.

Long ago, inspired by an idea he'd obtained from studying ancient Aztec priests, he had sewn a double hood for the shoulders of his jacket. The lower layer protected his shoulders from rain. The upper layer, descending over his broad shoulders like a short cape, could be drawn up in a hood to prevent excessive heat loss from his head, which accounted for sixty percent of heat loss in the open air. It was a unique and functional design, and Hunter had learned from experience that a hood was indispensable in frigid temperatures.

Traveling so light, he resembled an early American frontier scout—an appearance made all the more apparent when contrasted to the high-tech profile and weaponry of the Special Response Squads he often worked beside.

For shelter and food he would simply live off nature. He would forage as he went, kill quickly and efficiently when necessary, but always moving. At night he would take fifteen minutes to rig a simple but effective fish trap in a stream which would capture a half dozen mountain trout for breakfast before morning. The fish that he didn't immediately eat he would eat as hunger came on him through the day. From years of practice he had discovered that it was a simple, effective means of traveling quickly across cold, high country.

He assumed that this mysterious military team would bear the standard forty pounds of survival gear necessary for Arctic survival. In general, that included a load-bearing vest, or LBV, probably armored with Kevlar. Then they would have a small backpack that held individual water purifiers, cold-weather tents, Arctic sleeping bags, extra clothes and socks, de-hydrated food, propane ovens, field radios and microphones, night-vision equipment, teargas, and flares, as well as bionic listening devices—either those worn as earphones or the laser-guided sort for pinpointing distant disturbance.

In addition to that, they would be heavily armed with a variety of weapons from M-16's to Benelli shotguns and MH-40 cylindrical grenade launchers. And, doubtless, they would rely upon the Magellan Global Positioning System for orientation—a fist-sized device that triangulated off satellites to provide exact location, accurate to within six feet. It was standard equipment for maneuvers.

Hunter was familiar with the technology and had used it himself. But it was still a machine, and machines could break down in primitive conditions. So he preferred to rely upon a map and compass and had cultivated his skills at dead reckoning so that he could accurately navigate using only the sun and stars, or nothing at all.

But Hunter knew that the most essential ingredient for survival in this land wasn't something so simple as equipment: it was mindset. For it was all too easy to panic when disaster struck and there was no one to rely upon for assistance.

He had learned long ago, mostly by necessity, to be supremely self-reliant under any circumstance. And up here there would be no substitute for a lack of strength or willpower.

He remembered a conversation he had with a grizzled old trapper during his first trip to Alaska. As he was preparing to venture into the mountains, he asked the old man if it was possible to survive a winter in the mountains with only a knife and rifle. Experienced with the lethal brutality of the wilderness, the trapper had taken a surprisingly long time to reply.

"Well," he said finally, turning a weathered face, "I reckon it could be done." His tone indicated that he had no intention of trying. "But you'd have to have Injun in you. You'd have to be an animal. 'Cause there ain't no God nor mercy up there, boy. Damn sure ain't." He paused. "When I go up high, I got my horse and two pack mules, 'cause a mule is worth any three horses in them woods. I break camp late and set up early, and I don't break at all if it looks like a hard cold might be settin in." He chewed a toothpick. "You ain't planning to try nuthin' like that, are ya?"

"No," Hunter assured him. "Just asking."

The old man nodded slowly and pointed toward the mountains. "The big ol' Out There ain't no place for a human bein', son. I seen some go in and winter it out, and them that made it home ... well, they wudn't the same. It changes a man, more ways 'an one."

Hunter knew the words were true.

There were few areas in the world as brutal with rain and cold, and as unforgiving of fools. He knew that if he was injured and forced to survive in those mountains for months, sheer determination would be his greatest ally. Pain could be ignored but any wound must be very carefully tended. Just as food would have to be attentively protected and harbored; it would be endless work to stay alive.

Patience and discipline would be vital, as would whatever tenuous grip he managed to maintain on his sanity. Although under the current conditions of this trip there would be little chance of a disaster, he had learned to always be prepared: conditions, no matter how certain they seem, could change completely and without warning.

As Hunter surfaced from his thoughts he was suddenly aware of the dull thundering engines of the military C-141, its four huge jet engines roaring outside the fuselage.

He smiled at the sudden awareness, for absolute concentration to the point of ignoring everything else was a faculty he had unconsciously perfected. And it was a vital skill when he was tracking.

Amazingly, although Hunter could effortlessly ignore a loud conversation directly behind him, he could simultaneously pick up the whispered clicks of a woodlark a quarter mile away. To the uninitiated, the sound would mean nothing, but it could tell Hunter what the bird was experiencing, what it was looking at, whether it was searching for its mate or just frightened, and of what.

For instance, the woodlark, more than any bird, hated water snakes like cottonmouths. So when a viper was moving in the water the woodlark would virtually set the forest on fire with that distinctive, hysterical high-pitched cry—a sound far different from its other songs and calls.

And, just as Hunter could identify the call to know that a snake was moving close, he knew that particular snakes would not be moving at all during certain times of the day unless something was forcing them. So, in a thousand ways similar to this, the forest could tell you about hidden movement and unseen activity. One had only to know the language of the forest, the native calls of the wild.

Ghost, sleeping soundly, lay beside him on a tarp and Hunter reached out to caress the wolf's thick mane.

Military officials had refused to allow Ghost among the other passengers, fearing the massive wolf's potential for violence if, for some reason, he decided to demonstrate his prowess. And, rather than engage them in a doomed debate, Hunter elected to travel in the cargo hold with what he knew was his closest and most loyal friend.

He remembered when he had found Ghost. The wolf was only three weeks old, and his sire, an enormous gray wolf, had been killed by poachers, along with the mother and siblings.

Though wounded by a bullet graze, Ghost had survived by hiding beneath a deadfall, buried deep beneath tons of logs. Starving, sick and wounded, the cub would have died within days but Hunter coaxed him out with a piece of raw meat and carried him back to the cabin.

It was a month before the malnourished cub could clamber around the three-room structure, but after that he grew rapidly, eventually surpassing the strength and size of his gigantic father. Yet it was his spirit that caught Hunter's early attention and made him laugh; something he rarely did.

Hunter had never attempted to train him, but the wolf's keen intelligence was evident from the first moments. Without being taught, Ghost knew where to find food, how to communicate his needs, when he wanted to go outside. And his curiosity was endless, as was his unconcealed joy every time Hunter returned from a trip.

When he was six months old Hunter let him sleep on the porch, sheltered by a fairly luxurious doghouse that Hunter built from spare lumber. Hunter filled the bottom with a thick layer of straw and an old blanket and installed a heat lamp for cold nights, but he never leashed the wolf. If Ghost wished to leave, he was free to go.

For endless nights Hunter went to bed knowing Ghost was staring and listening to the calls of the wild, summoned by the wolf packs that surrounded the cabin. And then when Ghost was two years old, near full size, he began disappearing for days at a time, often returning with bloody wounds—slash marks of other wolves.

http://wbp.bz/huntera

Other WildBlue Press Books By James Byron Huggins

The Reckoning: Separated from the secret world he once dominated, he chose a life of exile, pursuing a lonely peace, a solitary faith. Only the murder of his mentor and the mysterious theft of an ancient manuscript can compel him to emerge from solitude. Now his greatest battle begins. Bound by a promise to a dying friend, he wages war once more in the dark world he left behind. **wbp.bz/reckoninga**

Hunter: In yet another experiment to extend human life, scientists accidentally unleash a force that might well be a terrible curse. Now an infected creature is loose in the Alaskan wilderness, and the America military is forced to ask the world's greatest tracker, Nathaniel Hunter, to locate the beast and destroy it before it reaches a populated area. **wbp. bz/huntera**

Cain: Grotesquely transformed, Cain has become the ultimate predator: A killing machine with the soul of a devil. And the only force that can stop him is a trio of flawed people: a soldier who lost his family and his soul to a terrorist's bullets, a priest who has lost his faith, and the scientist who created Cain and then lost control of him. **wbp.bz/caina**

Dark Visions: Joe Mac was a legendary homicide detective until his vision was lost in the line of duty and he was forced into retirement. But when Joe Mac's grandson is murdered by an unknown killer, Joe emerges from his self-imposed solitude to resurrect the skills of the detective he once was. **wbp.bz/darkvisionsa**

Leviathan: On an Icelandic Island, an illegal experiment intended to create the perfect biological weapon has transformed a once-innocent creature into the biblical Leviathan that once terrorized the world. Able to shatter steel and granite as easily as it can melt the strongest containment shields, Leviathan escapes from its pen and is loose in a vast underground chamber harboring soldiers and scientists. **wbp.bz/leviathana**

www.ingramcontent.com/pod-product-compliance
Lightning Source LLC
Chambersburg PA
CBHW051004180726
48291CB00006B/1974